Praise for

STEPHEN

and the #1 *New York T*

THE OUTSIDER

"More than fifty novels published, and [King's] still adding new influences to his work. . . . This expansiveness allows King to highlight the idea that . . . people the world over tell certain stories for reasons that feel much the same: to understand the mysteries of our universe, the improbable and inexplicable . . . here's to the strange and to Stephen King. Still inspiring."

—Victor LaValle, *The New York Times Book Review*

"Plenty of shadowy . . . supernatural goings-on . . . yet the most unsettling stuff—that which will leave you uncomfortable when you sit and devour this first-rate read—probes the monstrous side of human nature. . . . In King's hands, real darkness is just as pervasive as the supernatural."

—*USA Today*

"The master of horror hits a home run. . . . Gives King fans exactly what they want at the same time as cramming in new ideas, proving the least surprising thing of all: that his novels are as strong as they ever were."

—*The Guardian* (UK)

"Remarkable and deeply pleasurable."

—*The A. V. Club*

"Absolutely riveting . . . intoxicating . . . another shockingly dark book—perfect for longtime fans, of whom there are, well, zillions."

—*Booklist*

STEPHEN KING

THE OUTSIDER

A NOVEL

GALLERY BOOKS
NEW YORK LONDON TORONTO SYDNEY NEW DELHI

Gallery Books
An Imprint of Simon & Schuster, Inc.
1230 Avenue of the Americas
New York, NY 10020

This book is a work of fiction. Any references to historical events, real people, or real places are used fictitiously. Other names, characters, places, and events are products of the author's imagination, and any resemblance to actual events or places or persons, living or dead, is entirely coincidental.

Copyright © 2018 by Stephen King

All rights reserved, including the right to reproduce this book or portions thereof in any form whatsoever. For information, address Scribner Subsidiary Rights Department, 1230 Avenue of the Americas, New York, NY 10020.

First Gallery Books trade paperback edition June 2019

GALLERY BOOKS and colophon are registered trademarks of Simon & Schuster, Inc.

For information about special discounts for bulk purchases, please contact Simon & Schuster Special Sales at 1-866-506-1949 or business@simonandschuster.com.

The Simon & Schuster Speakers Bureau can bring authors to your live event. For more information or to book an event, contact the Simon & Schuster Speakers Bureau at 1-866-248-3049 or visit our website at www.simonspeakers.com.

Interior design by Erich Hobbing

Manufactured in the United States of America

1 3 5 7 9 10 8 6 4 2

ISBN: 978-1-5011-8098-9
ISBN: 978-1-5011-8100-9 (pbk)
ISBN: 978-1-5011-8101-6 (ebook)

For Rand and Judy Holston

Thought only gives the world an appearance of order to anyone weak enough to be convinced by its show.

     Colin Wilson
     "The Country of the Blind"

THE OUTSIDER

THE ARREST

July 14th

1

It was an unmarked car, just some nondescript American sedan a few years old, but the blackwall tires and the three men inside gave it away for what it was. The two in front were wearing blue uniforms. The one in back was wearing a suit, and he was as big as a house. A pair of black boys standing on the sidewalk, one with a foot on a scuffed orange skateboard, the other with a lime-colored board under his arm, watched it turn into the parking lot of the Estelle Barga Recreational Park, then looked at each other.

One said, "That's Five-O."

The other said, "No shit."

They headed off with no further conversation, pumping their boards. The rule was simple: when Five-O shows up, it's time to go. Black lives matter, their parents had instructed them, but not always to Five-O. At the baseball field, the crowd began to cheer and clap rhythmically as the Flint City Golden Dragons came to bat in the bottom of the ninth, one run down.

The boys didn't look back.

2

Statement of Mr. Jonathan Ritz {July 10th, 9:30 PM, interviewed by Detective Ralph Anderson}

Detective Anderson: I know you're upset, Mr. Ritz,

it's understandable, but I need to know exactly what you saw earlier this evening.

Ritz: I'll never get it out of my mind. Never. I think I could use a pill. Maybe a Valium. I've never taken any of that stuff, but I sure could use something now. My heart still feels like it's in my throat. Your forensic people should know that if they find puke at the scene, and I guess they will, it's mine. I'm not ashamed, either. Anyone would have lost their supper if they saw something like that.

Detective Anderson: I'm sure a doctor will prescribe something to calm you down when we're done. I think I can arrange for that, but right now I need you clearheaded. You understand that, don't you?

Ritz: Yes. Of course.

Detective Anderson: Just tell me everything you saw, and we'll be finished for this evening. Can you do that for me, sir?

Ritz: All right. I went out to walk Dave right around six o'clock this evening. Dave is our beagle. He has his evening meal at five. My wife and I eat at five thirty. By six, Dave is ready to take care of his business—Number One and Number Two, I mean. I walk him while Sandy—my wife—does up the dishes. It's a fair division of labor. A fair division of labor is very important in a marriage, especially after the children have grown up, that's the way we look at it. I'm rambling, aren't I?

Detective Anderson: That's okay, Mr. Ritz. Tell it your way.

Ritz: Oh, please call me Jon. I can't stand Mr. Ritz. Makes me feel like a cracker. That's what the kids called me when I was in school, Ritz Cracker.

THE OUTSIDER

Detective Anderson: Uh-huh. So you were walking your dog—

Ritz: That's right. And when he got a strong scent—the scent of death, I suppose—I had to hold him back on his leash with both hands, even though Dave's just a little dog. He wanted to get at what he was smelling. The—

Detective Anderson: Wait, let's go back. You left your house at 249 Mulberry Avenue at six o'clock—

Ritz: It might have been a little before. Dave and I walked down the hill to Gerald's, that grocery on the corner where they sell all the gourmet stuff, then up Barnum Street, and then into Figgis Park. That's the one the kids call Frig Us Park. They think adults don't know what they say, that we don't listen, but we do. At least some of us do.

Detective Anderson: Was this your usual evening walk?

Ritz: Oh, sometimes we change it up a little so we don't get bored, but the park is where we almost always end up before heading home, because there's always lots for Dave to smell. There's a parking lot, but at that time of the evening it's almost always empty, unless there are some high school kids playing tennis. There weren't any that night, because the courts are clay and it rained earlier. The only thing parked there was a white van.

Detective Anderson: A commercial van, would you say?

Ritz: That's right. No windows, just double doors in the back. The kind of van small companies use to haul stuff in. It might have been an Econoline, but I couldn't swear to that.

Detective Anderson: Was there a company name written on it? Like Sam's Air Conditioning or Bob's Custom Windows? Something like that?

Ritz: No, uh-uh. Nothing at all. It was dirty, though, I can tell you that. Hadn't been washed in some time. And there was mud on the tires, probably from the rain. Dave sniffed at the tires, then we went along one of the gravel paths through the trees. After about a quarter of a mile, Dave started to bark and ran into the bushes on the right. That's when he got that scent. He almost dragged the leash out of my hand. I tried to pull him back and he wouldn't come, just flopped over and dug at the ground with his paws and kept on barking. So I snubbed him up close—I have one of those retractable leashes, and it's very good for that kind of thing—and went after him. He doesn't bother about squirrels and chipmunks so much now that he's not a puppy anymore, but I thought he might have scented up a raccoon. I was going to make him come back whether he wanted to or not, dogs need to know who's boss, only that was when I saw the first few drops of blood. They were on a birch leaf, about chest-high to me, which would make it I guess five feet or so off the ground. There was another drop on another leaf a little further on, then a whole splash of it on some bushes further on still. Still red and wet. Dave sniffed at that one, but wanted to keep going. And listen, before I forget, right about then I heard an engine start up behind me. I might not have noticed, except it was pretty loud, like the muffler was shot. Kind of rumbling, do you know what I mean?

Detective Anderson: Uh-huh, I do.

Ritz: I can't swear it was that white van, and I didn't go back that way, so I don't know if it was gone, but I bet it was. And you know what that means?

Detective Anderson: Tell me what you think it means, Jon.

Ritz: That he might have been watching me. The killer. Standing in the trees and watching me. It gives me the creeps, just thinking about it. Now, I mean. Then, I was pretty much fixated on the blood. And keeping Dave from yanking my arm right out of its socket. I was getting scared, and don't mind admitting it. I'm not a big man, and although I try to stay in shape, I'm in my sixties now. Even in my twenties I wasn't much of a brawler. But I had to see. In case someone was hurt.

Detective Anderson: That's very commendable. What time would you say it was when you first saw the blood-trail?

Ritz: I didn't check my watch, but I'm guessing twenty past six. Maybe twenty-five past. I let Dave lead the way, keeping him snubbed up so I could push through the branches he could just go under with his little short legs. You know what they say about beagles—they're high-toned but low-slung. He was barking like crazy. We came into a clearing, a sort of . . . I don't know, sort of a nook where lovers might sit and smooch a little. There was a granite bench in the middle of it, and it was covered in blood. So much of it. More underneath. The body was lying on the grass beside it. That poor boy. His head was turned toward me, and his eyes were open, and his throat was just gone. Nothing there but a red hole. His bluejeans and underpants were pulled down to his ankles, and I saw something . . . a dead branch, I guess . . . sticking out of his . . . his . . . well, you know.

Detective Anderson: I do, but I need you to say it for the record, Mr. Ritz.

Ritz: He was on his stomach, and the branch was sticking out of his bottom. That was bloody, too. The branch. Part of the bark was stripped, and there was a handprint. I saw that clear as day. Dave wasn't barking anymore, he was howling, poor thing, and I just don't know who would do something like that. He must have been a maniac. Will you catch him, Detective Anderson?

Detective Anderson: Oh, yes. We'll catch him.

3

The Estelle Barga parking lot was almost as big as the one at the Kroger's where Ralph Anderson and his wife shopped on Saturday afternoons, and on this July evening it was totally filled. Many of the bumpers bore Golden Dragons stickers, and a few rear windows had been soaped with exuberant slogans: WE WILL ROCK YOU; DRAGONS WILL BURN BEARS; CAP CITY HERE WE COME; THIS YEAR IT'S OUR TURN. From the field, where the lights had been turned on (although it would be daylight for quite a while yet), there arose cheering and rhythmic clapping.

Troy Ramage, a twenty-year veteran, was behind the wheel of the unmarked. As he cruised up one packed row and down another, he said, "Whenever I come here, I always wonder who the hell Estelle Barga was, anyway."

THE OUTSIDER

Ralph made no reply. His muscles were tight, his skin was hot, and his pulse felt like it was red-lining. He had arrested plenty of bad doers over the years, but this was different. This was particularly awful. And personal. That was the worst: it was personal. He had no business being part of the arrest, and knew it, but following the last round of budget cuts, there were only three full-time detectives on the Flint City police force's roster. Jack Hoskins was on vacation, fishing somewhere in the back of beyond, and good riddance. Betsy Riggins, who should have been on maternity leave, would be assisting the State Police with another aspect of this evening's work.

He hoped to God they weren't going too fast. He had expressed that worry to Bill Samuels, the Flint County district attorney, just that afternoon, in their pre-arrest conference. Samuels was a little young for the post, just thirty-five, but he belonged to the right political party, and he was sure of himself. Not cocksure, there was that, but undoubtedly gung-ho.

"There are still some rough edges I'd like to smooth out," Ralph said. "We don't have all the background. Plus, he's going to say he has an alibi. Unless he just gives it up, we can be sure of that."

"If he does," Samuels had replied, "we'll knock it down. You know we will."

Ralph had no doubt of it, he knew they had the right man, but he still would have preferred a little more investigation before pulling the trigger. Find the holes in the sonofabitch's alibi, punch them wider, wide enough to drive a truck through, *then* bring him in. In most cases that would have been the correct procedure. Not in this one.

"Three things," Samuels had said. "Are you ready for them?"

Ralph nodded. He had to work with this man, after all.

"One, people in this town, particularly the parents of small children, are terrified and angry. They want a quick arrest so they can feel safe again. Two, the evidence is beyond doubt. I've never seen a case so ironclad. Are you with me on that?"

"Yes."

"Okay, here's number three. The big one." Samuels had leaned forward. "We can't say he's done it before—although if he has, we'll probably find out once we really start digging—but he sure as hell has done it now. Broken loose. Busted his cherry. And once that happens . . ."

"He could do it again," Ralph finished.

"Right. Not the likeliest scenario so soon after Peterson, but possible. He's with kids all the time, for Christ's sake. Young boys. If he killed one of them, never mind losing our jobs, we'd never forgive ourselves."

Ralph was already having problems forgiving himself for not seeing it sooner. That was irrational, you couldn't look into a man's eyes at a backyard barbecue following the conclusion of the Little League season and know he was contemplating an unspeakable act—stroking it and feeding it and watching it grow—but the irrationality didn't change the way he felt.

Now, leaning forward to point between the two cops in the front seat, Ralph said, "Over there. Try the handicap spaces."

From the shotgun seat, Officer Tom Yates said, "Two-hundred-dollar fine for that, boss."

"I think we'll get a pass this time," Ralph said.

"I was joking."

Ralph, in no mood for cop repartee, made no reply.

"Crip spaces ahoy," Ramage said. "And I see two empties."

He pulled into one of them, and the three men got out. Ralph saw Yates unsnap the strap over the butt of his Glock and shook his head. "Are you out of your mind? There's got to be fifteen hundred people at that game."

"What if he runs?"

"Then you'll catch him."

Ralph leaned against the hood of the unmarked and watched as the two Flint City officers started toward the field, the lights, and the crammed bleachers, where the clapping and the cheering were still rising in volume and intensity. Arresting Peterson's killer fast had been a call he and Samuels had made together (however reluctantly). Arresting him at the game had been strictly Ralph's decision.

Ramage looked back. "Coming?"

"I am not. You do the deed, and read him his rights nice and goddam loud, then bring him here. Tom, when we roll, you're going to ride in back with him. I'll be up front with Troy. Bill Samuels is waiting for my call, and he'll be at the station to meet us. This one's A-Team all the way. As for the collar, it's all yours."

"But it's your case," Yates said. "Why wouldn't you want to be the one to bust the motherfucker?"

Still with his arms crossed, Ralph said, "Because the man who raped Frankie Peterson with a tree branch and tore open his throat coached my son for four years, two in Peewee and two in Little League. He had his hands on my son, showing him how to hold a bat, and I don't trust myself."

"Got it, got it," Troy Ramage said. He and Yates started toward the field.

"And listen, you two."

They turned back.

"Cuff him right there. And cuff him in front."

"That's not protocol, boss," Ramage said.

"I know, and I don't care. I want everyone to see him led away in handcuffs. Got it?"

When they were on their way, Ralph took his cell phone off his belt. He had Betsy Riggins on speed-dial. "Are you in position?"

"Yes indeed. Parked in front of his house. Me and four State Troopers."

"Search warrant?"

"In my hot little hand."

"Good." He was about to end the call when something else occurred to him. "Bets, when's your due date?"

"Yesterday," she said. "So hurry this shit up." And ended the call herself.

4

Statement of Mrs. Arlene Stanhope {July 12th, 1:00 PM, interviewed by Detective Ralph Anderson}

Stanhope: Will this take long, Detective?

Detective Anderson: Not long at all. Just tell me what you saw on the afternoon of Tuesday, July 10th, and we'll be done.

Stanhope: All right. I was coming out of Gerald's Fine Groceries. I always do my shopping there on Tuesdays. Things are more expensive at Gerald's, but I don't go to the Kroger since I stopped driving. I gave up my license the year after my husband died because I didn't trust my reflexes anymore. I had a couple of accidents. Just fender-benders, you know, but that was enough for me. Gerald's is only two blocks from the apartment I've been living in since I sold the house, and the doctor says walking is good for me. Good for my heart, you know. I was coming out with my three bags in my little cart—three bags is all I can afford now, the prices are so awful, especially meat, I don't know the last time I've had bacon—and I saw the Peterson boy.

Detective Anderson: You're sure it was Frank Peterson you saw?

Stanhope: Oh yes, it was Frank. Poor boy, I'm so sorry about what happened to him, but he's in heaven now, and his pain is over. That's the consolation. There are two Peterson boys, you know, both redheads, that awful carroty red, but the older one—Oliver, that's his name—is at least five years older. He used to deliver our newspaper. Frank has a bicycle, one of those that have the high handlebars and the narrow seat—

Detective Anderson: A banana seat, it's called.

Stanhope: I don't know about that, but I know it was bright lime green, an awful color, really, and there was a sticker on the seat. It said Flint City High. Only he'll never go to high school, will he? Poor, poor boy.

Detective Anderson: Mrs. Stanhope, would you like a short break?

Stanhope: No, I want to finish. I need to go home and feed my cat. I always feed her at three, and she'll be hungry. She'll also wonder where I am. But if I could have a tissue? I'm sure I'm a mess. Thank you.

Detective Anderson: You could see the sticker on the seat of Frank Peterson's bicycle because—?

Stanhope: Oh, because he wasn't on it. He was walking it across the Gerald's parking lot. The chain was broken, and dragging on the pavement.

Detective Anderson: Did you notice what he was wearing?

Stanhope: A tee-shirt with some rock and roll band on it. I don't know bands, so I can't say which one it was. If that's important, I'm sorry. And he was wearing a Rangers cap. It was pushed back on his head, and I could see all that red hair. Those carrot-tops usually go bald very early in life, you know. He'll never have to worry about that now, will he? Oh, it's just so sad. Anyway, there was a dirty white van parked at the far end of the lot, and a man got out and came over to Frank. He was—

   Detective Anderson: We'll get to that, but first I want to hear about the van. This was the kind with no windows?

   Stanhope: Yes.

   Detective Anderson: With no writing on it? No company name, or anything of that nature?

   Stanhope: Not that I saw.

   Detective Anderson: Okay, let's talk about the man you saw. Did you recognize him, Mrs. Stanhope?

   Stanhope: Oh, of course. It was Terry Maitland. Everyone on the West Side knows Coach T. They call him that even at the high school. He teaches English there, you know. My husband taught with him before he retired. They call him Coach T because he coaches Little League, and the City League baseball team when Little League is done, and in the fall he coaches little boys who like to play football. They have a name for that league, too, but I don't remember it.

   Detective Anderson: If we could get back to what you saw on Tuesday afternoon—

   Stanhope: There's not much more to tell. Frank talked to Coach T, and pointed at his broken chain. Coach T nodded and opened the back of the white van, which couldn't have been his—

   Detective Anderson: Why do you say that, Mrs. Stanhope?

   Stanhope: Because it had an orange license plate. I don't know which state that would be, my long vision isn't what it used to be, but I know Oklahoma plates are blue and white. Anyway, I couldn't

THE OUTSIDER

see anything in the back of the van except for a long green thing that looked like a toolbox. Was it a toolbox, Detective?

Detective Anderson: What happened then?

Stanhope: Well, Coach T put Frank's bicycle in the back and shut the doors. He clapped Frank on the back. Then he went around to the driver's side and Frank went around to the passenger side. They both got in, and the van drove away, onto Mulberry Avenue. I thought Coach T was going to drive the lad home. Of course I did. What else would I think? Terry Maitland has lived on the West Side for going on twenty years, he has a very nice family, a wife and two daughters . . . could I have another tissue, please? Thank you. Are we almost done?

Detective Anderson: Yes, and you've been very helpful. I believe that before I started to record, you said this was around three o'clock?

Stanhope: Exactly three. I heard the bell in the Town Hall clock chiming the hour just as I came out with my little cart. I wanted to go home and feed my cat.

Detective Anderson: The boy you saw, the redheaded boy, was Frank Peterson.

Stanhope: Yes. The Petersons live right around the corner. Ollie used to deliver my newspaper. I see those boys all the time.

Detective Anderson: And the man, the one who put the bike in the back of the white van and drove away with Frank Peterson, that was Terence Maitland, also known as Coach Terry or Coach T.

Stanhope: Yes.

Detective Anderson: You're sure of that.

Stanhope: Oh, yes.

Detective Anderson: Thank you, Mrs. Stanhope.

Stanhope: Who could believe Terry would do such a thing? Do you suppose there have been others?

Detective Anderson: We may find that out in the course of our investigation.

5

Since all City League tournament games were played at Estelle Barga Field—the best baseball field in the county, and the only one with lights for night games—home team advantage was decided by a coin toss. Terry Maitland called tails before the game, as he always did—it was a superstition handed down from his own City League coach, back in the day—and tails it was. "I don't care where we're playing, I just like to get my lasties," he always told his boys.

And tonight he needed them. It was the bottom of the ninth, the Bears were up in this league semifinal by a single run. The Golden Dragons were down to their last out, but they had the bases loaded. A walk, a wild pitch, an error, or an infield single would tie it, a ball hit into the gap would win it. The crowd was clapping, stamping the metal bleachers, and cheering as little Trevor Michaels stepped into the lefthand batter's box. His batting helmet was the smallest one they had, but it still shaded his eyes and he had to keep pushing it up. He twitched his bat nervously back and forth.

Terry had considered pinch-hitting for the boy, but at just an inch over five feet, he drew a lot of walks. And while he was no home run hitter, he was sometimes able to put the bat on the ball. Not often, but sometimes. If Terry lifted him for a pinch hitter, the poor kid would have to live with the humiliation through the whole next year of middle school. If, on the other hand, he managed a single, he would recall it over beers and backyard barbecues for the rest of his life. Terry knew. He'd been there himself, once upon a time, in the antique era before the game was played with aluminum bats.

The Bears pitcher—their closer, a real fireballer—wound up and threw one right down the heart of the plate. Trevor watched it go by with an expression of dismay. The umpire called strike one. The crowd groaned.

Gavin Frick, Terry's assistant coach, paced up and down in front of the boys on the bench, the scorebook rolled up in one hand (how many times had Terry asked him not to do that?), and his XXL Golden Dragons tee-shirt straining over his belly, which was XXXL at least. "I hope letting Trevor bat for himself wasn't a mistake, Ter," he said. Sweat was trickling down his cheeks. "He looks scared to death, and I don't b'lieve he could hit that kid's speedball with a tennis racket."

"Let's see what happens," Terry said. "I've got a good feeling about this." He didn't, not really.

The Bears pitcher wound up and released another burner, but this one landed in the dirt in front of home plate. The crowd rose to its feet as Baibir Patel, the Dragons' tying run at third, jinked a few steps down the line. They settled back with a groan as the ball bounced into the catcher's mitt. The Bears catcher turned to third, and Terry could read his expression, even through the mask: *Just try it, homeboy.* Baibir didn't.

The next pitch was wide, but Trevor flailed at it, anyway.

"Strike him out, Fritz!" a leather-lung shouted from high up in the bleachers—almost surely the fireballer's father, from the way the kid snapped his head in that direction. "Strike him *owwwwwt!*"

Trevor didn't offer at the next pitch, which was close—too close to take, really, but the ump called it a ball, and it was the Bears' fans' turn to groan. Someone suggested that the ump needed stronger glasses. Another fan mentioned something about a seeing-eye dog.

Two and two now, and Terry had a strong sense that the Dragons' season hung on the next pitch. Either they would play the Panthers for the City championship, and go on to compete in the States—games that were actually televised—or they would go home and meet just one more time, at the barbecue in the Maitland backyard that traditionally marked the end of the season.

He turned to look at Marcy and the girls, sitting where they always did, in lawn chairs behind the home plate screen. His daughters were flanking his wife like pretty bookends. All three waved crossed fingers at him. Terry gave them a wink and a smile and two thumbs up, although he still didn't feel right. It wasn't just the game. He hadn't felt right for some time now. Not quite.

Marcy's return smile faltered into a puzzled frown. She was looking to her left, and jerked a thumb that way. Terry turned and saw two city cops walking in lockstep down the third base line, past Barry Houlihan, who was coaching there.

"Time, time!" the home plate umpire bellowed, stopping the Bears pitcher just as he went into his wind-up. Trevor Michaels stepped out of the batter's box, and with an expression of relief, Terry thought. The crowd had grown quiet, looking at the two cops. One of them was reaching behind his back. The other had his hand on the butt of his holstered service weapon.

"Off the field!" the ump was shouting. *"Off the field!"*

Troy Ramage and Tom Yates ignored him. They walked into the Dragons' dugout—a makeshift affair containing a long bench, three baskets of equipment, and a bucket of dirty practice balls—and directly to where Terry was standing. From the back of his belt, Ramage produced a pair of handcuffs. The crowd saw them, and raised a murmur that was two parts confusion and one part excitement: *Ooooo.*

"Hey, you guys!" Gavin said, hustling up (and almost tripping over Richie Gallant's discarded first baseman's mitt). "We've got a game to finish here!"

Yates pushed him back, shaking his head. The crowd was dead silent now. The Bears had abandoned their tense defensive postures and were just watching, their gloves dangling. The catcher trotted out to his pitcher, and they stood together halfway between the mound and home plate.

Terry knew the one holding the cuffs a little; he and his brother sometimes came to watch the Pop Warner games in the fall. "Troy? What is this? What's the deal?"

Ramage saw nothing on the man's face except what looked like honest bewilderment, but he had been a cop since the nineties, and knew that the really bad ones had that *Who, me?* look down to a science. And this guy was as bad as they came. Remembering Anderson's instructions (and not minding a bit), he raised his voice so he could be heard by the entire crowd, which the next day's paper would announce as 1,588.

"Terence Maitland, I am arresting you for the murder of Frank Peterson."

Another *Ooooo* from the bleachers, this one louder, the sound of a rising wind.

Terry frowned at Ramage. He understood the words, they were simple English words forming a simple declarative sentence, he knew who Frankie Peterson was and what had happened to him, but the *meaning* of the words eluded him. All he could say was "What? Are you kidding?" and that was when the sports photographer from the *Flint City Call* snapped his picture, the one that appeared on the front page the next day. His mouth was open, his eyes were wide, his hair was sticking out around the edges of his Golden Dragons cap. In that photo he looked both enfeebled and guilty.

"*What* did you say?"

"Hold out your wrists, please."

Terry looked at Marcy and his daughters, still sitting in their chairs behind the chickenwire, staring at him with identical expressions of frozen surprise. Horror would come later. Baibir Patel left third base and started to walk toward the dugout, taking off his batting helmet to show the sweaty mat of his black hair, and Terry saw the kid was starting to cry.

"Get back there!" Gavin shouted at him. "Game's not over."

But Baibir only stood in foul territory, staring at Terry and bawling. Terry stared back, positive (*almost* positive) he was dreaming all this, and then Tom Yates grabbed him and yanked his arms out with enough force to make Terry stumble forward. Ramage snapped on the cuffs. Real ones, not the plastic strips, big and heavy, gleaming in the late sun. In that same rolling voice, he proclaimed: "You have the right to remain silent and refuse to answer questions, but if you choose to speak, anything you say can be held against you in a court of law. You have the right to an attorney during questioning now or in the future. Do you understand?"

"Troy?" Terry could hardly hear his own voice. He felt as if the wind had been punched out of him. "What in God's name is this?"

Ramage took no notice. "Do you understand?"

Marcy came to the chickenwire, hooked her fingers through it, and shook it. Behind her, Sarah and Grace were crying. Grace was on her knees beside Sarah's lawn chair; her own had fallen over and lay in the dirt. "What are you doing?" Marcy shouted. "What in God's name are you doing? And why are you doing it *here?*"

"Do you understand?"

What Terry understood was that he had been handcuffed and was now being read his rights in front of almost sixteen hundred staring people, his wife and two young daughters among them. It was not a dream, and it was not simply an arrest. It was, for reasons he could not comprehend, a public shaming. Best to get it over as fast as possible, and get this thing straightened out. Although, even in his shock and bewilderment, he understood that his life would not be going back to normal for a long time.

"I understand," he said, and then: "Coach Frick, get back."

Gavin, who had been approaching the cops with his fists clenched and his fat face flushed a hectic red, lowered his arms and stepped back. He looked through the chickenwire at Marcy, raised his enormous shoulders, spread his pudgy hands.

In the same rolling tones, like a town crier belting out the week's big news in a New England town square, Troy Ramage continued. Ralph Anderson could hear him from where he stood leaning against the unmarked unit. He was doing a good job, was Troy. It was ugly, and Ralph supposed he might be reprimanded for it, but he would not be reprimanded by Frankie Peterson's parents. No, not by them.

"If you cannot afford an attorney, one will be provided to you before any questioning, if you desire. Do you understand?"

"Yes," Terry said. "I understand something else, too." He turned to the crowd. *"I have no idea why I'm being arrested! Gavin Frick will finish coaching the game!"* And then, as an afterthought: "Baibir, get back to third, and remember to run in foul territory."

There was a smatter of applause, but only a smatter. The leather-lung in the bleachers yelled again, *"What'd you say he did?"* And the crowd responding to the question, muttering the two words that would soon be all over the West Side and the rest of the city: Frank Peterson's name.

Yates grabbed Terry by the arm and started hustling him toward the snack shack and the parking lot beyond. "You can preach to the multitudes later, Maitland. Right now you're going to jail. And guess what? We have the needle in this state, and we use it. But you're a teacher, right? You probably knew that."

They hadn't gotten twenty steps from the makeshift dugout before Marcy Maitland caught up and grabbed Tom Yates's arm. "What in God's name do you think you're doing?"

Yates shrugged her off, and when she tried to grasp her husband's arm, Troy Ramage pushed her away, gently but firmly. She stood where she was for a moment, dazed, then saw Ralph Anderson walking to meet his arresting officers. She knew him from Little League, when Derek Anderson had played for Terry's team, the Gerald's Fine Groceries Lions. Ralph hadn't been able to come to all the games, of course, but he came to as many as possible. Back then he'd still been in uniform; Terry had sent him a congratulatory email when he was promoted to detective. Now she ran toward him, fleet over the grass in her old tennis shoes, which she always wore to Terry's games, claiming there was good luck in them.

"Ralph!" she called. "What's going on? This is a mistake!"

"I'm afraid it isn't," Ralph said.

This part he didn't like, because he liked Marcy. On the other hand, he had always liked Terry, as well—the man had probably changed Derek's life only a little, given the boy just a smatter of confidence-building, but when you were eleven years old, a little confidence was a big deal. And there was something else. Marcy might have known what her husband was, even if she didn't allow herself to know on a conscious level. The Maitlands had been married a long time, and horrors like the Peterson boy's murder simply did not come out of thin air. There was always a build-up to the act.

"You need to go home, Marcy. Right away. You may want to leave the girls with a friend, because there will be police waiting for you."

She only looked at him, uncomprehending.

From behind them came the chink of an aluminum bat making good contact, although there were few cheers; those in attendance were still shocked, and more interested in what they'd just witnessed than the game before them. Which was sort of a shame. Trevor Michaels had just hit the ball harder than ever before in his life, harder even than when Coach T was throwing meatballs in practice. Unfortunately, it was a line drive straight to the Bears shortstop, who didn't even have to jump to make the catch.

Game over.

6

Statement of June Morris {July 12th, 5:45 PM, interviewed by Detective Ralph Anderson, Mrs. Francine Morris in attendance}

Detective Anderson: Thank you for bringing your daughter down to the station, Mrs. Morris. June, how's that soda?

June Morris: It's good. Am I in trouble?

Detective Anderson: Not at all. I just want to ask you a couple of questions about what you saw two evenings ago.

June Morris: When I saw Coach Terry?

Detective Anderson: That's right, when you saw Coach Terry.

Francine Morris: Since she turned nine, we've let her go down the street by herself to see her friend Helen. As long as it's daylight. We don't believe in being helicopter parents. I won't after this, you can be sure of that.

Detective Anderson: You saw him after you had your supper, June? Is that right?

June Morris: Yes. We had meatloaf. Last night we had fish. I don't like fish, but that's how it goes.

Francine Morris: She doesn't have to cross the street, or anything. We thought it would be okay, since we live in such a good neighborhood. At least I thought we did.

Detective Anderson: It's always hard to know when

to start giving them responsibilities. Now June—you went down the street, and that took you right past the Figgis Park parking lot, is that right?

June Morris: Yes. Me and Helen—

Francine Morris: Helen and I—

June Morris: Helen and I were going to finish our map of South America. It's for our day camp project. We use different colors for the different countries, and we were mostly done, but we forgot Paraguay, so we were going to start all over again. That's also how it goes. After that we were going to play Angry Birds and Corgi Hop on Helen's iPad until my daddy came to walk me home. Because by then it might be getting dark.

Detective Anderson: This would have been at what time, Mom?

Francine Morris: The local news was on when Junie left. Norm was watching while I did the dishes. So, between six and six thirty. Probably quarter past, because I think the weather was on.

Detective Anderson: Tell me what you saw when you were walking past the parking lot, June.

June Morris: Coach Terry, I told you. He lives up the street, and once when our dog got lost, Coach T brought him back. Sometimes I play with Gracie Maitland, but not too much. She's a year older, and likes boys. He was all bloody. Because of his nose.

Detective Anderson: Uh-huh. What was he doing when you saw him?

June Morris: He came out of the trees. He saw me looking at him and waved. I waved back and said, "Hey, Coach Terry, what happened to you?" and he said a branch hit him in the face. He said, "Don't be scared, it's just a bloody nose, I get them all the time." And I said, "I'm not scared, but you won't be able to wear that shirt anymore, because blood doesn't come out, that's what my mom says." He smiled and said, "Good thing I've got lots of shirts." But it was on his pants, too. Also on his hands.

Francine Morris: She was that close to him. I can't stop thinking about it.

June Morris: Why, because he had a bloody nose? Rolf Jacobs got one on the playground last year when he fell down, and it didn't scare me. I was going to give him my handkerchief, but Mrs. Grisha took him to the nurse's office before I could.

Detective Anderson: How close were you?

June Morris: Gee, I don't know. He was in the parking lot and I was on the sidewalk. How far is that?

Detective Anderson: I don't know, either, but I'm sure I'll find out. Is that soda good?

June Morris: You already asked me that.

Detective Anderson: Oh, right, so I did.

June Morris: Old people are forgetful, that's what my grandpa says.

Francine Morris: Junie, that's impolite.

Detective Anderson: It's okay. Your grandpa sounds like a wise man, June. What happened then?

June Morris: Nothing. Coach Terry got into his van and drove away.

Detective Anderson: What color was the van?

June Morris: Well, it would be white if it was

washed, I guess, but it was pretty dirty. Also, it made a lot of noise and all this blue smoke. Phew.

Detective Anderson: Was anything written on the side? Like a company name?

June Morris: Nope. It was just a white van.

Detective Anderson: Did you see the license plate?

June Morris: Nope.

Detective Anderson: Which way did the van go?

June Morris: Down Barnum Street.

Detective Morris: And you're sure the man, the one who told you he had a bloody nose, was Terry Maitland?

June Morris: Sure, Coach Terry, Coach T. I see him all the time. Is he all right? Did he do something wrong? My mom says I can't look at the newspaper or watch the TV news, but I'm pretty sure something bad happened in the park. I'd know if school was in, because everybody blabs. Did Coach Terry fight with a bad person? Is that how he got the bloody—

Francine Morris: Are you almost done, Detective? I know you need information, but remember that I'm the one who has to put her to bed tonight.

June Morris: I put myself to bed!

Detective Anderson: Right, almost done. But June, before you go, I'm going to play a little game with you. Do you like games?

June Morris: I guess so, if they're not boring.

Detective Anderson: I'm going to put six photographs of six different people on the table . . . like this . . . and they all look a little like Coach Terry. I want you to tell me—

June Morris: That one. Number four. That's Coach Terry.

7

Troy Ramage opened one of the rear doors of the unmarked car. Terry looked over his shoulder and saw Marcy behind them, halted at the edge of the parking lot, her face a study in agonized bewilderment. Behind her came the *Call* photographer, snapping pictures even as he jogged across the grass. *Those won't be worth a damn*, Terry thought, and with a certain amount of satisfaction. To Marcy he shouted, "Call Howie Gold! Tell him I've been arrested! Tell him—"

Then Yates had his hand on top of Terry's head, pushing him down and in. "Slide over, slide over. And keep your hands in your lap while I fasten your seatbelt."

Terry slid over. He kept his hands in his lap. Through the windshield he could see the ballfield's big electronic scoreboard. His wife had led the fund drive for that two years before. She was standing there, and he would never forget the expression on her face. It was the look of some woman in a third world country, watching as her village burned.

Then Ramage was behind the wheel, Ralph Anderson was in the passenger seat, and even before Ralph could get his door closed, the unmarked was backing out of the handicap space with a chirp of the tires. Ramage turned tight, spinning the wheel with the heel of his hand, then headed for Tinsley Avenue. They rode *sans* siren, but a blue bubble-light stuck to the dashboard began to swing and flash. Terry realized that the car smelled of Mexican food. Strange, the things you noticed when your day—your *life*—suddenly went over a cliff you hadn't even known was there. He leaned forward.

"Ralph, listen to me."

Ralph was looking straight ahead. His hands were clenched tightly together. "You can talk all you want down at the station."

"Hell, let him tell it," Ramage said. "Save us all some time."

"Shut up, Troy," Ralph said. Still watching the road unroll. Terry could see two tendons standing out on the back of his neck, making the number 11.

"Ralph, I don't know what led you to me, or why you'd want to arrest me in front of half the town, but you're totally off the rails."

"So say they all," Tom Yates remarked from beside him in a just-passing-the-time voice. "Keep those hands in your lap, Maitland. Don't even scratch your nose."

Terry's head was clearing now—not a lot, but a little—and he was careful to do as Officer Yates (his name was pinned to his uniform shirt) had instructed. Yates looked as if he'd like an excuse to take a poke at his prisoner, cuffs or no cuffs.

Someone had been eating enchiladas in this car, Terry was sure of it. Probably from Señor Joe's. It was a favorite of his daughters, who always laughed a lot during the meal—hell, they all did—and accused each other of farting on their way home. "Listen to me, Ralph. Please."

He sighed. "Okay, I'm listening."

"We all are," Ramage said. "Open ears, buddy, open ears."

"Frank Peterson was killed on Tuesday. Tuesday afternoon. It was in the papers, it was on the news. I was in Cap City on Tuesday, Tuesday night, and most of Wednesday. Didn't get back until nine or nine thirty on Wednesday night. Gavin Frick, Barry Houlihan, and Lukesh Patel—Baibir's father—practiced the boys both days."

For a moment there was silence in the car, not even interrupted by the radio, which had been turned off. Terry had a golden moment in which he believed—yes, absolutely—that Ralph would now tell the big cop behind the wheel to pull over. Then he would turn to Terry with wide, embarrassed eyes and say, *Oh Christ, we really goofed, didn't we?*

What Ralph said, still without turning around, was, "Ah. Comes the famous alibi."

"What? I don't understand what you m—"

"You're a smart guy, Terry. I knew that from the first time I met you, back when you were coaching Derek in Little League. If you didn't confess outright—which I was hoping for, but didn't really expect—I was pretty sure you'd offer some kind of alibi." He turned around at last, and the face Terry looked into was that of an absolute stranger. "And I'm equally sure we'll knock it down. Because we've got you for this. We absolutely do."

"What were you doing in Cap City, Coach?" Yates asked, and all at once the man who had told Terry to not even scratch his nose sounded friendly, interested. Terry almost told him what he had been doing there, then decided against it. Thinking was beginning to replace reacting, and he realized this car, with its fading aroma of enchiladas, was enemy territory. It was time to shut up until Howie Gold arrived at the station. The two of them could sort this mess out together. It shouldn't take long.

He realized something else, as well. He was angry, probably angrier than he'd ever been in his life, and as they turned onto Main Street and headed for the Flint City police station, he made himself a promise: come fall, maybe even sooner, the man in the front seat, the one he'd considered a friend, was going to be looking for a new job. Possibly as a bank guard in Tulsa or Amarillo.

8

Statement of Mr. Carlton Scowcroft {July 12th, 9:30 PM, interviewed by Detective Ralph Anderson}

```
Scowcroft: Will this take long, Detective? Because
I usually go to bed early. I work maintenance on the
railroad, and if I don't clock in by seven, I'll be
in dutch.
```

Detective Anderson: I'll be as quick as I can, Mr. Scowcroft, but this is a serious matter.

Scowcroft: I know. And I'll help all I can. There's just, I don't have much to tell you, and I want to get home. I don't know how well I'll sleep, though. I haven't been in this station since a drinking party I went to when I was seventeen. Charlie Borton was chief then. Our fathers got us out, but I was grounded for the whole summer.

Detective Anderson: Well, we appreciate you coming in. Tell me where were you at seven PM on the night of July 10th.

Scowcroft: Like I told the gal at the desk when I came in, I was at Shorty's Pub, and I seen that white van, and I seen the guy who coaches baseball and Pop Warner over on West Side. I don't remember his name, but his picture's in the paper all the time because he's got a good City League team this year. Paper said they might go all the way. Moreland, is that his name? He had blood all over him.

Detective Anderson: How was it you happened to see him?

Scowcroft: Well, I got a routine for when I clock off work, not having a wife to go home to and not being much of a chef myself, if you know what I mean. Mondays and Wednesdays, it's the Flint City Diner. Fridays I go to Bonanza Steakhouse. And on Tuesdays and Thursdays, I usually go to Shorty's for a plate of ribs and a beer. That Tuesday I got to Shorty's at, oh, I'm gonna say quarter past six. Kid was already long dead by then, wasn't he?

Detective Anderson: But at around seven, you were out back, correct? Behind Shorty's Pub.

Scowcroft: Yeah, me and Riley Franklin. I ran into him there, and we ate together. Out back, that's where people go to smoke. Down the hall between the restrooms and out the back door. There's an ash bucket and everything. So we ate—I had the ribs, he had the mac and cheese—and we ordered dessert, and went out back to have a smoke before it came. While we were standing there, shooting the shit, this dirty white van pulled in. Had a New York plate on it, I remember that. It parked beside a little Subaru wagon—I think it was a Subaru—and that guy got out. Moreland, or whatever his name is.

Detective Anderson: What was he wearing?

Scowcroft: Well, I'm not sure about the pants—Riley might remember, they could've been chinos—but the shirt was white. I remember that because there was blood down the front of it, quite a bit. Not so much on the pants, just some spatters. There was blood on his face, too. Under his nose, around his mouth, on his chin. Man, he was gory. So Riley—I think he must have had a couple of beers before I showed up, but I only had the one—Riley says, "How's the other guy look, Coach T?"

Detective Anderson: He called him Coach T.

Scowcroft: Sure. And the coach, he laughs and says, "There was no other guy. Something let go in my nose, that's all, and it went like Old Faithful. Is there a doc-in-the-box anywhere around here?"

Detective Anderson: Which you took to mean a walk-in facility, like MedNOW or Quick Care?

Scowcroft: That's what he meant, all right, because he wanted to see if he needed it cauterized up there inside. Ouch, huh? Said he had it happen to him once before. I told him to go down Burrfield about a mile, turn left at the second light, and he'd see a sign. You know that billboard by Coney Ford? It tells you about how long you'll have to wait and everything. Then he asked if he could leave his van in that little parking area behind the pub, which is not for customers—as the sign on the back of the building says—but for employees. And I said, "It's not my lot, but if you don't leave it too long, it should be all right." Then he says—and it struck both of us as weird, times being what they are—that he'd leave the keys in the cup holder in case somebody had to move it. Riley said, "That's a good way to get it stoled, Coach T." But he said again that he wouldn't be long, and about how someone might want to move it. You know what I think? I think maybe he wanted someone to steal it, maybe even me or Riley. You think that could be, Detective?

   Detective Anderson: What happened then?

   Scowcroft: He got into that little green Subaru, and off he went. Which also struck me as weird.

   Detective Anderson: What was weird about it?

   Scowcroft: He asked if he could leave his van for a little while—like he thought it might get towed, or something—but his car was there all along, safe and sound. Weird, right?

   Detective Anderson: Mr. Scowcroft, I'm going to put six photographs of six different men down in front of you, and I want you to pick out the man you saw behind Shorty's. They all look similar, so I want you to take your time. Can you do that for me?

   Scowcroft: Sure, but I don't need to take my

time. That's him right there. Moreland, or whatever his name is. Can I go home now?

9

No one in the unmarked said anything else until they turned into the police station lot and parked in one of the spaces marked OFFICIAL VEHICLES ONLY. Then Ralph turned to survey the man who had coached his son. Terry Maitland's Dragons cap had been knocked slightly askew, so it sat in a kind of gangsta twist. His Dragons tee-shirt had come untucked on one side, and his face was streaked with sweat. In that moment he looked guilty as hell. Except, maybe, for his eyes, which met Ralph's dead-on. They were wide and silently accusing.

Ralph had a question that couldn't wait. "Why him, Terry? Why Frankie Peterson? Was he on the Lions Little League team this year? Did you have your eye on him? Or was it just a crime of opportunity?"

Terry opened his mouth to reiterate his denial, but what was the point? Ralph wasn't going to listen, at least not yet. None of them were. Better to wait. That was hard, but it might save time in the end.

"Go on," Ralph said. He spoke softly, conversationally. "You wanted to talk before, so talk now. Tell me. Make me understand. Right here, before we even get out of this car."

"I think I'll wait for my lawyer," Terry said.

"If you're innocent," Yates said, "you don't need one. Put a pin in this, if you can. We'll even give you a ride home."

Still looking into Ralph Anderson's eyes, Terry spoke almost too softly to hear. "This is bad behavior. You never even checked on where I might have been on Tuesday, did you? I wouldn't have thought it of you." He paused, as if thinking, then said: "You *bastard.*"

Ralph had no intention of telling Terry that he had discussed that with Samuels, but not for long. It was a small town. They hadn't wanted to start asking questions that could get back to Maitland. "This was a rare case where we didn't need to check." Ralph opened his door. "Come on. Let's get you booked and printed and photographed before your lawyer gets h—"

"Terry! *Terry!*"

Instead of taking Ralph's advice, Marcy Maitland had followed the police car from the field in her Toyota. Jamie Mattingly, a neighbor, had stepped up and taken Sarah and Grace to her house. Both girls had been crying. Jamie had been, too.

"Terry, what are they doing? What should *I* be doing?"

He twisted momentarily free of Yates, who had him by the arm. "Call Howie!"

It was all he had time for. Ramage opened the door marked POLICE PERSONNEL ONLY and Yates hustled Terry inside, none too gently, with a hand planted in the middle of his back.

Ralph stayed behind for a moment, holding the door. "Go home, Marcy," he said. "Go before the news people get there." He almost added *I'm sorry about this*, and didn't. Because he wasn't. Betsy Riggins and the State Police would be waiting for her, but it was still the best thing she could do. The only thing, really. And maybe he owed her. For her girls, certainly—they were the true innocents in all of this—but also . . .

This is bad behavior. I wouldn't have expected it of you.

There was no reason for Ralph to feel guilty at the reproach of a man who had raped and murdered a child, but for a moment he still did. Then he thought of the crime scene pictures, photos so ugly you almost wished you were blind. He thought of the branch sticking out of the little boy's rectum. He thought of a bloody mark on smooth wood. Smooth because the hand that left the print had shoved down so hard it had peeled the bark away.

Bill Samuels had made two simple points. Ralph had agreed, and so had Judge Carter, to whom Samuels had gone for the various warrants. First, it was a slam-dunk. There was no sense waiting when they already had everything they needed. Second, if they gave Terry time, he might take off, and then they'd have to find him before he found another Frank Peterson to rape and murder.

10

Statement of Mr. Riley Franklin {July 13th, 7:45 AM, interviewed by Detective Ralph Anderson}

Detective Anderson: I'm going to show you six photographs of six different men, Mr. Franklin, and I'd like you to pick out the man you saw behind Shorty's Pub on the evening of July 10th. Take your time.

Franklin: I don't need to. It's that one there. Number two. That's Coach T. I can't believe it. He coached my son in Little League.

Detective Anderson: It so happens he also coached mine. Thank you, Mr. Franklin.

Franklin: The needle's too good for him. They ought to hang him with a slow rope.

11

Marcy pulled into the parking lot of the Burger King on Tinsley Avenue, and took her cell phone out of her purse. Her hands were trembling, and she dropped it on the floor. She bent over to get it, thumped her head on the steering wheel, and began to cry again. She thumbed through her contacts and found Howie Gold's number—not because the Maitlands had a reason to keep a lawyer on speed-dial, but because Howie had coached Pop Warner with Terry during the last two seasons. He answered on the second ring.

"Howie? This is Marcy Maitland. Terry's wife?" As if they hadn't had dinner together once every month or so since 2016.

"Marcy? Are you crying? What's wrong?"

It was so enormous that at first she couldn't say it.

"Marcy? Are you still there? Were you in an accident or something?"

"I'm here. It's not me, it's Terry. They've arrested Terry. Ralph Anderson arrested Terry. For the murder of that boy. That's what they said. For the murder of the Peterson boy."

"*What?* Are you *shitting* me?"

"He wasn't even in town!" Marcy wailed. She heard herself doing it, thought she sounded like a teenager throwing a tantrum, but couldn't stop. "They arrested him, and they said the police are waiting at home!"

"Where are Sarah and Grace?"

"I sent them with Jamie Mattingly, from the next street over. They'll be okay for now." Although after just seeing their father arrested and led away in handcuffs, how okay could they be?

She rubbed her forehead, wondering if the steering wheel had left a mark, wondering why she cared. Because there might be news people waiting already? Because if there were, they might see the mark and think Terry had hit her?

"Howie, will you help me? Will you help us?"

"Of course I will. They took Terry to the station?"

"Yes! In handcuffs!"

"All right. I'm on my way. Go home, Marce. See what the police want. If they have a search warrant—that must be why they're there, I can't think of anything else—read it, see what they're after, let them in, but don't say anything. Have you got that? Don't say *anything*."

"I . . . yes."

"The Peterson boy was killed last Tuesday, I think. Wait—" There was murmuring in the background, first Howie, followed by a woman, probably Howie's wife, Elaine. Then Howie was back. "Yes, it was Tuesday. Where was Terry on Tuesday?"

"Cap City! He went—"

"Never mind that now. The police may ask you about that. They may ask you all sorts of things. Tell them you're keeping silent on advice from your lawyer. Got it?"

"Y-Yes."

"Don't let them coax, coerce, or bait you. They're good at all three."

"Okay. Okay, I won't."

"Where are you now?"

She knew, she'd seen the sign, but had to look at it again to be sure. "Burger King. The one on Tinsley. I pulled in to call you."

"Are you okay to drive?"

She almost told him she'd bumped her head, then didn't. "Yes."

"Take a deep breath. Take three. Then drive home. Speed limit all the way, signal every turn. Does Terry have a computer?"

"Sure. In his office. Plus an iPad, although he doesn't use it much. And we both have laptops. The girls have their own iPad Minis. And phones, of course, we all have phones. Grace just got hers for her birthday three months ago."

"They'll give you a list of the stuff they mean to take."

"Can they really do that?" She wasn't wailing again, but she was close. "Just take our stuff? It's like something out of Russia or North Korea!"

"They can take what their warrant says they can take, but I want you to keep your own list. Do the girls have their cell phones with them?"

"Are you kidding? Those things are practically grafted to their hands."

"Okay. The cops may want to take yours. Refuse."

"What if they take it, anyway?" And did it matter? Did it really?

"They won't. If you haven't been charged with anything, they can't. Go on now. I'll be with you just as soon as I can. We are going to sort this out, I promise you."

"Thank you, Howie." She began to cry again. "Thank you very, very much."

"You bet. And remember: speed limit, full stops, turnblinkers. Got it?"

"Yes."

"Headed to the station now." And he was gone.

Marcy put her car in drive, then put it back in park. She took a deep breath. Then two. Then three. *This is a nightmare, but at least it will be a short one. He was in Cap City. They'll see that, and they'll let him go.*

"Then," she told her car (it seemed so empty without the girls giggling and squabbling in the backseat), "we will sue their asses off."

That straightened her spine and brought the world back into focus. She drove home to Barnum Court, keeping to the speed limit and coming to a full stop at every stop sign.

12

Statement of Mr. George Czerny, {July 13th, 8:15 AM, interviewed by Officer Ronald Wilberforce}

```
Officer Wilberforce: Thank you for coming in, Mr.
Czerny—
   Czerny: You say it "Zurny." C-Z-E-R-N-Y. The C is
silent.
```

Officer Wilberforce: Uh-huh, thanks, I'll make a note of that. Detective Ralph Anderson will also want to talk to you, but right now he's busy with another interview, and he asked me to get the basic facts while they're fresh in your mind.

Czerny: Are you towing that car? That Subaru? You ought to get it impounded so no one can pollute the evidence. There's plenty of evidence, I can tell you that.

Officer Wilberforce: Being taken care of as we speak, sir. Now I believe you were out fishing this morning?

Czerny: Well, that was the plan, but as it turned out, I never even wet a line. I went out just after sunrise, to what they call the Iron Bridge. You know, out on Old Forge Road?

Officer Wilberforce: Yes, sir.

Czerny: It's a great place to catch catfish. Many people don't like to fish for them because they're ugly—not to mention that they'll bite you sometimes while you're trying to get the hook out of them—but my wife fries them up with salt and lemon juice, and they taste pretty damn good. The lemon's the secret, you know. And you have to use an iron skillet. What my ma used to call a spider.

Officer Wilberforce: So you parked at the end of the bridge—

Czerny: Yes, but off the highway. There's an old boat landing down there. Someone bought the land it's on a few years back and put up a wire fence with NO TRESPASSING signs on it. Never built anything yet, though. Those few acres just sit there growing weeds, and the landing's half under water.

I always park my truck on the little spur road that goes down to that wire fence. Which is what I did this morning, and what do I see? The fence is knocked down, and there's a little green car parked on the edge of that sunken boat landing, so close to the water that the front tires were half-sunk in the mud. So I went down there, because I figured some guy must've left the titty-bar drunk the night before, and run off the main road. Had an idea he might still be inside, passed out.

Officer Wilberforce: When you say titty-bar, you mean Gentlemen, Please, just out at the town line?

Czerny: Yeah. Yes. Men go there, they get loaded, they stuff ones and fives into the girls' panties until they're broke, then they drive home drunk. Don't understand the attraction of such places, myself.

Officer Wilberforce: Uh-huh. So you went down and looked in the car.

Czerny: It was a little green Subaru. Nobody in it, but there were bloody clothes on the passenger seat, and I thought right away of the little boy that was murdered, because the news said the police were looking for a green Subaru in connection with the crime.

Officer Wilberforce: Did you see anything else?

Czerny: Sneakers. On the floor of the passenger side footwell. They had blood on 'em, too.

Officer Wilberforce: Did you touch anything? Try the doors, maybe?

Czerny: Hell no. The wife and I never missed an episode of CSI when it was on.

Officer Wilberforce: What did you do?

Czerny: Called 911.

13

Terry Maitland sat in an interview room, waiting. The handcuffs had been removed so his lawyer wouldn't raise hell when he got here—which would be soon. Ralph Anderson stood at parade rest, hands clasped behind his back, watching his son's old coach through the one-way glass. He had sent Yates and Ramage on their way. He had spoken to Betsy Riggins, who told him Mrs. Maitland hadn't arrived home yet. Now that the arrest had been made and his blood had cooled a little, Ralph again felt uneasy about the speed at which this thing was progressing. It wasn't surprising that Terry was claiming an alibi, and it would surely prove as thin, but—

"Hey, Ralph." Bill Samuels hurried up, straightening the knot in his tie as he came. His hair was as black as Kiwi shoe polish, and worn short, but a cowlick stuck up in back, making him look younger than ever. Ralph knew Samuels had prosecuted half a dozen capital murder cases, all successfully, with two of his convicted murderers (he called them his "boys") currently on death row at McAlester. That was all to the good, nothing wrong with having a child prodigy on your team, but tonight the Flint County district attorney bore an eerie resemblance to Alfalfa in the old *Little Rascals* shorts.

"Hello, Bill."

"So there he is," Samuels said, looking in at Terry. "Don't like to see him in his game jersey and Dragons hat, though. I'll be happy when he's in a nice pair of county browns. Happier still when he's in a cell twenty feet from the go-to-sleep table."

Ralph said nothing. He was thinking of Marcy, standing at the edge of the police parking lot like a lost child, wringing her hands and staring at Ralph as if he were a complete stranger. Or the boogeyman. Except it was her husband who was the boogeyman.

As if reading his thoughts, Samuels asked, "Doesn't look like a monster, does he?"

"They rarely do."

Samuels reached into the pocket of his sportcoat and brought out several folded sheets of paper. One was a copy of Terry Maitland's fingerprints, taken from his file at Flint City High School. All new teachers had to be fingerprinted before they ever stepped before a class. The other two sheets were headed STATE CRIMINALISTICS. Samuels held them up and shook them. "The latest and the greatest."

"From the Subaru?"

"Yep. The state guys lifted over seventy prints in all, and fifty-seven are Maitland's. According to the tech who ran the comparisons, the others are much smaller, probably from the woman in Cap City who reported the car stolen two weeks ago. Barbara Nearing, her name is. Hers are much older, which lets her out of any part in the Peterson murder."

"Okay, but we still need DNA. He refused the swabs." Unlike fingerprints, DNA cheek swabs were considered *invasive* in this state.

"You know damn well we don't need them. Riggins and the Staties will take his razor, his toothbrush, and any hairs they find on his pillow."

"Not good enough until we match what we've got against samples we take right here."

Samuels looked at him, head tilted. Now he looked not like Alfalfa from *The Little Rascals*, but an extremely intelligent rodent. Or maybe a crow with its eye on something shiny. "Are you having second thoughts? Please tell me you're not. Especially when you were as raring to go as I was this morning."

Then I was thinking about Derek, Ralph thought. *That was before Terry looked me in the eye, as if he had a right to. And before he called me a bastard, which should have bounced right off and somehow didn't.*

"No second thoughts. It's just that moving so fast makes me nervous. I'm used to building a case. I didn't even have an arrest warrant."

"If you saw a kid dealing crack out of his knapsack in City Square, would you need a warrant?"

"Of course not, but this is different."

"Not much, not really, but as it so happens, I do have a warrant, and it was executed by Judge Carter before you made the arrest. It should be sitting in your fax machine right now. So . . . shall we go in and discuss the matter?" Samuels's eyes were brighter than ever.

"I don't think he'll talk to us."

"No, probably not."

Samuels smiled, and in that smile Ralph saw the man who had put two murderers on death row. And who would, Ralph had little doubt, soon put Derek Anderson's old Little League coach there, as well. Just one more of Bill's "boys."

"But we can talk to *him*, can't we? We can show him that the walls are closing in, and that he'll soon be so much strawberry jelly between them."

14

Statement of Ms. Willow Rainwater {July 13th, 11:40 AM, interviewed by Detective Ralph Anderson}

```
Rainwater: Go on and admit it, Detective—I'm the
least willowy Willow you ever saw.
   Detective Anderson: Your size isn't at issue
here, Ms. Rainwater. We're here to discuss—
   Rainwater: Oh yeah, it is, you just don't know
it. My size is why I was out there. There are ten,
maybe twelve cabs waiting around at that panty
palace by eleven o'clock most nights, and I'm the
```

only woman. Why? Because none of the customers try to hit on me, no matter how drunk they are. I could have played left tackle back in high school, if they let women on their football team. And hey, half those guys don't even realize I'm a gal when they get in my cab, and many still don't know when they get out of it. Which is just hunky-dunky with me. Only thought you might want to know what I was doing there.

  Detective Anderson: Okay, thanks.

  Rainwater: But this wasn't eleven, this was about eight thirty.

  Detective Anderson: On the night of Tuesday, July 10th.

  Rainwater: That's right. Weeknights are slow all over town since the oil patch more or less dried up. A lot of the drivers just hang around the garage, shooting the shit and playing poker and telling dirty stories, but I got no use for any of that, so I'm apt to go out to the Flint Hotel or the Holiday Inn or the Doubletree. Or I go out to Gentlemen, Please. They got a cab-stand there, you know, for those who haven't drunk themselves stupid enough to try driving home, and if I get there early, I'm usually first in line. Second or third at worst. I sit there and read on my Kindle while I wait for a fare. Hard to read a regular book once it gets dark, but the Kindle's just fine. Great fucking invention, if you'll pardon me for lapsing into my Native American tongue for a minute.

  Detective Anderson: If you could tell me—

  Rainwater: I am telling you, but I've got my own way of telling, been this way since I was in rompers, so be quiet. I know what you want, and I'll give it to you. Here and in court, too. Then, when they send that kid-murdering sonofabitch to hell, I'll put on my buckskins and my feathers and goofy-dance until I drop. We straight?

Detective Anderson: We are.

Rainwater: That night, early as it was, I was the only cab. I didn't see him go in. I got a theory about that, and I'll bet you five dollars I'm right. I don't think he went in to see the pussy-prancers. I think he turned up before I arrived—maybe just before—and just went in to call a cab.

Detective Anderson: You would have won that bet, Ms. Rainwater. Your dispatcher—

Rainwater: Clint Ellenquist was on dispatch Tuesday night.

Detective Anderson: That's correct. Mr. Ellenquist told the caller to check the cab-stand in the parking lot, and a cab would be there soon, if not already. That call was logged at eight forty.

Rainwater: Sounds about right. So he comes out, right over to my cab—

Detective Anderson: Can you tell me what he was wearing?

Rainwater: Bluejeans and a nice button-up shirt. The jeans were faded, but clean. Hard to tell under those arc-sodium parking lot lights, but I think the shirt was yellow. Oh, and his belt had a fancy buckle—a horse's head. Rodeo shit. Until he bent down, I thought he was probably just another Oil-patch Pete who somehow held onto his job when the price of crude went to hell, or a construction worker. Then I saw it was Terry Maitland.

Detective Anderson: You're sure of that.

Rainwater: Hand to God. The lights in that parking lot are bright as day. They keep it that way to discourage muggings and fistfights and drug deals. Because their clientele is such a bunch of gentlemen, you know. Also, I coach Prairie League basketball down at the YMCA. Those teams are coed, but they're mostly boys. Maitland used to come down—not every Saturday, but a lot of 'em—and sit on the bleachers with the parents and watch the kids play. He told me he was scouting talent for City League baseball, said you could tell a kid with natural defensive talent by watching 'em play hoops, and like a fool I believed him. He was probably sitting there and trying to decide which one he'd like to cornhole. Judging them the way men judge women in a bar. Fucking pervo deviant asshole. Scouting talent, my wide Indian ass!

Detective Anderson: When he came to your cab, did you tell him you recognized him?

Rainwater: Oh yeah. Discretion may be somebody's middle name, but it ain't mine. I say, "Hey there, Terry, does your wife know where you are tonight?" And he says, "I had a spot of business to do." And I say, "Would your spot of business have involved a lap dance?" And he says, "You should call in and tell your dispatcher I'm all set." So I say, "I'll do that. Are we headed home, Coach T?" And he says, "Not at all, ma'am. Drive me to Dubrow. The train station." I say, "That's gonna be a forty-dollar fare." And he says, "Make it in time for me to catch the train to Dallas, and I'll tip you twenty." So I say, "Jump in and hold onto your jock, Coach, here we go."

THE OUTSIDER

Detective Anderson: So you drove him to the Amtrak station in Dubrow?

Rainwater: I did indeed. Got him there in plenty of time to catch the night train to Dallas–Fort Worth.

Detective Anderson: Did you make conversation with him on the way? I ask because you seem like the conversational type.

Rainwater: Oh, I am! My tongue runs like a supermarket conveyor belt on payday. Just ask anybody. I started by asking him about the City League Tourney, were they gonna beat the Bears, and he said, "I expect good things." Like getting an answer from a Magic 8 Ball, right? I bet he was thinking about what he'd done, and making a quick getaway. Stuff like that must put a hole in your small talk. My question for you, Detective, is why the hell did he come back to FC? Why didn't he run all the way across Texas and down to Old Meh-hee-co?

Detective Anderson: What else did he say?

Rainwater: Not much. He said he was going to try and catch a nap. He closed his eyes, but I think he was faking. I think he might have been peeking at me, like maybe he was thinking of trying something. I wish he had. And I wish I'd known then what I know now, about what he done. I would have pulled him out of my cab and tore off his plumbing. I ain't lying.

Detective Anderson: And when you got to the Amtrak station?

Rainwater: I pulled up to the drop-off and he tossed three twenties on the front seat. I started to tell him to say hello to his wife, but he was already gone. Did he also go into Gentlemen to change his clothes in the men's room? Because there was blood on them?

Detective Anderson: I'm going to put six pictures of six different men down in front of you, Ms. Rainwater. They all look similar, so take your t—

Rainwater: Don't bother. That's him right there. That's Maitland. Go get him, and I hope he resists arrest. Save the taxpayers a piece of change.

15

When Marcy Maitland was in junior high (that was what it was still called when she went there), she sometimes had a nightmare that she turned up in home room naked, and everyone laughed. *Stupid Marcy Gibson forgot to get dressed this morning! Look, you can see everything!* By the time she got to high school, this anxiety dream had been replaced by a slightly more sophisticated one where she arrived in class clothed but realizing she was about to take the biggest test of her life and had forgotten to study.

When she turned off Barnum Street and onto Barnum Court, the horror and the helplessness of those dreams returned, and this time there would be no sweet relief and muttered *Thank God* when she woke up. In her driveway was a cop car that could have been the twin of the one which had conveyed Terry to the police station. Parked behind it was a windowless truck with STATE POLICE MOBILE CRIME UNIT printed on the side in big blue letters. Bookending the driveway was a pair of black OHP cruisers, with their lightbars strobing in the day's growing gloom. Four large troopers, their County Mounty hats making them look at least seven feet tall, stood on the sidewalk, their legs spread (*as if their balls are too big to keep them together*, she thought). These things were bad enough, but not the worst. The worst was her neighbors, standing out on their lawns and watching. Did they know why this police presence had suddenly materialized in front of the neat Maitland ranchhouse? She guessed that most already did—the curse of cell phones—and they would tell the rest.

One of the troopers stepped into the street, holding up a hand. She stopped and powered down her window.

"Are you Marcia Maitland, ma'am?"

"Yes. I can't get into my garage with those vehicles in my driveway."

"Park at the curb there," he said, pointing behind one of the cruisers.

Marcy felt an urge to lean through the open window, get right up in his face, and scream, *MY driveway! MY garage! Get your stuff out of my way!*

Instead, she pulled over and got out. She needed to pee, and badly. Probably had needed to since the cop had handcuffed Terry, and she just hadn't realized until now.

One of the other cops was talking into his shoulder mic, and from around the corner of the house, walkie-talkie in one hand, came the crowning touch of this evening's malignant surrealism: a hugely pregnant woman in a sleeveless flower-print dress. She cut across the Maitland lawn in that peculiar duck-footed walk—almost a waddle—that all women seem to have when they arrive at the far end of their last trimester. She did not smile as she approached Marcy. A laminated ID hung from her neck. Pinned to her dress, riding the slope of one enormous breast and as out of place as a dog biscuit on a communion plate, was a Flint City police badge.

"Mrs. Maitland? I'm Detective Betsy Riggins."

She held out her hand. Marcy did not shake it. And although Howie had already told her, she said, "What do you want?"

Riggins looked over Marcy's shoulder. One of the state cops was standing there. He was apparently the bull goose of the quartet, because he had stripes on his shirtsleeve. He was holding out a sheet of paper. "Mrs. Maitland, I'm Lieutenant Yunel Sablo. We have a warrant to search these premises and take out any items belonging to your husband, Terence John Maitland."

She snatched the paper. SEARCH WARRANT was printed at the top in gothic type. There followed a bunch of legalistic blah-blah, and it was signed at the bottom by a name she at first misread as Judge Crater. *Didn't he disappear a long time ago?* she thought, then blinked water from her eyes—maybe sweat, maybe tears—and saw the name was Carter, not Crater. The warrant bore today's date and had apparently been signed less than six hours ago.

She turned it over and frowned. "There's nothing listed here. Does that mean you can even take his underwear, if you want to?"

Betsy Riggins, who knew they *would* take any underwear they happened to find in the Maitlands' dirty clothes hamper, said, "It's at our discretion, Mrs. Maitland."

"Your discretion? Your *discretion*? What is this, Nazi Germany?"

Riggins said, "We are investigating the most heinous murder to occur in this state during my twenty years as a policewoman, and we will take what we need to take. We have done you the courtesy of waiting until you got home—"

"To hell with your courtesy. If I'd turned up late, you would have what? Broken down the door?"

Riggins looked vastly uncomfortable—not because of the question, Marcy thought, but because of the passenger she was lugging around on this hot July night. She should have been sitting at home, with the air conditioning on and her feet up. Marcy didn't care. Her head was pounding, her bladder was throbbing, and her eyes were welling with tears.

"That would have been a last resort," said the trooper with the shit on his sleeve, "but within our legal right, as defined by the warrant I have just shown you."

"Let us in, Mrs. Maitland," Riggins said. "The sooner we get started, the sooner we'll be out of your hair."

"Yo, Loot," one of the other troopers said. "Here come the vultures."

Marcy turned. From around the corner came a TV truck, with its satellite dish still folded against the roof. Behind it was an SUV with KYO decaled on the hood in big white letters. Behind that, almost kissing the KYO vehicle's bumper, came another TV truck from another station.

"Come inside with us," Riggins said. Almost coaxed. "You don't want to be on the sidewalk when they get here."

Marcy gave in, thinking this might be the first surrender of many. Her privacy. Her dignity. Her kids' sense of security. And her husband? Would she be forced to surrender Terry? Surely not. What they were accusing him of was insane. They might as well have accused him of kidnapping the Lindbergh baby.

"All right. But I'm not going to talk to you, so don't even try. And I don't have to give you my phone. My lawyer said so."

"That's fine." Riggins took her by the arm, when—given the size of her—Marcy should have been taking hers, to make sure she didn't trip and fall on her enormous belly.

The Chevy Tahoe from KYO—"Ki-Yo," as they styled themselves—stopped in the middle of the street, and one of their correspondents, the pretty blond one, got out so fast that her skirt slid most of the way to her waist. The troopers did not miss this.

"Mrs. Maitland! Mrs. Maitland, just a couple of questions!"

Marcy couldn't remember taking her purse when she exited the car, but it was over her shoulder and she got the house key out of the side pocket with no trouble. The trouble came when she tried to get it into the lock. Her hand was trembling too badly. Riggins didn't take the key, but closed her hand over Marcy's to steady it, and it finally slid home.

From behind her: "Is it true that your husband has been arrested for the murder of Frank Peterson, Mrs. Maitland?"

"Keep back," one of the troopers said. "Not one step off the sidewalk."

"Mrs. Maitland!"

Then they were inside. That was good, even with the pregnant detective beside her, but the house looked different, and Marcy knew it would never look quite the same. She thought of the woman who had left here with her daughters, all of them laughing and excited, and it was like thinking of a woman you had loved, but who had died.

Her legs gave out and she plopped onto the bench in the hall where the girls sat to put on their boots in winter. Where Terry sometimes sat (as he had tonight) to go over his lineup one final time before leaving for the field. Betsy Riggins sat down beside her with a grunt of relief, her meaty right hip thwacking against Marcy's less padded left one. The cop with the shit on his sleeve, Sablo, and two others passed them without a look, drawing on thick blue plastic gloves. They were already wearing booties of a matching blue. Marcy assumed the fourth one was doing crowd control. Crowd control in front of their house on sleepy Barnum Court.

"I have to pee," she said to Riggins.

"As do I," Riggins said. "Lieutenant Sablo! A word?"

The one with the shit on his sleeve returned to the bench. The other two continued on into the kitchen, where the most evil thing they'd find was half a devil's food cake in the fridge.

To Marcy, Riggins asked, "Do you folks have a downstairs bathroom?"

"Yes, through the pantry. Terry added it himself last year."

"Uh-huh. Lieutenant, the ladies need to pee, so that's where you start, and make it as fast as you can." And, to Marcy: "Does your husband have an office?"

"Not as such. He uses the far end of the dining room."

"Thank you. That's your next stop, Lieutenant." She turned back to Marcy. "Mind one little question while we wait?"

"Yes."

Riggins paid this no mind. "Have you noticed anything odd about your husband's behavior over the last few weeks?"

Marcy gave a humorless laugh. "You mean was he building up to committing murder? Walking around, rubbing his hands together, maybe drooling and muttering to himself? Has your pregnancy affected your mind, Detective?"

"I take it that's a no."

"It is. Now please stop *nagging* me!"

Riggins sat back and folded her hands on her belly. Leaving Marcy with her throbbing bladder and a memory of something Gavin Frick had said only last week, after practice: *Where's Terry's mind lately? Half the time he seems somewhere else. It's like he's fighting the flu, or something.*

"Mrs. Maitland?"

"What?"

"You look like you had a thought there."

"I did, actually. I was thinking that sitting next to you on this bench is very uncomfortable. It's like sitting next to an oven that knows how to breathe."

Fresh color rose in Betsy Riggins's already flushed cheeks. On one hand, Marcy was horrified at what she had just said—the cruelty of it. On the other, she was delighted that she had gotten in a thrust that seemed to have gone home.

In any case, Riggins asked no more questions.

What seemed like an endless time later, Sablo came back, holding a clear plastic bag that contained all the pills from the downstairs medicine cabinet (OTC stuff, their few prescriptions were in the two bathrooms upstairs), and Terry's tube of hemorrhoid cream. "All clear," he said.

"You first," Riggins said.

Under other circumstances, Marcy surely would have deferred to the pregnant lady and held her water a bit longer, but not under these. She went in, closed the door, and saw the cover of the toilet tank was on crooked. They had been probing in there for God knew what—drugs, seemed most likely. She urinated with her head lowered and her face in her hands, so she didn't have to look at the rest of the disarray. Was she going to bring Sarah and Grace back here tonight? Was she going to escort them through the glare of the TV lights, which would undoubtedly be set up by then? And if not here, where? A hotel? Wouldn't they (*the vultures*, the trooper had called them) still find them? Of course they would.

When she finished emptying out, Betsy Riggins went. Marcy slipped into the dining room, having no wish to share the hall bench again with Officer Shamu. The cops were going through Terry's desk—*raping* his desk, really, all the drawers out, most of the contents piled on the floor. His computer had already been dismantled, the various components plastered with yellow stickers, as if in preparation for a tag sale.

Marcy thought, *An hour ago the most important thing in my life was a Golden Dragons win and a trip to the finals.*

Betsy Riggins returned. "Oh, that's so much better," she said, sitting down at the dining room table. "And will be, for a whole fifteen minutes."

Marcy opened her mouth and what almost came out was *I hope your baby dies.*

Instead of that she said, "It's nice that someone's feeling better. Even for fifteen minutes."

16

Statement of Mr. Claude Bolton {July 13th, 4:30 PM, interviewed by Detective Ralph Anderson}

Detective Anderson: Well, Claude, it must be nice for you to be here when you're not in trouble. Refreshing.

Bolton: You know, it kind of is. And to get a ride in the front of a police car instead of in the back. Ninety miles an hour most of the way back from Cap City. Lights, siren, the whole works. You're right. It was nice.

Detective Anderson: What were you doing in Cap?

Bolton: Seeing the sights. Had a couple of nights off, so why not? No law against it, is there?

Detective Anderson: I understand you were seeing them with Carla Jeppeson, known as Pixie Dreamboat when she's working.

Bolton: You should know, since she came back in the cruiser with me. She also appreciated the ride, by the way. Said it beat the hell out of Trailways.

Detective Anderson: And the sights you saw, most of those would have been in Room 509 of the Western Vista Motel out on Highway 40?

Bolton: Oh, we didn't spend all our time there. Went to Bonanza for dinner twice. They give you a damn good meal there, and for cheap. Also, Carla wanted to go to the mall, so we spent some time there. They have a climbing wall, and I killed that sucker.

Detective Anderson: I'll bet you did. Were you aware that a boy had been murdered here in Flint City?

Bolton: I might have seen something on the news. Listen, you don't think I had anything to do with that, do you?

Detective Anderson: No, but you may have information concerning the person who did.

Bolton: How could I—

Detective Anderson: You work as a bouncer at Gentlemen, Please, isn't that correct?

Bolton: I'm part of the security staff. We don't use the term bouncer. Gentlemen, Please is a high-class establishment.

Detective Anderson: We won't argue the point. You were working Tuesday night, I'm told. Didn't leave FC until Wednesday afternoon.

Bolton: Was it Tony Ross told you me and Carla went to Cap City?

Detective Anderson: Yes.

Bolton: We got a rate at that motel because Tony's uncle owns it. Tony was also on duty Tuesday night, that's when I asked him to call his unc. We're tight, me and Tony. We were on the door from four until eight, then in the pit from eight to midnight. The pit is in front of the stage, where the gentlemen sit.

Detective Anderson: Mr. Ross also told me that on or around eight thirty, you saw someone you recognized.

Bolton: Oh, you mean Coach T. Hey, you don't think he was the one who did that kid, do you? Because Coach T's a straight arrow. He coached Tony's nephews in Pop Warner and in Little League. I was surprised to see him in our place, but not shocked. You'd never guess some of the people we see in the pit—bankers, lawyers, even a couple of men of the cloth. But it's like they say about Vegas: what happens in Gent's stays in—

Detective Anderson: Uh-huh, I'm sure you're as discreet as priests in the confessional.

Bolton: Joke about it if you want, but we are. If you want repeat business, you have to be.

Detective Anderson: Also for the record, Claude, when you say Coach T, you're talking about Terry Maitland.

Bolton: Sure.

Detective Anderson: Tell me how you happened to see him.

Bolton: We don't spend all of our time in the pit, okay? There's more to the job than that. Most of the time we're there, circulating, making sure none of the guys get their hands on the girls, and stopping fights before they get going—when guys get randy, they also can get aggressive, you must know that in your line of work. But the pit's not the only place trouble can start, it's just the most likely place, so one of us stays there all the time. The other one floats—checks the bar, the little alcove where there's a few video games and a coin-op pool table, the private dance cubbies, and of course the men's room. That's where your drug deals are apt to go down, and if we see them, we put a stop to them and kick the guys out.

Detective Anderson: Says the man who's got a jacket for possession and possession with intent to sell.

Bolton: All due respect, sir, but that's just mean. I've been clean for six years. Go to NA and all. You want me to drop a urine? Happy to oblige.

Detective Anderson: That won't be necessary, and I congratulate you on your sobriety. So you were circulating around eight thirty—

Bolton: That's right. I checked the bar, then I started down the hall to take a peek in the men's, and that's where I saw Coach T, just hanging up the phone. There are two pay phones back there, but only one of them works. He was . . .

Detective Anderson: Claude? You kind of dropped out on me there.

Bolton: Just thinking. Remembering. He looked kind of funny. In a daze, like. You really think he killed that kid? I thought it was just because it was his first visit to a place where young ladies take off their clothes. It gets some guys that way, makes them kinda stupid. Or he might've been high. I said, "Hey, Coach, how's that team of yours looking?" And he gives me this stare like he's never seen me before, although I went to just about every one of the Pop Warner games Stevie and Stanley played in, and told him about how to run a double reverse, which he never did because he said it was too complex for little kids. Although if they can learn long division, they ought to be able to learn something like that, don't you think?

Detective Anderson: You're sure it was Terence Maitland.

Bolton: Oh God, yes. He said the team was fine, and told me he just stopped in to call a cab. Sort of like the way we all used to say we only read *Playboy* for the articles when our wives saw it in the bathroom beside the toilet. But I went along with it, the customer is always right at Gentlemen's as long as he doesn't try to grab a handful of tit. Told him there might be a cab or two outside already. He said the dispatcher already told him that, and thanked me, and off he went.

   Detective Anderson: What was he wearing?

   Bolton: Yellow shirt, jeans. Belt buckle with a horse's head on it. Fancy sneakers. I remember those, because they looked pretty expensive.

   Detective Anderson: Were you the only one who saw him in the club?

   Bolton: No, I saw a couple of guys tip him a wave as he went out. Don't know who they were, and you might have trouble finding them, because a lot of guys don't want to admit they like to visit places like Gent's. Just a fact of life. I wasn't surprised he got recognized, because Terry's pretty close to famous around here. Even won some sort of award a few years back, I saw that in the paper. Call it Flint City all you want, it's really just a small town where most everybody knows everybody else, at least by face. And anybody with sons who are what you'd call athletically inclined, they know Coach T from baseball or football.

   Detective Anderson: Thank you, Claude. This has been helpful.

   Bolton: I remember one other thing, no big deal but kind of spooky if he really was the one who killed that kid.

   Detective Anderson: Go on.

   Bolton: It was just one of those things that happen, nobody's fault. He was on his way out to see if there was a cab, right? I stuck out my hand and said, "I want to thank you for everything you did for Tony's nephews, Coach. They're good boys, but a little rambunctious, maybe because of their folks getting divorced and all. You gave 'em something to do besides hell around town." I think I surprised him, because he jerked back a little before he shook with me. He had a good strong grip, though, and . . . see this little scab on the back of my hand? He did it with his pinky nail when we shook. It's pretty much healed up already, wasn't no more than a nick in the first place, but it took me back to my drug days for a second or two.

Detective Anderson: Why is that?

Bolton: Some guys—Hells Angels and Devils Disciples, mostly—used to grow out one of their pinky nails. I've seen some as long as those Chinese emperors used to have. Some of the bikers even decorate 'em with decals, like the ladies do on theirs. They call it their coke nail.

17

After the arrest at the baseball field there was no possibility of Ralph playing the good cop in a good cop/bad cop scenario, so he simply stood leaning against the wall of the interview room, looking on. He was prepared for another of those accusing stares, but Terry only glanced at him briefly, and with no expression at all, before turning his attention to Bill Samuels, who had taken a seat in one of the three chairs on the other side of the table.

Studying Samuels now, Ralph began to get an idea of how he

had risen so high so quickly. While the two of them were standing on the other side of the one-way glass, the DA had simply looked a bit young for the job. Now, facing Frankie Peterson's rapist and killer, he looked even younger, like a law office intern who had (due to some mixup, probably) landed this interview with a big-time perp. Even the little Alfalfa cowlick sticking up from the back of his head added to the role the man had slipped into: untried youth, just happy to be here. *You can tell me anything*, said those wide, interested eyes, *because I'll believe it. This is my first time playing with the big boys, and I just don't know any better.*

"Hello, Mr. Maitland," Samuels said. "I work in the county DA's office."

Good start, Ralph thought. *You* are *the county DA's office.*

"You're wasting your time," Terry said. "I'm not going to talk to you until my lawyer gets here. I will say that I see a sizeable wrongful arrest suit in your future."

"I understand that you're upset, in your position, anyone would be. Maybe we can iron it out right here. Can you just tell me where you were when the Peterson boy was killed? That was on last Tuesday afternoon. If you were somewhere else, then—"

"I was," Terry said, "but I intend to discuss that with my lawyer before I discuss it with you. His name is Howard Gold. When he gets here, I'll want to talk to him privately. I assume that's my right? Since I'm presumed innocent until proven guilty?"

Quick recovery, Ralph thought. *A career criminal couldn't have done it better.*

"It is indeed," Samuels said. "But if you haven't done anything—"

"Don't try, Mr. Samuels. You didn't bring me here because you're a nice guy."

"Actually, I am," Samuels said earnestly. "If there's been a mistake, I'm as interested in getting it straightened out as you are."

"You have some hair sticking up in back," Terry said. "Might want to do something about that. It makes you look like Alfalfa in the old comedies I used to watch when I was a kid."

Ralph didn't even come close to laughing, but one corner of his mouth twitched. That he couldn't help.

Momentarily put off-balance, Samuels raised a hand to smooth down the cowlick. It laid flat for a moment, then sprang back up.

"Are you sure you don't want to clear this up?" Samuels leaned forward, his earnest expression suggesting that Terry was making a bad mistake.

"I'm sure," Terry said. "And I'm sure about the suit, too. I don't think there's a settlement large enough to pay for what you sorry sons of bitches did tonight—not just to me, but to my wife and girls—but I intend to find out."

Samuels sat where he was for a moment longer—leaning forward, innocently hopeful eyes locked on Terry's—and then he stood up. The innocent look disappeared. "Okay. Fine. You can confer with your lawyer, Mr. Maitland, that's your right. No audio, no video, we'll even draw the curtain. If you two are quick about it, maybe we can get this squared away tonight. I've got an early tee time in the morning."

Terry looked as if he had misheard. *"Golf?"*

"Golf. It's a game where you try to knock the little ball into the cup. I'm not very good at it, but I'm *very* good at this game, Mr. Maitland. And as the estimable Mr. Gold will tell you, we can hold you here for forty-eight hours without charging you. It won't actually be that long. If we can't clarify this, we'll take you for arraignment bright and early on Monday morning. Your arrest will be statewide news by then, so there will be plenty of coverage. I'm sure the photographers will get your good side."

Having gotten what he assumed was the last word, Samuels almost strutted to the door (Ralph guessed Terry's comment about the cowlick still rankled). Before he could open it, Terry said, "Hey, Ralph."

Ralph turned. Terry looked calm, which was extraordinary under the circumstances. Or maybe not. Sometimes the really cold ones, the sociopaths, found that calm after the initial shock, and buckled down for the long haul. Ralph had seen it before.

"I'm not going to discuss any of this until Howie gets here, but I want to tell you one thing."

"Go ahead." That was Samuels, trying not to sound eager, but his face fell at what Terry said next.

"Derek was the best drag bunter I ever had."

"Oh, no," Ralph said. He could hear the rage trembling in his voice, a kind of vibrato. "Don't go there. I don't want to hear my son's name come out of your mouth. Not tonight, not ever."

Terry nodded. "I can relate, because I never wanted to be arrested in front of my wife and daughters and a thousand other people, many of them my neighbors. So never mind what you don't want to hear. Just listen a minute. I think you owe me that for doing it the nasty way."

Ralph opened the door, but Samuels put a hand on his arm, shook his head, and raised his eyes slightly to the camera in the corner with its small red light. Ralph closed the door again and turned back to Terry, crossing his arms over his chest. He had an idea that Terry's idea of payback for the public arrest was going to hurt, but he knew Samuels was right. A suspect talking was always better than a suspect clamming up until his lawyer arrived. Because one thing had a way of leading to another.

Terry said, "Derek couldn't have been more than four-ten or -eleven back in Little League. I've seen him since—tried to get him to play for City last year, as a matter of fact—and he's grown six inches since then. He'll be taller than you by the time he graduates from high school, I bet."

Ralph waited.

"He was a shrimp, but he was never afraid in the batter's box. A lot of them are, but Derek would stand in even against the kids who'd wind up and fling the ball with no idea of where it was going. Got hit half a dozen times, but he never gave in."

It was the truth. Ralph had seen the bruises after some of the games, when D peeled off his uniform: on the butt, on the thigh, on the arm, on the shoulder. Once there had been a perfect black and blue circle on the nape of his neck. Those hits had driven Jeanette crazy, and the batting helmet Derek wore didn't comfort her; every time D stepped into the batter's box, she had gripped Ralph's arm almost hard enough to bring blood, afraid the kid would eventually take one between the eyes and wind up in a coma. Ralph assured her it wouldn't happen, but he had been almost as glad as Jeannie was when Derek decided tennis was more his game. The balls were softer.

Terry leaned forward, actually smiling a little.

"A kid that short usually gets a lot of walks—as a matter of fact, that's sort of what I was hoping for tonight, when I let Trevor Michaels bat for himself—but Derek wasn't going to get cheated. He'd flail at just about anything—inside, outside, over his head or in the dirt. Some of the kids started calling him Whiffer Anderson, then one of them changed it to Swiffer, like the mop, and that stuck. At least for awhile."

"Very interesting," Samuels said, "but why don't we talk about Frank Peterson, instead?"

Terry's eyes remained fixed on Ralph.

"Long story short, when I saw he wouldn't take a walk, I taught him to bunt. Lot of boys his age—ten, eleven—they won't do it. They get the idea, but they don't like dropping the bat over the plate, especially against a kid who can really bring it. They keep thinking about how much their fingers are going to hurt if they get hit with their bare hands out front like that. Not Derek, though. He had a yard of guts, your boy. Besides, he could really scoot down the line, and a lot of times when I sent him up to sacrifice, he ended up getting a base hit."

Ralph didn't nod or give any sign at all that he cared about this, but he knew what Terry was talking about. He had cheered plenty of those bunts, and had seen his kid fly down the line like his hair was on fire and his ass was catching.

"It was just a matter of teaching him the right bat angles," Terry said, and held up his hands to demonstrate. They were still smudged with dirt, probably from throwing batting practice before tonight's game. "Angle to the left, the ball squirts up the third base line. Angle to the right, first base line. Don't shove the bat, most times that does nothing but send an easy pop-up to the pitcher, just give it a little nudge at the last split-second. He caught on fast. The kids stopped calling him Swiffer and gave him a new nickname. We'd have a runner on first or third late in the game and the other team knew he was going to lay one down—there was no faking, he'd drop the bat across the plate as soon as the pitcher went into his motion, and the kids on the bench would all be yelling 'Push it, Derek, push it!' Me and Gavin, too. And that was what they called him that whole last year, when we won the district. Push It Anderson. Did you know that?"

Ralph hadn't, maybe because it was strictly a team thing. What he did know was that Derek had grown up a lot that summer. He laughed more, and wanted to hang around after the games were over instead of just heading for the car with his head down and his glove dangling.

"He did most of it himself—practiced like a mother until he had it right—but I was the one who talked him into trying it." He paused, then said, very softly, "And you do this to me. In front of everyone, you do this to me."

Ralph felt his cheeks heat up. He opened his mouth to reply, but Samuels was escorting him out the door, almost pulling him along. He paused just long enough to say one thing over his shoulder. "Ralph didn't do it to you, Maitland. Neither did I. You did it to yourself."

Then the two of them were looking through the one-way glass again, and Samuels was asking if Ralph was all right.

"Fine," Ralph said. His cheeks were still burning.

"Some of them are masters at getting under your skin. You know that, right?"

"Yes."

"And you know he did this, right? I've never had a case sewn up so tight."

Which bothers me, Ralph thought. *It didn't before, but it does now. It shouldn't, because Samuels is right, but it does.*

"Did you notice his hands?" Ralph asked. "When he was showing how he taught Derek to bunt, did you see his hands?"

"Yes. What about them?"

"No long pinky fingernail," Ralph said. "Not on either hand."

Samuels shrugged. "So he clipped it. Are you sure you're all right?"

"Fine," Ralph said. "I just—"

The door between the office area and the detention wing buzzed, then banged open. The man who came hurrying down the hallway was dressed in his Saturday night relaxing-at-home clothes—faded jeans and a TCU tee-shirt with SuperFrog hopping on the front—but the boxy briefcase he was carrying was all lawyer.

"Hello, Bill," he said. "And hello to you, Detective Anderson. Would either of you like to tell me why you have arrested Flint City's 2015 Man of the Year? Is it just a mistake, one we can perhaps smooth over, or have you lost your fucking minds?"

Howard Gold had arrived.

18

To: County District Attorney William Samuels
Flint City Chief of Police Rodney Geller

THE OUTSIDER

Flint County Sheriff Richard Doolin
Capt. Avery Rudolph, State Police Post 7
Det. Ralph Anderson, Flint City PD

From: Det. Lieutenant Yunel Sablo, State Police Post 7
Date: July 13th

Subject: Vogel Transportation Center, Dubrow

As per request of DA Samuels and Detective Anderson, I arrived at the Vogel Transportation Center at 2:30 PM on the date referenced above. Vogel is the main depot for land transportation in the southern part of the state, housing three major bus lines (Greyhound, Trailways, Mid-State) as well as Amtrak service. There are also the usual car rental agencies (Hertz, Avis, Enterprise, Alamo). Since all areas of the Transportation Center are well monitored by surveillance cameras, I went directly to the security office, where I was met by Michael Camp, Vogel's Security Director. He was ready for me. Surveillance footage is kept for 30 days, and the whole operation is computerized, so I was able to review everything from the night of July 10th, as seen from a total of 16 cameras.

According to Mr. Clinton Ellenquist, the Flint City Cab Company dispatcher who was on duty on the night of July 10th, driver Willow Rainwater called in at 9:30 PM to report she had delivered her fare. The Southern Limited, which Ms. Rainwater has stated is the train the subject under investigation meant to take, pulled into the Vogel at 9:50 PM.

Passengers disembarked at Track 3. Passengers going on to Dallas—Fort Worth were given the go-ahead to embark at Track 3 seven minutes later, at 9:57. The Southern Limited pulled out at 10:12. Times are exact, as all arrivals and departures are monitored and recorded by computer.

Security Director Camp and I reviewed surveillance footage from all 16 cameras, beginning at 9:00 PM on July 10th (just to be on the safe side) and ending at 11:00 PM, approximately 50 minutes after the Southern Limited left the station. I have all camera references on my iPad, but due to the stated (by DA Samuels) urgency of the situation, I will only summarize in this preliminary report.

9:33 PM: Subject enters the station through the north portal, which is the usual drop-off point for taxis and where most travelers enter. He crosses the main concourse. Yellow shirt, bluejeans. He has no luggage. Clear view of his face for 2 to 4 seconds as he looks up at the large overhead clock (still image emailed to DA Samuels and Detective Anderson).

9:35 PM: Subject stops at the newsstand in the center of the concourse. He buys a paperback book, paying cash. The title cannot be read, and the clerk does not remember, but we can probably get this if needed. In this footage, the horse's head belt buckle can be seen (still image emailed to DA Samuels and Detective Anderson).

9:39 PM: Subject exits the station via the Montrose Avenue door (south portal). Although this entrance/exit point is open to the public, it is mostly used by Vogel personnel, as the employee parking lot is on that side of the building. Two cameras are placed

THE OUTSIDER

to monitor this lot. Subject does not appear on either camera, but both Camp and I detected a momentary shadow, which we believe may have been the subject, heading to the right, toward a service alley.

Subject did not buy a ticket on the Southern Limited, either for cash at the station or by credit card. After several reviews of the Track 3 footage, which is clear and in my opinion complete, I can state with reasonable certainty that the subject did not re-enter the station and board the train.

My conclusion is that the subject's trip to Dubrow may have been an effort to lay a false trail and thus confuse pursuit. My speculation is that the subject may have returned to Flint City, either with the help of an accomplice or by hitchhiking. It is also possible that he stole a car. The Dubrow Police Department has no reports of vehicles reported stolen in the vicinity of the Vogel Transportation Center on the night in question, but as Security Director Camp points out, one could be taken from the long-term parking lot without being reported for a week or even longer.

Security footage of the long-term lot is available, and will be reviewed upon request, but the coverage there is far from complete. In addition, Security Director Camp informs me that those cameras are due to be replaced and often malfunction. I think that, for the time being, at least, we would be better served pursuing other lines of investigation.

RESPECTFULLY SUBMITTED
Det. Lt. Y. Sablo
See attachments

19

Howie Gold shook hands with Samuels and Ralph Anderson. Then he gazed through the one-way glass at Terry Maitland, in his Golden Dragons jersey and lucky game hat. Terry's back was straight, his head was up, and his hands were folded neatly on the table. There was no twitching, no fidgeting, no nervous sideways glances. He was not, Ralph admitted to himself, the picture of guilt.

At last Gold turned back to Samuels. "Speak," he said. As if inviting a dog to do a trick.

"Not much to say at this point, Howard." Samuels's hand went to the back of his head. He smoothed the cowlick down. It stayed put for a moment, then sprang up again. Ralph found himself remembering an Alfalfa quote he and his brother used to giggle over when they were kids: *You only meet your once-in-a-lifetime friends once in a lifetime.* "Just that it's not a mistake, and no, we haven't lost our fucking minds."

"What does Terry say?"

"So far, nothing," Ralph said.

Gold swung his way, bright blue eyes glittering and slightly magnified behind the round lenses of his spectacles. "You misunderstand me, Anderson. Not tonight, I know he didn't say anything to you tonight, he knows better. I mean at the initial interview. You might as well tell me, because he will."

"There was no initial interview," Ralph said. And there was no need to feel uncomfortable about that, not with the case they'd put together in just four short days, but he did, all the same. Part of it had to do with Howie Gold calling him by his last name, as if they had never bought each other drinks in the Wagon Wheel across from the county courthouse. He felt a ridiculous urge to tell Howie, *Don't look at me, look at the guy beside me. He's the one with the pedal to the metal.*

"What? Wait. Wait just a goddam minute."

Gold stuck his hands in his front pockets and began to rock back and forth on the balls of his feet. Ralph had seen this many times, in county and district court, and braced himself. Being cross-examined on the stand by Howie Gold was never a pleasant experience. Ralph had never held it against him, though. It was all part of the due process dance.

"Are you telling me you arrested him in front of two thousand people without even giving him a chance to *explain himself*?"

Ralph said, "You're a fine defense attorney, but God himself couldn't get Maitland out from under this one. And by the way, there might have been twelve hundred people there, fifteen hundred at most. Estelle Barga Field won't hold two thousand. The bleachers would collapse."

Gold ignored this feeble stab at lightening the atmosphere. He was staring at Ralph as though he were some new kind of bug. "But you arrested him in a public place, at what one could argue was the moment of his apotheosis—"

"His apothie-*whatsis*?" Samuels asked, smiling.

Gold ignored this, as well. He was still studying Ralph. "You did it even though you could have put a quiet police presence around the field and then arrested him at his home, after the game was over. You did it in front of his wife and daughters, which had to be deliberate. What possessed you? What on God's green earth *possessed* you?"

Ralph felt his face heating up again. "You really want to know, counselor?"

"Ralph," Samuels said warningly. He put a restraining hand on Ralph's arm.

Ralph shook it off. "I wasn't the one who arrested him. I had a couple of officers do that, because I was afraid I might put my hands around his throat and choke him blue. Which would give a smart lawyer like you a little too much to work with." He stepped forward, getting into Gold's space to make him stop the back and forth rocking. "He grabbed Frank Peterson and took him to Figgis Park. There he raped the kid with a tree branch, and there he killed him. Do you want to know *how* he killed him?"

"Ralph, that's privileged!" Samuels squawked.

Ralph paid no attention. "Preliminary forensics suggests he tore the kid's throat open with his *teeth*. He may even have swallowed some of the flesh, okay? All that got him so excited that he dropped trou and spilled his spunk all over the back of the kid's thighs. Nastiest, vilest, most *unspeakable* murder any of us will ever see, God willing. He must have been building up to it for a long time. None of us who were at the scene will ever get it out of our minds. And Terry Maitland did it. *Coach T* did it, and not so long ago he had his hands on my son's hands, showing him how to bunt. He just told me all about it, like it was supposed to exonerate him, or something."

Gold was no longer staring at him like he was a bug. Now there was a kind of wonder on his face, as if he had stumbled upon an artifact left behind by some unknowable extraterrestrial race. Ralph didn't care. He was beyond caring.

"You've got a boy yourself—Tommy, right? Isn't that why you started coaching Pop Warner with Terry, because Tommy was playing? He had his hands on your son, too. And now you're going to defend him?"

Samuels said, "For Christ's sake, shut your trap."

Gold had stopped rocking, but he gave no ground, and he was still staring at Ralph with that expression of almost anthropological wonder. "Didn't even interview him," he breathed. "Didn't. Even. I have never . . . I have *never* . . ."

"Oh, come on," Samuels said with forced jollity. "You've seen everything, Howie. Most of it twice."

"I want to conference with him now," Gold said briskly, "so turn off your audio shit and close the curtain."

"Fine," Samuels said. "You can have fifteen minutes, then we'll join you. See if the coach has anything to say."

Gold said, "I will have an hour, Mr. Samuels."

"Half an hour. Then we'll either take his confession—which could conceivably make a difference between life in McAlester and the needle—or he's going into a cell until his arraignment on Monday. Up to you. But if you think we did this lightly, you were never more wrong in your life."

Gold went to the door. Ralph swiped his card across the lock, listened to the clunk as the double bolts let go, then returned to the window to watch the attorney enter. Samuels tensed when Maitland rose from his seat and started toward Gold with his arms out, but the expression on Maitland's face was one of relief, not aggression. He embraced Gold, who dropped his boxy briefcase and hugged him back.

"Bro hug," Samuels said. "Ain't that just the sweetest."

Gold turned as if he had heard, and pointed to the camera with its little red light. "Turn it off," came his voice through the overhead speaker. "Sound as well. Then draw the curtain."

The switches were on a wall-mounted console that also held audio and video recorders. Ralph flipped them. The red light on the camera in the corner of the interview room went out. He nodded to Samuels, who yanked the curtain. The sound it made as it covered the glass brought Ralph an unpleasant memory. On three occasions—all before Bill Samuels's day—Ralph had attended executions at McAlester. There was a similar curtain (perhaps made by the same company!) over the long glass window between the execution chamber and the viewing room. It was pulled open when the witnesses entered the viewing room, and closed as soon as the prisoner was pronounced dead. It made that same unpleasant rasping sound.

"I'm going across the street to Zoney's for a soda and a burger," Samuels said. "I was too nervous to eat any dinner. Do you want anything?"

"I could do with a coffee. No milk, one sugar."

"You sure? I've had Zoncy's coffee, and they don't call it the Black Death for nothing."

"I'll take the chance," Ralph said.

"Okay. I'll be back in fifteen. If they break early, don't start without me."

No chance of that. As far as Ralph was concerned, this was now Bill Samuels's show. Let him have all the glory, if there was any to be had in a horror like this. There were chairs lining the far side of the hall. Ralph took the one next to the photocopier, which was droning softly in its sleep. He stared at the drawn curtain and wondered what Terry Maitland was saying in there, what outlandish alibi he was trying out for his Pop Warner co-coach.

Ralph found himself thinking of the big Native American woman who had picked Maitland up at Gentlemen, Please and taken him to the train station in Dubrow. *I coach Prairie League basketball down at the YMCA*, she'd said. *Maitland used to come down and sit on the bleachers with the parents and watch the kids play. He told me he was scouting talent for City League baseball . . .*

She had known him, and he must have known her—given her size and ethnicity, she'd be a hard woman to forget. Yet in the cab he had called her ma'am. Why was that? Because even if he knew her face from the Y, he didn't remember her name? That was possible, but Ralph didn't like it much. As names went, Willow Rainwater wasn't all that forgettable, either.

"Well, he was under stress," Ralph muttered, either to himself or to the drowsing photocopier. "Also . . ."

Another memory came to him, and with it a reason for Maitland's use of *ma'am* that he liked better. His kid brother, Johnny, three years younger, had not been much good when it came to hide-and-seek. Many times he'd just run into his bedroom and throw the covers over his head, apparently thinking that if he couldn't see Ralphie, Ralphie couldn't see him. Wasn't it possible that a man who had just committed a terrible murder might be prone to the same sort of magical thinking? *If I don't know you, you don't know me.* Mad logic, sure, but it had been a madman's crime, and it could explain more than just Terry's reaction to Rainwater; it could explain why he'd thought he could get away with it even though he was well-known to lots of folks in Flint City, and an actual celebrity to sports fans.

But then there was Carlton Scowcroft. If he closed his eyes, Ralph could almost see Gold underlining a key passage in Scowcroft's statement, and preparing for his summation to the jury, perhaps stealing an idea from OJ's attorney. *If the glove does not fit, you must acquit*, Johnnie Cochran had said. Gold's version, almost as catchy, might be, *Since he didn't know, you must let him go.*

It wouldn't work, it wasn't even close to the same, but—

According to Scowcroft, Maitland had explained the blood on his face and clothes by saying something in his nose had ruptured. *It went like Old Faithful*, Terry told him. *Is there a doc-in-the-box anywhere around here?*

Only Terry Maitland had, with the exception of four years in college, lived in Flint City all his life. He wouldn't have needed the Quick Care billboard near Coney Ford to direct him; he wouldn't have needed to ask in the first place. So why had he?

Samuels came back with a Coke, a burger wrapped in foil, and a go-cup of coffee, which he handed to Ralph. "All quiet in there?"

"Yep. They've got another twenty minutes, by my watch. When they finish, I'm going to try to get him to give us a DNA swab."

Samuels unwrapped his burger and cautiously lifted the bun for a peek. "Oh my God," he said. "It looks like something a paramedic scraped off a burn victim." Nevertheless, he began to eat it.

Ralph thought about mentioning Terry's conversation with Rainwater, and Terry's odd question about the doc-in-the-box, and didn't. He thought about bringing up Terry's failure to disguise himself or even to try to hide his face with sunglasses, and didn't mention that, either. He had raised these issues before, and Samuels had swatted them aside, maintaining—and rightly—that they had no significance when stacked against the eyewitnesses and the damning forensic evidence.

The coffee was as awful as Samuels had predicted, but Ralph sipped at it anyway, and the cup was almost empty when Gold buzzed to be let out of the interview room. His expression made Ralph Anderson's stomach contract. It wasn't worry, anger, or the theatrical indignation some lawyers could muster up when they realized a client was in deep shit. No, this was sympathy, and it looked genuine.

"Oy vey," he said. "You two guys are in big trouble."

20

FLINT CITY GENERAL HOSPITAL
DEPARTMENT OF PATHOLOGY AND SEROLOGY

To: Detective Ralph Anderson
Lieutenant Yunel Sablo
District Attorney William Samuels

From: Dr. Edward Bogan

Date: July 14th

Subject: Blood Typing and DNA

<u>Blood:</u>
Several items were tested for blood type.
The first was the branch used to sodomize the victim, Frank Peterson, a white male child, 11 years of age. This branch was approximately 22" long and

3" in diameter. A section about halfway down has been stripped of its loose bark, likely because of rough handling by the perpetrator of the crime (see attached photograph). Fingerprints were found on this smooth section of the branch; they were photographed and lifted by State Criminalistics before the evidence was conveyed to me by Detective Ralph Anderson (Flint City PD) and Trooper Yunel Sablo (State Police Post 7). I therefore state that the chain of evidence remains intact.

The blood on the last 5" of this piece of branch is O+, which is the victim's type, as confirmed by Frank Peterson's family doctor, Horace Connolly. There are many other traces of O+ on the branch, caused by a phenomenon called "splashback" or "sudsing." These likely flew up as the victim was sexually violated, and it is fair to assume that the perpetrator also sustained splashback on his skin and clothes.

Traces of a second blood type were also found on the specimen. This was AB+, a much rarer type (3% of the population). I believe this to be the perpetrator's blood, and speculate that he may have cut the hand he used to manipulate the branch, which he must have done with great force.

A great deal of O+ blood was discovered on the driver's seat, steering wheel, and dashboard of a 2007 Econoline van found abandoned in the employees' parking lot behind Shorty's Pub (1124 Main Street). Spots of AB+ blood were also found on the steering wheel of the van. These samples were conveyed to me by Sgts. Elmer Stanton and Richard Spencer of the State Criminalistics Division, and I therefore state that the chain of evidence remains intact.

A great deal of O+ blood was also found on the clothes (shirt, pants, socks, Adidas sneakers, Jockey underpants) retrieved from a 2011 Subaru discovered at an abandoned boat landing near Route 72 (also known as Old Forge Road). There is also a spot of AB+ blood on the left cuff of the shirt. These samples were conveyed to me by Trooper John Koryta (Post 7) and Sgt. Spencer of the SCD, and I therefore state that the chain of evidence remains intact. No AB+ blood has been found in the Subaru Outback as of this report. Such blood may be found, but it's possible that any scratches the perpetrator suffered in the commission of the crime had clotted by the time he abandoned the Subaru. It is also possible that he may have bandaged them, although the samples are so small that I think this is unlikely. They would be minor cuts, at best.

I recommend that any suspect's blood type be ascertained quickly, due to the relative rarity of the AB+ type.

DNA:

The line of samples awaiting DNA testing in Cap City is always a very long one, and under ordinary circumstances, results cannot be obtained for weeks or even months. However, due to the extreme brutality of this crime and the age of the victim, samples obtained at the crime scene have been put "at the head of the line."

Chief among these is semen found on the victim's thighs and buttocks, but skin samples were also obtained from the branch used to sodomize the Peterson boy, and of course there are the blood samples I have already discussed. A DNA report from the semen found at the scene should be available for potential matching next week. Sgt. Stanton told me the report might be available even sooner, but I have dealt with the DNA issue many times before, and would suggest that next Friday seems more likely, even in a priority case such as this.

Although it is outside protocol, I am compelled to add a personal note here. I have dealt with evidence from many murder victims, but this is by far the worst crime I have ever been called upon to examine, and the person who did it needs to be captured ASAP.

Memo dictated at 11 AM by Dr. Edward Bogan

21

Howie Gold finished his private conference with Terry at 8:40 PM, a full ten minutes before the half hour he had been allotted was up. By then, Ralph and Bill Samuels had been joined by Troy Ramage and Stephanie Gould, a patrolwoman who had come on duty at eight. She had a DNA kit, still in its plastic bag. Ignoring Howie's *oy vey, big trouble* comment, Ralph asked the lawyer if he and his client would okay a DNA swab.

Howie was holding the door to the interview room open with his foot so it wouldn't re-lock. "They want to take cheek swabs, Terry. You okay with that? They're going to get them anyway, and I need to make a couple of quick phone calls."

"All right," Terry said. Dark circles had begun to form under his eyes, but he sounded calm. "Let's do everything we have to do so I can get out of here before midnight."

The man sounded absolutely sure that was going to happen.

Ralph and Samuels exchanged a glance. Samuels raised his eyebrows, which made him look more like Alfalfa than ever.

"Call my wife," Terry said. "Tell her I'm okay."

Howie grinned. "Number one on my list."

"Go up to the end of the hall," Ralph said. "You'll get five bars."

"I know," Howie said. "I've been here before. It's kind of like reincarnation." And, to Terry: "Say nothing until I get back."

Officer Ramage took the swabs, one from each inner cheek, and held them up to the camera before putting each into its little vial. Officer Gould placed the vials back in the bag and held it up to the camera as she sealed it with a red evidence sticker. She then signed the chain-of-custody sheet. The two officers would take the samples down to the closet-sized room that served as the Flint City PD's evidence locker. There it would once more be shown to an overhead camera before being filed. Two more officers, probably State Police, would convey it to Cap City the following day. Chain of evidence therefore remains intact, as Dr. Bogan would have said. Which might sound a bit prissy, but was no joke. Ralph intended that there should be absolutely no weak links in that chain. No slip-ups. No way to break free. Not in this case.

DA Samuels started to return to the interview room while Howie was making his calls by the door to the main office, but Ralph held him back, wanting to listen. Howie conversed briefly with Terry's wife—Ralph heard him say *It's going to be okay, Marcy*—and then made a second, even briefer call, telling someone where Terry's daughters were and reminding the someone that there would be press clogging up Barnum Court, and to proceed accordingly. Then he came back to the interview room. "Okay, let's see if we can't sort this mess out."

Ralph and Samuels sat down across the table from Terry. The chair between them remained vacant. Howie elected to stand beside his client, a hand on his shoulder.

Smiling, Samuels began.

"You like little boys, don't you, Coach?"

There was no hesitation on Terry's part. "Very much. I also like little girls, having two of my own."

"And I'm sure your daughters play sports, with Coach T for a dad, how could they not? But you don't coach any girls' teams, do you? No soccer, no softball, no lacrosse. You stick to the boys. Baseball in the summer, Pop Warner in the fall, and Y basketball in the winter, although I guess you just spectate at that one. All those Saturday afternoon trips to the Y were what you might call scouting expeditions, right? Looking for boys with speed and agility. And maybe checking out how they looked in their shorts, while you were at it."

Ralph waited for Howie to put a stop to this, but Howie kept silent, at least for the time being. His face had become an absolute blank, nothing moving but the eyes, going from one speaker to the next. *He's probably one hell of a poker player*, Ralph thought.

Terry, however, had actually begun to smile. "You got that from Willow Rainwater. Must have. She's a piece of work, isn't she? You should hear her bellowing on Saturday afternoons. *'Box out, box out, pick up your feet, now GO TO THE HOLE!'* How's she doing?"

"You tell me," Samuels said. "After all, you saw her Tuesday night."

"I didn't—"

Howie grabbed Terry's shoulder and squeezed before he could say anything else. "Why don't we stop Interrogation 101, okay? Just tell us why Terry's here. Lay it out."

"Tell us where you were on Tuesday," Samuels countered. "You started, go ahead and finish."

"I was—"

But Howie Gold squeezed Terry's shoulder again, this time harder, before he could go on. "No, Bill, it's not going to work that way. Tell us what you've got, or I'll go right to the press and tell them you've arrested one of Flint City's premier citizens for the murder of Frank Peterson, thrown mud all over his reputation, terrified his wife and daughters, and won't say why."

Samuels looked at Ralph, who shrugged. If the DA hadn't been present, Ralph would already have been laying out the evidence, in hopes of a quick confession.

"Go on, Bill," Howie said. "This man needs to get home and be with his family."

Samuels smiled, but there was no humor in his eyes; it was your basic show of teeth. "He'll see them in court, Howard. At the arraignment on Monday."

Ralph could feel the fabric of civility fraying, and put most of the blame for that on Bill, who was genuinely enraged at the crime, and at the man who had done the crime. As anyone would be . . . but that didn't pull the plow, as Ralph's grandfather would have said.

"Hey, before we get started, I've got a question," Ralph said, striving for cheeriness. "Just one. Okay, counselor? It's nothing we won't find out, anyway."

Howie seemed grateful enough to turn his attention away from Samuels. "Let's hear it."

"What's your blood type, Terry? Do you know?"

Terry looked at Howie, who shrugged, then back at Ralph. "I ought to. I give six times a year at the Red Cross, because it's pretty rare."

"AB positive?"

Terry blinked. "How did you know that?" And then, realizing what the answer must be: "But not *that* rare. If you want really rare, you want AB negative. One per cent of the population. The Red Cross has people with that type on speed-dial, believe me."

"When it comes to rare, I always think of fingerprints," Samuels remarked, as if just passing the time of day. "I suppose because they come up so often in court."

"Where they rarely figure in the jury's decision," Howie said.

Samuels ignored him. "No two sets exactly alike. There are even minute variations in the prints of identical twins. You don't happen to have an identical twin, do you, Terry?"

"You're not saying you have mine at the scene where the Peterson boy was killed, are you?" Terry's expression was pure incredulity. Ralph had to give it to him; he was a hell of an actor, and apparently meant to play the string out right to the end.

"We've got so many fingerprints I can barely count them," Ralph said. "They're all over the white van you used to abduct the Peterson boy. They're on the boy's bike, which we found in the back of the van. They're on the toolbox that was in the van. They're all over the Subaru you switched to behind Shorty's Pub." He paused. "And they're on the branch that was used to sodomize the Peterson boy, an attack so vicious that the internal injuries alone might well have killed him."

"No need for fingerprint powder or UV light on those," Samuels said. "Those prints are in the boy's blood."

This was where most perps—like ninety-five per cent—would break down, lawyer or no lawyer. Not this one. Ralph saw shock and amazement on the man's face, but no guilt.

Howie rallied. "You have prints. Fine. It wouldn't be the first time fingerprints were planted."

"A few, maybe," Ralph said. "But seventy? Eighty? And in blood, on the weapon itself?"

"We also have a chain of witnesses," Samuels said. He began ticking them off on his fingers. "You were seen accosting Peterson in the parking lot of Gerald's Fine Groceries. You were seen putting his bicycle in the back of the van you used. He was seen getting into the van with you. You were seen exiting the woods where the murder took place, covered with blood. I could go on, but my mother always told me that I should save some for later."

"Eyewitnesses are rarely reliable," Howie said. "The fingerprints are iffy, but eyewitnesses . . ." He shook his head.

Ralph jumped in. "I'd agree, at least in most cases. Not in this one. I interviewed someone recently who said Flint City is really just a small town. I don't know if I buy that completely, but the West Side is pretty tightly knit, and Mr. Maitland here is widely known. Terry, the woman who ID'd you at Gerald's is a neighbor, and the girl who saw you coming out of the woods in Figgis Park knows you very well, not just because she lives a little way down from you, on Barnum Street, but because you once brought back her lost dog."

"June Morris?" Terry was looking at Ralph with frank disbelief. *"Junie?"*

"There are others," Samuels said. "Many."

"Willow?" Terry sounded out of breath, as if he'd been punched. "Her, too?"

"Many," Samuels repeated.

"Every one of them picked you out of six-packs," Ralph said. "No hesitation."

"And was the photo of my client perhaps wearing a Golden Dragons cap and a shirt with a big C on it?" Howie asked. "Was that one perhaps tapped by the finger of the questioning officer?"

"You know better," Ralph said. "At least I hope you do."

Terry said, "This is a nightmare."

Samuels smiled sympathetically. "I understand that. And all you have to do to end it is to tell us why you did it."

As if there might be a reason on God's green earth that any sane person could understand, Ralph thought.

"It might make a difference." Samuels was almost wheedling now. "But you should do it before the DNA comes back. We've got plenty, and when it matches those cheek swabs . . ." He shrugged.

"Tell us," Ralph said. "I don't know if it was temporary insanity, or something you did in a fugue state, or a sexual compulsion, or just what, but tell us." He heard his voice rising, thought about clamping down on it, then thought what the hell. *"Be a man and tell us!"*

Speaking more to himself than to the men on the other side of the table, Terry said, "I don't know how any of this can be. I wasn't even in town on Tuesday."

"Where were you, then?" Samuels asked. "Go ahead, lay it on us. I love a good story. Read my way through most of Agatha Christie in high school."

Terry turned to look up at Gold, who nodded. But Ralph thought Howie looked worried now. The stuff about the blood type and the fingerprints had rocked him hard, the eyewitnesses even harder. He'd been rocked most of all, perhaps, by little Junie Morris, whose lost dog had been returned by good old reliable Coach T.

"I was in Cap City. Left at ten on Tuesday morning, got back late Wednesday night. Well, nine thirty or so, late for me."

"I don't suppose you had anyone with you," Samuels said. "Just off on your own and kind of gathering your thoughts, right? Getting ready for the big game?"

"I—"

"Did you take your car or the white van? By the way, where did you have that van stashed? And how did you happen to steal one with New York plates in the first place? I've got a theory about that, but I'd love to have you confirm or deny—"

"Do you want to hear this or not?" Terry asked. He had, incredibly, begun to smile again. "Maybe you're afraid to hear it. And maybe you should be afraid. You're in shit up to your waist, Mr. Samuels, and it's getting deeper."

"Is that so? Then why am I the one who can walk out of here and go home when this interview is over?"

"Cool it," Ralph said quietly.

Samuels turned to him, cowlick springing back and forth. Ralph saw nothing comical about it now. "Don't tell me to cool it, Detective. We're sitting here with a man who raped a kid with a tree branch and then tore out his throat like . . . like a fucking cannibal!"

Gold looked directly up at the camera in the corner, now speaking for some future judge and jury. "Stop acting like an angry child, Mr. District Attorney, or I'll terminate this interview right here."

"I wasn't alone," Terry said, "and I don't know anything about a white van. I went with Everett Roundhill, Billy Quade, and Debbie Grant. The entire Flint High School English Department, in other words. My Expedition was in the shop because the air conditioner died, so we took Ev's car. He's the department chairman, and he's got a BMW. Plenty of room. We left from the high school at ten."

Samuels looked temporarily too perplexed by this to ask the obvious question, so Ralph did it. "What was in Cap City that would take four English teachers there in the middle of summer vacation?"

"Harlan Coben," Terry said.

"Who's Harlan Coben?" Bill Samuels asked. His interest in mystery stories had apparently peaked with Agatha Christie.

Ralph knew; he wasn't much of a fiction reader, but his wife was. "The mystery writer?"

"The mystery writer," Terry agreed. "Look, there's a group called the Tri-State Teachers of English, and every year they hold a three-day midsummer conference. It's the only time everyone can get together. There are seminars and panel discussions, that sort of thing. It's held in a different city each year. This year it was Cap City's turn. Only English teachers are like anyone else, it's hard to get them together even in summer, because they've got so many other things going on—all the paint-up, fix-up stuff that didn't get done during the school year, family vacations, plus various summer activities. For me it's Little League and City League. So the TSTE always tries to get a big-name speaker as a draw for the middle day, which is when most attendees show up."

"Which in this case was last Tuesday?" Ralph asked.

"Right. This year's conference was at the Sheraton, from July 9th—the Monday—to July 11th, the Wednesday. I haven't been to one of those conferences in five years, but when Ev told me that Coben was going to be the keynote speaker, and the other English teachers were going, I arranged for Gavin Frick and Baibir Patel's dad to take the practices on Tuesday and Wednesday. It killed me to do it, with the semifinal game coming up, but I knew I'd be back for the practices on Thursday and Friday, and I didn't want to miss Coben. I've read all his books. He's great on plot, and he has a sense of humor. Also, the theme of this year's conference was teaching popular adult fiction in grades seven through twelve, and that's been a hot-button issue for years, especially in this part of the country."

"Save the exposition," Samuels said. "Get to the bottom line."

"Fine. We went. We were there for the banquet lunch, we were there for Coben's speech, we were there for the evening panel discussion at eight PM, we spent the night. Ev and Debbie had single rooms, but I split the cost of a double with Billy Quade. That was his idea. He said he was building an addition on his house, and had to economize. They'll vouch for me." He looked at Ralph and lifted his hands, palms out. "*I was there.* That's the bottom line."

Silence in the room. At last Samuels said, "What time was Coben's speech?"

"Three o'clock," Terry said. "Three o'clock on Tuesday afternoon."

"How convenient," Samuels said acidly.

Howie Gold smiled widely. "Not for you."

Three o'clock, Ralph thought. Almost the same time that Arlene Stanhope claimed to have seen Terry putting Frank Peterson's bicycle into the back of the stolen white van, and then riding away with the boy in the passenger seat. No, not even almost. Mrs. Stanhope said she'd heard the bell in the Town Hall clock announce the hour.

"The speech was in the Sheraton's big meeting room?" Ralph asked.

"Yes. Right across from the banquet room."

"And you're sure it started at three."

"Well, that's when the TSTE chairman started her introduction. Which droned on for at least ten minutes."

"Uh-huh, and how long did Coben speak?"

"I think about forty-five minutes. After that he took questions. It was probably four thirty by the time he finished."

Ralph's thoughts were whirling around in his head like loose paper caught in a draft. He could not remember ever having been so completely blindsided. They should have checked Terry's movements out in advance, but that was Monday morning quarterbacking. He, Samuels, and Yune Sablo of the State Police had all agreed that questions about Maitland ahead of his arrest would risk alerting a very dangerous man. And it had seemed unnecessary, given the weight of evidence. Now, however . . .

He glanced at Samuels, but saw no immediate help there; the man's expression was a mixture of suspicion and perplexity.

"You've made a bad mistake here," Gold said. "Surely you two gentlemen see that."

"No mistake," Ralph said. "We have his prints, we have eyewitnesses who know him, and pretty soon we'll have the first DNA result. A match there will clinch it."

"Ah, but we may also have something else pretty soon," Gold said. "My investigator is on it as we speak, and confidence is high."

"What?" Samuels snapped.

Gold smiled. "Why spoil the surprise before we see what Alec comes up with? If what my client told me is correct, I think it's going to put another hole in your boat, Bill, and your boat is already leaking badly."

The Alec in question was Alec Pelley, a retired State Police detective who now worked exclusively for lawyers defending criminal cases. He was expensive, and good at his job. Once, over drinks, Ralph had asked Pelley why he had gone over to the Dark Side. Pelley replied that he'd put away at least four men he later came to believe were innocent, and felt he had a lot to atone for. "Also," he'd said, "retirement sucks if you don't play golf."

No use speculating about what Pelley was chasing this time . . . always supposing it wasn't just some chimera, or a defense attorney bluff. Ralph stared at Terry, again looking for guilt and seeing only worry, anger, and bewilderment—the expression of a man who has been arrested for something he hasn't done.

Except he *had* done it, all the evidence said so, and the DNA would put the final nail in his coffin. His alibi was an artfully constructed piece of misdirection, something straight out of an Agatha Christie novel (or one by Harlan Coben). Ralph would begin the job of dismantling the magic trick tomorrow morning, starting with interviews of Terry's colleagues and moving on to a back-check of the conference, focusing on the start and end times of Coben's appearance.

Even before beginning that work—his bread and butter—he saw one possible gap in Terry's alibi. Arlene Stanhope had seen Frank Peterson getting into the white van with Terry at three. June Morris had seen Terry in Figgis Park, covered with blood, at around six thirty—the girl's mother had said the weather was on the local news when June left, and that pegged it. That left a gap of three and a half hours, which was more than enough time to drive the seventy miles from Cap City to Flint City.

Suppose it *hadn't* been Terry Maitland Mrs. Stanhope had seen in the parking lot of Gerald's Fine Groceries? Suppose it had been an accomplice who looked like Terry? Or maybe just *dressed* like Terry, in a Golden Dragons cap and shirt? It seemed unlikely until you factored in Mrs. Stanhope's age . . . and the thick glasses she'd been wearing . . .

"Are we done here, gentlemen?" Gold asked. "Because if you

really intend to hold Mr. Maitland, I have a great deal to do. High on the list is speaking to the press. Not my favorite thing, but—"

"You lie," Samuels said sourly.

"But it may draw them away from Terry's house, and give his children a chance to get indoors without being hounded and photographed. Most of all, it will give that family a little bit of the peace you have so recklessly stolen from them."

"Save it for the TV cameras," Samuels said. He pointed to Terry, also playing for some judge and jury. "Your client tortured and murdered a child, and if his family is collateral damage, he himself is responsible."

"You're unbelievable," Terry said. "You didn't even question me before you arrested me. Not one single question."

Ralph said, "What did you do after the speech, Terry?"

Terry shook his head, not in negation but as if to clear it. "After? I got in line with everyone else. But we were pretty far back, thanks to Debbie. She had to use the bathroom, and wanted us to wait for her so we'd all be together. She was gone for a long time. A lot of guys also broke for the johns as soon as the Q-and-A was over, but it always takes the women longer, because . . . well, you know, only so many stalls. I went down to the newsstand with Ev and Billy and we hung out there. By the time she met us, the line was all the way out into the lobby."

"What line?" Samuels asked.

"Do you live under a rock, Mr. Samuels? The *autograph* line. Everyone had a copy of his new book, *I Told You I Would*. It came with the price of the conference ticket. I've got mine, signed and dated, and will be happy to show it to you. Assuming you haven't already taken it out of the house with the rest of my stuff, that is. By the time we got to the autograph table, it was past five thirty."

If so, Ralph thought, his imagined gap in Terry's alibi had just closed to a pinhole. It was theoretically possible to drive from Cap to Flint in an hour, the turnpike speed limit was seventy and the cops wouldn't give you a second look unless you were doing eighty-five or even ninety—but how would Terry have had time to commit the murder? Unless the look-alike accomplice had done it, and how did that work, with Terry's fingerprints everywhere, including on the branch? Answer: it didn't. Also, why would Terry want an accomplice who looked like him, dressed like him, or both? Answer: he wouldn't.

"Were the other English teachers with you the whole time you were standing in line?" Samuels asked.

"Yes."

"The signing was also in the big room?"

"Yes. I think they call it the ballroom."

"And once you all had your autographs, what did you do then?"

"Went out to dinner together with some English teachers from Broken Arrow we met while we were standing in line."

"Out to dinner where?" Ralph asked.

"Place called the Firepit. It's a steakhouse about three blocks from the hotel. Got there around six, had a couple of drinks before, had dessert after. It was a good time." He said this almost wistfully. "There were nine of us in all, I think. We walked back to the hotel together, and sat in on the evening panel, which had to do with how to handle challenges to books like *To Kill a Mockingbird* and *Slaughterhouse-Five*. Ev and Debbie left before it was over, but Billy and I stayed to the end."

"Which was when?" Ralph asked.

"Nine thirty or so."

"And then?"

"Billy and I had a beer in the bar, then we went up to the room and went to bed."

Listening to a speech by a noted mystery writer when the Peterson boy was snatched, Ralph thought. At dinner with at least eight other people when the Peterson boy was killed. Attending a panel discussion on banned books when Willow Rainwater claimed to have taken him in her cab from Gentlemen, Please to the train station in Dubrow. He must know we'll go to his colleagues, that we'll track down the teachers from Broken Arrow, that we'll talk to the bartender in the Sheraton lounge. He must know we'll check the hotel's security footage, and even the autograph in his copy of the latest Harlan Coben barnburner. He *must* know these things, he's not a stupid man.

The conclusion—that his story would check out—was both unavoidable and unbelievable.

Samuels leaned forward over the table, his chin jutting. "Do you expect us to believe that you were with others the entire time between three o'clock and eight o'clock on Tuesday? The *entire* time?"

Terry gave him a look of which only high school teachers are capable: *We both know you're an idiot, but I will not embarrass you in front of your peers by saying so.* "Of course not. I used the john myself before Coben's speech started. And I went once at the restaurant. Maybe you can convince a jury that I came back to Flint, killed poor Frankie Peterson, and returned to Cap City in the minute and a half it took me to empty my bladder. Think they'll buy it?"

Samuels looked at Ralph. Ralph shrugged.

"I think we have no further questions now," Samuels said. "Mr. Maitland will be escorted to the county jail and kept in custody until his arraignment on Monday."

Terry's shoulders slumped.

"You intend to go through with this," Gold said. "You really do."

Ralph expected another explosion from Samuels, but this time the district attorney surprised him. He sounded almost as weary as Maitland looked. "Come on, Howie. You know I have no choice, given the evidence. And when the DNA comes back a match, it's going to be game over."

He leaned forward again, once more invading Terry's space.

"You still have a chance to avoid the needle, Terry. Not a good one, but it's there. I urge you to take it. Drop the bullshit and confess. Do it for Fred and Arlene Peterson, who've lost their son in the worst way imaginable. You'll feel better."

Terry did not draw back, as Samuels might have expected. He leaned forward instead, and it was the district attorney who pulled away, as if afraid the man on the other side of the table had something contagious that he, Samuels, might catch. "There is nothing to confess to, sir. I didn't kill Frankie Peterson. I would never hurt a child. You have the wrong man."

Samuels sighed and stood up. "Okay, you had your chance. Now . . . God help you."

22

FLINT CITY GENERAL HOSPITAL
DEPARTMENT OF PATHOLOGY AND SEROLOGY

```
To: Detective Ralph Anderson
SP Lt. Yunel Sablo
District Attorney William Samuels


From: Dr. F. Ackerman, Head of Pathology


Date: July 12th


Subject: Autopsy Addendum/PERSONAL AND
CONFIDENTIAL
```

As requested, my opinion follows.

Although Frank Peterson might or might not have survived the act of sodomy noted in the autopsy report (performed July 11th, by myself, with Dr.

Alvin Barkland assisting), there can be no doubt that the immediate cause of death was exsanguination (i.e., massive loss of blood).

Teeth marks were found on the remains of Peterson's face, throat, shoulder, chest, right side, and torso. The injuries, coupled with photographs of the murder scene, suggest the following sequence: Peterson was thrown violently to the ground on his back and bitten at least six times, perhaps as many as a dozen. This was frenzied behavior. He was then turned over and sodomized. By then Peterson was almost certainly unconscious. Either during the sodomy or directly after, the perpetrator ejaculated.

I have marked this addendum <u>personal and confidential</u> because certain aspects of this case, if disclosed, will be sensationalized in the press not just locally but nationwide. Parts of Peterson's body, most specifically the right earlobe, right nipple, and parts of the trachea and esophagus, are missing. The perpetrator may have taken these body parts, along with a considerable section of flesh from the nape of the neck, as trophies. That is actually the best case scenario. The alternative hypothesis is that the perpetrator ate them.

Being in charge of the case, you will do as you see fit, but it is my strong recommendation that these facts, and my subsequent conclusions, be kept not only from the press, but out of any trial, unless absolutely necessary to secure a conviction. The reaction of the parents to such information can of course be imagined, but who would want to? My apologies if I have overstepped my bounds, but in this case I felt it necessary. I am a doctor, I am the county's medical examiner, but I am also a mother.

I beg you to catch the man who defiled and murdered this child, and soon. If you don't, he will almost certainly do it again.

Felicity Ackerman, M.D.
Flint City General Hospital
Head of Pathology
Flint County Chief Medical Examiner

23

The main room of the Flint City PD was large, but the four men waiting for Terry Maitland seemed to fill it—two State Police and two correctional officers from the county jail, widebodies one and all. Even though he remained stunned by what had happened to him (what was *still* happening), Terry could not help being a bit amused. The county jail was only four blocks away. A great deal of beef had been assembled to take him a little more than half a mile.

"Hands out," one of the correctional officers said.

Terry put them out and watched as a new pair of handcuffs was snapped onto his wrists. He looked for Howie, suddenly as anxious as he had been at five, when his mother let go of his hand on his first day of kindergarten. Howie was seated on the corner of a vacant desk, talking on his cell phone, but when he saw Terry's look, he ended the call and hurried over.

"Do not touch the prisoner, sir," said the officer who had cuffed Terry.

Gold ignored him. He put an arm around Terry's shoulders and murmured, "It's going to be all right." Then—to Gold's surprise as much as his client's—he kissed Terry on the cheek.

Terry took that kiss with him as the four men escorted him down the front steps to where a county van waited behind a State Police cruiser with its jackpot lights pulsing. And the words. Them especially, as the cameras flashed and the TV lights came on and the questions flew at him like bullets: *Have you been charged, did you do it, are you innocent, have you confessed, what can you say to Frank Peterson's parents.*

It's going to be all right, Gold had said, and that was what Terry hung onto.

But of course it wasn't.

SORRY

July 14th–July 15th

1

The battery-powered bubble-light Alec Pelley kept in the center console of his Explorer was in sort of a gray area. It might no longer be strictly legal, since he was retired from the State Police, but on the other hand, since he was a member in good standing of the Cap City Police Reserve, maybe it was. Either way, it seemed necessary to plonk it on the dashboard and light it up on this occasion. With its help, he made the run from Cap to Flint in record time and was knocking on the door of 17 Barnum Court at quarter past nine. There were no news people here, but further up the street he could see the harsh glare of TV lights in front of what he assumed was the Maitland house. Not all the blowflies had been drawn to the fresh meat of Howie's impromptu press conference, it seemed. Not that he had expected it.

The door was opened by a short sandy-haired fireplug of a man, his brow creased, his lips pressed so tightly together that his mouth was almost nonexistent. All ready to let fly with his go-to-hell speech. The woman standing behind him was a green-eyed blonde, three inches taller than her husband and much better looking, even with no makeup and her eyes swollen. She wasn't currently crying, but somewhere deeper in the house, someone was. A child. One of Maitland's, Alec assumed.

"Mr. and Mrs. Mattingly? I'm Alec Pelley. Did Howie Gold call you?"

"Yes," the woman said. "Come in, Mr. Pelley."

Alec started forward. Mattingly, eight inches shorter but undaunted, stepped in his way. "Could we see some identification first, please?"

"Of course." Alec could have shown them his driver's license, but opted for his Police Reserve ID instead. No need for them to know that most of his duty shifts these days were a kind of charity function, usually as a glorified security guard at rock shows, rodeos, pro wrestling fuckarees, and the thrice-yearly Monster Truck Jam at the Coliseum. He also worked the Cap City business area with a chalk-stick when one of the meter maids called in sick. This was a humbling experience for a man who had once commanded a squad of four State Police detectives, but Alec didn't mind; he liked being outside in the sunshine. Also, he was something of a Bible scholar, and James 4, verse 6, proclaims, "God opposeth the proud, but giveth grace to the humble."

"Thank you," Mr. Mattingly said, simultaneously stepping aside and holding out his hand. "Tom Mattingly."

Alec shook with him, prepared for a strong grip. He was not disappointed.

"I'm not normally suspicious, this is a nice quiet neighborhood, but I told Jamie that we had to be super careful while we've got Sarah and Grace under our roof. Lot of people angry at Coach T already, and believe me, this is just the beginning. Once what he did gets around, it's gonna be a whole lot worse. Glad you're here to take them off our hands."

Jamie Mattingly gave him a reproachful look. "Whatever their father may have done—if he did anything—it's not their fault." And, to Alec: "They're devastated, especially Gracie. They saw their father led away in handcuffs."

"Ah, Jesus, wait until they find out why," Mattingly said. "And they will. These days kids always do. Goddam Internet, goddam Facebook, goddam Tweeter birds." He shook his head. "Jamie's right, innocent until proven guilty, it's the American way, but when they make a public arrest like that . . ." He sighed. "Want something to drink, Mr. Pelley? Jamie made iced tea before the game."

"Thank you, but I better get the girls home. Their mother will be waiting." And delivering her children was only his first job tonight. Howie had rattled off a to-do list with machine-gun rapidity just before stepping into the glare of the television lights, and item number two meant racing back to Cap City, making calls (and calling in favors) as he went. Back in harness, which was good—a lot better than chalking tires on Midland Street—but this part was going to be hard.

The girls were in a room that, judging from the stuffed fish leaping on the knotty pine walls, had to be Tom Mattingly's man-cave. On the huge flatscreen, SpongeBob was capering in Bikini Bottom, but with the sound muted. The girls Alec had come to pick up were huddled on the sofa, still wearing their Golden Dragons teeshirts and baseball caps. They were also wearing black and gold facepaint—probably applied by their mother a few hours ago, before the previously friendly world had reared up on its hind legs and bitten a hole in their family—but the younger had cried most of hers off.

The older girl saw a strange man looming in the door and hugged her weeping sister tighter. Although Alec had no kids himself, he liked them fine, and Sarah Maitland's instinctive gesture hurt his heart: a child protecting a child.

He stood in the middle of the room, hands clasped before him. "Sarah? I'm a friend of Howie Gold's. You know him, don't you?"

"Yes. Is my father all right?" Her voice was little more than a whisper, and husky from her own tears. Grace never looked at Alec at all; she turned her face into the hollow of her big sister's shoulder.

"Yes. He asked me to take you home." Not strictly true, but this was hardly the time for splitting hairs.

"Is he there?"

"No, but your mother is."

"We could walk," Sarah said faintly. "It's only up the street. I could hold Gracie's hand."

Against the older girl's shoulder, Grace Maitland's head went back and forth in a gesture of negation.

"Not after dark, hon," Jamie Mattingly said.

And not tonight, Alec thought. Not for many nights to come. Days, either.

"Come on, girls," Tom said with manufactured (and rather ghoulish) good cheer. "I'll see you out."

On the stoop, under the porch light, Jamie Mattingly looked paler than ever; she had gone from soccer mom to cancer patient in three short hours. "This is awful," she said. "It's like the whole world turned upside down. Thank God our own girl is away at camp. We were only at the game tonight because Sarah and Maureen are best buds."

At the mention of her friend, Sarah Maitland also began to cry, and that got her sister cranked up again. Alec thanked the Mattinglys and led the girls to his Explorer. They walked slowly, heads down and holding hands like children in a fairy tale. He had cleared the front passenger seat of its usual load of crap, and they sat in it squeezed together. Grace once more had her face socked into the hollow of her sister's shoulder.

Alec didn't bother trying to buckle them in; it was no more than two tenths of a mile to the circle of light illuminating the sidewalk and the Maitland lawn. There was only a single crew left in front of the house. They were from the Cap City ABC affiliate, four or five guys standing around and drinking coffee from Styrofoam cups in the shadow of their truck's satellite dish. When they saw the Explorer turn into the Maitland driveway, they scrambled into action.

Alec powered down his window and spoke to them in his best halt-and-put-your-hands-up voice. *"Not one camera! Not one camera on these children!"*

That stopped them for a few seconds, but only a few. Telling media blowflies not to film was like telling mosquitoes not to bite. Alec could remember when things had been different (back in the antique days when a gentleman still held the door for a lady), but that time was gone. The lone reporter who had elected to stay here on Barnum Court—a Hispanic guy that Alec recognized vaguely, the one who was partial to bowties and did the weather on weekends—was already grabbing his mic and checking the power pack on his belt.

The front door of the Maitland house opened. Sarah saw her mother there and started to get out. "Wait one, Sarah," Alec said, and reached behind him. He had taken a couple of towels from the downstairs bathroom before leaving his house, and now he handed one to each girl.

"Put these over your faces, except for your eyes." He smiled. "Like bandits in a movie, okay?"

Grace only stared at him, but Sarah got it, and draped one of the towels over her sister's head. Alec swept it over Grace's mouth and nose while Sarah fixed her own towel. They got out and hurried through the harsh light from the TV truck, holding the towels closed below their chins. They didn't look like bandits; they looked like midget Bedouins in a sandstorm. They also looked like the saddest, most desperate kiddos Alec had ever seen.

Marcy Maitland had no towel to hide her face, and it was her that the cameraman focused on.

"Mrs. Maitland!" Bowtie shouted at her. "Do you have any comment on your husband's arrest? Have you spoken to him?"

Stepping in front of the camera (and moving with it nimbly when the cameraman tried to get a clear angle), Alec pointed to Bowtie. "Not one step on the lawn, *hermano*, or you can ask Maitland your bullshit questions from the next cell."

Bowtie gave him an insulted look. "Who you calling *hermano*? I have a job to do here."

"Hassling a distraught woman and two little kids," Alec said. "That's some job."

But his own job here was over. Mrs. Maitland had gathered her daughters to her and taken them inside. They were safe—as safe as they could be, anyway, although he had a feeling those two kids weren't going to feel safe anywhere for a very long time.

Bowtie trotted down the sidewalk, motioning for the cameraman to follow as Alec returned to his car. "Who are you, sir? What's your name?"

"Puddentane. Ask me again and I'll tell you the same. Your story isn't here, so leave these people alone, okay? They had nothing to do with this."

Knowing he might as well have been speaking in Russian. Already the neighbors were back on their lawns, eager to view the next episode of Barnum Court's continuing drama.

Alec backed down the driveway and headed west, also knowing that the cameraman would be videoing his license plate, and soon they would know who he was, and who he was working for. Not big news, but a cherry to put on top of the sundae they would serve the viewers who tuned in for the eleven o'clock news. He thought briefly of what was now going on in that house—the stunned and terrified mother trying to comfort two stunned and terrified girls still wearing their game-day facepaint.

"Did he do it?" he'd asked Howie when Howie called and gave him a quick shorthand version of the situation. It didn't matter, the work was the work, but he always liked to know. "What do you think?"

"I don't know *what* to think," Howie had replied, "but I know what your next move is, as soon as you get Sarah and Gracie home."

As he saw the first sign pointing him toward the turnpike, Alec called the Cap City Sheraton and asked for the concierge, with whom he had done business in the past.

Hell, he'd done business with most of them.

2

Ralph and Bill Samuels sat in Ralph's office with their ties yanked down and their collars loosened. The TV lights outside had gone off ten minutes before. All four buttons on Ralph's desk phone were lit up, but Sandy McGill was handling the incoming, and would until Gerry Malden arrived at eleven. For the time being, her job was simple, if repetitive: *The Flint City Police Department has no comment at this time. The investigation is ongoing.*

Meanwhile, Ralph had been working his own phone. Now he put it back in his coat pocket.

"Yune Sablo and his wife went upstate to see his in-laws. He says he put it off twice already, and this time he had no choice, unless he wanted to spend a week on the couch. Which, he says, is very uncomfortable. He'll be back tomorrow, and of course he'll be at the arraignment."

"We'll send someone else to the Sheraton, then," Samuels said. "Too bad Jack Hoskins is on vacation."

"No, it isn't," Ralph said, and that made Samuels laugh.

"Okay, you got me there. Our Jackie-boy might not be the worst detective in the state, but I admit he's right up there. You know every detective on the Cap City force. Start calling until you get a live one."

Ralph shook his head. "It should be Sablo. He knows the case, and he's our liaison with the State Police. This is no time to risk pissing them off, considering the way things went tonight. Which was not quite as we expected."

This was the understatement of the year, if not the century. Terry's complete surprise and seeming lack of guilt had shaken Ralph even more than the impossible alibi. Was it possible that the monster inside him had not only killed the boy, but erased all memory of what he had done? And then . . . what? Filled in the blank with a detailed false history of a teachers' conference in Cap City?

"If you don't send someone ASAP, that guy Gold uses—"

"Alec Pelley."

"Yeah, him. He'll beat us to the hotel's security footage. If they still have it, that is."

"They will. They keep everything for thirty days."

"You know that for a fact?"

"Yes. But Pelley doesn't have a warrant."

"Come on. Do you think he'll need one?"

In truth, Ralph did not. Alec Pelley had been a detective with the SP for over twenty years. He would have made a great many contacts during that time, and working for a successful criminal lawyer like Howard Gold, he would be sure to keep them current.

"Your idea to arrest him in public is now looking like a bad call," Samuels said.

Ralph gave him a hard look. "It was one you went along with."

"Not very enthusiastically," Samuels said. "Let's have the truth, since everyone else has gone home and it's just us girls. With you it was close to home."

"Damn straight," Ralph said. "It still is. And since it's just us girls, let me remind you that you did a little more than just go along. You've got an election coming up in the fall, and a dramatic high-profile arrest wouldn't exactly hurt your chances."

"That never entered my mind," Samuels said.

"Fine. It never entered your mind, you just went with the flow, but if you think arresting him at the ballpark was just about my son, you need to take another look at those crime scene pictures, and think about Felicity Ackerman's autopsy addendum. Guys like this never stop at one."

Color began to mount in Samuels's cheeks. "You think I haven't?

Christ, Ralph, I was the one who called him a fucking cannibal, *on the record*."

Ralph slid a palm up his cheek. It rasped. "Arguing over who said what and who did what is pointless. The thing to remember is it doesn't matter who gets to the security footage first. If it's Pelley, he can't just put it under his arm and carry it away, can he? Nor can he erase it."

"That's true," Samuels said. "And it's not apt to be conclusive, in any case. We may see a man in some of the footage who *looks* like Maitland—"

"Right. But proving it's him, based on a few glimpses, would be a different kettle of fish. Especially when stacked up against our eye-wits and the fingerprints." Ralph stood and opened the door. "Maybe the footage isn't the most important thing. I need to make a phone call. Should have made it already."

Samuels followed him into the reception area. Sandy McGill was on the telephone. Ralph approached her and made a throat-cutting gesture. She hung up and looked at him expectantly.

"Everett Roundhill," he said. "Chairman of the high school English department. Track him down and get him on the phone."

"Tracking him down won't be a problem, since I've already got his number," Sandy said. "He's called twice already, asking to speak to the lead investigator, and I basically told him to get in line." She picked up a sheaf of WHILE YOU WERE OUT notes and waved them at him. "I was going to put these on your desk for tomorrow. I know it's Sunday, but I've been telling people I'm pretty sure you'll be in."

Speaking very slowly, and looking at the floor instead of at the man beside him, Bill Samuels said, "Roundhill called. Twice. I don't like that. I don't like it at all."

3

Ralph arrived home at quarter to eleven on that Saturday night. He hit the garage door opener, drove inside, then hit it again. The door rattled obediently back down on its tracks, at least one thing in the world that remained sane and normal. Push Button A and, assuming Battery Compartment B is loaded with relatively fresh Duracells, Garage Door C opens and closes.

He turned off the engine and just sat there in the dark, tapping the steering wheel with his wedding ring, remembering a rhyme from his raucous teenage years: *Shave and a haircut . . . you bet! Sung by the whorehouse . . . quartet!*

The door opened and Jeanette came out, wrapped in her housecoat. In the spill of light from the kitchen, he saw that she was wearing the bunny slippers he'd given her as a joke present on her last birthday. The real present had been a trip to Key West, just the two of them, and they'd had a great time, but now it was just a blurry remnant in his mind, the way all vacations were later on: things with no more substance than the aftertaste of candy floss. The joke slippers were the things that had lasted, pink slippers from the Dollar Store with their ridiculous little eyes and their comical floppy ears. Seeing her in them made his eyes sting. He felt as if he had aged twenty years since stepping into that clearing at Figgis Park and viewing the bloody ruin that had been a little boy who probably idolized Batman and Superman.

He got out and hugged his wife hard, pressing his beard-stubbly cheek to her smooth one, saying nothing at first, concentrating on holding back the tears that wanted to come.

"Honey," she said. "Honey, you got him. You got him, so what's wrong?"

"Maybe nothing," he said. "Maybe everything. I should have brought him in for questioning. But Jesus Christ, I was so sure!"

"Come in," she said. "I'll make tea, and you can tell me about it."

"Tea will keep me awake."

She drew back and looked at him with eyes as lovely and dark at fifty as they had been at twenty-five. "Are you going to sleep, anyway?" And when he didn't reply: "Case closed."

Derek was away at camp in Michigan, so they had the house to themselves. She asked him if he wanted to watch the eleven o'clock news on the kitchen TV, and he shook his head. The last thing he wanted was ten minutes of coverage on how the Flint City Monster had been brought to bay. Jeannie made raisin toast to go with the tea. Ralph sat at the kitchen table, looking at his hands, and told her everything. He saved Everett Roundhill for last.

"He was furious with all of us," Ralph said, "but since I was the one who finally called him back, I was the one who took the incoming fire."

"Are you saying he confirmed Terry's story?"

"Every word. Roundhill picked up Terry and the other two teachers—Quade and Grant—at the high school. Ten o'clock Tuesday morning, as arranged. They got to the Sheraton in Cap City around 11:45, just in time to pick up their conference IDs and be seated for the banquet lunch. Roundhill says he lost track of Terry for an hour or so after the lunch was over, but he thinks Quade was with him. In any case, they were all back together by three, which is when Mrs. Stanhope saw him putting Frank Peterson's bike—and Frank himself—into a dirty white van seventy miles south."

"Have you talked to Quade?"

"Yes. On the way home. He wasn't angry—Roundhill's so pissed he's threatening to call for a full-scale investigation by the AG—but he was disbelieving. Stunned. Said that he and Terry went to a used bookstore called Second Edition after the banquet lunch, browsed, then came back for Coben."

"And Grant? What about him?"

"He's a she—Debbie Grant. Haven't reached her yet, her husband said she went out with some other women, and when she does that she always turns off her phone. I'll get her tomorrow morning, and when I do, I have no doubt that she'll confirm what Roundhill and Quade told me." He took a small bite of his toast, then put it back on the plate. "This is my fault. If I'd pulled Terry in for questioning Thursday night, after Stanhope and the Morris girl ID'd him, I'd have known we had a problem and this wouldn't be all over TV and the Internet now."

"But by then you'd matched the fingerprints to Terry Maitland's, isn't that right?"

"Yes."

"Fingerprints in the van, a fingerprint on the van's ignition key, fingerprints in the car he abandoned by the river, on the branch he used to . . ."

"Yes."

"And then more eyewitnesses. The man behind Shorty's Pub, and his friend. Plus the cab driver. And the bouncer at the strip club. They all knew him."

"Uh-huh, and now that he's been arrested, I have no doubt we'll get a few more eye-wits from Gentlemen, Please. Bachelors, mostly, who won't have to explain to their wives what they were doing there. I still should have waited. Maybe I should have called the high school to check on his movements on the day of the murder, except it made no sense, being summer vacation and all. What could they have told me except 'He's not here'?"

"And you were afraid that if you started asking questions, it would get back to him."

That had seemed obvious at the time, but now it only seemed stupid. Worse, careless. "I've made some mistakes in my career, but nothing like this. It's as if I went blind."

She shook her head vehemently. "Do you remember what I said when you told me that was how you meant to do it?"

"Yes."

Go ahead. Get him away from those boys as fast as you can.

That was what she'd said.

They sat there, looking at each other across the table.

"This is impossible," Jeannie said at last.

He pointed a finger at her. "I think you've reached the heart of the matter."

She sipped her tea thoughtfully, then looked at him over the rim of her cup. "There's an old saying that everyone has a double. I think Edgar Allan Poe even wrote a story about it. 'William Wilson,' it was called."

"Poe wrote his stories before fingerprints and DNA. We don't have the DNA yet—that's pending—but if it comes back as his, it's him and I'm probably okay. If it comes back as someone else's, they'll cart me off to the loonybin. After I lose my job and get sued for false arrest, that is."

She lifted her own piece of toast, then lowered it again. "You have his fingerprints *here.* And you'll have his DNA *here*, I'm sure of it. But Ralph . . . you don't have any fingerprints or DNA from *there.* From whoever attended that conference in Cap City. What if Terry Maitland killed the boy and it was the *double* at that conference?"

"If you're saying Terry Maitland has a lost identical twin with the same fingerprints and DNA, it's not possible."

"I'm *not* saying that. I'm saying that you don't have any forensic proof that it was Terry in Cap City. If Terry was *here*, and the forensic evidence says he was, then the double *must* have been there. It's the only thing that makes sense."

Ralph understood the logic, and in the detective novels Jeannie liked to read—the Agatha Christies, the Rex Stouts, the Harlan Cobens—it would have been the centerpiece of the final chapter, when Miss Marple, Nero Wolfe, or Myron Bolitar revealed all. There was one rock-hard fact, as unassailable as gravity: a man could not be in two places at the same time.

But if Ralph had confidence in the eyewitnesses *here*, he had to have equal confidence in the eyewitnesses who said they had been in Cap City with Maitland. How could he doubt them? Roundhill, Quade, and Grant all taught in the same department. They saw Maitland every day. Was he, Ralph, supposed to believe those three teachers had colluded in the rape-murder of a child? Or that they had spent two days with a double so perfect they had never even suspected? And even if he could make *himself* believe it, could Bill Samuels ever convince a jury, especially when Terry had a seasoned and crafty defense lawyer like Howie Gold on his side?

"Let's go up to bed," Jeanette said. "I'll give you one of my Ambiens and rub your back. This will look better in the morning."

"You think so?" he asked.

4

As Jeanette Anderson was rubbing her husband's back, Fred Peterson and his older son (now, with Frankie gone, his only son) were picking up dishes and setting the living room and the den to rights. And although it had been a remembrance gathering, the remains were pretty much the same as after any large and long houseparty.

Ollie had surprised Fred. The boy was your typical self-involved teenager who ordinarily wouldn't pick up his socks from under the coffee table unless told twice or three times, but tonight he'd been an efficient and uncomplaining helper since Arlene had at ten o'clock turned out the last of that day's unending stream of guests. The gathering of friends and neighbors had been winding down by seven, and Fred had hoped it would be over by eight—God, he was so tired of nodding when people told him Frankie was in heaven now—but then came the news that Terence Maitland had been arrested for Frankie's murder, and the damn thing had cranked up all over again. That second cycle almost *had* been a party, albeit a grim one. Again and again Fred had been told that a, it was unbelievable, that b, Coach T had always seemed so *normal*, and c, the needle at McAlester was too good for him.

Ollie went back and forth from the living room to the kitchen, carrying glasses and piles of dishes, loading them into the dishwasher with an efficiency Fred never would have expected. When the dishwasher was full, Ollie set it going and rinsed more dishes, stacking them in the sink for the next load. Fred brought in the dishes that had been left in the den, and found yet more on the picnic table in the backyard, where some of their visitors had gone to smoke. Fifty or sixty people must have washed through the house before it was finally over, everyone in the neighborhood, plus well-wishers from other parts of town, not to mention Father Brixton and his various hangers-on (his *groupies*, Fred thought) from St. Anthony's. On and on they had come, a stream of mourners and gawkers.

Fred and Ollie did their clean-up work silently, each wrapped up in his own thoughts and his own grief. After receiving condolences for hours—and to be fair, even those from total strangers had been heartfelt—they were unable to condole with each other. Maybe that was strange. Maybe it was sad. Maybe it was what literary types called irony. Fred was too tired and heartsick to think about it.

During all of this, the dead boy's mother sat on the sofa in her best meet-the-public silk dress, her knees together, her hands cupping her fat upper arms as if she were cold. She'd said nothing since the last of the evening's guests—old Mrs. Gibson from next door, who had predictably held on until the bitter end—finally took her leave.

She can go now, she's got it all stored up, Arlene Peterson had said to her husband as she locked the front door and then leaned her bulk against it.

Arlene Kelly had been a slender vision in white lace when Father

Brixton's predecessor married them. She had still been slender and beautiful after giving birth to Ollie, but that had been seventeen years ago. She had begun to put on weight after giving birth to Frank, and now she was on the verge of obesity ... although she was still beautiful to Fred, who hadn't the heart to take Dr. Connolly's advice, at his last physical: *You're good to go for another fifty years, Fred, as long as you don't fall off a building or step in front of a truck, but your wife has type two diabetes, and needs to lose fifty pounds if she's going to stay healthy. You need to help her. After all, you've both got a lot to live for.*

Only with Frankie not just dead but murdered, most of the things they had to live for seemed stupid and insignificant. Only Ollie retained his former precious importance in Fred's mind, and even in his grief, he knew that he and Arlene had to be careful about how they treated him in the weeks and months ahead. Ollie was also grieving. Ollie could shoulder his share (more than that, really) of clearing away the remains of this last act in the tribal death-rites of Franklin Victor Peterson, but tomorrow they would have to let him start going back to being a boy. It would take time, but he would get there eventually.

The next time I see Ollie's socks under the coffee table, I will rejoice, Fred promised himself. *And I will break this horrible, unnatural silence as soon as I can think of something to say.*

But he could think of nothing, and as Ollie sleepwalked past him into the den, pulling their vacuum cleaner by its hose, Fred thought—with no idea of how wrong he was—that at least things could not get worse.

He went to the doorway of the den, and watched as Ollie began vacuuming the gray pile with that same eerie, unguessed-at efficiency, taking long, even strokes, first pushing the nap one way and then pulling it the other. The crumby remains of Nabs, Oreos, and Ritz crackers disappeared as if they had never been there, and Fred finally found something to say. "I'll do the living room."

"I don't mind," Ollie said. His eyes were red and swollen. Given the age difference between the two brothers—seven years—they had been amazingly close. Or maybe it wasn't so amazing, maybe that was just enough space to keep sibling rivalry to a bare minimum. To make Ollie something like Frank's second father.

"I know," Fred said, "but share and share alike."

"Okay. Just don't say, 'It's what Frankie would have wanted.' I'd have to strangle you with the vacuum hose."

Fred smiled at that. Probably not his first smile since the policeman had come to the door last Tuesday, but maybe the first real one. "It's a deal."

Ollie finished the carpet and trundled the vacuum to his father. When Fred pulled it into the living room and started in on the carpet, Arlene got to her feet and trudged toward the kitchen without looking back. Fred and Ollie glanced at each other. Ollie shrugged. Fred shrugged back and began vacuuming again. People had reached out to them in their grief, and Fred supposed that was nice, but golly-willikers, what a mess they had left behind. He consoled himself with the thought that it would have been much worse if it had been an Irish wake, but Fred had quit the booze after Ollie was born, and the Petersons kept a dry house.

From the kitchen came a most unexpected sound: laughter.

Fred and Ollie stared at each other again. Ollie hurried for the kitchen, where his mother's laughter, which had seemed natural and easy to begin with, was now rising to a hysterical pitch. Fred stepped on the vacuum cleaner's power button, killing it, and followed.

Arlene Peterson was standing with her back to the sink, holding her considerable belly and nearly screaming with laughter. Her face had gone bright red, as if she were running a high fever. Tears coursed down her cheeks.

"Ma?" Ollie asked. "What the hell?"

Although the dishes had been cleared from the living room and den, there was still a ton of work to be done here. There were two counters on either side of the sink, and a table in the kitchen nook, where the Peterson family had taken most of their evening meals. All these surfaces were loaded with partially eaten casseroles, Tupperware containers, and leftovers wrapped in aluminum foil. Resting on top of the stove was the carcass of a partially eaten chicken and a gravy boat full of congealed brown sludge.

"We've got enough leftovers for a month!" Arlene managed. She doubled over, guffawing, then straightened up. Her cheeks had turned purple. Her red hair, which she had bequeathed to both the son standing before her and the one now underground, had come loose from the clips with which she had temporarily tamed it, and now stood out around her congested face in a frizzy corona. "Bad news, Frankie's dead! Good news, I won't have to go shopping for a *long . . . long . . . time!*"

She began to howl. It was a sound that belonged in an insane asylum, not in their kitchen. Fred told his legs to move, to go to her and embrace her, but at first they wouldn't obey. It was Ollie who moved, but before he could get to her, Arlene picked up the chicken and threw it. Ollie ducked. The chicken flew end over end, shedding stuffing, and hit the wall with a horrible *crunch-splat*. It left a circle of grease on the wallpaper below the clock.

"Mom, stop. Stop it."

Ollie tried to take her by the shoulders and pull her into a hug, but Arlene slipped under his hands and darted toward one of the counters, still laughing and howling. She grabbed a serving dish of lasagna in both hands—it had been brought by one of Father Brixton's sycophants—and dumped it on her head. Cold pasta fell into her hair and onto her shoulders. She heaved the dish into the living room.

"Frankie is dead and we've got a fucking Italian buffet!"

Fred got moving then, but Arlene slid away from him, too. She was laughing like an overexcited girl playing a spirited game of tag. She grabbed a Tupperware container full of Marshmallow

Delite. She started to raise it, then dropped it between her feet. The laughter stopped. One hand cupped her large left breast. The other lay flat on her chest above it. She looked at her husband with wide eyes that were still swimming with tears.

Those eyes, Fred thought. *Those are what I fell in love with.*

"Mom? Mom, what's wrong?"

"Nothing," she said, and then: "I think my heart." She bent to look at the chicken and the marshmallow dessert. Pasta fell from her hair. "Look what I did."

She gave a long, whooping, rattling gasp. Fred grabbed her, but she was too heavy, and slithered through his arms. Before she went down on her side, Fred saw that the color was already fading from her cheeks.

Ollie screamed and dropped to his knees beside her. "Mom! Mom! *Mom!*" He looked up at his father. "I don't think she's breathing!"

Fred pushed his son aside. "Call 911."

Without looking to see if Ollie was doing it, Fred slipped a hand around his wife's big neck, feeling for a pulse. He got one, but it was disorganized, chaotic: *beat-beat, beatbeatbeat, beat-beat-beat.* He straddled her, gripped his left wrist in his right hand, and began to push down in a steady rhythm. Was he doing it right? Was it even CPR? He didn't know, but when her eyes opened, his own heart seemed to give an upward leap in his chest. There she was, she was back.

It wasn't really a heart attack. She overexerted herself, that's all. Fainted. I think they call that a syncope. But we're getting you on a diet, my dear, and your birthday present is going to be one of those wristbands that measure your—

"Made a mess," Arlene whispered. "Sorry."

"Don't try to talk."

Ollie was on their kitchen wall phone, talking fast and loud, almost shouting. Giving their address. Telling them to hurry.

"You'll have to clean up the living room again," she said. "I'm sorry. Fred, I'm so, so sorry."

Before Fred could tell her again to stop talking, to just lie still until she felt better, Arlene drew another of those great, rattling breaths. As she let it out, her eyes rolled up in her head. The bloodshot whites bulged, turning her into a horror-movie deathmask Fred would afterwards try to erase from his mind. He would fail.

"Dad? They're on their way. Is she all right?"

Fred didn't reply. He was too busy applying more half-assed CPR and wishing he had taken a class—why had he never found time to do that? There were so many things he wished for. He would have traded his immortal soul to be able to turn the calendar back one lousy week.

Press and release. Press and release.

You'll be all right, he told her. *You have to be all right.* Sorry *cannot be your last word on this earth. I will not allow it.*

Press and release. Press and release.

5

Marcy Maitland was glad to take Grace into bed with her when Grace asked, but when she asked Sarah if she wanted to join them, her older daughter shook her head.

"All right," Marcy said, "but if you change your mind, I'll be here."

An hour passed, then another. The worst Saturday of her life became the worst Sunday. She thought of Terry, who should have been beside her now, fast asleep (perhaps dreaming about the upcoming City League championship, now that the Bears had been disposed of), and was instead in a jail cell. Was he also awake? Of course he was.

She knew there were going to be some hard days ahead, but

Howie would put things right. Terry had once told her that his old Pop Warner co-coach was the best defense lawyer in the southwest, and might someday sit on the state's supreme court. Given Terry's cast-iron alibi, there was no way Howie could fail. But each time she drew almost enough comfort from this idea to drop off, she thought of Ralph Anderson, the Judas sonofabitch she'd thought of as a friend, and she came wide awake again. As soon as this was over, they would sue the Flint City PD for false arrest, defamation of character, anything else Howie Gold could think of, and when Howie began dropping his legal smart-bombs, she would make sure Ralph Anderson was standing on ground zero. Could they sue him personally? Strip him of everything he owned? She hoped so. She hoped they could send him, his wife, and the son with whom Terry had taken such pains, out into the street, barefoot and dressed in rags, with begging bowls in their hands. She guessed such things were not likely in this advanced and supposedly enlightened day and age, but she could see the three of them that way with utter clarity—mendicants in the streets of Flint City—and each time she did, the vision brought her wide awake again, vibrating with rage and satisfaction.

It was quarter past two by the clock on the nightstand when her older daughter appeared in the doorway, only her legs clearly visible below the oversized Okie City Thunder tee she wore as a nightshirt.

"Mom? Are you awake?"

"I am."

"Can I get in with you and Gracie?"

Marcy threw back the sheet and moved over. Sarah got in, and when Marcy hugged her and kissed the nape of her neck, Sarah began to cry.

"Shh, you'll wake your sister."

"I can't help it. I keep thinking about the handcuffs. I'm sorry."

"Quietly, then. Quietly, hon."

Marcy held her until Sarah had gotten it all out. When she was quiet for five minutes or so, Marcy thought the girl had gone to sleep, and felt that now, with both of her girls here, bookending her, she might be able to sleep herself. But then Sarah rolled over to look at her. Her wet eyes shone in the dark.

"He won't go to prison, will he, Mom?"

"No," she said. "He didn't do anything."

"But innocent people *do* go to prison. Sometimes for years, until someone finds out they were innocent after all. Then they get out, but they're *old*."

"That isn't going to happen to your father. He was in Cap City when the thing happened that they arrested him for—"

"I know what they arrested him for," Sarah said. She wiped her eyes. "I'm not *stupid*."

"I know you're not, honey."

Sarah stirred restlessly. "They must have had a reason."

"They probably think so, but their reasons are wrong. Mr. Gold will explain where he was, and they'll have to let him go."

"All right." A long pause. "But I don't want to go back to community camp until this is over, and I don't think Gracie should, either."

"You won't have to. And when fall comes around, all of this will just be a memory."

"A bad one," Sarah said, and sniffled.

"Agreed. Now go to sleep."

Sarah did. And with her girls to warm her, so did Marcy, although her dreams were bad ones in which Terry was marched away by those two policemen, while the crowd watched and Baibir Patel cried and Gavin Frick stared in disbelief.

6

Until midnight, the county jail sounded like a zoo at feeding time—drunks singing, drunks crying, drunks standing at the bars of their cells and holding shouted conversations. There was even what sounded like a fistfight, although since all the cells were singles, Terry didn't see how that could be, unless there were two guys punching at each other through the bars. Somewhere, at the far end of the corridor, a guy was bellowing the first phrase of John 3:16 over and over at the top of his lungs: *"For God so loved the world! For God so loved the world! For God so loved THE WHOLE FUCKIN WORLD!"* The stench was piss, shit, disinfectant, and whatever sauce-soaked pasta had been served for supper.

My first time in jail, Terry marveled. *After forty years of life, I have landed in stir, the calaboose, the joint, the old stone hotel. Think of that.*

He wanted to feel anger, *righteous* anger, and he supposed that feeling might arise with daylight, when the world came back into focus, but now, at three o'clock on Sunday morning, as the shouts and singing subsided to snores, farts, and the occasional groan, all he felt was shame. As if he really *had* done something. Except he would have felt nothing of the kind if he had really done what he was accused of doing. If he had been sick and evil enough to commit such an obscene act upon a child, he would have felt nothing but the desperate cunning of an animal in a trap, willing to say anything or do anything in order to get out. Or was that true? How did he know what a man like that would think or feel? It was like trying to guess what might be in the mind of an alien from space.

He had no doubt that Howie Gold would get him out of this; even now, in the darkest ditch of the night, with his mind still trying to get a grip on the way his whole life had changed in a matter of minutes, he didn't doubt it. But he also knew that not all of the shit would wash off. He would be released with an apology—if not tomorrow, then at the arraignment, if not at the arraignment, then at the next step, which would probably be a grand jury hearing in Cap City—but he knew what he would see in the eyes of his students the next time he stepped in front of a class, and his career as a youth sports coach was probably finished. The various governing bodies would find some excuse if he wouldn't do what they'd see as the honorable thing and step down himself. Because he was never going to be completely innocent again, not in the eyes of his neighbors on the West Side, or in those of Flint City as a whole. He would always be the man who was arrested for the murder of Frank Peterson. He would always be the man of whom people would say, *No smoke without fire.*

If it was just him, he thought he could deal with it. What did he tell his boys when they whined that a call was unfair? *Suck it up and get back in there. Play the game.* But it wasn't just him who would have to suck this up, not just him who would have to play the game. Marcy would be branded. The whispers and sidelong looks at work and at the grocery store. The friends who would no longer call. Jamie Mattingly might be an exception, but he had his doubts even about her.

Then there were the girls. Sarah and Gracie would be subjected to the sort of vicious gossip and wholesale shunning of which only kids their age were capable. He guessed Marcy would have sense enough to keep them close until this was sorted out, if only to keep them away from the reporters who would otherwise hound them, but even in the fall, even after he was cleared, they would be marked. *See that girl over there? Her father was arrested for killing a kid and shoving a stick up his ass.*

Lying on his bunk. Staring up into the dark. Smelling the jailhouse stench. Thinking, *We'll have to move. Maybe to Tulsa, maybe to Cap City, maybe down to Texas. Somebody will give me a job, even if they won't allow me within a country mile of boys' baseball, football, or* basketball practice. My references are good, and they'll be afraid of a discrimination suit if they say no.

Only the arrest—and the reason for the arrest—would follow them like this jailhouse stink. Especially the girls. Facebook alone would be enough to hunt them down and single them out. *These are the girls whose father got away with murder.*

He had to stop thinking this way and get some sleep, and he had to stop feeling ashamed of himself because someone else—Ralph Anderson, to be specific—had made a horrible mistake. These things always looked worse in the small hours, that was what he had to remember. And given his current position, in a cell and wearing a baggy brown uniform with DOC on the back of the shirt, it was inevitable that his fears would grow as big as the floats in a holiday parade. Things would look better in the morning. He was sure of it.

Yes.

But still, the shame.

Terry covered his eyes.

7

Howie Gold slipped from bed at six thirty on Sunday morning, not because there was anything he could do at that hour, and not from personal preference. Like many men in their early sixties, his prostate had grown along with his IRA, and his bladder seemed to have shrunk along with his sexual aspirations. Once he was awake, his brain slipped from park into drive, and going back to sleep was an impossibility.

He left Elaine to dream what he hoped were pleasant dreams, and padded barefoot into the kitchen to start the coffee and check his phone, which he'd silenced and left on the counter before going to bed. He had a text from Alec Pelley, delivered at 1:12 AM.

Howie drank his coffee, and was eating a bowl of Raisin Bran when Elaine came into the kitchen, knotting the belt of her robe and yawning. "What's up, powderpuff?"

"Time will tell. In the meantime, do you want some scrambled eggs?"

"Breakfast, he offers me." She was pouring her own cup of coffee. "Since it's not Valentine's Day or my birthday, should I find that suspicious?"

"I'm killing time. Got a text from Alec, but I can't call him until seven."

"Good news or bad?"

"No idea. So do you want some eggs?"

"Yes. Two. Fried, not scrambled."

"You know I always break the yolks."

"Since I get to sit and watch, I will restrain my criticism. Wheat toast, please."

For a wonder, only one of the yolks broke. As he set the plate in front of her, she said, "If Terry Maitland killed that child, the world has gone insane."

"The world *is* insane," Howie said, "but he didn't do it. He has an alibi as strong as the S on Superman's chest."

"Why did they arrest him, then?"

"Because they believe they have proof as strong as the S on Superman's chest."

She considered this. "Unstoppable force meets immovable object?"

"There is no such thing, sweetheart."

He looked at his watch. Five minutes of seven. Close enough. He called Alec's cell.

His investigator answered on the third ring. "You're early, and I'm shaving. Can you call back in five minutes? At seven, in other words, as I suggested?"

"No," Howie said, "but I'll wait until you wipe the shaving cream off the phone side of your face, how's that?"

"You're a tough boss," Alec said, but he sounded good-humored in spite of the hour, and in spite of being interrupted at a task most men preferred to do while occupied by nothing but their own thoughts. Which gave Howie hope. He had a lot to work with already, but he could always use more.

"Is it good news or bad news?"

"Give me a second, will you? I'm getting this shit all over my phone."

It was more like five, but then Alec was back. "The news is good, boss. Good for us and bad for the DA. Very bad."

"You saw the security footage? How much is there, and from how many cameras?"

"I saw the footage, and there's plenty." Alec paused, and when he spoke again, Howie knew he was smiling; he could hear it in the man's voice. "But there's something better. *Much* better."

8

Jeanette Anderson rose at quarter of seven and found her husband's side of the bed empty. The kitchen smelled of fresh coffee, but Ralph wasn't there, either. She looked out the window and saw him sitting at the picnic table in the backyard, still in his striped pajamas and sipping from the joke cup Derek had given him last Father's Day. On the side, in big blue letters, it said YOU HAVE THE RIGHT TO REMAIN SILENT UNTIL I DRINK MY COFFEE. She got her own cup, went out to him, and kissed his cheek. The day was going to be a hot one, but now this early morning was cool and quiet and pleasant.

"Can't let go of it, can you?" she asked.

"None of us will be letting go of this one," he said. "Not for awhile."

"It's Sunday," she said. "Day of rest. And you need it. I don't like the way you look. According to an article I read in the *New York Times* Health section last week, you have entered heart attack country."

"That's cheering."

She sighed. "What's first on your list?"

"Checking with that other teacher, Deborah Grant. Just a *t* to cross. I have no doubt she'll confirm that Terry was on the trip to Cap City, although there's always a chance that she noticed something off about him that Roundhill and Quade missed. Women can be more observant."

Jeannie considered this idea doubtful, perhaps even sexist, but it wasn't the time to say so. She reverted to their discussion of the night before, instead. "Terry *was* here. He *did* do it. What you need is some forensic evidence from there. I guess DNA is out of the question, but fingerprints?"

"We can dust the room where he and Quade stayed, but they checked out Wednesday morning, and the room will have been cleaned and occupied since then. Almost certainly more than once."

"But it's still possible, isn't it? Some hotel maids are conscientious, but plenty just make the beds and wipe the rings and smudges off the coffee table and call it good. What if you found Mr. Quade's fingerprints, but not Terry Maitland's?"

He liked the flush of Junior Detective excitement on her face, and wished he didn't have to dampen it. "It wouldn't prove anything, hon. Howie Gold would tell the jury they couldn't convict anyone on the *absence* of prints, and he'd be right."

She considered this. "Okay, but I still think you should gather prints from that room, and identify as many as possible. Can you do that?"

"Yes. And it's a good idea." It was at least another *t* to cross. "I'll find out which room it was, and try to have the Sheraton move out whoever is in there now. I think they'll cooperate, given the play this is going to have in the media. We'll dust it top to bottom and side to side. But what I really want is to see the security footage from the days that convention was in session, and since Detective Sablo—he's the State Police's lead on this—won't be back until later today, I'm going to take a run up there myself. I'll be hours behind Gold's investigator, but that can't be helped."

She put a hand over his. "Just promise me you'll stop every once in a while and acknowledge the day, honey. It's the only one you'll have until tomorrow."

He smiled at her, squeezed her hand, then let go. "I keep thinking about the vehicles he used, the one he used to kidnap the Peterson boy and the one he left town in."

"The Econoline van and the Subaru."

"Uh-huh. The Subaru doesn't bother me much. That one was a straight steal from a municipal parking lot, and we've seen plenty of similar thefts since 2012 or so. The new keyless ignitions are the car thief's best friend, because when you stop somewhere, thinking about whatever errands you have to run or what you're going to put on for supper, you don't see your keys dangling from the ignition. It's easy to leave the electronic fob behind, especially if you're wearing earbuds or yakking on your phone, and don't hear the car chiming at you to take them. The Subaru's owner—Barbara Nearing—left her fob in the cup holder and the parking ticket on the dashboard when she went to work at eight. Car was gone when she came back at five."

"The attendant doesn't remember who drove it out?"

"No, and that's not surprising. It's a big garage, five levels, there are people coming and going all the time. There's a camera at the exit, but the footage gets wiped every forty-eight hours. The van, though . . ."

"What about the van?"

"It belonged to a part-time carpenter and handyman named Carl Jellison, who lives in Spuytenkill, New York, a little town between Poughkeepsie and New Paltz. He took his keys, but there was a spare in a little magnetic box under the rear bumper. Someone found the box and drove the van away. Bill Samuels's theory is that the thief drove it from mid-state New York to Cap City . . . or Dubrow . . . or maybe right here to FC . . . and then left it with that spare key still in the ignition. Terry found it, *re*-stole it, and stashed it somewhere. Maybe in a barn or shed outside of town. God knows there are plenty of abandoned farms since everything went blooey in 2008. He ditched the van behind Shorty's Pub with the key still in it, hoping—not unreasonably—that someone would steal it a third time."

"Only no one did," Jeannie said. "So you have the van in impound, and you have the key. Which has a Terry Maitland thumbprint on it."

Ralph nodded. "We actually have a *ton* of prints. That thing's ten years old and hasn't been cleaned for at least the last five, if ever. Some of the prints we've eliminated—Jellison, his son, his wife, two guys who worked for him. Had those by Thursday afternoon, courtesy of the New York State Police, and God bless them. Some states, *most* states, we'd still be waiting. We've also got Terry Maitland's and Frank Peterson's, of course. Four of Peterson's were on the inside of the passenger door. That's a greasy area, and they're as clear as fresh-minted pennies. I'm thinking those were made in the Figgis Park parking lot, when Terry was trying to pull him out of the passenger seat and the kid was trying to resist."

Jeannie winced.

"There are others from the van we're still waiting on; they've been out on the wire since last Wednesday. We may get hits, we may not. We assume some of them belong to the original car thief, up in Spuytenkill. The others could belong to anyone from friends of Jellison's to hitchhikers the car thief picked up. But the freshest ones, other than the boy's, are Maitland's. The original thief doesn't matter, but I *would* like to know where he dumped the van." He paused, then added, "It makes no sense, you know."

"Not wiping away the prints?"

"Not just that. How about stealing the van and the Subaru in the first place? Why steal vehicles to use while you do your dirt if you're going to flash your face to anyone who cares to look at it?"

Jeannie listened to this with growing dismay. As his wife, she couldn't ask the questions that his prompted: *If you had such doubts, why in God's name did you act the way you did? And why so fast?* Yes, she had encouraged him, and so maybe she owned a little of this current trouble, but she hadn't had all the information. *A cheap out, but mine own*, she thought . . . and winced again.

As if reading her mind (and after almost twenty-five years of marriage, he could probably do that), he said, "This isn't all buyer's remorse, you know—don't get that idea. Bill Samuels and I talked about it. He says it doesn't *have* to make sense. He says Terry did it the way he did because he went crazy. That the impulse to do it—the *need* to do it, for all I know, although you'd never get me to put it that way in court—kept building up and up. There have been similar cases. Bill says, 'Oh yes, he planned to do something, and he put some of the pieces in place, but when he saw Frank Peterson last Tuesday, pushing that bike with the broken chain, all the planning went out the window. The top blew off, and Dr. Jekyll turned into Mr. Hyde.'"

"A sexual sadist in a full-blown frenzy," she murmured. "Terry Maitland. Coach T."

"It made sense then and it makes sense now," he said, almost belligerently.

Maybe, she could have replied, *but what about after, honey? What about when it was over, and he was sated? Did you and Bill consider that? How come he* still *didn't wipe his fingerprints, and went right on showing his face?*

"There was something under the driver's seat of the van," Ralph said.

"Really? What?"

"A scrap of paper. Part of a take-out menu, maybe. Probably

means nothing, but I want to take a good close look at it. Pretty sure it was checked into evidence." He threw what remained of his coffee into the grass and stood up. "What I want more is a look at the Sheraton security footage for last Tuesday and Wednesday. Also any footage from the restaurant where he says that bunch of teachers went to dinner."

"If you get a good look at his face in any of the footage, send me a screen-grab." And when he raised his eyebrows: "I've known Terry as long as you have, and if that wasn't him in Cap City, I'll know." She smiled. "After all, women are more observant than men. You said so yourself."

9

Sarah and Grace Maitland ate almost no breakfast, which didn't disturb Marcy so much as the unaccustomed absence of phones and mini-tablets from their immediate vicinity. The police had let them keep their electronics, but after a few quick looks, Sarah and Grace left their gadgets in their bedrooms. Whatever news or social chatter they had found was nothing either girl wanted to pursue. And after her own quick look out the living room window, where she saw two news vans and a Flint City PD cruiser parked at the curb, Marcy pulled the curtains. How long was this day going to be? And what in God's name was she going to do with it?

Howie Gold answered that for her. He called at quarter past eight, sounding remarkably upbeat.

"We're going to see Terry this afternoon. Together. Ordinarily, visitors have to be requested by the inmate twenty-four hours in advance and pre-approved, but I was able to cut through that. The one thing I couldn't get past was the non-contact thing. He's on a maximum security hold. It means talking to him through glass, but it's better than the way it looks in the movies. You'll see."

"Okay." Feeling breathless. "What time?"

"I'll pick you up at one thirty. You should have his best suit, plus a nice dark tie. For the arraignment. And you can bring him something nice to eat. Nuts, fruit, candy. Put it in a see-through bag, okay?"

"Okay. What about the girls? Should I—"

"No, the girls stay home. County is no place for them. Find someone to sit with them, in case the press guys get pushy. And tell them all is well."

She didn't know if she could find anyone—she hated to impose on Jamie after last night. Surely if she spoke to the cop in the cruiser out front, he would keep the press off the lawn. Wouldn't he?

"*Is* all well? Is it really?"

"I think it is. Alec Pelley just busted a jumbo-sized piñata in Cap City, and all the prizes fell into our laps. I'm going to send you a link to something. Up to you whether or not you share it with your chickadees, but I know I would, if they were mine."

Five minutes later, Marcy was seated on the couch, with Sarah on one side and Grace on the other. They were looking at Sarah's mini-tablet. Terry's desktop or one of the laptops would have been better, but the police had taken those. The tablet was good enough, as it turned out. Soon all three of them were laughing and screaming with joy and giving each other high fives.

This isn't just light at the end of the tunnel, Marcy thought, *it's a whole damn rainbow.*

10

Thuck-thuck-thuck.

At first Merl Cassidy thought he was hearing it in a dream, one of the bad ones where his stepfather was getting ready to tune up on him. The bald bastard had a way of rapping on the kitchen table, first with his knuckles, then with his whole fist, as he asked the preparatory questions that led up to that evening's beating: *Where were you? Why do you bother wearing that watch if you're always going to be late for supper? Why don't you ever help your mother? Why do you bother bringing those books home if you're never going to do any fucking homework?* His mother might try to protest, but she was ignored. If she tried to intervene, she was pushed away. Then the fist that had been hitting the table with ever increasing force would start hitting him.

Thuck-thuck-thuck.

Merl opened his eyes to get away from the dream, and had just a moment to savor the irony: he was fifteen hundred miles away from that bullying asshole, fifteen hundred at least . . . and still as close as any night's sleep. Not that he'd gotten a full night; he rarely had since running away from home.

Thuck-thuck-thuck.

It was a cop, tapping with his nightstick. Patient. Now making a cranking gesture with his free hand: roll it down.

For a moment Merl had no idea where he was, but when he looked through the windshield at the big-box store looming across what seemed like a mile of mostly empty parking lot, it snapped into place. El Paso. This was El Paso. The Buick he was driving was almost out of gas, and he was almost out of money. He had pulled into the Walmart Supercenter lot to catch a few hours' sleep. Maybe in the morning he would have an idea of what to do next. Only now there probably was no next.

Thuck-thuck-thuck.

He rolled down the window. "Good morning, Officer. I was driving late, and I pulled in to get a little sleep. I thought it would be all right to coop a little here. If I was wrong, I'm sorry."

"Uh-huh, that's actually admirable," said the cop, and when he smiled, Merl had a moment of hope. It was a friendly smile. "Lots of people do it. Only most of them don't look fourteen years old."

"I'm eighteen, just small for my age." But he felt an immense weariness that had nothing to do with the short sleep he'd had over the last weeks.

"Uh-huh, and people are always mistaking me for Tom Hanks. Some even ask for my autograph. Let's see your license and registration."

One more effort, as weak as the final twitch of a dying man's foot. "They were in my coat. Someone stole it while I was in the restroom. At McDonald's, this was."

"Uh-huh, uh-huh, okay. And where are you from?"

"Phoenix," Merl said without conviction.

"Uh-huh, so how come that's an Oklahoma plate on this beauty?"

Merl was silent, out of answers.

"Step out of the car, son, and even though you look about as dangerous as a little yellow dog shitting in a rainstorm, keep your hands where I can see them."

Merl got out of the car without too much regret. It had been a good run. More, really; when you thought of it, it had been a miraculous run. He should have been collared a dozen times since leaving home in late April, but he hadn't been. Now that he had been, so what? Where had he been going, anyway? Nowhere. Anywhere. Away from the bald bastard.

"What's your name, kiddo?"

"Merl Cassidy. Merl, short for Merlin."

A few early shoppers looked at them, then went on their way into the round-the-clock wonders of Walmart.

"Just like the wizard, uh-huh, okay. You got any ID, Merl?"

He reached into his back pocket and brought out a cheap wallet with frayed buckskin stitching, a birthday present given to him by his mother when he was eight. Back then it had just been the two of them, and the world had made some sense. Inside the billfold was a five and two ones. From the compartment where he kept a few pictures of his mom, he brought out a laminated card with his photo on it.

"Poughkeepsie Youth Ministry," the cop mused. "You from New York?"

"Yes, sir." The *sir* was a thing his stepfather had beaten into him early.

"You from there?"

"No, sir, but close by. A little town called Spuytenkill. That means 'a lake that spouts.' At least that's what my mother told me."

"Uh-huh, okay, interesting, you learn a new thing every day. How long have you been on the run, Merl?"

"Going on three months, I guess."

"And who taught you to drive?"

"My uncle Dave. In the fields, mostly. I'm a good driver. Standard or automatic, makes no difference. My uncle Dave, he had a heart attack and died."

The cop considered this, tapping the laminated card against one thumbnail, not *thuck-thuck-thuck* now but *tick-tick-tick*. On the whole, Merl liked him. At least so far.

"Good driver, uh-huh, you must be to get all the way from New York to this dusty puckered asshole of a border town. How many cars have you stolen, Merl?"

"Three. No, four. This one's the fourth. Only the first one was a van. From my neighbor down the road."

"Four," the cop said, considering the dirty child standing in front of him. "And how did you finance your southward safari, Merl?"

"Huh?"

"How did you eat? Where did you sleep?"

"Mostly sleep in whatever I was driving. And I stole." He hung his head. "From ladies' purses, mostly. Sometimes they didn't see me, but when they did . . . I can run fast." The tears began to come.

He had cried quite a bit on what the cop called his southward safari, mostly at night, but those tears had brought no real relief. These did. Merl didn't know why and didn't care.

"Three months, four cars," the cop said, and *tick-tick-tick* went Merl's youth ministry card. "What were you running from, kiddo?"

"My stepfather. And if you send me back to that sonofabitch, I'll run away again, first chance I get."

"Uh-huh, uh-huh, I get the picture. And how old are you really, Merl?"

"Twelve, but I'll be thirteen next month."

"Twelve. I will be dipped in shit and spun backwards. You come with me, Merl. Let's see what we're gonna do with you."

At the cop shop on Harrison Avenue, while waiting for someone from social services to show up, Merl Cassidy was photographed, deloused, and fingerprinted. The prints went out on the wire. This was just a matter of routine.

11

When Ralph got to Flint City's much smaller cop shop, meaning to call Deborah Grant before picking up a cruiser for the run to Cap City, Bill Samuels was waiting for him. He looked sick. Even the Alfalfa cowlick was drooping.

"What's wrong?" Ralph asked. Meaning *what else?*

"Alec Pelley texted me. With a link."

He unbuckled his briefcase, brought out his iPad (the big one, of course, the Pro), and powered it up. He tapped a couple of times, then passed it to Ralph. The text from Pelley read, **Are you sure you want to pursue a case against T. Maitland? Check this first.** The link was beneath. Ralph tapped it.

What came up was a website for Channel 81: CAP CITY'S PUBLIC ACCESS RESOURCE! Beneath it was a block of videos showing City Council meetings, a bridge re-opening, a tutorial called YOUR LIBRARY AND HOW TO USE IT, and one called NEW ADDITIONS TO THE CAP CITY ZOO. Ralph looked at Samuels questioningly.

"Scroll down."

Ralph did, and found one titled HARLAN COBEN SPEAKS TO TRI-STATE ENGLISH TEACHERS. The PLAY icon was superimposed over a bespectacled woman with hair so arduously sprayed it looked as if you could bounce a baseball off it without hurting the skull beneath. She was at a podium. Behind her was the Sheraton Hotels logo. Ralph brought the video up to full screen.

"Hello, everybody! Welcome! I'm Josephine McDermott, this year's president of the Tri-State Teachers of English. I'm *so* happy to be here, and to officially welcome you to our yearly meeting of the minds. Plus, of course, a few adult beverages." This brought a murmur of polite laughter. "Our attendance this year is particularly good, and while I'd like to think my charming presence has something to do with it"—more polite laughter—"I think it probably has more to do with today's amazing guest speaker . . ."

"Maitland was right about one thing," Samuels said. "The fucking introduction goes on and on. She runs down just about every book the guy ever wrote. Go to nine minutes and thirty seconds. That's where she winds it up."

Ralph slid his finger along the counter at the bottom of the vid, now sure of what he was going to see. He didn't *want* to see it, and yet he did. The fascination was undeniable.

"Ladies and gentlemen, please give a warm welcome to today's guest speaker, Mr. *Harlan Coben*!"

From the wings strode a bald gentleman so tall that when he bent to shake hands with Ms. McDermott, he looked like a guy greeting a child in a grown-up's dress. Channel 81 had deemed this event interesting enough to spring for two cameras, and the picture now switched to the audience, which was giving Coben a standing O. And there, at a table near the front, were three men and a woman. Ralph felt his stomach take the express elevator down. He tapped the video, pausing it.

"Christ," he said. "It's him. Terry Maitland with Roundhill, Quade, and Grant."

"Based on the evidence we have in hand, I don't see how it can be, but it sure as hell looks like him."

"Bill . . ." For a moment Ralph couldn't go on. He was utterly flabbergasted. "Bill, the guy coached my son. It doesn't just look like him, it *is* him."

"Coben speaks for about forty minutes. It's mostly just him at the podium, but every now and then there are shots of the audience, laughing at some of the witty stuff he says—he's a witty guy, I'll give him that—or just listening attentively. Maitland—if it is Maitland—is in most of those shots. But the nail in the coffin is right around minute fifty-six. Go there."

Ralph went to minute fifty-four, just to be safe. By then Coben was taking questions from the audience. "I never use profanity in my books for profanity's sake," he was saying, "but under certain circumstances, it seems absolutely appropriate. A man who hits his thumb with a hammer doesn't say, 'Oh, pickles.'" Laughter from the audience. "I have time for one or two more. How about you, sir?"

The picture switched from Coben to the next questioner. It was Terry Maitland, in a big fat close-up, and Ralph's last hope that they were dealing with a double, as Jeannie had suggested, evaporated. "Do you always know who did it when you sit down to write, Mr. Coben, or is it sometimes a surprise even to you?"

The picture switched back to Coben, who smiled and said, "That's a very good question."

Before he could give a very good answer, Ralph backed up to Terry, standing to ask his question. He stared at the image for twenty seconds, then handed the iPad back to the district attorney.

"Poof," Samuels said. "There goes our case."

"DNA's still pending," Ralph said . . . or rather, heard himself say. He felt divorced from his own body. He supposed it was how boxers felt just before the ref stopped the fight. "And I still need to talk to Deborah Grant. After that I'm going up to Cap City to do some old-school detective work. Get off my ass and knock on doors, like the man said. Talk to people at the hotel, and at the Firepit, where they went to dinner." Then, thinking of Jeannie: "I want to look into the possibility of forensic evidence, as well."

"Do you know how unlikely that is in a big city hotel, the best part of a week after the day in question?"

"I do."

"As for the restaurant, it probably won't even be open." Samuels sounded like a kid who's just been pushed down on the sidewalk by a bigger kid and scraped his knee. Ralph was coming to realize he didn't like this guy very much. He came across more and more as a quitter.

"If it's near the hotel, chances are they'll be open for brunch."

Samuels shook his head, still peering at the frozen image of Terry Maitland. "Even if we get a DNA match . . . which I'm starting to doubt . . . you've been in this job long enough to know that juries rarely convict based on DNA and fingerprints. The OJ trial is an excellent case in point."

"The eye-wits—"

"Gold will demolish them on cross. Stanhope? Old and half-blind. 'Isn't it true you gave up your driver's license three years ago, Mrs. Stanhope?' June Morris? A kid who saw a bloody man from across the street. Scowcroft was drinking, and so was his buddy. Claude Bolton's got a drug jacket. The best you've got is Willow Rainwater, and I've got news for you, buddy, in this state people still don't care much for Indians. Don't much trust them."

"But we're in too deep to back out," Ralph said.

"That happens to be the dirty truth."

They sat silently for a bit. Ralph's office door was open, and the station's main room was almost deserted, as it usually was on Sunday mornings in this small southwestern city. Ralph thought of telling Samuels that the video had jolted them away from the elephant in the room: a child had been murdered, and according to every bit of evidence they had gleaned, they had the man who'd done it. That Maitland appeared to have been seventy miles away was something that had to be addressed and clarified. There could be no rest for either of them until it was.

"Come up to Cap City with me, if you want to."

"Not going to happen," Samuels said. "I'm taking my ex-wife and the kids to Lake Ocoma. She's bringing a picnic. We're finally back on good terms, and I'd like not to jeopardize that."

"Okay." The offer had been half-hearted, anyway. Ralph wanted to be by himself. He wanted to try to get his head around what had seemed so straightforward and was now looking like a colossal clusterfuck.

He stood up. Bill Samuels put his iPad back in his briefcase and then stood up beside him. "I think we could lose our jobs over this, Ralph. And if Maitland walks, he'll sue. You know he will."

"Go on to your picnic. Eat some sandwiches. This isn't over yet."

Samuels left the office ahead of him, and something about his walk—the slumped shoulders, the briefcase banging dispiritedly at his knee—infuriated Ralph. "Bill?"

Samuels turned.

"A child in this town was viciously raped. Either before or just after, he may have been *bitten* to death. I'm still trying to get my head around that. Do you think his parents give a rodent's behind if we lose our jobs or the city gets sued?"

Samuels made no reply, only crossed the deserted squadroom and went out into the early morning sunshine. It was going to be a great day for a picnic, but Ralph had an idea the DA wasn't going to enjoy it much.

12

Fred and Ollie had arrived in the Mercy Hospital ER waiting room shortly before Saturday night became Sunday morning, no more than three minutes behind the ambulance carrying Arlene Peterson. At that hour, the big waiting room had been jammed with the bruised and bleeding, the drunk and complaining, the crying and coughing. Like most ERs, the one at Mercy was extremely busy on Saturday nights, but by nine o'clock on Sunday morning, it was almost deserted. A man was holding a makeshift bandage over a bleeding hand. A woman sat with a feverish child in her lap, both of them watching Elmo caper on the TV set bolted high in one corner. A teenage girl with frizzy hair sat with her head back and her eyes closed and her hands clasped to her midriff.

And there was them. The remains of the Peterson family. Fred had closed his eyes around six and drifted off to sleep, but Ollie only sat, staring at the elevator into which his mother had disappeared, sure that if he dozed, she would die. "Could you not have watched with me one hour?" Jesus had asked Peter, and that was a very good question, one you couldn't answer.

At ten minutes past nine, the door of that elevator slid open and the doctor they had spoken to shortly after arriving stepped out. He was wearing blue scrubs and a sweat-stained blue surgical cap decorated with dancing red hearts. He looked very tired, and when he saw them, he turned to one side, as if wishing he could retreat. Ollie only had to see that involuntary flinch to know. He wished he could let his father sleep through the initial blast of bad news, but that would be wrong. Dad had known and loved her longer than Ollie had been alive, after all.

"Huh!" Fred said, sitting up when Ollie shook his shoulder. "What?"

Then he saw the doctor, who was removing his cap to expose

a thatch of sweaty brown hair. "Gentlemen, I'm sorry to tell you that Mrs. Peterson has passed away. We tried hard to save her, and at first I thought we were going to be successful, but the damage was simply too great. Again, I'm very, very sorry."

Fred stared at him unbelievingly for a moment, then let out a cry. The girl with the frizzy hair opened her eyes and stared at him. The feverish toddler cringed.

Sorry, Ollie thought. *That's the word of the day. Last week we were a family, now there's just Dad and me. Sorry's the word for that, all right. The very one, there is no other.*

Fred was weeping with his hands over his face. Ollie took him in his arms and held him.

13

After lunch, which Marcy and her girls only picked at, Marcy went into the bedroom to explore Terry's side of the closet. He was half of their partnership, but his clothes only took up a quarter of the space. Terry was an English teacher, a baseball and football coach, a fund-raiser when funds were required—which was like always—a husband, and a father. He was good at all of those jobs, but only the teaching gig paid, and he wasn't overloaded with dressy clothes. The blue suit was the best, it brought out the color of his eyes, but it was showing signs of wear, and no one with an eye for men's fashions was going to mistake it for Brioni. It was Men's Wearhouse, and four years old. She sighed, took it down, added a white shirt and a dark blue tie. She was putting them in a suit bag when the doorbell rang.

It was Howie, dressed in duds much nicer than the ones Marcy had just bagged up. He gave the girls a quick hug and bussed Marcy on the cheek.

"Are you going to bring my daddy home?" Gracie asked.

"Not today, but soon," he said, taking the suit bag. "What about a pair of shoes, Marcy?"

"Oh, God," she said. "I'm such a klutz."

The black ones were okay, but they needed a polish. No time for that now, though. She put them in a bag and went back into the living room. "Okay, I'm ready."

"All right. Step lively and pay no attention to the coyotes. Girls, keep the doors locked until your mom gets back, and don't answer the phone unless you recognize the number. Got it?"

"We'll be okay," Sarah said. She didn't look okay. Neither of them did. Marcy wondered if it was possible for preteen girls to lose weight overnight. Surely not.

"Here we go," Howie said. He was bubbling over, cheerful.

They left the house with Howie carrying the suit and Marcy carrying the shoes. The reporters once more surged to the edge of the lawn. *Mrs. Maitland, have you talked to your husband? What have the police told you? Mr. Gold, has Terry Maitland responded to the charges? Are you going to request bail?*

"We have nothing to say at this time," Howie said, stone-faced, escorting Marcy to his Escalade through a glare of television lights (surely not necessary on this brilliant July day, Marcy thought). At the foot of the driveway, Howie powered down his window and leaned out to speak to one of the two cops on duty. "The Maitland girls are inside. You guys are responsible for seeing they're not bothered, right?"

Neither responded, only looked at Howie with expressions that were either blank or hostile. Marcy couldn't tell which, but she leaned toward the latter.

The joy and relief she'd felt after looking at that video—God bless Channel 81—hadn't left her, but there were still TV trucks and microphone-waving reporters in front of her house. Terry was still locked up—"in county," as Howie had put it, and what a terrible phrase that was, like something out of a lonesome country-

and-western song. Strangers had searched their house and taken anything they pleased. The wooden faces of the policemen and their lack of response were the worst, though, far more unsettling than the TV lights and the shouted questions. A machine had swallowed her family. Howie said they would get out of it unharmed, but it hadn't happened yet.

No, not yet.

14

Marcy was given a quick patdown by a sleepy-eyed female officer, who told her to dump her purse in the plastic basket provided and step through the metal detector. The officer also took their driver's licenses, put them in a Baggie, and tacked it to a bulletin board with many others. "Also the suit and shoes, missus."

Marcy handed them over.

"I want to see him in that suit and looking sharp when I come for him tomorrow morning," Howie said, and walked through the metal detector, which went off.

"We'll be sure to tell his butler," said the officer on the far side of the detector. "Now get rid of whatever you've still got in your pockets and try again."

The problem turned out to be his keyring. Howie handed it to the female officer and went through the detector a second time. "I've been here at least five thousand times, and I always forget my keys," he told Marcy. "It must be some kind of Freudian thing."

She smiled nervously and made no reply. Her throat was dry, and she thought anything she said would come out in a croak.

Another officer led them through one door, then another. Marcy heard laughing children and a buzz of adult conversation. They passed through a visiting area with brown industrial carpet on the floor. Children were playing. Prisoners in brown jumpsuits were talking with their wives, sweethearts, mothers. A large man with a purple birthmark dripping down one side of his face and a healing cut on the other was helping his young daughter rearrange the furniture in a dollhouse.

This is all a dream, Marcy thought. *An incredibly vivid one. I'll wake up with Terry beside me and tell him how I had a nightmare that he'd been arrested for murder. We'll laugh about it.*

One of the inmates pointed her out, with no attempt made to hide the gesture. The woman beside him stared, round-eyed, then whispered to another woman. The officer who was guiding them seemed to be having some trouble with the key-card that opened the door on the far side of the visiting area, and Marcy couldn't quite dismiss the idea that he was lollygagging on purpose. Before the lock clunked and he led them through, it seemed that everyone was staring at them. Even the kids.

On the far side of the door was a hallway lined with small rooms divided by what looked like cloudy glass. Terry was sitting in one of these. At the sight of him, floating inside a brown jumpsuit that was far too big, Marcy began to cry. She stepped into her side of the booth and looked at her husband through what was not glass at all but a thick sheet of Perspex. She put a hand up, fingers splayed, and he put his up against it. There was a circle of small holes, like those in an old-fashioned telephone receiver, to talk through. "Stop crying, honey. If you don't, I'll start. And sit down."

She sat, Howie crowding onto the bench beside her.

"How are the girls?"

"Fine. Worried about you, but better today. We've got some very good news. Honey, did you know Mr. Coben's speech was taped by the public access channel?"

For a moment Terry just gaped. Then he began to laugh. "You know what, I think the woman who introduced him said something about that, but she was so long-winded I mostly tuned out. Holy shit."

"Yes, it's an authentic holy shit," Howie said, smiling.

Terry leaned forward until his forehead was almost touching the barrier. His eyes were bright, intent. "Marcy... Howie... I asked Coben something during the Q-and-A. I know it's a longshot, but maybe it got picked up on the audio. If it was, maybe they can run voice-recognition or something and do a match!"

Marcy and Howie looked at each other and began to laugh. It was an uncommon sound in Maximum Security Visiting, and the guard at the end of the short corridor looked up, frowning.

"What? What did I say?"

"Terry, you're on *video* asking your question," Marcy said. "Do you understand? *You are on the video.*"

For a moment Terry didn't seem to comprehend what she was saying. Then he raised his fists and shook them beside his temples, a gesture of triumph she had seen often when one of his teams scored or pulled off a cool defensive play. Without thinking about it, she raised her own hands and copied him.

"Are you sure? Like a hundred per cent? It seems too good to be true."

"It's true," Howie said, grinning. "As a matter of fact you're on the tape half a dozen times, when they cut away from Coben to show the audience laughing or applauding. The question you asked is just icing on the cake, the whipped cream on top of the banana split."

"So it's case closed, right? I'll walk free tomorrow?"

"Let's not get ahead of ourselves." Howie's grin faded to a rather grim smile. "Tomorrow is just the arraignment, and they've got a heap of forensic evidence that they're very proud of—"

"How can they?" Marcy burst out. "How *can* they, when Terry was obviously *there*? The tape *proves* it!"

Howie put a hand up in a *Stop* gesture. "We'll worry about the conflict later, although I can tell you right now that what we've got trumps what they've got. *Easily* trumps it. But certain machinery has been set in motion."

"The machine," Marcy said. "Yes. We know about the machine, don't we, Ter?"

He nodded. "It's like I fell into a Kafka novel. Or *1984*. And pulled you and the girls in along with me."

"Whoa, whoa," Howie said. "You didn't pull anyone, they did. This is going to work out, guys. Uncle Howie promises it, and Uncle Howie always keeps his promises. You're going to be arraigned tomorrow at nine o'clock, Terry, in front of Judge Horton. You will be looking reet and complete in the nice suit your wife brought, which is now hanging in the prisoner storage closet. I intend to meet with Bill Samuels to discuss bail—tonight, if he'll take the meeting, tomorrow morning if he won't. He won't like it, and he's going to insist on home confinement, but we'll get it, because by then someone in the press will have discovered that Channel 81 tape, and the problems with the prosecution's case will become public knowledge. I imagine you'll have to put your home up to secure the bond, but that shouldn't be much of a risk, unless you plan to cut off the ankle monitor and run for the hills."

"I'm not going anywhere," Terry said grimly. Color had risen in his cheeks. "What did some Civil War general say? 'I intend to fight it out on this line if it takes all summer.'"

"Okay, so what's the next battle?" Marcy asked.

"I will tell the DA that it would be a bad idea to present an indictment to the grand jury. And that argument will prevail. You will then walk free."

But will he? Marcy wondered. *Will* we? *When they claim to have his fingerprints, and people who saw him abducting that little boy, and then coming out of Figgis Park covered in blood? Will we ever be free as long as the real killer stays uncaught?*

"Marcy." Terry was smiling at her. "Take it easy. You know what I tell the boys—one base at a time."

"I want to ask you something," Howie said. "Just a shot in the dark."

"Ask away."

"They claim to have all sorts of forensic evidence, although the DNA's still pending—"

"That *can't* come back a match," Terry said. "It's not possible."

"I would have said that about the fingerprints," Howie said.

"Maybe someone set him up," Marcy blurted. "I know how paranoid that sounds, but . . ." She shrugged.

"But why?" Howie asked. "That's the question. Can either of you think of someone who would go to such extraordinary lengths to do that?"

The Maitlands considered, one on each side of the scuffed Perspex, then shook their heads.

"Me, either," Howie said. "Life rarely if ever imitates the novels of Robert Ludlum. Still, they've got evidence strong enough for them to have rushed into an arrest I'm sure they now regret. My fear is that, even if I can get you out of the machine, the *shadow* of the machine may remain."

"I was thinking about that most of last night," Terry said.

"I'm still thinking about it," Marcy said.

Howie leaned forward, hands clasped. "It would help if we had some physical evidence to match theirs. The Channel 81 tape is fine, and when you add in your colleagues, it's probably all we need, but I'm greedy. I want more."

"Physical evidence from one of the busiest hotels in Cap City, and four days later?" Marcy asked, unaware that she was echoing Bill Samuels not long before. "That seems unlikely."

Terry was looking off into space, brows drawn together. "Not *entirely* unlikely."

"Terry?" Howie asked. "What are you thinking about?"

He looked around at them, smiling. "There might be something. There just might be."

15

The Firepit was indeed open for brunch, so Ralph went there first. Two of the staff who had been working on the night of the murder were currently on duty: the hostess and a crewcut waiter who looked about old enough to buy a beer. The hostess was no help ("We were mobbed that night, Detective"), and while the waiter vaguely remembered serving a large group of teachers, he was equivocal when Ralph showed him Terry's picture from the previous year's FCHS yearbook. He said that, yes, he "sorta" remembered a guy who looked like that, but he couldn't swear it was the guy in the picture. He said he wasn't even sure the guy had been with that bunch of teachers. "Hey, man, I might have just served him a Hot Wing Platter at the bar."

So that was that.

Ralph's luck at the Sheraton was at first no better. He was able to confirm that Maitland and William Quade had stayed in room 644 on Tuesday night, and the hotel manager was able to show him the bill, but it was Quade's signature. He had used his MasterCard. The manager also told him that room 644 had been occupied every night since Maitland and Quade checked out, and had been cleaned every morning.

"And we offer turn-down service," said the manager, adding insult to injury. "That means on most days the room was cleaned twice."

Yes, Detective Anderson was welcome to review the security footage, and Ralph did it without any complaints about how Alec Pelley had already been allowed to do so. (Ralph was not a Cap City police officer, which meant diplomacy was the better part of valor.) The footage was in full color, and sharp—no elderly Zoney's Go-Mart cameras for the Cap City Sheraton. He saw a man who looked like Terry in the lobby, in the gift shop, doing a quick

Wednesday morning workout in the hotel's fitness room, and outside the hotel ballroom, waiting in the autograph line. The stuff from the lobby and gift shop was iffy, but there could be little doubt—at least in his mind—that the guy signing in to use the exercise equipment and the guy waiting in line for an autograph was his son's old coach. The one who'd taught Derek to bunt, thus changing his nickname from Swiffer to Push It.

In his mind, Ralph could hear his wife telling him that forensic evidence from Cap City was the missing piece, the Golden Ticket. *If Terry was* here, she'd said—meaning in Flint City, committing murder—*then the double must have been* there. *It's the only thing that makes sense.*

"None of it makes sense," he muttered, looking at the monitor. On it was a frozen image of a man who certainly looked like Terry Maitland, caught laughing about something as he stood in the autograph line with his department head, Roundhill.

"Pardon?" asked the hotel dick who had shown him the footage.

"Nothing."

"Can I show you anything else?"

"No, but thanks." This had been a fool's errand. The Channel 81 tape of the lecture had pretty much rendered the security footage moot, anyway, because it was Terry during the Q-and-A. No one could doubt it.

Except in one corner of his mind, Ralph still did. The way Terry had stood to ask his question, as if he'd known that a camera would be on him . . . it was just so goddam *perfect.* Was it possible that the whole thing was a set-up? An amazing but ultimately explicable act of legerdemain? Ralph didn't see how it could be, but he didn't know how David Copperfield had walked through the Great Wall of China, and Ralph had seen that on TV. If it *was* so, Terry Maitland wasn't just a murderer, he was a murderer who was laughing at them.

"Detective, just a heads-up," said the hotel dick. "I've got a note from Harley Bright—he's the boss—saying all the stuff you just looked at is supposed to be saved for a lawyer named Howard Gold."

"I don't care what you do with it," Ralph said. "Mail it off to Sarah Palin in Whistledick, Alaska, for all I care. I'm going home." Yes. Good idea. Go home, sit in his backyard with Jeannie, split a six with her—four for him, two for her. And try not to go crazy thinking about this goddam paradox.

The dick walked him to the door of the security office. "News says you got the guy who killed that kid."

"News says a lot of things. Thank you for your time, sir."

"Always a pleasure to help the police."

If only you had, Ralph thought.

He halted on the far side of the lobby, hand out to push the revolving door, struck by a thought. There was one other place he should check, as long as he was here. According to Terry, Debbie Grant had booked for the women's room as soon as Coben's lecture ended, and she had been gone a long time. *I went down to the newsstand with Ev and Billy*, Terry had said. *She met us there.*

The newsstand, it turned out, was a kind of auxiliary gift shop. An overly made-up woman with graying hair was behind the counter, rearranging bits of inexpensive jewelry. Ralph showed her his ID and asked her if she had been working the previous Tuesday afternoon.

"Honey," she said, "I work here *every* day, unless I'm sick. I don't get anything extra from the books and magazines, but when it comes to this jewelry and the souvenir coffee cups, I'm on commission."

"Would you remember this man? He was here last Tuesday with a bunch of English teachers, for a lecture." He showed her Terry's picture.

"Sure, I remember him. He asked about the Flint County book. First one to do that in Jesus knows how long. I didn't stock it, the darn thing was here when I started running this place back in 2010. I should take it down, I guess, but replace it with what? Anything way above or way below eye-level doesn't move, you find that out quick running a place like this. At least the stuff down low is cheap. That top shelf is your expensive stuff with photographs and glossy pages."

"What book are we talking about, Ms.—" He looked at her name-tag. "Ms. Levelle?"

"That one," she said, pointing. "*A Pictorial History of Flint County, Douree County, and Canning Township.* Jawbreaker title, huh?"

He turned and saw two racks of reading material next to a shelf of souvenir cups and plates. One rack held magazines; the other held a mixture of paperback and current hardcover fiction. On the top shelf of the latter were half a dozen larger volumes, what Jeannie would have called coffee table books. They were shrink-wrapped so that browsers couldn't smudge the pages or dog-ear the corners. Ralph walked over and looked up at them. Terry, who had a good three inches on him, wouldn't have had to look up, or stand on tiptoe to take one of them down.

He started to reach for the book she'd mentioned, then changed his mind. He turned back to Ms. Levelle. "Tell me what you remember."

"What, about that guy? Nothing much to tell. The gift shop got way busy after the lecture broke, I remember that, but I only got a trickle of custom. You know why, don't you?"

Ralph shook his head, trying to be patient. There was something here, all right, and he thought—*hoped*—he knew what it was.

"They didn't want to lose their place in line, of course, and they all had the new book by Mr. Coben to read while they waited. But these three gentlemen did come in, and one of them—the fat one—bought that new Lisa Gardner hardback. The other two just browsed. Then a lady poked her head in and said she was all set, so they left. To get their autographs, I suppose."

"But one of them—the tall one—expressed an interest in the Flint County book."

"Yes, but I think it was the Canning Township part of the title that caught his eye. Did he say his family lived there for a long time?"

"I don't know," Ralph said. "You tell me."

"Pretty sure he did. He took it down, but when he saw the pricetag—seventy-nine ninety-nine—he put it back on the shelf."

And whoomp, there it was. "Has anyone looked at that book since? Taken it down and handled it?"

"That one? You're kidding."

Ralph went to the rack, stood on his toes, and took down the shrink-wrapped book. He held it by the sides, using his palms. On the front was a sepia-toned photograph of a long-ago funeral procession. Six cowboys, all wearing battered hats and holstered pistols, were carrying a plank coffin into a dusty cemetery. A preacher (also wearing a holstered gun) was waiting for them at the head of an open grave with a Bible in his hands.

Ms. Levelle brightened considerably. "You actually want to buy that?"

"Yes."

"Well, hand it over so I can scan it."

"I don't think so." He held the book up with the bar code stickered to the shrink-wrap facing her, and she beeped it.

"That's eighty-four fourteen with the tax, but we'll call it eighty-four even."

Ralph set the book carefully on end to hand over his credit card. He tucked his receipt into his breast pocket, then once again picked the book up using just his palms, holding it out like a chalice.

"He handled it," he said, less to make sure of her than to confirm his own absurd luck. "You're sure the man in the picture I showed you handled this book."

"Took it down and said that cover picture was taken in Canning Township. Then he looked at the price and put it back. Just like I told you. Is it evidence, or something?"

"I don't know," Ralph said, looking down at the antique mourners gracing the cover. "But I'm going to find out."

16

Frank Peterson's body had been released to the Donelli Brothers Funeral Home on Thursday afternoon. Arlene Peterson had arranged for this and everything else, including the obituary, the flowers, the Friday morning memorial service, the funeral itself, the graveside service, and the Saturday evening gathering of friends and family. It had to be her. Fred was useless at making any kind of social arrangements at the best of times.

But this time it has to be me, Fred told himself when he and Ollie got home from the hospital. *It has to be, because there is no one else. And that guy from Donelli will help me. They're experts at this.* Only how was he supposed to pay for a *second* funeral, so soon after the first? Would insurance cover it? He didn't know. Arlene had handled all that stuff, too. They had a deal: he made the money and she paid the bills. He would have to look through her desk for the insurance paperwork. The thought of it made him tired.

They sat in the living room. Ollie turned on the television. There was a soccer match on. They watched it awhile, although neither of them really cared for the game; they were pro football guys. At last Fred got up, trudged into the hall, and brought back Arlene's old red address book. He turned to the Ds, and yes, there was Donelli Brothers, but her usual neat script was shaky, and why not? She wouldn't have noted down the number of a funeral parlor *before* Frank died, now would she? The Petersons were supposed to have years before needing to worry about burial rites. Years.

Looking at the address book, its red leather faded and scuffed, Fred thought of all the times he had seen it in her hands, jotting down return addresses from envelopes in the old days, from the Internet more recently. He began to cry.

"I can't," he said. "I just can't. Not so soon after Frankie."

On TV, the announcer screamed *"GOAL!"* and the players in the red shirts started to jump all over each other. Ollie turned it off and held out his hand.

"I'll do it."

Fred looked at him, eyes red and streaming.

Ollie nodded. "It's okay, Dad. Really. I'll take care of it, the whole deal. Why don't you go upstairs and lie down?"

And although Fred knew it was probably wrong to leave his seventeen-year-old son with this burden, he did just that. He promised himself he would carry his share of the weight in time, but right now he needed to take a nap. He was really very tired.

17

Alec Pelley wasn't able to break free of his own family commitments that Sunday until three thirty. It was after five when he reached the Cap City Sheraton, but the afternoon sun was still burning a hole in the sky. He parked in the hotel turnaround, slipped the parking valet a ten, and told him to keep his car close. In the newsstand, Lorette Levelle was once more rearranging her bits of jewelry. Alec's visit there was brief. He went back outside, leaned against his Explorer, and called Howie Gold.

"I beat Anderson to the security footage—plus the TV tape—but he beat me to the book. And bought it. I guess you'd have to call that a wash."

"Fuck," Howie said. "How did he even know about it?"

"I don't think he did. I think it was a combination of luck and old-fashioned police work. The woman who works in the newsstand says a guy took it down on the day of Coben's lecture, saw the pricetag—almost eighty bucks—and put it back. Didn't seem to know the guy was Maitland, so I guess she doesn't watch the news. She told Anderson, and Anderson bought the book. She says he walked out holding it by the sides, and with the palms of his hands."

"Hoping to raise prints that don't match Terry's," Howie said, "thus suggesting that whoever handled that book was *not* Terry. Won't work. God knows how many people may have taken that book down and handled it."

"The woman who runs the newsstand would beg to disagree. She says that one just sat up there, month in and month out."

"Makes no difference." Howie didn't sound worried, which left Alec free to worry for both of them. It wasn't much, but it was something. A small flaw in a case that had been shaping up as pretty as a painting in a museum. A *possible* flaw, he reminded himself, and Howie could easily work around it; juries didn't care much about what *wasn't* there.

"Just wanted you to know, boss. It's what you pay me for."

"Okay, now I know. You'll be there for the arraignment tomorrow, right?"

"Wouldn't miss it," Alec said. "Did you talk to Samuels about bail?"

"I did. The conversation was brief. He said he would fight it with every fiber of his being. His very words."

"Jesus, does the guy have an off button?"

"A good question."

"Will you get it anyway?"

"I have a good chance. Nothing's a sure thing, but I'm almost positive."

"If you do, tell Maitland not to take any neighborhood strolls.

Lots of people keep a home protection weapon handy, and right now he's the least popular guy in Flint City."

"He'll be restricted to his home, and you can be sure the cops will be keeping the house under surveillance." Howie sighed. "A shame about that book."

Alec ended the call and jumped back in his car. He wanted to be home in plenty of time to make popcorn before *Game of Thrones*.

18

Ralph Anderson and State Police Detective Yunel Sablo met with the Flint County DA that evening in the den of Bill Samuels's home on the city's north side, an almost-posh neighborhood of large houses that aspired to McMansion status and didn't quite make it. Outside, Samuels's two girls were chasing each other through the backyard sprinkler as dusk slowly dissolved into dark. Samuels's ex-wife had stayed around to cook dinner for them. Samuels had been in fine fettle all through the meal, often patting his ex's hand and even holding it for brief periods, to which she did not seem to object. *Pretty chummy for a couple living in splitsville*, Ralph thought, and good for them. But now dinner was finished, the ex was packing up the girls' things, and Ralph had an idea that DA Samuels's good mood would soon be finished, too.

A Pictorial History of Flint County, Douree County, and Canning Township sat on the den's coffee table. It was in a clear plastic Baggie, taken from one of Ralph's kitchen drawers and slipped carefully over the book. The funeral cortege now looked blurry, because the shrink-wrap had been dusted with fingerprint powder. A single print—a thumb—stood out on the book's front cover, near the spine. It was as clear as the date on a new penny.

"There are four more good ones on the back," Ralph said. "It's how you pick up a heavy book—thumb in front, fingers on the back, slightly splayed, to support. I would have printed it right there in Cap City, but I didn't have Terry's prints for comparison purposes. So I grabbed what I needed at the station and did it at home."

Samuels elevated his brows. "You took his print-card out of evidence?"

"Nah, photocopied it."

"Don't keep us in suspense," Sablo said.

"I won't," Ralph said. "They match. The prints on this book belong to Terry Maitland."

The Mr. Sunshine who'd sat beside his ex at the dinner table disappeared. Mr. Gonna Rain A Bitch took his place. "You can't be sure of that without a computer match."

"Bill, I was doing this before there was such a thing." *Back in the days when you were still trying to look up girls' skirts in high school study hall.* "They're Maitland's prints, and computer comparison will confirm it. Look at these."

He took a small bundle of cards from the inner pocket of his sportcoat and laid them out in two rows on the coffee table. "Here are Terry's prints from his booking last night. And here are Terry's prints from the shrink-wrap. Now you tell me."

Samuels and Sablo leaned forward, looking from the row of cards on the left to the ones on the right. Sablo sat back first. "I buy it."

"I won't without a computer comparison," Samuels said. The words came out sounding stilted because his jaw was jutting. Under other circumstances, that might have been funny.

Ralph made no immediate reply. He was curious about Bill Samuels, and hopeful (he was hopeful by nature) that his earlier judgement about the man—that he might cut and run if faced with a really spirited counterattack—had been wrong. Samuels's ex-wife still held him in some regard, that had been obvious, and the little girls loved him bigtime, but such evidence only spoke to one facet of a man's character. A guy at home wasn't necessarily the same guy at work, especially when the fellow in question was ambitious and faced with a sudden obstacle that might nip all his big plans in the bud. These things mattered to Ralph. They mattered a great deal, because he and Samuels were bound together by this case, win or lose.

"It's impossible," Samuels said, one hand going to brush down the cowlick, but tonight the cowlick wasn't there. Tonight it was behaving. "He can't have been in two places at the same time."

"Yet so it appears," Sablo said. "Until today, there was no forensic evidence in Cap City. Now there is."

Samuels brightened momentarily. "Maybe he handled the book at some prior date. Preparing his alibi. All part of the set-up." Apparently forgetting his previous assessment that the murder of Frank Peterson had been the impulse act of a man who could no longer control his urges.

"The idea can't be discounted," Ralph said, "but I've seen a lot of prints, and these look fairly fresh. The quality of the friction ridge detail is very good. That wouldn't be the case if these had been made weeks or months ago."

Speaking almost too softly to hear, Sablo said, " '*Mano*, it's like you took a hit on twelve and got a face-card."

"What?" Samuels snapped his head around.

"Blackjack," Ralph said. "He's saying it would have been better if we hadn't found it. If we'd just stood pat."

They considered this. When Samuels spoke, he sounded almost pleasant—a man just passing the time. "Here's a hypothetical for you. What if you had dusted down that shrink-wrap and found nothing? Or just a few unidentifiable blurs?"

"We wouldn't be better off," Sablo said, "but we wouldn't be worse off."

Samuels nodded. "In that case—hypothetically speaking—Ralph would just be a guy who'd bought a fairly expensive book. He wouldn't throw it away, he'd call it a good idea that didn't pan out and put it on his shelf. After stripping off the shrink-wrap and throwing it away, of course."

Sablo looked from Samuels to Ralph, his face giving nothing away.

"And these fingerprint cards?" Ralph asked. "What about them?"

"What cards?" Samuels asked. "I don't see any cards. Do you, Yune?"

"I don't know if I do or not," Sablo said.

"You're talking about destroying evidence," Ralph said.

"Not at all. This is all just hypothetical." Samuels again raised his hand to brush at the cowlick that wasn't there. "But here's something to think about, Ralph. You went to the station first, but did the comparison at your home. Was your wife there?"

"Jeannie was at her book club."

"Uh-huh, and look. The book's in a Glad bag instead of an official one. Not entered into evidence."

"Not yet," Ralph said, but instead of thinking about the different facets of Bill Samuels's character, he was now forced to think about the different facets of his own.

"I'm just saying that the same hypothetical possibility might have been in the back of your own mind."

Had it been? Ralph could not honestly say. And if it had been, *why* had it been? To save an ugly black mark on his career, now that this thing was not just going sideways but in danger of tipping over?

"No," he said. "This will be logged into evidence, and will become part of discovery. Because that kid is dead, Bill. What happens to us is small shit compared to that."

"I agree," Sablo said.

"Of course you do," Samuels said. He sounded tired. "Lieutenant Yune Sablo will survive either way."

"Speaking of survival," Ralph said, "what about Terry Maitland's? What if we really do have the wrong man?"

"We don't," Samuels said. "The evidence says we don't."

And on that note, the meeting ended. Ralph went back to the station. There he logged in *A Pictorial History of Flint County, Douree County, and Canning Township* and stored it in the accumulating file. He was glad to be rid of it.

As he went around the building to retrieve his personal car, his cell rang. It was his wife's picture on the screen, and when he answered, he was alarmed by the sound of her voice. "Honey? Have you been crying?"

"Derek called. From camp."

Ralph's heart kicked up a notch. "Is he all right?"

"He's fine. *Physically* fine. But some of his friends emailed him about Terry, and he's upset. He said it must be wrong, that Coach T would never do a thing like that."

"Oh. Is that all." He started moving again, feeling for his keys with his free hand.

"No, it's not *all*," she said fiercely. "Where are you?"

"At the station. Then headed home."

"Can you go to county first? And talk to him?"

"To Terry? I guess I could, if he'll agree to see me, but why?"

"Set aside all the evidence for a minute. All of it on both sides, and answer me one question, truly and from your heart. Will you do that?"

"Okay . . ." He could hear the faraway drone of semis on the interstate. Closer, the peaceful summer sound of crickets in the grass growing alongside the brick building where he had worked for so many years. He knew what she was going to ask.

"Do *you* think Terry Maitland killed that little boy?"

Ralph thought of how the man who'd taken Willow Rainwater's cab to Dubrow had called her ma'am instead of by her name, which he should have known. He thought about how the man who'd parked the white van behind Shorty's Pub had asked directions to the nearest doc-in-the-box, although Terry Maitland had lived in Flint City all his life. He thought about the teachers who would swear Terry had been with them, both at the time of the abduction and at the time of the murder. Then he thought about how convenient it was that Terry had not just asked a question at Mr. Harlan Coben's talk, but had *risen to his feet*, as if to make sure he would be seen and recorded. Even the fingerprints on the book . . . how perfect was that?

"Ralph? Are you still there?"

"I don't know," he said. "Maybe if I'd coached with him like Howie . . . but I only watched him coach Derek. So the answer to your question—truly, and from my heart—is I just don't know."

"Then go there," she said. "Look him in the eyes and *ask* him."

"Samuels is apt to rip me a new one if he finds out," Ralph said.

"I don't care about Bill Samuels, but I care about our son. And I know you do, too. Do it for him, Ralph. For Derek."

19

It turned out that Arlene Peterson did have burial insurance, so that was all right. Ollie found the pertinent papers in the bottom drawer of her little desk, in a folder between MORTGAGE AGREEMENT (said mortgage now almost paid off) and APPLIANCE WARRANTIES. He called the funeral parlor, where a man with the soft voice of a professional mourner—maybe a Donelli brother, maybe not—thanked him and told him that "your mother has arrived." As if she'd gotten there on her own, maybe in an Uber. The professional mourner asked if Ollie needed an obituary form for the newspaper. Ollie said no. He was looking at two blank forms right there on the desk. His mother—careful, even in her grief—must have made photocopies of the one she'd gotten for Frank, in case she made a mistake. So that was all right, too. Would he want to come in tomorrow and make arrangements for the funeral and the burial? Ollie said he didn't think so. He thought his father should be the one to do that.

Once the question of paying for his mother's final rites was put to rest, Ollie dropped his head onto her desk and cried for awhile. He did it quietly, so as not to wake his father. When the tears dried up, he filled out one of the obituary forms, printing everything because his handwriting sucked. Once that chore was finished, he went out to the kitchen and surveyed the mess there: pasta on the linoleum, chicken carcass lying under the clock, all those Tupperwares and covered dishes on the counters. It reminded him of something his mom used to say after big family meals—*the pigs ate here.* He got a Hefty bag from under the sink and dumped everything in, starting with the chicken carcass, which looked especially gruesome. Then he washed the floor. Once everything was spick (something else his mother used to say), he discovered he was hungry. That seemed wrong but was still a fact. People were basically animals, he realized. Even with your mother and little brother dead, you had to eat and shit out what you ate. The body demanded it. He opened the fridge and discovered it was packed top to bottom and side to side with more casseroles, more Tupperware containers, more cold cuts. He selected a shepherd's pie, its surface a snowy plain of mashed potato, and stuck it in the oven at 350. While he was leaning against the counter and waiting for it to heat, feeling like a visitor inside his own head, his dad wandered in. Fred's hair was a mess. *You're all sticky-uppy*, Arlene Peterson would have said. He needed a shave. His eyes were puffy and dazed.

"I took one of your mother's pills and slept too long," he said.

"Don't worry about it, Dad."

"You cleaned up the kitchen. I should have helped you."

"It's okay."

"Your mother . . . the funeral . . ." Fred didn't seem to know how to go on, and Ollie noticed that his fly was unzipped. This filled him with an inchoate pity. Yet he didn't feel like crying again, he seemed to be cried out, at least for the time being. Something else that was all right. *Must count my blessings*, Ollie thought.

"We're in good shape," he told his dad. "She had burial insurance, you both do, and she's . . . there. At the place. You know, the parlor." He was afraid to say *funeral*, because that might get his father going. Which might get *him* going again.

"Oh. Good." Fred sat down and put the heel of his hand against his forehead. "I should have done that. It was my job. My responsibility. I never meant to sleep so long."

"You can go down tomorrow. Pick out the coffin, and all."

"Where?"

"Donelli Brothers. Same as Frank."

"She's dead," Fred marveled. "I don't even know how to think of it."

"Yeah," Ollie said, although he had been able to think of nothing else. How she'd kept trying to apologize, right to the end. As if it was all her fault when none of it was. "The funeral guy says there's stuff you'll have to decide about. Will you be able to do that?"

"Sure. I'll be better tomorrow. Something smells good."

"Shepherd's pie."

"Did your mother make it, or did someone bring it?"

"I don't know."

"Well, it smells good."

They ate at the kitchen table. Ollie put their dishes in the sink, because the dishwasher was full. They went into the living room. Now it was baseball on ESPN, Phillies against the Mets. They watched without talking, each in his own way exploring the edges of the hole that had appeared in their lives, so as not to fall in. After awhile Ollie went out on the back steps and sat looking up at the stars. There were plenty of them. He also saw a meteor, an earth satellite, and several planes. He thought about how his mother was dead, and would see none of these things again. It was totally absurd that such a thing should be so. When he went back in, the baseball game was going into the ninth all tied up, and his father had gone to sleep in his chair. Ollie kissed him on the top of his head. Fred didn't stir.

20

Ralph got a text on his way to the county jail. It was from Kinderman, in State Police Computer Forensics. Ralph pulled over at once and called back. Kinderman answered on the first ring.

"Don't you guys take Sunday night off?" Ralph asked.

"What can I say, we're geeks." In the background, Ralph could hear the bellow of a heavy metal band. "Besides, I always think that good news can wait, but bad news should be passed on right away. We're not done exploring Maitland's hard drives for hidden files, and some of these kiddy-fiddlers can be pretty clever about that, but on the surface, he's clean. No kiddie porn, no porn of any kind. Not on his desktop, not on his laptop, not on his iPad, not on his phone. He looks like Mr. White Hat."

"What about his history?"

"There's plenty, but all stuff you'd expect—shopping sites like Amazon, news blogs like *Huffington Post*, half a dozen sports sites. He keeps track of the Major League standings, and he appears to be a fan of the Tampa Bay Rays. That alone suggests there's something wrong with his head. He watches *Ozark* on Netflix, and *The Americans* on iTunes. I enjoy that one myself."

"Keep digging."

"It's what they pay me for."

Ralph parked in an OFFICIAL VEHICLES ONLY slot behind the county jail, took his on-duty card from the glove compartment, and put it on the dashboard. A corrections officer—L. KEENE, according to his name-tag—was waiting for him, and escorted him to one of the interview rooms. "This is irregular, Detective. It's almost ten o'clock."

"I'm aware of the time, and I'm not here for recreational purposes."

"Does the DA know you're here?"

"Above your pay grade, Officer Keene."

Ralph sat down on one side of the table and waited to see if Terry would agree to make an appearance. No porn on Terry's computers, and no stashes of porn in the house, at least that they had found so far. But, as Kinderman had pointed out, pedos could be clever.

How clever was it for him to show his face, though? And leave fingerprints?

He knew what Samuels would say: Terry was in a frenzy. Once (it seemed like a long time ago) this had made sense to Ralph.

Keene led Terry in. He was wearing county browns and cheap plastic flip-flops. His hands were cuffed in front of him.

"Take off the bracelets, Officer."

Keene shook his head. "Protocol."

"I'll take responsibility."

Keene smiled without humor. "No, Detective, you will not. This is my house, and if he decides to leap across the table and choke you, it's on me. But tell you what, I won't tether him to the cuff-bolt. How's that?"

Terry smiled at this, as if to say *You see what I have to deal with?*

Ralph sighed. "You can leave us, Officer Keene. And thanks."

Keene left, but he would be watching through the one-way glass. Probably listening, as well. This was going to get back to Samuels; there was simply no way around it.

Ralph looked at Terry. "Don't just stand there. Sit down, for God's sake."

Terry sat and folded his hands on the table. The handcuff chain rattled. "Howie Gold wouldn't approve of me meeting you." He continued to smile as he said it.

"Samuels wouldn't either, so we're even."

"What do you want?"

"Answers. If you're innocent, why do I have half a dozen witnesses who've identified you? Why are your fingerprints on the branch used to sodomize that boy, and all over the van that was used to abduct him?"

Terry shook his head. The smile was gone. "I'm as mystified as you are. I just thank God, his only begotten son, and all the saints that I can prove I was in Cap City. What if I couldn't, Ralph? I think we both know. I'd be in the death house up in McAlester before the end of summer, and two years from now I'd be riding the needle. Maybe sooner, because the courts are rigged to the right all the way to the top and your pal Samuels would plow over my appeals like a bulldozer over a kid's sand castle."

The first thing that rose to Ralph's lips was *he's not my pal.* What he said was, "The van interests me. The one with the New York plates."

"Can't help you there. The last time I was in New York was on my honeymoon, and that was sixteen years ago."

It was Ralph's turn to smile. "I didn't know that, but I knew you hadn't been there recently. We back-checked your movements over the last six months. Nothing but a trip to Ohio in April."

"Yes, to Dayton. The girls' spring vacation. I wanted to see my dad, and they wanted to go. Marcy did, too."

"Your father lives in Dayton?"

"If you can call what he's doing these days living. It's a long story, and nothing to do with this. No sinister white vans involved, not even the family car. We flew Southwest. I don't care how many of my fingerprints you found in the van that guy used to abduct Frank Peterson, I didn't steal it. I've never even seen it. I don't expect you to believe it, but it's the truth."

"Nobody thinks you stole the van in New York," Ralph said. "Bill Samuels's theory is that whoever did steal it dumped it somewhere in this vicinity, with the ignition key still in it. You *re*-stole it, and cached it somewhere until you were ready to . . . to do what you did."

"Pretty careful, for a man who went about his business with his bare face hanging out."

"Samuels will tell the jury you were in a kill-frenzy. And they'll believe it."

"Will they still believe it after Ev, Billy, and Debbie testify? And after Howie shows the jury that tape of Coben's lecture?"

Ralph didn't want to go there. At least not yet. "Did you know Frank Peterson?"

Terry uttered a bark of laughter. "That's one of those questions Howie wouldn't want me to answer."

"Does that mean you won't?"

"As a matter of fact, I will. I knew him to say hi to—I know most of the kids on the West Side—but I didn't *know* him know him, if you see what I mean. He was still in grade school and didn't play sports. Couldn't miss that red hair, though. Like a stop sign. Him and his brother both. I had Ollie in Little League, but he didn't move up to City League when he turned thirteen. He wasn't bad in the outfield, and he could hit a little, but he lost interest. Some of them do."

"So you didn't have your eye on Frankie?"

"No, Ralph. I have no sexual interest in children."

"Didn't just happen to see him walking his bike across the parking lot of Gerald's Fine Groceries and say 'Aha, here's my chance'?"

Terry looked at him with a silent contempt that Ralph found hard to bear. But he didn't drop his eyes. After a moment, Terry sighed, raised his cuffed hands to the mirror side of the one-way glass, and called, "We're done here."

"Not quite," Ralph said. "I need you to answer one more question, and I want you to look me right in the eyes when you do it. Did you kill Frank Peterson?"

Terry's gaze didn't waver. "I did not."

Officer Keene took Terry away. Ralph sat where he was, waiting for Keene to come back and escort him through the three locked doors between this interview room and free air. So now he had the answer to the question Jeannie had told him to ask, and the answer, given with unwavering eye contact, was *I did not.*

Ralph wanted to believe him.

And *could* not.

THE ARRAIGNMENT

July 16th

1

"No," Howie Gold said. "No, no, no."

"It's for his own protection," Ralph said. "Surely you see—"

"What I see is a front-page photograph in the paper. What I see is lead story footage on every channel, showing my client walking into district court wearing a bulletproof vest over his suit. Looking already convicted, in other words. The cuffs are bad enough."

There were seven men in the county jail's visitors' room, where the toys had been neatened away in their colorful plastic boxes and the chairs had been upturned on the tables. Terry Maitland stood with Howie at his side. Facing them were County Sheriff Dick Doolin, Ralph Anderson, and Vernon Gilstrap, the assistant district attorney. Samuels would already be at the county courthouse, awaiting their arrival. Sheriff Doolin continued to hold out the bulletproof vest, saying nothing. On it, in bright accusatory yellow, were the letters FCDC, standing for Flint County Department of Corrections. Its three Velcro straps—one for each arm, one to cinch the waist—hung down.

Two jail officers (call them guards and they would correct you) stood by the door to the lobby, meaty arms folded. One had supervised Terry as he shaved with a disposable razor; the other had gone through the pockets of the suit and shirt Marcy had brought, not neglecting to check the seam down the back of the blue tie.

ADA Gilstrap looked at Terry. "What do you say, chum? Want

to risk getting shot? Okay by me if you do. Save the state the expense of a bunch of appeals before you take the needle."

"That's uncalled-for," Howie said.

Gilstrap, a long-timer who would almost certainly choose to retire (and with a fat pension) if Bill Samuels lost the upcoming election, only smirked.

"Hey, Mitchell," Terry said. The guard who had monitored Terry's shave, making sure the prisoner did not try to cut his throat with a single-blade Bic, raised his eyebrows but didn't unfold his arms. "How hot is it outside?"

"Eighty-four when I came in," Mitchell said. "Going up close on a hundred come noon, they said on the radio."

"No vest," Terry said to the sheriff, and broke into a smile that made him look very young. "I don't want to stand in front of Judge Horton in a sweaty shirt. I coached his grandson in Little League."

Gilstrap, looking alarmed at this, took a notebook from inside his plaid jacket and jotted something.

"Let's get going," Howie said. He took Terry by the arm.

Ralph's cell phone rang. He took it from the left side of his belt (his holstered service weapon was on the right) and looked at the screen. "Hold it, hold it, I have to take this."

"Oh, come *on*," Howie said. "What is this, an arraignment or a dog-and-pony show?"

Ralph ignored him and walked to the far side of the room, where there were coin-op snack and soda vending machines. He stood beneath a sign reading FOR VISITOR USE ONLY, spoke briefly, listened. He ended the call and returned to the others. "Okay. Let's do it."

Officer Mitchell had stepped between Howie and Terry long enough to snap cuffs on Terry's wrists. "Too tight?" he asked.

Terry shook his head.

"Then let's walk."

Howie took off his suit coat and draped it over the cuffs. The two officers led Terry out of the room with Gilstrap in the lead, strutting like a majorette.

Howie fell in step next to Ralph. He spoke in a low voice. "This is a clusterfuck." And when Ralph made no reply: "Okay, fine, clam up all you want to, but between now and the grand jury, we have to sit down—you, me, and Samuels. Pelley too, if you want. The facts of the case aren't going to come out today, but they *will* come out, and then you won't have to worry about just state or regional news coverage. CNN, FOX, MSNBC, the Internet blogs—they'll all be here, savoring the weirdness. It'll be OJ meets *The Exorcist*."

Yes, and Ralph had an idea Howie would do all he could to make that happen. If he could get reporters to focus on the question of a man who appeared to have been in two places at the same time, he wouldn't have to worry about them focusing on the boy who had been raped and murdered, perhaps partially eaten.

"I know what you're thinking, but I'm not the enemy here, Ralph. Unless you don't give a shit about anything except seeing Terry convicted, that is, and I don't believe it. That's Samuels, not you. Don't you want to know what happened?"

Ralph made no reply.

Marcy Maitland was waiting in the lobby, looking very small between the hugely pregnant Betsy Riggins and Yune Sablo from the State Police. When she saw her husband and started forward, Riggins attempted to hold her back, but Marcy shook her off easily. Sablo only stood pat, watching. Marcy had just time enough to look into her husband's face and kiss his cheek before Officer Mitchell took her by the shoulders and pushed her gently but firmly back toward the sheriff, who was still holding the bulletproof vest, as if he didn't know what to do with it now that it had been refused.

"Come on, now, Mrs. Maitland," Mitchell said. "That's not allowed."

"I love you, Terry," Marcy called as the officers moved him toward the door. "And the girls send theirs."

"Same goes back to all of you doubled," Terry said. "Tell them it's going to be all right."

Then he was outside, into the hot morning sunshine and the incoming fire of two dozen questions, all hurled at once. To Ralph, still in the lobby, those mingled voices sounded more like invective than interrogation.

Ralph had to give Howie points for persistence. He still hadn't given up.

"You're one of the good ones. Never took a bribe, never pitted evidence, always walked a straight path."

I think I came close to pitting some evidence last night, Ralph thought. *I think it was close. If Sablo hadn't been there, if it had just been me and Samuels . . .*

Howie's expression was almost pleading. "You've never had a case like this. None of us have. And it's not just the little boy anymore. His mother is dead, too."

Ralph, who hadn't turned on the television that morning, stopped and stared at Howie. "You say *what*?"

Howie nodded. "Yesterday. Heart attack. That makes her victim number two. So come on—don't you want to know? Don't you want to get this right?"

Ralph couldn't hold back any longer. "I *do* know. And because I do, I'm going to give you one for free, Howie. That call I just took was from Dr. Bogan, in the Pathology and Serology Department at General. He doesn't have all of the DNA back yet, and won't for at least another couple of weeks, but they crashed the semen sample they took from the backs of the boy's legs. It matches the cheek swabs we took Saturday night. Your client killed Frank Peterson, and buggered him, and tore away pieces of his flesh. And all that got him so excited that he spunked on the corpse."

He strode away quickly, leaving Howie Gold temporarily unable to move or speak. Which was good, because the central paradox still remained. DNA didn't lie. But Terry's colleagues weren't lying, either, Ralph was sure of it. Add to that the fingerprints on the book from the newsstand, and the Channel 81 video.

Ralph Anderson was a man of two minds, and the double vision was driving him crazy.

2

Until 2015, the Flint County courthouse had stood next to the Flint County jail, which was convenient. Prisoners up for arraignment were simply led from one gothic heap of stones to the other, like overgrown children going on a field trip (except, of course, kids going on field trips were rarely handcuffed). Now a half-constructed Civic Center stood next door, and prisoners had to be transported six blocks to the new courthouse, a nine-story glass box that wags had dubbed the Chicken Coop.

At the curb in front of the jail, waiting to make the trip: two police cars with flashing lights, a short blue bus, and Howie's gleaming black SUV. Standing on the sidewalk next to the latter, and looking like a chauffeur in his dark suit and darker shades, was Alec Pelley. On the other side of the street, behind police department sawhorses, were the reporters, the camerapersons, and a small crowd of lookie-loos. Several of the latter were carrying signs. One read, EXECUTE THE CHILD KILLER. Another read, MAITLAND YOU WILL BURN IN HELL. Marcy stopped on the top step and stared at these signs with dismay.

The county jail corrections officers halted at the foot of the steps, their job done. Sheriff Doolin and ADA Gilstrap, the men technically in charge of this morning's legal ritual, escorted Terry to the lead police car. Ralph and Yunel Sablo headed for the one behind. Howie took Marcy's hand and led her toward his Escalade.

"Don't look up. Don't give the photographers anything but the top of your head."

"Those signs . . . Howie, those *signs* . . ."

"Never mind them, just keep moving."

Because of the heat, the windows of the blue bus were open. The prisoners inside, most of them weekend warriors bound for their own arraignments on an array of lesser charges, caught sight of Terry. They pressed their faces against the wire mesh, catcalling.

"Hey, faggot!"

"Did you bend your dick getting it in?"

"You're bound for the needle, Maitland!"

"Did you suck his cock before you bit it off?"

Alec started around the Escalade to open the passenger door, but Howie shook his head, motioned him back, and pointed to the rear door on the curb side instead. He wanted to keep Marcy as far as possible from the crowd across the street. Her head was lowered, and her hair obscured her face, but as Howie led her to the door Alec was holding open, he could hear her sobbing even in the general tumult.

"Mrs. Maitland!" That was a leather-lunged reporter, calling from beyond the sawhorse barricade. *"Did he tell you he was going to do it? Did you try to stop him?"*

"Don't look up, don't respond," Howie said. He wished he could tell her not to listen. "This is all under control. Just get in, and off we go."

As he handed her in, Alec murmured in his ear. "Beautiful, isn't it? Half the city police are on vacation, and FC's fearless sheriff can barely manage crowd control at the Elks Barbecue."

"Just get us there," Howie said. "I'll ride in back with Marcy."

Once Alec was behind the wheel and all the doors were closed, the yells from the crowd and the bus were muted. Ahead of the Escalade, the police cars and the blue bus were pulling out, moving as slowly as a funeral cortege. Alec fell into line. Howie could see the reporters sprinting up the sidewalk, oblivious of the heat, just wanting to be at the Chicken Coop when Terry arrived. The TV trucks would already be there, parked nose to tail like a herd of grazing mastodons.

"They hate him," Marcy said. The little eye makeup she had put on—mostly to hide the bags beneath them—had run, giving her a raccoon-like aspect. "He never did anything but good for this town, and they all hate him."

"That will change when the grand jury refuses to indict," Howie said. "And they will. I know it, and Samuels knows it, too."

"Are you sure?"

"I am. In some cases, Marcy, you have to struggle to find even one reasonable doubt. This case is *made* of them. No way can the grand jury indict."

"That isn't what I meant. Are you sure that people will change their minds?"

"Of course they will."

In the rearview mirror he saw Alec grimace at that, but sometimes a lie was necessary, and this was one of those times. Until the real killer of Frank Peterson was found—if he ever was—the people of Flint City were going to believe that Terry Maitland had gamed the system and gotten away with murder. They would treat him accordingly. But for now all Howie could do was focus on the arraignment.

3

As long as Ralph was dealing with prosaic day-to-day affairs, things like what was for supper, a grocery run with Jeannie, an evening call from Derek at camp (these were less frequent now that the kiddo's homesickness was abating), he was more or less okay. But when his attention centered on Terry—as it had to now—a kind of *uber* consciousness set in, as if his mind was trying to reassure itself that everything was just as it always had been: up was up, down was down, and it was just the summer heat in this badly air-conditioned car that was producing fine droplets of sweat under his nose. Each day was to be relished because life was short, he understood that, but too much was just too much. When the mind's filter disappeared, the big picture disappeared with it. There was no forest, only trees. At its worst, there were no trees, either. Just bark.

When the little procession reached the Flint County courthouse, Ralph snuggled in behind the sheriff, noting every hot point of sun on the rear bumper of Doolin's cruiser: four points in all. The reporters who had been at the county jail were already arriving, streaming into a crowd twice the size of the one that had been waiting at the county jail. They were crammed shoulder to shoulder on the lawn flanking the steps. He could see various station logos on the TV reporters' polo shirts, and the dark circles of sweat under their arms. The pretty blond anchor from Channel 7 out of Cap City arrived with her hair in a tangle and sweat cutting trenches in her showgirl makeup.

Sawhorses had been set up here, too, but the ebb and flow of the jostling crowd had already knocked some of them askew. A dozen cops, half city police and half sheriff's department, tried their best to keep the steps and the sidewalk clear. Twelve weren't enough, in Ralph's estimation, not nearly, but summer always depleted the ranks.

The reporters jostled for the prime spots on the lawn, unapologetically elbowing the spectators back. The blond anchor from Channel 7 tried to make a place for herself in front, flashing her locally famous smile, and was thwacked by a hastily made sign for her pains. The sign featured a crudely drawn hypodermic needle below the message MAITLAND TAKE YOUR MEDICINE. Her cameraman shoved the guy with the sign backward, shouldering an elderly woman off her feet in the process. Another woman caught her and fetched the cameraman a good one upside the head with her purse. The purse, Ralph noticed (he was currently helpless not to), was *faux* alligator, and red.

"How did the vultures get here so quick?" Sablo marveled. "Man, they scurry faster than cockroaches when someone turns on the light."

Ralph only shook his head, looking at the crowd with mounting dismay, trying to see it as a whole, and unable to in his current state of hyper-vigilance. As Sheriff Doolin exited his car (brown uniform shirt untucked on one side above his Sam Browne belt; roll of pink fat peeking through the gap) and opened the rear door so that Terry could get out, someone began shouting, *"Needle, needle!"*

The crowd picked it up, chanting like fans at a football game. *"NEEDLE! NEEDLE! NEEDLE!"*

Terry stared at them, one lock of his neatly combed hair coming loose and hanging down above his left eyebrow. (Ralph felt he could count every strand.) There was a look of pained bewilderment on his face. *Seeing people he knows*, Ralph thought. *People whose kids he taught, people whose kids he coached, people he had to his house for end-of-season barbecues. All of them rooting for him to die.*

One of the sawhorse barricades clattered into the street, the crossbar sliding away. People surged onto the sidewalk, a few of them reporters with mics and notebooks, the rest local citizens who looked ready to string Terry Maitland up from the nearest lamppost. Two of the cops on crowd control rushed over and pushed them back, none too gently. Another replaced the barricade, which left the crowd free to break through at another location. Ralph saw what looked like two dozen cell phones taking photos and video.

"Come on," he said to Sablo. "Let's get him the fuck inside before they clog the steps."

They exited the car and hurried toward the courthouse steps, Sablo motioning Doolin and Gilstrap forward. Now Ralph could see Bill Samuels standing inside one of the courthouse doors, looking dumbfounded . . . but why? How could he have not expected this? How could Sheriff Doolin not have expected it? Nor was he himself blameless—why hadn't he insisted they bring Terry around to the rear doors, where most of the courthouse staff entered?

"Get back, folks!" Ralph shouted. *"This is the process, let the process work!"*

Gilstrap and the sheriff started Terry toward the steps, one holding each arm. Ralph had time to register (again) Gilstrap's horrible plaid coat, and to wonder if the man's wife had picked it out. If so, she must secretly hate him. Now the prisoners in the short bus—who would wait there in the day's strengthening heat, stewing in their own sweat until the star prisoner's arraignment was disposed of—added their voices to the auditory melee, some chanting *Needle, Needle*, others just yipping like dogs or howling like coyotes, pistoning their fists against the mesh covering the open windows.

Ralph turned to the Escalade and raised his open palm to it in a *Stop* gesture, wanting Howie and Alec Pelley to keep Marcy where she was until Terry was inside and the crowd settled down. It did no good. The streetside back door opened and then she was out, dipping one shoulder and eluding Howie Gold's grasping hand as easily as she had slipped away from Betsy Riggins in the county jail's lobby. As she ran to catch up with her husband, Ralph noted her low heels and a shaving cut on one calf. *Her hand must have trembled*, he thought. When she called Terry's name, the cameras swung toward her. There were five in all, their lenses like glazed eyes. Someone threw a book at her. Ralph couldn't read the title, but he knew that green jacket. *Go Set a Watchman*, by Harper Lee. His wife had read it for her book club. The cover came loose and one of the flaps fluttered. The book hit her shoulder and bounced off. She didn't seem to notice.

"Marcy!" Ralph shouted, leaving his place by the steps. "Marcy, over here!"

She looked around, perhaps searching for him, perhaps not. She looked like a woman in a dream. Terry stopped, turning at the sound of his wife's name, and resisted when Sheriff Doolin tried to continue pulling him toward the steps.

Howie reached Marcy before Ralph could. As he took her arm, a burly man in mechanic's coveralls overturned one of the sawhorses and rushed her. "Did you cover up for him, you evil cunt? Did you?"

Howie was sixty, but still in good shape. And he wasn't shy. As Ralph watched, he flexed his knees and drove a shoulder into the right side of the burly man's midsection, knocking him aside.

"Let me help," Ralph said.

"I can take care of her," Howie said. His face was flushed all the way to his thinning hair. He had an arm around Marcy's waist. "We don't want your help. Just get him inside. Now! Jesus, man, what were you thinking? This is a circus!"

Ralph thought to say, *It's the sheriff's circus, not mine*, only it *was* at least partly his. And what about Samuels? Had he perhaps foreseen this? Even hoped for it, because of the wide news coverage it would surely garner?

He turned in time to see a man in a cowboy shirt duck around one of the crowd control cops, sprint across the sidewalk, and hock a mouthful of spit in Terry's face. Before the guy could rush away, Ralph stuck out a foot and sent him sprawling in the street. Ralph could read the tag on his jeans: LEVI'S BOOT CUT. He could see the faded circle of a Skoal can on the right back pocket. He pointed at one of the crowd control cops. "Cuff that man and stick him in your cruiser."

"Our c-cars are all around b-back," the cop said. He was a county guy, and looked not much older than Ralph's son.

"Then stick him on the short bus!"

"And leave these people to—"

Ralph lost the rest, because he was seeing something amazing. While Doolin and Gilstrap stared at the spectators, Terry was helping the man in the cowboy shirt to his feet. He said something to Cowboy Shirt that Ralph missed, even with his ears seemingly attuned to the whole universe. Cowboy Shirt nodded and started away, hunching one shoulder to blot a scrape on his cheek. Later, Ralph would remember this little moment in the larger play. He would consider it deeply on long nights when sleep wouldn't come: Terry helping the guy get up with his cuffed hands even as the spit ran down his cheek. Like something out of the fucking Bible.

The spectators had become a crowd, and now the crowd teetered on the edge of mob-ism. Some of them had made it onto the twenty or so granite steps leading up to the courthouse doors in spite of the cops' efforts to push them back. A couple of bailiffs—one male and portly, the other female and scrawny—came out and attempted to help clear them away. Some people went, but others surged into their places.

Now, God save the queen, Gilstrap and Doolin were arguing. Gilstrap wanted Terry back in the car until authority could be reasserted. Doolin wanted him inside immediately, and Ralph knew the sheriff was right.

"Come on," he said to them. "Yune and I will take point."

"Draw your guns," Gilstrap panted. "That will make them clear the way."

This, of course, was not only against protocol but insane, and both Doolin and Ralph knew it. The sheriff and the ADA began to move forward again, once more holding Terry's arms. At least the sidewalk was clear at the base of the steps. Ralph could see flecks of mica gleaming in the cement. *Those will leave afterimages once we're inside*, he thought. *They'll hang there in front of my eyes like a little constellation.*

The blue bus began rocking on its springs as the gleeful inmates threw themselves from one side to the other, still chanting *Needle, Needle* along with the crowd outside. A car alarm began to blurt as two young men danced atop someone's previously pristine Camaro, one on the hood and the other on the roof. Ralph saw the cameras filming the crowd, and knew exactly how the people of his town were going to look to the rest of the state when this footage aired on the six o'clock news: like hyenas. Everyone stood out in bright relief, and everyone was a grotesque. He saw the blond anchor from Channel 7 again knocked to her knees by the hypodermic sign, saw her pick herself up, saw a kind of unbelieving sneer twist her pretty face as she touched her head and looked at the drops of blood on her fingers. He saw a man with tattoos on his hands, a yellow kerchief on his head, and most of his features blanked out by what were probably old burn scars that surgeries hadn't been able to correct. *A grease fire*, Ralph thought, *maybe while he was drunk and trying to cook pork chops.* He saw a man waving a cowboy hat as if this was the Cap City ro-*day*-o. He saw Howie leading Marcy toward the steps, their heads bent as if they were moving into a stiff wind, and saw a woman lean forward to give her the finger. He saw a man with a canvas newspaper sack over his shoulder and a watch cap crammed down on his head in spite of the heat of the day. He saw the portly bailiff shoved from behind and only saved from a nasty tumble when a broad-shouldered black woman grabbed him by the belt. He saw a teenage boy with his girlfriend perched on his shoulders. The girl was shaking her fists and laughing, one of her bra straps hanging down to her elbow. The strap was bright yellow. He saw a boy with a cleft lip wearing a tee-shirt with Frank Peterson's smiling face on it. REMEMBER THE VICTIM, the shirt said. He saw waving signs. He saw open, shouting mouths, all white teeth and red satin lining. He heard someone blowing a bicycle horn: *hooga-hooga-hooga*. He looked at Sablo, who was now standing with his arms outstretched to hold people back, and read the SP detective's expression: *This is so fucked.*

Doolin and Gilstrap finally made it to the foot of the steps with Terry between them. Howie and Marcy joined them. Howie shouted something at the assistant district attorney, something else at the sheriff. Ralph couldn't tell what it was over the chanting, but it got them moving again. Marcy reached out to her husband. Doolin pushed her back. Now someone began shouting "Die, Maitland, die!" and the crowd picked up that chant as Terry and his escorts started up the steep flight of steps.

Ralph's gaze was drawn back to the man with the canvas newspaper sack. READ THE *FLINT CITY CALL* was printed on the side in fading red letters, as if the bag had been left outside in the rain. The man who was wearing a knit watch cap on a summer morning when the temperature was already in the mid-eighties. The man who was now reaching into his bag. Ralph suddenly remembered his interview with Mrs. Stanhope, the old lady who had witnessed Frank Peterson getting into the white van with Terry. *Are you sure it was Frank Peterson you saw?* he had asked. *Oh yes*, she'd said, *it was Frank. There are two Peterson boys, both redheads.* And wasn't that red hair Ralph saw sticking out from beneath the watch cap?

He used to deliver our newspaper, Mrs. Stanhope had said.

Watch Cap's hand came out of the bag, and it wasn't holding a newspaper.

Ralph drew in all his breath even as he drew his Glock. *"Gun! GUN!"*

The people around Ollie screamed and scattered. ADA Gilstrap had been holding one of Terry's arms, but when he saw the old-fashioned long-barreled Colt, he let go, dropped into a toad-like crouch and backpedaled. The sheriff also let go of Terry, but to draw his own weapon . . . or attempt to. The safety strap was still fastened, and the gun stayed where it was.

Ralph didn't have a clear shot. The blond anchor from Channel 7, still dazed from the blow to her head, was standing almost directly in front of Ollie Peterson. Blood trickled down her left cheek.

"Down, lady, down!" Sablo shouted. He was on one knee, holding his own Glock in his right hand and bracing with his left.

Terry took his wife by the forearms—the handcuff chain was just long enough—and pushed her away from him just as Ollie fired over the blond anchor's shoulder. She shrieked and clapped a hand to her no doubt deafened ear. The bullet grooved the side of Terry's head, making his hair fly up and sending a cascade of blood onto the shoulder of the suit Marcy had been at such pains to press.

"*My brother wasn't enough, you had to kill my mother, too!*" Ollie shouted, and fired again, this time striking the Camaro across the street. The young men who had been dancing on it jumped for safety, shouting.

Sablo leaped up the steps, grabbed the blond reporter, pulled her down, and landed on top of her. "*Ralph, Ralph, do it!*" he shouted.

Now Ralph had a clear shot, but just as he fired, one of the fleeing spectators crashed into him. Instead of hitting Ollie, the bullet struck a shoulder-mounted TV camera, shattering it. The cameraman dropped it and staggered backward with his hands over his face. Blood streamed through his fingers.

"*Bastard!*" Ollie screamed. "*Murderer!*"

He fired a third time. Terry grunted and stepped back onto the sidewalk. He held his cuffed hands up to his chin, as if struck by a thought that needed serious pondering. Marcy scrambled to him and threw her arms around his waist. Doolin was still yanking at the strapped butt of his service automatic. Gilstrap was running down the street with the split tail of his awful plaid sportcoat flapping behind him. Ralph took careful aim and fired again. This time no one jostled him, and the boy's forehead collapsed inward as if struck with a hammer. His eyes bulged from their sockets in an expression of cartoon surprise as the 9 mm slug exploded his brains. His knees unhinged. He fell on top of his newsboy's bag, the revolver slipping from his fingers and clattering down two or three steps before coming to rest.

We can go up those steps now, Ralph thought, still in his shooter's stance. *No problem, all clear.* Except Marcy's shout—"*Somebody help him! Oh God, somebody please help my man!"*—told him that there was no longer any reason to climb them. Not today, perhaps not ever.

4

Ollie Peterson's first bullet had only grooved the side of Terry Maitland's head, a bloody injury but superficial, something that would have left Terry with a scar and a story to tell. The third one, however, had punched through the coat of his suit on the left side of his chest, and the shirt below was turning purple as the blood from the wound spread.

It would have hit the vest if he hadn't refused it, Ralph thought.

Terry lay on the sidewalk. His eyes were open. His lips were moving. Howie tried to crouch next to him. Ralph swung an arm hard and shoved the lawyer away. Howie went over on his back. Marcy was clinging to her husband, babbling "It's not bad, Ter, you're okay, stay with us." Ralph put the heel of his hand against the soft springiness of her breast and pushed her away, too. Terry Maitland was still conscious, but there wasn't much time.

A shadow fell over him, one of those goddam cameramen from one of the goddam TV stations. Yune Sablo grabbed him around the waist and spun him away. The cameraman's feet stuttered, then crossed, and he went down, holding his camera up to keep it from harm.

"Terry," Ralph said. He could see drops of sweat from his forehead falling onto Terry's face, where they mixed with the blood from the head wound. "Terry, you're going to die. Do you understand me? He got you, and he got you good. *You are going to die.*"

"*No!*" Marcy shrieked. "*No, he can't! The girls need their daddy! He can't!*"

She was trying to get to him, and this time it was Alec Pelley—

pale and grave—who held her back. Howie had gotten to his knees, but he did not attempt to interfere again, either.

"Where . . . get me?"

"Your chest, Terry. He got you in the heart, or just above it. You need to make a dying declaration, okay? You need to tell me you killed Frank Peterson. This is your chance to clear your conscience."

Terry smiled, and a thin trickle of blood spilled from either side of his mouth. "But I didn't," he said. His voice was low, little more than a whisper, but perfectly audible. "I didn't, so tell me, Ralph . . . how are you going to clear yours?"

His eyes closed, then struggled open again. For a moment or two there was something in them. Then there wasn't. Ralph put his fingers in front of Terry's mouth. Nothing.

He turned to look at Marcy Maitland. It was hard, because his head seemed to weigh a thousand pounds. "I'm sorry," he said. "Your husband has passed on."

Sheriff Doolin said dolefully, "If he'd been wearing the vest . . ." He shook his head.

The new-minted widow looked unbelievingly at Doolin, but it was Ralph Anderson she sprang at, leaving Alec Pelley with nothing but a shredded piece of her blouse in his left hand. *"This is your fault! If you hadn't arrested him in public, these people never would have been here! You might as well have shot him yourself!"*

Ralph let her rake her fingers down the left side of his face before grabbing her wrists. Letting her blood him, because maybe he had that coming . . . and maybe there was no maybe about it.

"Marcy," he said. "It was Frank Peterson's brother who did the shooting, and *he* would have been here no matter where we arrested Terry."

Alec Pelley and Howie Gold helped Marcy to her feet, being careful not to step on the body of her husband as they did so. Howie said, "That might be true, Detective Anderson, but there wouldn't have been a fuck-ton of other people all around him. He would have stood out like a sore thumb."

Alec only looked at Ralph with a species of stony contempt. Ralph turned to Yunel, but Yune looked away and bent to help the sobbing blond anchor from Channel 7 to her feet.

"Well, you got your dying statement, at least," Marcy said. She held out her palms to Ralph. They were red with her husband's blood. "Didn't you?" When he made no reply, she turned away from him and saw Bill Samuels. He had come out of the courthouse at last and was standing between the bailiffs at the top of the steps.

"He said he didn't do it!" she screamed at him. *"He said he was innocent! We all heard it, you son of a bitch! As my husband lay dying, HE SAID HE WAS INNOCENT!"*

Samuels didn't reply, only turned and went back inside.

Sirens. The Camaro car alarm. The excited babble of people who were returning now that the shooting was over. Wanting to see the body. Wanting to photograph it, and put it on their Facebook pages. Howie's coat, which the lawyer had draped over Terry's hands to conceal the cuffs from the press and the cameras, now lay in the street, streaked with dirt and splotched with blood. Ralph picked it up and used it to cover Terry's face, eliciting a terrible howl of grief from his wife. Then he went to the courthouse steps, sat down, and lowered his head between his knees.

FOOTSTEPS AND CANTALOUPE

July 18th–July 20th

1

Because Ralph hadn't told Jeannie about his darkest suspicion concerning the Flint County prosecutor—that he might have hoped for a crowd of righteously angry citizens at the courthouse—she let Bill Samuels in when he appeared at the door of the Anderson home on Wednesday evening, but she made it clear that she didn't have much use for him.

"He's out back," she said, turning away and heading back into the living room, where Alex Trebek was putting that evening's *Jeopardy* contestants through their paces. "You know the way."

Samuels, tonight clad in jeans, sneakers, and a plain gray tee-shirt, stood in the front hall for a moment, considering, then followed her. There were two easy chairs in front of the television, the bigger, more lived-in one empty. He picked up the remote from the table between the two and muted the sound. Jeannie continued looking at the television, where the contestants were currently munching their way through a category called Literary Villains. The answer onscreen was *She demanded Alice's head.*

"That's an easy one," Samuels said. "The Red Queen. How is he, Jeannie?"

"How do you think he is?"

"I'm sorry about the way things turned out."

"Our son found out that his father's been suspended," she said, still looking at the TV. "It was on the Internet. He's very upset by that, of course, but he's also upset because his favorite coach was gunned down in front of the courthouse. He wants to come home. I told him to give it a few days and see if he doesn't change his mind. I didn't want to tell him the truth, that his father isn't ready to see him yet."

"He hasn't been suspended. He's just on administrative leave. With pay. And it's mandatory after a shooting incident."

"You say to-may-to, I say to-mah-to." Now the answer onscreen was *This nurse was wretched.* "He says he may be off for as long as six months, and that's if he agrees to the mandatory psych evaluation."

"Why would he not?"

"He's thinking of pulling the pin."

Samuels raised his hand to the top of his head, but tonight the cowlick was behaving—at least so far—and he lowered it again. "In that case, maybe we can go into business together. This town needs a good car wash."

Now she did look at him. "What are you talking about?"

"I've decided not to run for re-election."

She favored him with a thin stiletto of a smile that her own mother might not have recognized. "Going to quit before Johnny Q. Public can fire you?"

"If you want to put it that way," he said.

"I do," Jeannie said. "Go on out back, Mr. Prosecutor For Now, and feel free to suggest a partnership. But you should be ready to duck."

2

Ralph was sitting in a lawn chair with a beer in his hand and a Styrofoam cooler beside him. He glanced around when the kitchen's screen door slammed, saw Samuels, and then returned his attention to a hackberry tree just beyond the back fence.

"Yonder's a nuthatch," he said, pointing. "Haven't seen one of those in a dog's age."

There was no second chair, so Samuels lowered himself to the bench of the long picnic table. He had sat here several times before, under happier circumstances. He looked at the tree. "I don't see it."

"There he goes," Ralph said, as a small bird took wing.

"I think that's a sparrow."

"Time to get your eyes checked." Ralph reached into the cooler and handed Samuels a Shiner.

"Jeannie says you're thinking about retiring."

Ralph shrugged.

"If it's the psych eval you're worried about, you'll pass with flying colors. You did what you had to do."

"It's not that. It's not even the cameraman. You know about him? When the bullet hit his camera—the first one I fired—the pieces went everywhere. Including one into his eye."

Samuels did know this, but kept quiet and sipped his beer, although he loathed Shiner.

"He's probably going to lose it," Ralph said. "The doctors at Dean McGee up in Okie City are trying to save it, but yeah, he's probably going to lose it. You think a cameraman with one eye can still work? Probably, maybe, or no way?"

"Ralph, someone slammed into you as you fired. And listen, if the guy hadn't had the camera up to his face, he'd probably be dead now. That's the upside."

"Yeah, and fuck a bunch of upside. I called his wife to apologize. She said, 'We're going to sue the Flint City PD for ten million dollars, and once we win that one, we'll start on you.' Then she hung up."

"That will never fly. Peterson had a gun, and you were in performance of your duty."

"As that camera-jockey was in performance of his."

"Not the same. He had a choice."

"No, Bill." Ralph swung around in his chair. "He had a *job*. And that was a nuthatch, goddammit."

"Ralph, you need to listen to me now. Maitland killed Frank Peterson. Peterson's brother killed Maitland. Most people see that as frontier justice, and why not? This state *was* the frontier not that long ago."

"Terry said he didn't do it. That was his dying declaration."

Samuels got to his feet and began to pace. "What else was he going to say with his wife kneeling right there beside him and crying her eyes out? Was he going to say, 'Oh yes, right, I buggered the kid, and I bit him—not necessarily in that order—and then I ejaculated on him for good measure'?"

"There's a wealth of evidence to support what Terry said at the end."

Samuels stalked back to Ralph and stood looking down at him. "It was his fucking DNA in the semen sample, and DNA trumps *everything*. Terry killed him. I don't know how he set up the rest, but he did."

"Did you come here to convince me or yourself?"

"I don't need any convincing. I only came to tell you that we now know who originally stole that white Econoline van."

"At this point does it make any difference?" Ralph asked, but Samuels at last detected a gleam of interest in the man's eyes.

"If you're asking if it casts any light on this mess, no. But it's fascinating. Do you want to hear or not?"

"Sure."

"It was stolen by a twelve-year-old boy."

"*Twelve?* Are you kidding me?"

"Nope, and he was on the road for months. Made it all the way to El Paso before a cop bagged him in a Walmart parking lot, sleeping in a stolen Buick. He stole four vehicles in all, but the van was the first. He drove it as far as Ohio before he ditched it and switched to another one. Left the ignition key in it, just the way we thought." He said this with some pride, and Ralph supposed he had a right; it was nice that at least one of their theories going in had proved correct.

"But we still don't know how it got down here, do we?" Ralph asked. Something was nagging him, though. Some small detail.

"No," Samuels said. "It's just a loose thread that isn't loose anymore. I thought you'd like to know."

"And now I do."

Samuels drank a swallow of beer, then set the can on the picnic table. "I'm not running for re-election."

"No?"

"No. Let that lazy asshole Richmond have the job, and see how people like him when he refuses to prosecute eighty per cent of the cases that land on his desk. I told your wife, and she didn't exactly overwhelm me with sympathy."

"If you think I've been telling her this is all your fault, Bill, you're wrong. I haven't said a word against you. Why would I? Arresting him at that fucking ballgame was my idea, and when I talk to the IA shooflies on Friday, I'll make that clear."

"I'd expect nothing less."

"But as I may have already mentioned, you didn't exactly try to talk me out of it."

"We believed him guilty. I *still* believe him guilty, dying declaration or no dying declaration. We didn't check for an alibi because he knows everyone in the goddam town and we were afraid of spooking him—"

"Also we didn't see the point, and boy, were we wrong about tha—"

"Yes, okay, your fucking point is fucking taken. We also believed he was extremely dangerous, especially to young boys, and on last Saturday night he was surrounded by them."

"When we got to the courthouse, we should have taken him around back," Ralph said. "I should have insisted on it."

Samuels shook his head vehemently enough to cause the cowlick to come loose and spring to attention. "Don't take that on yourself. Transfer from county jail to the courthouse is the sheriff's purview. *Not* the city's."

"Doolin would've listened to me." Ralph dropped his empty can back into the cooler and looked directly at Samuels. "And he would have listened to you. I think you know that."

"Water over the dam. Or under the bridge. Or whatever the hell that saying is. We're done. I guess the case might technically stay in the open file, but—"

"The technical term is OBI, open but inactive. It will stay that way even if Marcy Maitland brings a civil suit against the department, claiming her husband was killed as a result of negligence. And that's a suit she could win."

"Is she talking about doing that?"

"I don't know. I haven't scraped up enough nerve to speak to her yet. Howie might give you an idea of what she's thinking."

"Maybe I'll talk to him. Try to pour a little oil on troubled waters."

"You're a fountain of wise sayings this evening, counselor."

Samuels picked up his can of beer, then put it back with a small grimace. He saw Jeannie Anderson at the kitchen window, looking out at them. Just standing there, her face unreadable. "My mother used to subscribe to *Fate*."

"Me too," Ralph said moodily, "but after what happened to Terry, I'm not so sure. That Peterson kid came right out of nowhere. *Nowhere.*"

Samuels smiled a little. "I'm not talking about predestination, just a little digest-sized magazine full of stories about ghosts and crop circles and UFOs and God knows what else. Mom used to read me some of them when I was a kid. There was one in particular that fascinated me. 'Footsteps in the Sand,' it was called. It was about a newly married couple that went on their honeymoon in the Mojave Desert. Camping, you know. Well, one night they pitched their little tent in a grove of cottonwoods, and when the young bride woke up the next morning, her husband was gone. She walked out of the grove to where the sand started, and saw his tracks. She called to him, but there was no answer."

Ralph made a horror-movie sound: *Ooooo-oooo.*

"She followed the tracks over the first dune, then over the second. The tracks kept getting fresher. She followed them over the third . . ."

"And the fourth, and the fifth!" Ralph said in an awed voice. "*And she's still walking to this day!* Bill, I hate to cut your campfire story short, but I think I'm going to eat a piece of pie, take a shower, and go to bed."

"No, listen to me. The third dune was as far as she got. His tracks went halfway down the far side, then stopped. Just stopped, with nothing but acres of sand all around. She never saw him again."

"And you believe that?"

"No, I'm sure it's bullshit, but belief isn't the point. It's a metaphor." Samuels tried to soothe the cowlick down. The cowlick refused. "We followed *Terry's* tracks, because that's our job. Our duty, if you like that word better. We followed them until they stopped on Monday morning. Is there a mystery? Yes. Will there always be unanswered questions? Unless some new and amazing piece of information drops into our laps, there will be. Sometimes that happens. It's why people continue to wonder what happened to Jimmy Hoffa. It's why people keep trying to figure out what happened to the crew of the *Mary Celeste*. It's why people argue about whether or not Oswald acted alone when he shot JFK. Sometimes the tracks just stop, and we have to live with that."

"One big difference," Ralph said. "The woman in your story about the footsteps could believe her husband was still alive somewhere. She could go on believing that until she was an old woman instead of a young bride. But when Marcy got to the end of her husband's tracks, Terry was right there, dead on the sidewalk. She's burying him tomorrow, according to the obituary in today's paper. I imagine it'll just be her and her girls. Along with fifty news vultures outside the fence, that is, yelling questions and snapping pictures."

Samuels sighed. "Enough. I'm going home. I told you about the kid—Merlin Cassidy's his name, by the way—and I can see you don't want to listen to anything else."

"No, wait, sit back down a minute," Ralph said. "You told me one, now I'm going to tell you one. Not out of a psychic magazine, though. This is personal experience. Every word true."

Samuels lowered himself back to the bench.

"When *I* was a kid," Ralph said, "ten or eleven—around Frank Peterson's age—my mother sometimes used to bring home cantaloupes from the farmers' market, if they were in season. Back then I loved cantaloupe. They've got this sweet, dense flavor watermelon can't get close to. So one day she brought home three or four in a net bag, and I asked her if I could have a piece. 'Sure,' she said. 'Just remember to scrape the seeds into the sink.' She didn't really have to tell me that, because I'd opened up my share of cantaloupes by then. You with me so far?"

"Uh-huh. I suppose you cut yourself, right?"

"No, but my mother thought I did, because I let out a screech they probably heard next door. She came on the run, and I just pointed at the cantaloupe, laying there on the counter, split in two. It was full of maggots and flies. I mean those bugs were squirming all over each other. My mother got the Raid and sprayed the ones on the counter. Then she got a dish towel, wrapped the pieces in it, and threw them in the swill bucket out back. Since that day I can't bear to look at a slice of cantaloupe, let alone eat one. That's *my* Terry Maitland metaphor, Bill. The cantaloupe looked fine. It wasn't spongy. The skin was whole. There was no way those bugs could have gotten inside, but somehow they did."

"Fuck your cantaloupe," Samuels said, "and fuck your metaphor.

I'm going home. Think before you quit the job, Ralph, okay? Your wife said I was getting out before Johnny Q. Public fired me, and she's probably right, but you don't have to face the voters. Just three retired cops that are this city's excuse for Internal Affairs, and a shrink collecting some municipal shekels to supplement a private practice on life support. And there's something else. If you quit, people will be even more sure that we screwed this thing up."

Ralph stared at him, then began laughing. It was hearty, a series of guffaws that came all the way up from the belly. "But we did! Don't you know that yet, Bill? We did. Royally. We bought a cantaloupe because it looked like a *good* cantaloupe, but when we cut it open in front of the whole town, it was full of maggots. No way for them to get in, but there they were."

Samuels trudged toward the kitchen door. He opened the screen, then whirled around, his cowlick springing jauntily back and forth. He pointed at the hackberry tree. "That was a *sparrow*, goddammit!"

3

Shortly after midnight (around the time the last remaining member of the Peterson family was learning how to make a hangman's noose, courtesy of Wikipedia), Marcy Maitland awoke to the sound of screams from her elder daughter's bedroom. It was Grace at first—a mother always knows—but then Sarah joined her, creating a terrible two-part harmony. It was the girls' first night out of the bedroom Marcy had shared with Terry, but of course the kids were still bunking together, and she thought they might do that for some time to come. Which was fine.

What wasn't fine were those screams.

Marcy didn't remember running down the hall to Sarah's bedroom. All she remembered was getting out of bed and then standing inside the open door of Sarah's room and beholding her daughters, sitting bolt upright in bed and clutching each other in the light of the full July moon that came flooding through the window.

"What?" Marcy asked, looking around for an intruder. At first she thought he (surely it was a he) was crouched in the corner, but that was only a pile of cast-off jumpers, tee-shirts, and sneakers.

"It was her!" Sarah cried. "It was G! She said there was a man! God, Mom, she scared me so bad!"

Marcy sat on the bed and pried her younger daughter from Sarah's arms and took Grace in her own. She was still looking around. Was he in the closet? He might be, the accordion doors were closed. He could have done that when he heard her coming. Or under the bed? Every childhood fear flooded back while she waited for a hand to close around her ankle. In the other would be a knife.

"Grace? Gracie? Who did you see? Where was he?"

Grace was crying too hard to answer, but she pointed at the window.

Marcy went there, her knees threatening to come unhinged at every step. Were the police still watching the house? Howie said they would be making regular passes for awhile, but that didn't mean they were there all the time, and besides, Sarah's bedroom window—*all* of their bedroom windows—looked out on either the backyard or the side yard, between their house and the Gundersons'. And the Gundersons were away on vacation.

The window was locked. The yard—every single blade of grass seeming to cast a shadow in the moonlight—was empty.

She came back to the bed, sat, and stroked Grace's hair, which was clumped and sweaty. "Sarah? Did you see anything?"

"I . . ." Sarah considered. She was still holding Grace, who was sobbing against her big sister's shoulder. "No. I might have thought I did, just for a second, but that was because she was screaming, 'The man, the man.' There was no one there." And, to Gracie, "No one, G. Really."

"You had a bad dream, honey," Marcy said. Thinking, *Probably the first of many.*

"He was *there*," Gracie whispered.

"He must have been floating, then," Sarah said, speaking with admirable reasonableness for someone who had been scared out of sleep only minutes before. "Because we're on the second floor, y'know."

"I don't care. I saw him. His hair was short and black and standing up. His face was lumpy, like Play-Doh. He had straws for eyes."

"Nightmare," Sarah said matter-of-factly, as if this closed the subject.

"Come on, you two," Marcy said, striving for that same matter-of-fact tone. "You're with me for the rest of the night."

They came without protest, and five minutes after she had them settled in, one on each side of her, ten-year-old Gracie had fallen asleep again.

"Mom?" Sarah whispered.

"What, honey?"

"I'm scared of Daddy's funeral."

"So am I."

"I don't want to go, and neither does G."

"That makes three of us, sweetheart. But we'll do it. We'll be brave. It's what your dad would have wanted."

"I miss him so much I can't think of anything else."

Marcy kissed the gently beating hollow of Sarah's temple. "Go to sleep, honey."

Sarah eventually did. Marcy lay awake between her daughters, looking up at the ceiling and thinking of Grace turning to the window in a dream so real she thought she was awake.

He had straws for eyes.

4

Shortly after three AM (around the time Fred Peterson was trudging out into his backyard with a footstool from the living room in his left hand and his hangrope over his right shoulder), Jeanette Anderson awoke, needing to pee. The other side of the bed was empty. After doing her little bit of business, she went downstairs and found Ralph sitting in his Papa Bear easy chair, staring at the blank screen of the TV set. She observed him with a wifely eye and noted that he had dropped weight since the discovery of Frank Peterson's body.

She put a gentle hand on his shoulder.

He didn't look around. "Bill Samuels said something that's nagging at me."

"What?"

"That's just it, I don't know. It's like having a word on the tip of your tongue."

"Was it about the boy who stole the van?"

Ralph had told her about his conversation with Samuels while the two of them were lying in bed prior to turning out the light, passing it on not because any of it was substantive but because a twelve-year-old boy making it all the way from mid-state New York to El Paso in a series of stolen vehicles was sort of amazing. Maybe not *Fate* magazine amazing, but still pretty wild. *He must really hate his stepdad*, Jeannie had said before turning out the light.

"I think it *was* something about the kid," Ralph said now. "And there was a scrap of paper in that van. I meant to check back on that, and it kind of got lost in the shuffle. I don't think I mentioned it to you."

She smiled and ruffled his hair, which—like the body under the pajamas—seemed thinner than it had in the spring. "You did, actually. You said it might be part of a take-out menu."

"I'm pretty sure it's in evidence."

"You told me that, too, hon."

"I might go down to the station tomorrow and take a peek. Maybe it will help me put a finger on whatever it was Bill said."

"I think that's a good idea. Time to do something besides brood. You know, I went back and re-read that Poe story. The narrator says that when he was at school, he kind of ruled the roost. But then this other boy arrived who had the same name."

Ralph took her hand and gave it an absent kiss. "Believable enough so far. William Wilson's not as common a name as Joe Smith, maybe, but it's not exactly Zbigniew Brzezinski, either."

"Yes, but then the narrator discovers that they have the same birth date, and they're going around in similar clothes. Worst of all, they look something alike. People get them mixed up. Sound familiar?"

"Yes."

"Well, William Wilson Number One keeps meeting William Wilson Number Two later in life, and these meetings always end badly for Number One, who turns to a life of crime and blames Number Two. Are you following this?"

"Considering it's quarter past three in the morning, I think I'm doing a fine job."

"Well, in the end, William Wilson Number One stabs William Wilson Number Two with a sword, only when he looks into a mirror, he sees he's stabbed himself."

"Because there never was any second William Wilson, I take it."

"But there was. Lots of other people *saw* the second one. In the end, though, William Wilson Number One had a hallucination and committed suicide. Because he couldn't stand the doubleness, I guess."

She expected him to scoff, but he nodded instead. "Okay, that actually makes sense. Pretty damn good psychology, in fact. Especially for . . . what? The middle of the nineteenth century?"

"Something like that, yes. I took a class in college called American Gothic, and we read a lot of Poe's stories, including that one. The professor said people had the mistaken idea that Poe wrote fantastic stories about the supernatural, when in fact he wrote realistic stories about abnormal psychology."

"But before fingerprints and DNA," Ralph said, smiling. "Let's go to bed. I think I can sleep now."

But she held him back. "I'm going to ask you something now, husband of mine. Probably because it's late and it's just the two of us. There's no one to hear you if you laugh at me, but please don't, because that would make me sad."

"I won't laugh."

"You might."

"I won't."

"You told me Bill's story about the footprints that just stopped, and you told me your story about the maggots that somehow got into the cantaloupe, but both of you were speaking in metaphors. Just as the Poe story is a metaphor for the divided self . . . or so my college prof said. But if you strip the metaphors away, what do you have?"

"I don't know."

"The inexplicable," she said. "So my question to you is pretty simple. What if the only answer to the riddle of the two Terrys is supernatural?"

He didn't laugh. He had no urge to laugh. It was too late at night for laughter. Or too early in the morning. Too something, anyway. "I don't believe in the supernatural. Not ghosts, not angels, not the divinity of Jesus Christ. I go to church, sure, but only because it's a peaceful place where I can sometimes listen to myself. Also because it's the expected thing. I had an idea that's why you went, too. Or because of Derek."

"I would like to believe in God," she said, "because I don't want to believe we just end, even though it balances the equation—

since we came from blackness, it seems logical to assume that it's to blackness we return. But I believe in the stars, and the infinity of the universe. That's the great Out There. Down here, I believe there are more universes in every fistful of sand, because infinity is a two-way street. I believe there's another dozen thoughts in my head lined up behind each one I'm aware of. I believe in my consciousness and my unconscious, even though I don't know what those things are. And I believe in A. Conan Doyle, who had Sherlock Holmes say, 'Once you eliminate the impossible, whatever remains, no matter how improbable, must be the truth.'"

"Wasn't he the guy who believed in fairies?" Ralph asked.

She sighed. "Come upstairs and let's get funky. Then maybe we'll both sleep."

Ralph went willingly enough, but even while they were making love (except at the moment of climax, when all thought was obliterated), he found himself remembering Doyle's dictum. It was smart. Logical. But could you amend it to *Once you eliminate the natural, whatever remains must be supernatural*? No. He could not believe in any explanation that transgressed the rules of the natural world, not just as a police detective but as a man. A real person had killed Frank Peterson, not a spook from a comic book. So what remained, no matter how improbable? Only one thing. Frank Peterson's killer had been Terry Maitland, now deceased.

5

On that Wednesday night, the July moon had risen as bloated and orange as a gigantic tropical fruit. By early Thursday morning, as Fred Peterson stood in his backyard, on the footstool where he had rested his feet during many a Sunday afternoon football game, it had shrunk to a cold silver coin riding high overhead.

He slipped the noose around his neck and yanked it until the knot rested against the angle of his jaw, as the Wikipedia entry had specified (complete with helpful illustration). The other end was attached to the branch of a hackberry tree like the one beyond Ralph Anderson's fence, although this one was a rather more elderly representative of Flint City's flora, having sprouted around the time an American bomber was dropping its payload on Hiroshima (surely a supernatural event to the Japanese who witnessed it at a distance great enough to save them from being vaporized).

The footstool rocked back and forth unsteadily beneath his feet. He listened to the crickets and felt the night breeze—cool and soothing after one hot day and before another he did not expect to see—on his sweaty cheeks. Part of his decision to draw a line under the Flint City Petersons and call the equation complete was a hope that Frank, Arlene, and Ollie had not gone far, at least not yet. It might still be possible to catch up. More of it was the unbearable prospect of attending a double funeral in the morning at the same mortuary—Donelli Brothers—that would bury the man responsible for their deaths in the afternoon. He couldn't do it.

He looked around one final time, asking himself if he really wanted to do *this*. The answer was yes, and so he kicked the footstool away, expecting to hear the crack of his neck breaking deep in his head before the tunnel of light opened before him—the tunnel with his family standing at the far end, beckoning him to a second and better life where harmless boys were not raped and murdered.

There was no crack. He had missed or ignored the part in the Wikipedia entry about how a certain drop was necessary to break the neck of a man weighing two hundred and five pounds. Instead of dying, he began to strangle. As his windpipe closed and his eyes bulged in their sockets, his previously drowsing survival instinct awakened in a clangor of alarm bells and a glare of interior security lights. In a space of three seconds his body overrode his brain and the desire to die became the brute will to live.

Fred raised his hands, groped, and found the rope. He pulled with all his strength. The rope slackened, and he was able to draw a breath—necessarily shallow, because the noose was still tight, the knot digging into the side of his throat like a swollen gland. Holding on with one hand, he groped for the branch to which he had tied the rope. His fingers brushed its underside, and loosed a few flakes of bark that fluttered down onto his hair, but that was all.

He was not a fit man in his middle age, most of his exercise consisting of trips to the fridge for another beer during one of his beloved Dallas Cowboys football games, but even as a high school kid in phys ed, five pull-ups had been the best he could do. He could feel his one-handed grip slipping, and grabbed the rope with his other hand again, holding it slack long enough to pull in another half-breath, but unable to yank himself any higher. His feet swung back and forth eight inches above the lawn. One of his slippers came off, then the other. He tried to call for help, but all he could manage was a rusty wheeze . . . and who would possibly be awake to hear him at this hour of the morning? Nosy old Mrs. Gibson next door? She would be asleep in her bed with her rosary in her hand, dreaming of Father Brixton.

His hands slipped. The branch creaked. His breath stopped. He could feel the blood trapped in his head pulsing, getting ready to burst his brains. He heard a rasping sound and thought, *It wasn't supposed to be like this.*

He flailed for the rope, a drowning man reaching for the surface of the lake into which he has fallen. Large black spores appeared in front of his eyes. They burst into extravagant black toadstools. But before they overwhelmed his sight, he saw a man standing on the patio in the moonlight, one hand resting possessively on the barbecue where Fred would never grill another steak. Or maybe it wasn't a man at all. The features were crude, as if punched into being by a blind sculptor. And the eyes were straws.

6

June Gibson happened to be the woman who had made the lasagna Arlene Peterson dumped over her head before suffering her heart attack, and she wasn't asleep. Nor was she thinking about Father Brixton. She was suffering herself, and plenty. It had been three years since her last attack of sciatica, and she had dared to hope it was gone for good, but here it was again, a nasty uninvited visitor who just barged in and took up residence. Only a telltale stiffness behind her left knee after the post-funeral gathering at the Petersons' next door, but she knew the signs and begged Dr. Richland for an oxycodone prescription, which he had reluctantly written. The pills only helped a little. The pain ran down her left side from the small of her back to her ankle, where it cinched her with a thorny manacle. One of the cruelest attributes of sciatica—hers, anyway—was that lying down intensified the pain instead of easing it. So she sat here in her living room, dressed in her robe and pajamas, alternately watching an infomercial for sexy abs on TV and playing solitaire on the iPhone her son had given her for Mother's Day.

Her back was bad and her eyes were failing, but she had muted the sound on the infomercial and there was nothing wrong with her ears. She heard a gunshot next door clearly, and leaped to her feet with no thought for the bolt of pain that pistoned down the entire left side of her body.

Dear God, Fred Peterson has just shot himself.

She grabbed her cane and hobbled, bent over and crone-like, to her back door. On the porch, and by the light of that heartless silver moon, she saw Peterson crumpled on his lawn. Not a gunshot after all. There was a rope around his neck, and it snaked a short distance to the broken branch around which it had been tied.

Dropping her cane—it would only slow her down—Mrs. Gibson sidesaddled down her back porch steps and negotiated the ninety feet between the two backyards at a lurching jog, unaware of her own cries of pain as her sciatic nerve went nuclear, ripping her from her skinny buttocks to the ball of her left foot.

She knelt beside Mr. Peterson, observing his swollen and empurpled face, the protruding tongue, and the rope half-buried in the ample flesh of his neck. She wriggled her fingers under the rope and pulled with all her strength, unleashing another blast of agony. The cry this occasioned she *was* aware of: a high, long, ululating scream. Lights went on across the street, but Mrs. Gibson didn't see them. The rope was finally loosening, thank God and Jesus and Mary and all the saints. She waited for Mr. Peterson to gasp in air.

He did not.

During the first phase of her working life, Mrs. Gibson had been a teller at Flint City First National. When she retired from that position at the mandatory age of sixty-two, she had taken the classes necessary to become a qualified Home Helper, a job she had done to supplement her retirement checks until the age of seventy-four. One of those classes had necessarily dealt with resuscitation. She now knelt beside Mr. Peterson's considerable bulk, tilted his head up, pinched his nostrils shut, yanked his mouth open, and pressed her lips to his.

She was on her tenth breath, and feeling decidedly woozy, when Mr. Jagger from across the street joined her and tapped her on one bony shoulder. "Is he dead?"

"Not if I can help it," said Mrs. Gibson. She clutched the pocket of her housecoat and felt the rectangle of her cell phone. She took it out and tossed it blindly behind her. "Call 911. And if I pass out, you'll have to take over."

But she didn't pass out. On her fifteenth breath—and just as she really was about to—Fred Peterson took a big, slobbery breath on his own. Then another. Mrs. Gibson waited for his eyes to open, and when they did not, she rolled up one lid. Beneath was nothing but the sclera, not white but red with burst blood vessels.

Fred Peterson took a third breath, then stopped again. Mrs. Gibson began the best chest compressions she could manage, not sure they would help but feeling they could not hurt. She was aware that the pain in her back and down her leg had lessened. Was it possible that sciatica could be shocked out of one's body? Of course not. The idea was ridiculous. It was adrenalin, and once the supply was exhausted, she would feel worse than ever.

A siren floated over the early morning darkness, approaching.

Mrs. Gibson returned to forcing her breath down Fred Peterson's throat (her most intimate contact with a man since her husband had died in 2004), stopping each time she felt on the verge of toppling into a gray faint. Mr. Jagger did not offer to take over, and she didn't ask him to. Until the ambulance came, this was between her and Peterson.

Sometimes when she stopped, Mr. Peterson would take one of those great slobbering breaths. Sometimes he would not. She was barely cognizant of the pulsing red ambulance lights when they began to zap the two adjacent yards, strobing across the jagged stub of branch on the hackberry tree where Mr. Peterson had tried to hang himself. One of the EMTs eased her to her feet, and she was able to stand on them almost without pain. It was amazing. No matter how temporary the miracle was, she'd accept it with thanks.

"We'll take over now, missus," the EMT said. "You did a hell of a job."

"You surely did," Mr. Jagger said. "You saved him, June! You saved that poor bugger's life!"

Wiping warm spittle from her chin—a mixture of hers and Peterson's—Mrs. Gibson said, "Maybe so. And maybe it would have been better if I hadn't."

7

At eight o'clock on Thursday morning, Ralph was cutting the grass in his backyard. With a day devoid of tasks stretching ahead of him, mowing was all he could think of to do with his time . . . although not with his mind, which ran on its own endless gerbil wheel: the mutilated body of Frank Peterson, the witnesses, the taped footage, the DNA, the crowd at the courthouse. Mostly that. It was the girl's dangling bra strap he kept fixing on for some reason—a bright yellow ribbon that jiggled up and down as she sat on her boyfriend's shoulders and pumped her fists.

He barely heard the xylophone rattle of his cell phone. He turned off the mower and took the call, standing there with his sneakers and bare ankles dusted with grass. "Anderson."

"Troy Ramage here, boss."

One of the two officers who had actually arrested Terry. That seemed a long time ago. In another life, as they said.

"What's up, Troy?"

"I'm at the hospital with Betsy Riggins."

Ralph smiled, an expression so lately unused that it felt foreign on his face. "She's having the baby."

"No, not yet. The chief asked her to come down because you're on leave and Jack Hoskins is still fishing on Lake Ocoma. Sent me along to keep her company."

"What's the deal?"

"EMTs brought in Fred Peterson a few hours ago. He tried to hang himself in his backyard, but the branch he tied his rope to broke. The lady next door, a Mrs. Gibson, gave him mouth-to-mouth and pulled him through. She came in to see how he was doing, and the chief wants a statement from her, which I guess is protocol, but this seems like a done deal to me. God knows the poor guy had plenty of reasons to pull the pin."

"What's his condition?"

"The docs say he's got minimal brain function. Chances of him ever coming back are like one in a hundred. Betsy said you'd want to know."

For a moment Ralph thought the bowl of cereal he'd eaten for breakfast was going to come back up, and he right-faced away from his Lawnboy to keep from spewing all over it.

"Boss? You there?"

Ralph swallowed back a sour mash of milk and Rice Chex. "I'm here. Where's Betsy now?"

"In Peterson's room with the Gibson woman. Detective Riggins sent me to call because ICU's a no-cell zone. The docs offered them a room where they could talk, but Gibson said she wanted to answer Detective Riggins's questions with Peterson. Almost like she thinks he could hear her. Nice old lady, but her back's killing her, you can see it by the way she walks. So why's she even here? This ain't *The Good Doctor*, and there ain't gonna be any miracle recovery."

Ralph could guess the reason. This Mrs. Gibson would have exchanged recipes with Arlene Peterson, and watched Ollie and Frankie grow up. Maybe Fred Peterson had shoveled out her driveway after one of Flint City's infrequent snowstorms. She was there out of sorrow and respect, perhaps even out of guilt that she hadn't just let Peterson go instead of condemning him to an indefinite stay in a hospital room where machines would do his breathing for him.

The full horror of the last eight days broke over Ralph in a wave. The killer hadn't been contented with taking just the boy; he'd taken the whole Peterson family. A clean sweep, as they said.

Not "the killer," no need to be so anonymous. Terry. The killer was Terry. There's no one else on the radar.

"Thought you'd want to know," Ramage repeated. "And hey, look on the bright side. Maybe Betsy'll go into labor while she's here. Save her husband from making a special trip."

"Tell her to go home," Ralph said.

"Roger that. And . . . Ralph? Sorry about the way things went down at the courthouse. It was a shit-show."

"That pretty well sums it up," Ralph said. "Thanks for calling."

He went back to the lawn, walking slowly behind the rackety old Lawnboy (he really ought to go down to Home Depot and buy a new one; it was a chore he no longer had an excuse to put off, with all this time on his hands), and was just finishing the last bit when his phone started playing its xylophone boogie again. He thought it would be Betsy. It wasn't, although this call had also originated at Flint City General.

"Still don't have all the DNA back," said Dr. Edward Bogan, "but we've got results from the branch used to sodomize the boy. The blood, plus skin fragments the perp's hand left behind when he . . . you know, grasped the branch and—"

"I know," Ralph said. "Don't keep me in suspense."

"No suspense about this, Detective. The samples from the branch match the Maitland cheek swabs."

"All right, Dr. Bogan, thank you for that. You need to pass it on to Chief Geller and Lieutenant Sablo at SP. I'm on administrative leave, and probably will be for the rest of the summer."

"Ridiculous."

"Regulations. I don't know who Geller will assign to work with Yune—Jack Hoskins is on vacation and Betsy Riggins is about to pop out her first kid at any minute—but he'll find somebody. And when you think of it, with Maitland dead there's no case to work. We're just filling in the blanks."

"The blanks are important," Bogan said. "Maitland's wife may decide to lodge a civil suit. This DNA evidence could get her lawyer to change her mind about that. Such a suit would be an obscenity, in my opinion. Her husband murdered that boy in the cruelest way imaginable, and if she didn't know about his . . . his proclivities . . . she wasn't paying attention. There are always warning signs with sexual sadists. Always. In my opinion, you should have gotten a medal instead of being put on leave."

"Thank you for saying that."

"Only speaking my mind. There are more samples pending. Many. Would you like me to keep you informed as they come in?"

"I would." Chief Geller might bring Hoskins back early, but the man was a waste of space even when he was sober, which wasn't often these days.

Ralph ended the call and sheared off the last stripe of lawn. Then he trundled the Lawnboy into the garage. He was thinking of another Poe story as he wiped down the housing, a tale about a man being bricked up in a wine cellar. He hadn't read it, but he'd seen the movie.

For the love of God, Montresor! the man being bricked up had screamed, and the man doing the interment had agreed: *For the love of God.*

In this case it was Terry Maitland who was being bricked up, only the bricks were DNA and he was already dead. There was conflicting evidence, yes, and that was troubling, but they now had DNA from Flint City and none from Cap City. There were the fingerprints on the book from the newsstand, true, but fingerprints could be planted. It wasn't as easy as the detective shows made it look, but it could be done.

What about the witnesses, Ralph? Three teachers who knew him for years.

Never mind them. Think about the DNA. Solid evidence. The most solid there is.

In the movie, Montresor had been undone by a black cat he had inadvertently entombed with his victim. Its yowling had alerted visitors to the wine cellar. The cat, Ralph supposed, was just another metaphor: the voice of the killer's own conscience. Only sometimes a cigar was just a smoke and a cat was just a cat. There was no reason to keep remembering Terry's dying eyes, or Terry's dying declaration. As Samuels had said, his wife had been kneeling there beside him when he went, holding his hand.

Ralph sat on his workbench, feeling very tired for a man who'd done nothing more than mow a modest patch of backyard lawn. The images of those final minutes leading up to the shooting would not leave him. The car alarm. The unlovely sneer of the blond anchor when she saw she had been bloodied—probably just a small cut, but good for ratings. The burned man with the tattoos on his hands. The boy with the cleft lip. The sun picking out complicated constellations of mica embedded in the sidewalk. The girl's yellow bra strap, flipping up and down. That most of all. It seemed to want to lead somewhere else, but sometimes a bra strap was just a bra strap.

"And a man can't be two places at the same time," he muttered.

"Ralph? Are you talking to yourself?"

He started and looked up. It was Jeannie, standing in the doorway.

"I must be, because there's no one else here."

"*I* am," she said. "Are you okay?"

"Not really," he said, and then told her about Fred Peterson. She sagged visibly.

"My God. That finishes that family. Unless he recovers."

"They're finished whether he recovers or not." Ralph got to his feet. "I'll go down to the station a little later, take a look at that scrap of paper. Menu or whatever it is."

"Shower first. You smell like oil and grass."

He made a smile and gave her a salute. "Yes, sir."

She stood on tiptoe and kissed his cheek. "Ralph? You'll get through this. You will. Trust me."

8

There were plenty of things Ralph didn't know about administrative leave, never having been on it before. One was whether or not he was even allowed in the cop shop. With that in mind he waited until mid-afternoon to go there, because the daily pulse of the station was slowest then. When he arrived, there was no one in the big main room except for Stephanie Gould, still in civvies, filling out reports on one of the old PCs the city council kept promising to replace, and Sandy McGill at the dispatch desk, reading *People*. Chief Geller's office was empty.

"Hey, Detective," Stephanie said, looking up. "What are you doing here? I heard you were on paid vacation."

"Trying to stay occupied."

"I could help you with that," she said, and patted the stack of files beside her computer.

"Maybe another time."

"I'm sorry about the way things went down. We all are."

"Thanks."

He went to the dispatch desk and asked Sandy for the key to the evidence room. She gave it to him without hesitation, hardly looking up from her magazine. Hanging from a hook beside the evidence room door was a clipboard and a ballpoint. Ralph thought about skipping the sign-in, then went ahead and entered name, date, and time: 1530 hours. No choice, really, when both Gould and McGill knew he was here and why he'd come. If anyone asked about what he'd wanted to look at, he would flat-out tell them. It was administrative leave he was on, after all, not a suspension.

The room, not much bigger than a closet, was hot and stuffy. The overhead fluorescent bars flickered. Like the ancient PCs, they needed to be replaced. Flint City, aided by federal dollars, made sure the PD had all the weaponry it needed, and more. So what if the infrastructure was falling apart?

Had Frank Peterson's murder been committed back when Ralph first came on the force, there might have been four boxes of Maitland evidence, maybe even half a dozen, but the computer age had done wonders for compression, and today there were only two, plus the toolbox that had been in the back of the van. That had contained the standard array of wrenches, hammers, and screwdrivers. Terry's prints had been on none of the tools, nor on the box itself. To Ralph that suggested that the toolbox had been in the van when it was stolen, and Terry had never examined the contents after stealing the van for his own purposes.

One of the evidence boxes was marked MAITLAND HOME. The second box was labeled VAN/SUBARU. This was the one Ralph wanted. He cut the tape. No reason not to, with Terry dead.

After a brief hunt, he came up with a plastic evidence bag containing the scrap of paper he remembered. It was blue, and roughly triangular. At the top, in bold black letters, was **TOMMY AND TUP**. Whatever came after **TUP** was gone. In the upper corner was a little drawing of a pie, with steam rising from its crust. Although Ralph hadn't remembered that specifically, it must have been the reason he'd thought this scrap had been part of a take-out menu. What had Jeannie said when they were talking early this morning? *I believe there's another dozen thoughts lined up behind each one I'm aware of.* If it was true, Ralph would have given a fair amount of money to get hold of the one lurking behind that yellow bra strap. Because there was one, he was almost sure of it.

Another thing he was almost sure of was how this scrap had happened to be lying on the van's floor. Someone had put menus under the windshield wipers of all the vehicles in the area where the van had been parked. The driver—maybe the kid who'd stolen it in New York, maybe whoever had stolen it after the kid dumped it—had torn it off rather than just lifting the wiper, leaving that triangular corner. The driver hadn't noticed then, but once he was rolling, he would have. Maybe he'd reached around and pulled it free, dropping it on the floor instead of just letting it fly away. Possibly because he wasn't a litterbug by nature, just a thief. Possibly because there'd been a cop car behind him, and he hadn't wanted to do anything, not even a little thing, that might attract attention. It was even possible that he'd *tried* to throw it out the window, and a vagary of wind had blown it right back into the cab. Ralph had investigated road accidents, one of them quite nasty, where that had happened with cigarette butts.

He took his notebook from his back pocket—carrying it was second nature, administrative leave or not—and printed TOMMY AND TUP on a blank sheet. He replaced the VAN/SUBARU box on the shelf it had come from, left the evidence room (not neglecting to jot down his out time), and re-locked the door. When he gave the key back to Sandy, he held his notebook open in front of her. She glanced up from the latest adventures of Jennifer Aniston to glance at it.

"Mean anything to you?"

"Nope."

She went back to her mag. Ralph went to Officer Gould, who was still entering hard copy info into some database and swearing under her breath when she hit a wrong key, which seemed to be often. She glanced at his notebook.

"Tup is old-timey British slang for screwing, I think—as in 'I tupped me girlfriend last night, mate'—but I can't think of anything else. Is it important?"

"I don't know. Probably not."

"Google it, why don't you?"

While he waited for his own out-of-date computer to boot up, he decided to try the database he was married to. Jeannie answered on the first ring, and didn't even need to think when he asked her. "It could be Tommy and Tuppence. They were cutie-poo detectives Agatha Christie wrote about when she wasn't writing about Hercule Poirot or Miss Marple. If that's the case, you'll probably find a restaurant run by a couple of British expats and specializing in things like bubble-and-squeak."

"Bubble and *what?*"

"Never mind."

"It probably means nothing," he repeated. But maybe it did. You chased this shit to make sure, one way or the other; chasing shit was, apologies to Sherlock Holmes, what most detective work was about.

"I'm curious, though. Tell me when you get home. Oh, and we're all out of orange juice."

"I'll stop by Gerald's," he said, and hung up.

He went to Google, typed in TOMMY AND TUPPENCE, then added RESTAURANT. The PD computers were old, but the Wi-Fi was new, and fast. He had what he was looking for in a matter of seconds. The Tommy and Tuppence Pub and Café was on Northwoods Boulevard in Dayton, Ohio.

Dayton. What was it about Dayton? Hadn't that come up once before in this sorry business? If so, where? He sat back in his chair and closed his eyes. Whatever connection he was trying to make courtesy of that yellow bra strap continued to elude him, but this new one he got. Dayton had come up during his last real conversation with Terry Maitland. They'd been talking about the van, and Terry had said he hadn't been in New York since he honeymooned there with his wife. The only trip Terry had taken recently had been to Ohio. To Dayton, in fact.

The girls' spring vacation. I wanted to see my dad. And when Ralph had asked if his father lived there, Terry had said, *If you can call what he's doing these days living.*

He called Sablo. "Hey, Yune, it's me."

"Hey, Ralph, how's retirement treating you?"

"It's good. You should see my lawn. I heard you're getting a commendation for covering that dipshit reporter's delectable body."

"So they say. Tell you what, life has been good for this son of a poor Mexican farming family."

"I thought you told me your father ran the biggest car dealership in Amarillo."

"I might have said that, I suppose. But when you have to decide between truth and legend, *ese*, print the legend. The wisdom of John Ford in *The Man Who Shot Liberty Valance*. What can I do for you?"

"Did Samuels tell you about the kid who originally stole the van?"

"Yeah. That's some story. Kid's name was Merlin, did you know that? And he sure must have been some kind of wizard to get all the way down to south Texas."

"Can you reach out to El Paso? That's where his run ended, but I know from Samuels that the kid ditched the van in Ohio. What I want to know is if it was somewhere near a pub and café called Tommy and Tuppence, on Northwoods Boulevard in Dayton."

"I could take a shot at that, I guess."

"Samuels told me this Merlin the Magician was on the road a long time. Can you also try to find out *when* he ditched the van? If maybe it was in April?"

"I can try to do that, too. Do you want to tell me why?"

"Terry Maitland was in Dayton in April. Visiting his father."

"Really?" Yune sounded totally engaged now. "Alone?"

"With his family," Ralph admitted, "and they flew both ways."

"So there goes that."

"Probably, but it still exercises a certain particular fascination over my consciousness."

"You'll have to 'splain that, Detective, for I am just the son of a poor Mexican farmer."

Ralph sighed.

"Let me see what I can find out."

"Thanks, Yune."

Just as he hung up, Chief Geller came in, toting a gym bag and looking freshly showered. Ralph tipped him a wave, and got a scowl in return. "You're not supposed to be here, Detective."

Ah, so that answered *that* question.

"Go home. Mow the lawn, or something."

"I already did that," Ralph said, getting up. "Cleaning out the cellar comes next."

"Fine, better get to it." Geller paused at his office door. "And Ralph . . . I'm sorry about all this. Sorry as hell."

People keep saying that, Ralph thought as he went out into the afternoon heat.

9

Yune called at quarter past nine that evening, while Jeannie was in the shower. Ralph wrote everything down. It wasn't much, but enough to be interesting. He went to bed an hour later, and fell into real sleep for the first time since Terry had been shot at the foot of the courthouse steps. He awoke at four on Friday morning from a dream of the teenage girl sitting on her boyfriend's shoulders and pumping her fists at the sky. He sat bolt upright in bed, still more asleep than awake, and unaware he was shouting until his frightened wife sat up beside him and grabbed him by the shoulders.

"What? Ralph, *what?*"

"Not the strap! The *color* of the strap!"

"What are you talking about?" She shook him. "Was it a dream, honey? A bad dream?"

I believe there's another dozen thoughts in my head lined up behind each one I'm aware of. That was what she had said. And that was what the dream—already dissolving, as dreams do—had been. One of those thoughts.

"I had it," he said. "In the dream I had it."

"Had what, honey? Something about Terry?"

"About the girl. Her bra strap was bright yellow. Only something else was, too. I knew what it was in the dream, but now . . ." He swung his feet out of bed and sat with his hands grasping his knees below the baggy boxers he slept in. "It's gone."

"It will come back. Lie down. You scared the hell out of me."

"I'm sorry." Ralph lay down again.

"Can you go back to sleep?"

"I don't know."

"What did Lieutenant Sablo say when he called?"

"I didn't tell you?" Knowing he hadn't.

"No, and I didn't want to push. You had your think-face on."

"I'll tell you in the morning."

"Since you scared me wide awake, might as well do it now."

"Not much to tell. Yune tracked the boy down through the officer who arrested him—the cop liked the kid, kind of took an interest, has been keeping track. For the time being, young Mr. Cassidy is in the foster care system down there in El Paso. He's got to face some kind of hearing in juvenile court for car theft, but nobody knows exactly where that will be yet. Dutchess County in New York seems the most likely, but they're not exactly champing at the bit to get him, and he's not champing at the bit to go back. So for the time being, he's in a kind of legal limbo, and according to Yune, he likes that fine. Stepfather tuned up on him pretty frequently, is the kid's story. While Mom pretended it wasn't happening. Pretty standard cycle of abuse."

"Poor kid, no wonder he ran away. What will happen to him?"

"Oh, eventually he'll be sent back. The wheels of justice grind slow, but exceedingly fine. He'll get a suspended sentence, or maybe they'll work out something about time served while in foster care. The cops in his town will be alerted to his home situation, but eventually the whole thing will start up again. Kid beaters sometimes hit pause, but they rarely hit stop."

He put his hands behind his head and thought of Terry, who had shown no previous signs of violence, not so much as bumping an umpire.

"The kid was in Dayton, all right," Ralph said, "and by then he was getting nervous about the van. He parked in a public lot because it was free, because there was no attendant, and because he saw the Golden Arches a few blocks up. He doesn't remember passing the Tommy and Tuppence café, but he does remember a young guy in a shirt that said Tommy something-or-other on the back. The guy had a stack of blue papers that he was putting under the windshield wipers of cars parked at the curb. He noticed the kid—Merlin—and offered him two bucks to put menus under the wipers of the vehicles in the parking lot. The kid said no thanks and went on up to Mickey D's to get his lunch. When he came back, the leaflet guy was gone, but there were menus on every car and truck in the lot. The kid was skittish, took it as a bad omen for some reason, God knows why. Anyway, he decided the time had come to switch rides."

"If he hadn't been skittish, he probably would have been caught a lot sooner," Jeannie observed.

"You're right. Anyway, he strolled around the lot, checking for cars that were unlocked. He told Yune he was surprised at how many were."

"I bet you weren't."

Ralph smiled. "People are careless. Fifth or sixth one he found unlocked, there was a spare key tucked behind the sun visor. It was perfect for him—a plain black Toyota, thousands of them on the road every day. Before our boy Merlin headed out in it, though, he put the van's key back in the ignition. He told Yune he hoped someone else would steal it because, and I quote, 'It might throw the po-po off my trail.' You know, like he was wanted for murder in six states instead of just being a runaway kid who never forgot to use his turn-signal."

"He said that?" She sounded amused.

"Yes. And by the way, he had to go back to the van for something else. A stack of smashed-down cartons he was sitting on to make him look taller behind the wheel."

"I kind of like this kid. Derek never would have thought of that."

We've never given him reason to, Ralph thought.

"Do you know if he left the menu under the van's windshield wiper?"

"Yune asked, and the kid said sure he did, why would he take it?"

"So the person who tore it off—and left the scrap which ended up inside—was the person who stole it from the parking lot in Dayton."

"Almost had to be. Now here's what had me wearing my thinkface. The kid said he thought it was in April. I take that with a grain of salt, because I doubt if keeping track of dates was very important to him, but he told Yune it was spring, with all the leaves pretty much out on the trees, and not real hot yet. So it *probably* was. And April is when Terry was in Dayton, visiting his father."

"Only he was with his family, and they flew round-trip."

"I know that. You could call it a coincidence. Only then the same van ends up here in Flint City, and it's hard for me to believe in two coincidences involving the same Ford Econoline van. Yune floated the idea that maybe Terry had an accomplice."

"One who looked exactly like him?" Jeannie hoisted an eyebrow. "A twin brother named William Wilson, maybe?"

"I know, the idea is ridiculous. But you see how weird it is, don't you? Terry is in Dayton, the van is in Dayton. Terry comes home to Flint City, and the van turns up in Flint City. There's a word for that, but I can't remember what it is."

"Confluence might be the one you're looking for."

"I want to talk to Marcy," he said. "I want to ask her about the trip the Maitlands made to Dayton. Everything she remembers. Only she won't want to talk to me, and I have absolutely no way of compelling her."

"Will you try?"

"Oh yes, I'll try."

"Can you sleep now?"

"I think so. Love you."

"Love you, too."

He was drifting away when she spoke into his ear, firm and almost harsh, trying to shock it out of him. "If it wasn't the bra strap, what was it?"

For a moment, clearly, Ralph saw the word CANT. Only the letters were bluey-green, not yellow. Something was there. He grasped for it, but it slipped away.

"Can't," he said.

"Not yet," Jeannie replied, "but you will. I know you."

They went to sleep. When Ralph woke up, it was eight o'clock and all the birds were singing.

10

By ten on that Friday morning, Sarah and Grace had reached the *Hard Day's Night* album, and Marcy thought she might actually lose her mind.

The girls had found Terry's record player—a steal on eBay, he had assured Marcy—in his garage workshop, along with his carefully assembled collection of Beatles albums. They had taken the player and the albums up to Grace's room and had begun with *Meet the Beatles!* "We're going to play all of them," Sarah told her mother. "To remember Daddy. If it's okay."

Marcy told them it was fine. What else could she say when

looking at their pale, solemn faces and red-rimmed eyes? Only she hadn't realized how hard those songs would hit her. The girls knew them all, of course; when Terry was in the garage, the record player's turntable was always spinning, filling his workshop with the British invasion groups he'd been born a little too late to have heard firsthand, but which he loved just the same: the Searchers, the Zombies, the Dave Clark Five, the Kinks, T. Rex, and—of course—the Beatles. Mostly them.

The girls loved those groups and those songs because their father did, but there was a whole emotional spectrum of which they were unaware. They hadn't heard "I Call Your Name" while making out in the back of Terry's father's car, Terry's lips on her neck, Terry's hand under her sweater. They hadn't heard "Can't Buy Me Love," the current track coming down from upstairs, while sitting on the couch in the first apartment where they'd lived together, holding hands, watching *A Hard Day's Night* on the battered VHS they'd picked up at a rummage sale for twenty dollars, the Fab Four young and running amok in black-and-white, Marcy knowing she was going to marry the young man sitting next to her even if he didn't know it yet. Had John Lennon already been dead when they watched that old tape? Shot down in the street just as her husband had been?

She didn't know, couldn't remember. All she knew was she, Sarah, and Grace had gotten through the funeral with their dignity intact, but now the funeral was over, her life as a single mom (oh, that horrible phrase) stretched ahead of her, and the cheerful music was driving her mad with sorrow. Every harmonized vocal, each clever George Harrison riff, was a fresh wound. Twice she had gotten up from where she sat at the kitchen table with a cooling cup of coffee in front of her. Twice she had gone to the foot of the stairs and drawn in breath to shout, *No more! Shut it off!* And twice she had gone back to the kitchen. They were grieving, too.

This time when she got up, Marcy went to the utensil drawer

and pulled it all the way out. She thought there would be nothing there, but her hand found a pack of Winston cigarettes. There were three left inside. No, make that four—one was hiding all the way in back. She hadn't smoked since her younger daughter's fifth birthday, when she'd had a coughing fit while mixing the batter for Gracie's cake, and had vowed there and then to quit forever. Yet instead of throwing these last soldiers of cancer out, she had tossed them in back of the utensil drawer, as if some dark and prescient part of her had known she would eventually need them again.

They're five years old. They'll be stale as hell. You'll probably cough until you pass out.

Good. So much the better.

She took one from the pack, greedy for it already. *Smokers never stop, they only pause*, she thought. She went to the stairs and cocked her head. "And I Love Her" had given way to "Tell Me Why" (that eternal question). She could imagine the girls sitting on Grace's bed, not talking, just listening. Holding hands, maybe. Taking the sacrament of Daddy. Daddy's albums, some bought at Turn Back the Hands of Time, the record store in Cap City, some bought online, all held in the hands that had once held his daughters.

She crossed the living room to the little potbellied stove they lit only on really cold winter nights, and reached blindly for the box of Diamond matches on the nearby shelf, blindly because on that shelf also stood a row of pictures she could not currently bear to look at. Maybe in a month she could. Maybe in a year. How long did it take to recover from the first, rawest stage of grief? She could probably find a fairly definitive answer on WebMD, but was afraid to look.

At least the reporters had gone away after the funeral, rushing back to Cap City to cover some fresh political scandal, and she wouldn't have to risk the back porch, where one of the girls might look out the window and see her renewing her old vice. Or in the garage, where they might smell the smoke if they came out for a fresh bundle of LPs.

She opened the front door, and there stood Ralph Anderson, with his fist raised to knock.

11

The horror with which she stared at him—as if he were some kind of monster, maybe a zombie from that TV show—struck Ralph like a blow to the chest. He had time to see the disarray of her hair, a splotch of something on the lapel of her robe (which was too big for her; maybe it was Terry's), the slightly bent cigarette between her fingers. And something else. She had always been a fine-looking woman, but she was losing her looks already. He would have called that impossible.

"Marcy—"

"No. You don't belong here. You need to get out of here." Her voice was low, breathless, as if someone had punched her.

"I need to talk to you. Please let me talk to you."

"You killed my husband. There's nothing else to say."

She started to swing the door closed. Ralph held it with his hand. "I didn't kill him, but yes, I played a part. Call me an accomplice, if that's what you want. I never should have arrested him the way I did. It was wrong on God knows how many different levels. I had my reasons, but they weren't good reasons. I—"

"Take your hand off the door. Do it now, or I'll have you arrested."

"Marcy—"

"*Don't call me that.* You have no *right* to call me that, not after what you did. The only reason I'm not screaming my head off is because my daughters are upstairs, listening to their dead father's records."

"Please." He thought to say, *Don't make me beg*, but that was wrong because it wasn't enough. "I'm begging you. Please talk to me."

She held up the cigarette and uttered a terrible toneless laugh.

"I thought, now that the little lice are gone, I can have a smoke on my doorstep. And look, here's the *big* louse, the louse of louses. Last warning, Mr. Louse who got my husband killed. *Get . . . the fuck . . . off my doorstep.*"

"What if he didn't do it?"

Her eyes widened and the pressure of her hand on the door slackened, at least for the moment.

"What if he . . . ? Jesus Christ, he *told* you he didn't do it! He told you as he lay there dying! What else do you want, a hand-delivered telegram from the Angel Gabriel?"

"If he didn't, whoever did is still out there, and he's responsible for the destruction of the Peterson family, as well as yours."

She considered this for a moment, then said: "Oliver Peterson is dead because you and that sonofabitch Samuels had to put on your circus. And *you* killed him, didn't you, Detective Anderson? Shot him in the head. Got your man. Excuse me, your *boy*."

She slammed the door in his face. Ralph again raised his hand to knock, thought better of it, and turned away.

12

Marcy stood trembling on her side of the door. She felt her knees go loose, and managed to make it to the bench near the door where people sat when they took off boots or muddy shoes. Upstairs, the Beatle who had been murdered was singing about all the things he was going to do when he got home. Marcy looked at the cigarette between her fingers as if unsure how it had gotten there, then snapped it in two and slipped the pieces into the pocket of the robe she was wearing (it was indeed Terry's). *At least he saved me from starting up that shit again*, she thought. *Maybe I should write him a thank-you note.*

The nerve of him coming to her door, after taking a wrecking bar to her family and flailing around with it until all was in ruins. The pure cruel in-your-face *nerve* of it. Only . . .

If he didn't, whoever did is still out there.

And how was she supposed to handle that, when she couldn't even find the strength to go on WebMD and find out how long the first stage of grief lasted? And why was she supposed to do *anything*? How was it her responsibility? The police had gotten the wrong man and stubbornly persisted even after checking Terry's alibi and finding it as solid as Gibraltar. Let them find the right one, if they had the guts to do so. Her job was to get through today without going insane, and then—in some future that was hard to contemplate—figure out what came next in her life. Was she supposed to live here, when half the town believed the man who had assassinated her husband was doing God's work? Was she supposed to condemn her daughters to those cannibal societies known as middle school and high school, where even wearing the wrong sneakers could get you ridiculed and ostracized?

Sending Anderson away was the right thing. I cannot have him in my house. Yes, I heard the honesty in his voice—at least I think I did—but how can I, after what he did?

If he didn't, whoever did . . .

"Shut up," she whispered to herself. "Just shut up, please shut up."

. . . is still out there.

And what if he did it again?

13

Most of the folks in Flint City's better class of citizenry thought Howard Gold had been born rich, or at least well-to-do. Although he wasn't ashamed of his catch-as-catch-can upbringing, not a bit, he didn't go out of his way to disabuse those folks. It so happened he was the son of an itinerant plowboy, sometime wrangler, and occasional rodeo rider who had traveled around the Southwest in an Airstream trailer with his wife and two sons, Howard and Edward. Howard had put himself through college, then helped to do the same for Eddie. He took care of his parents in their retirement (Andrew Gold had saved nary a nickel), and had plenty left over.

He was a member of Rotary and the Rolling Hills Country Club. He took important clients to dinner at Flint City's best restaurants (there were two), and supported a dozen different charities, including the athletic fields at Estelle Barga Park. He could order fine wine with the best of them and sent his biggest clients elaborate Harry & David gift boxes each Christmas. Yet when he was in his office by himself, as he was this Friday noon, he preferred to eat as he had as a boy on the road between Hoot, Oklahoma, and Holler, Nevada, and then back again, listening to Clint Black on the radio and studying his lessons at his mother's side when he wasn't in school someplace. He supposed his gall bladder would put a stop to his solitary, grease-soaked meals eventually, but he had reached his early sixties without hearing a peep from it, so God bless heredity. When the phone rang, he was working his way through a fried egg sandwich, heavy on the mayo, and French fries done just the way he liked them, cooked to a blackened crisp and slathered with ketchup. Waiting at the edge of the desk was a slice of apple pie with ice cream melting on top.

"Howard Gold speaking."

"It's Marcy, Howie. Ralph Anderson was here this morning."

Howie frowned. "He came to your house? He's got no business doing that. He's on administrative leave. Won't be active police again for some time, assuming he decides to come back at all. Did you want me to call Chief Geller, and put a bug in his ear?"

"No. I slammed the door in his face."

"Good for you!"

"It doesn't feel good. He said something I can't get out of my mind. Howard, tell me the truth. Do you think Terry killed that boy?"

"Jesus, no. I told you. There's evidence for it, we both know that, but there's too much against it. He would have walked. But never mind that, he just didn't have such an act in him. Also, there was his dying declaration."

"People will say that was because he didn't want to admit it in front of me. They're probably already saying it."

Honey, he thought, *I'm not sure he even knew you were there.*

"I think he was telling the truth."

"So do I, and if he was, whoever did it is still free, and if he killed one child, sooner or later he'll kill another one."

"So that's what Anderson put in your mind," Howie said. He pushed away what remained of his sandwich. He no longer wanted it. "I'm not surprised, the guilt-trip is an old police trick, but he was wrong to try it on you. Ralph needs to take some heat for it. A strong reprimand that goes in his jacket, at the very least. You just buried your husband, for God's sake."

"But what he said was true."

Maybe it was, Howie thought, *but that begs the question—why did he say it to you?*

"And there's something else," she said. "If the real killer isn't found, the girls and I will have to leave town. Maybe I could stand up to the whispers and the gossip if I was on my own, but it isn't fair to ask the girls to do that. The only place I can think of to go is my sister's in Michigan, and that wouldn't be fair to Debra and Sam. They've got two kids of their own, and the house is small. It would mean starting all over again for me, and I feel too tired to do that. I feel . . . Howie, I feel broken."

"I understand that. What is it you want me to do?"

"Call Anderson. Tell him I'll meet with him here at the house tonight, and he can ask his questions. But I want you here, too.

You and the investigator you use, if he's free and willing to come. Will you do that?"

"Of course, if it's what you want. And I'm sure Alec would come. But I want to . . . not warn you, exactly, but put you on your guard. I'm sure Ralph feels terrible about what happened, and I'm guessing he apologized—"

"He said he was begging me."

That was sort of amazing, but maybe not entirely out of character.

"He's not a bad man," Howie said. "He's a good man who made a bad mistake. But Marcy, he's still got a vested interest in proving it was Terry who killed the Peterson boy. If he can do that, his career is back on track. If it's never proved conclusively one way or the other, his career is still back on track. But if the real killer turns up, Ralph is finished as a member of the FC police. His next job will be working security in Cap City at half the salary. And that's not even figuring in the suits he might be facing."

"I understand that, but—"

"I'm not finished. Any questions he's got for you have to be about Terry. Maybe he's just flailing around, but it's possible he thinks he's got something that ties Terry to the murder in a different way. Now, do you still want me to set up a meeting?"

There was silence for a moment, and then Marcy said, "Jamie Mattingly is my best friend on Barnum Court. She took the girls in after Terry was arrested at the ballfield, but now she won't answer her phone when I call, and she's unfriended me on Facebook. My best friend has officially unfriended me."

"She'll come around."

"She will if the real killer is caught. Then she'll come to me on her hands and knees. Maybe I'll forgive her for knuckling under to her husband—because that's what happened, count on it—and maybe I won't. But that's a decision I can't make until things change for the better. If they ever do. Which is my way of saying go ahead and set up the meeting. You'll be there to protect me. Mr. Pelley, too. I want to know why Anderson got up enough guts to show his face at my door."

14

At four o'clock that afternoon, an old Dodge pickup rattled along a ranch road fifteen miles south of Flint City, pulling up a roostertail of dust. It passed an abandoned windmill with broken vanes, a deserted ranchhouse with glaring holes where the windows had been, a long-abandoned cemetery locally known as the Cowboy Graveyard, a boulder with TRUMP MAKE AMERICA GREAT AGAIN TRUMP painted on the side in fading letters. Galvanized milk cans rolled around in the truckbed and banged off the sides. Behind the wheel was a seventeen-year-old boy named Dougie Elfman. He kept checking his cell phone as he drove. By the time he got to Highway 79, he had two bars, and reckoned that would be enough. He stopped at the crossing, got out, and looked behind him. Nothing. Of course there was nothing. And still, he was relieved. He called his daddy. Clark Elfman answered on the second ring.

"Were those cans out there in that barn?"

"Yuh," Dougie said. "I got two dozen, but they'll have to be warshed out. Still smell like clabbered milk."

"What about the hoss-tack?"

"All gone, Daddy."

"Well, that ain't the best news of the week, but no more than what I expected. What you callin for, son? And where are you? Sound like you're on the dark side of the moon."

"I'm out at 79. Listen, Daddy, somebody been stayin out there."

"What? You mean like hobos or hippies?"

"It ain't that. There's no mess—beercans or wrappers or liquor bottles—and no sign anyone took a dump anywhere, unless they walked a quarter of a mile to the nearest bushes. No campfire sign, either."

"Thank Christ for that," Elfman said, "dry as it's been. What *did* you find? Not that I guess it matters, nothing left to steal and them old buildings half fallen down and not worth pea-turkey."

Dougie kept looking back. The road looked empty, all right, but he wished the dust would settle faster.

"I found a pair of bluejeans that look new, and Jockey underpants that look new, and some expensive sneakers, them with the gel insides, that also look new. Only they're all stained with something, and so's the hay they was lyin in."

"Blood?"

"No, it ain't blood. Turned the hay black, whatever it was."

"Oil? Motor oil? Somethin like 'at?"

"No, the *stuff* wasn't black, just the hay it got on. I don't know what it was."

But he knew what those stiff patches on the jeans and underpants looked like; he had been masturbating three and sometimes four times a day since he turned fourteen, using an old piece of towel to shoot his spunk into, and then using the backyard tap to rinse it out when his parents were gone. Sometimes he forgot, though, and that piece of toweling got pretty crusty.

Only there had been a lot of that stuff, a *lot*, and really, who would jizz off on a brand-new pair of Adipowers, high-class kicks that cost upward of a hundred and forty dollars, even at Wally World? Dougie might have thought about taking them for himself under other circumstances, but not with that crap on them, and not with the other thing he'd noticed.

"Well, let it go and just come on home," Elfman said. "You got those cans, at least."

"No, Daddy, you need to get the police out. There was a belt in them jeans, and it's got a shiny silver buckle in the shape of a horse's head."

"That means nothing to me, son, but I guess it does to you."

"On the news, they said that Terry Maitland was wearing a buckle like that when he was seen at the train station in Dubrow. After he killed that little boy."

"They said that?"

"Yes, Daddy."

"Well, shit. You wait there at the crossing until I call you back, but I guess the cops will want to come. I'll come, too."

"Tell them I'll meet them at Biddle's store."

"Biddle's . . . Dougie, that's five miles back toward Flint!"

"I know. But I don't want to stay here." The dust had settled now, and there was nothing to be seen, but Dougie still didn't feel right. Not a single car had passed on the main road since he started talking to his father, and he wanted to be where there were people.

"What's wrong, son?"

"When I was in that barn where I found the clothes—I'd already got the cans by then, and was lookin for that tack you said might be out there—I started to feel all wrong. Like someone was watchin me."

"You just got the creeps. The man who killed that boy is dead as dirt."

"I know, but tell the cops I'll meet em at Biddle's, and I'll take em out there, but I'm not staying here by myself." He ended the call before his father could argue with him.

15

The meeting with Marcy was set for eight o'clock that night at the Maitland home. Ralph got the green-light call from Howie Gold,

THE OUTSIDER

who told him Alec Pelley would also be there. Ralph asked if he could bring Yune Sablo, if Yune was available.

"Under no circumstances," Howie replied. "Bring Lieutenant Sablo or anyone else, even your lovely wife, and the meeting's off."

Ralph agreed. There was nothing else he could do. He puttered around in the cellar for awhile, mostly just shifting boxes from one side to the other and back again. Then he picked at his supper. With two hours still stretching before him, he pushed away from the table. "I'm going to the hospital to visit Fred Peterson."

"Why?"

"I just feel like I should."

"I'll come with you, if you want."

Ralph shook his head. "I'll go directly to Barnum Court from there."

"You're wearing yourself out. Running your guts to water, my grandmother would have said."

"I'm okay."

She gave him a smile that said she knew better, then stood on her toes to kiss him. "Call me. Whatever happens, call me."

He smiled. "Nuts to that. I'll come back and tell you in person."

16

As he was entering the hospital's lobby, Ralph met the department's missing detective on his way out. Jack Hoskins was a slight man, prematurely gray, with bags under his eyes and a red-veined nose. He was still wearing his fishing outfit—khaki shirt and khaki pants, both with many pockets—but his badge was clipped to his belt.

"What are you doing here, Jack? I thought you were on vacation."

"Called back three days early," he said. "Drove into town not an hour ago. My net, gumrubbers, poles, and tackle box are still in my truck. Chief thought he might like to have at least one detective on active duty. Betsy Riggins is upstairs on five, having the baby. Her labor started late this afternoon. I talked to her husband, who says she's got a long way to go. Like he'd have any idea. As for you . . ." He paused for effect. "You're in a hell of a mess, Ralph."

Jack Hoskins made no effort to hide his satisfaction. A year previous, Ralph and Betsy Riggins had been asked to fill out routine evaluation forms for Jack, when he became eligible for a pay bump. Betsy, the detective with the least seniority, had said all the right things. Ralph had turned his in to Chief Geller with only two words written in the space provided: *No opinion.* It hadn't kept Hoskins from getting his bump, but it was an opinion, all the same. Hoskins wasn't supposed to see the eval sheets, and maybe hadn't, but word of what had been on Ralph's had of course gotten back to him.

"Did you look in on Fred Peterson?"

"As a matter of fact, I did." Jack pursed his lower lip and blew scant hair off his forehead. "Lot of monitors in his room, and low lines on all of them. I don't think he's coming back."

"Well, welcome home."

"Fuck that, Ralph, I had three more days, the bass were running, and I'm not even going to get a chance to change my shirt, which stinks of fish guts. Got calls from both Geller and Sheriff Doolin. Have to go all the way out to that useless dustbowl known as Canning Township. I understand your buddy Sablo is already there. I probably won't actually make it home until ten or eleven."

Ralph could have said, *Don't blame me,* but who else was this mostly useless time-server going to blame? Betsy, for getting pregnant last November? "What's in Canning?"

"Jeans, underpants, and sneakers. Kid found them in a shed or a barn while he was hunting out milk cans for his father. Also a belt with a horse's head buckle. Of course the Mobile Crime Lab will already be there, I'll be about as useful as tits on a bull, but the chief—"

"There'll be fingerprints on the buckle," Ralph interrupted. "And there may be tire tracks from the van, or the Subaru, or both."

"Don't try teaching your daddy how to suck eggs," Jack said. "I was carrying a detective's shield while you were still in uniform." The subtext Ralph heard was *And I'll still be carrying it when you're working as a mall guard at Southgate.*

He left. Ralph was glad to see him go. He only wished he could go out there himself. Fresh evidence at this point could be precious. The silver lining was that Sablo had already gotten there, and would be supervising the Forensics Unit. They'd finish most of their work before Jack could arrive and maybe screw something up, as he had on at least two previous occasions that Ralph knew about.

He went up to the maternity waiting room first, but all the seats were empty, so maybe the delivery was going faster than Billy Riggins, a nervous novice at this, had expected. Ralph buttonholed a nurse and asked her to tell Betsy that he wished her all the best.

"I will when I get the chance," the nurse said, "but right now she's very busy. That little man is in a hurry to get out."

Ralph had a brief image of Frank Peterson's bloody, violated body and thought, *If the little man knew what this world was like, he'd be fighting to stay in.*

He took the elevator down two floors to ICU. The remaining member of the Peterson family was in room 304. His neck was heavily bandaged and in a cervical collar. A respirator wheezed, the little accordion gadget inside flopping up and down. The lines on the monitors surrounding the man's bed were, as Jack Hoskins had said, mighty low. There were no flowers (Ralph had an idea they weren't allowed in ICU rooms), but a couple of Mylar balloons had been tethered to the foot of the bed and floated near the ceiling. They were imprinted with cheerful exhortations Ralph didn't like to look at. He listened to the wheeze of the machine that was breathing for Fred. He stared at those low lines and thought of Jack saying *I don't think he's coming back.*

As he sat down by the bed, a memory from his high school days came to him, back when what was now called environmental studies had been plain old Earth science. They had been studying pollution. Mr. Greer had produced a bottle of Poland Spring water and poured it into a glass. He invited one of the kids—Misty Trenton, it had been, she of the deliciously short skirts—up to the front of the room and asked her to take a sip. She had done so. Mr. Greer then produced an eyedropper and dipped it into a bottle of Carter's Ink. He squeezed a drop into the glass. The students watched, fascinated, as that single drop sank, trailing an indigo tentacle behind it. Mr. Greer rocked the glass gently from side to side, and soon all the water in the glass was tinted a weak blue. *Would you drink it now?* Mr. Greer asked Misty. She shook her head so emphatically that one of her hair clips came loose, and everybody, Ralph included, had laughed. He wasn't laughing now.

Less than two weeks ago, the Peterson family had been perfectly fine. Then had come the drop of polluting ink. You could say it was the chain on Frankie Peterson's bike, that he would have made it home unharmed if it hadn't broken, but he *also* would have made it home unharmed—only pushing his bike instead of riding it—if Terry Maitland hadn't been waiting in that grocery store parking lot. *Terry* was the drop of ink, not the bike chain. It was Terry who had first polluted and then destroyed the entire Peterson family. Terry, or whoever had been wearing Terry's face.

Strip away the metaphors, Jeannie had said, *and you are left with the inexplicable. The supernatural.*

Only that's not possible. The supernatural may exist in books and movies, but not in the real world.

No, not in the real world, where drunk incompetents like Jack

Hoskins got pay bumps. All Ralph had experienced in his nearly fifty years of life denied the idea. Denied there was even the possibility of such a thing. Yet as he sat here looking at Fred (or what remained of him), Ralph had to admit there was something devilish about the way the boy's death had spread, taking not just one or two members of his nuclear family, but the whole shebang. Nor did the damage stop with the Petersons. No one could doubt that Marcy and her daughters would carry scars for the rest of their lives, perhaps even permanent disabilities.

Ralph could tell himself that similar collateral damage followed every atrocity—hadn't he seen it time and again? Yes. He had. Yet this one seemed so personal, somehow. Almost as if these people had been targeted. And what about Ralph himself? Was he not part of the collateral damage? And Jeannie? Even Derek, who was going to come home from camp to discover that a good many things he'd taken for granted—his father's job, for instance—were now at risk.

The respirator wheezed. Fred Peterson's chest rose and fell. Every now and then he made a thick noise that sounded weirdly like a chuckle. As if it were all a cosmic joke, but you had to be in a coma to get it.

Ralph couldn't stand it anymore. He left the room, and by the time he got to the elevator, he was nearly running.

17

Once outside, he sat on a bench in the shade and called the station. Sandy McGill picked up, and when Ralph asked if she'd heard anything from Canning Township, there was a pause. When she finally spoke, she sounded embarrassed. "I'm not supposed to talk about that with you, Ralph. Chief Geller left specific instructions. I'm sorry."

"That's okay," Ralph said, getting up. His shadow stretched long, the shadow of a hanged man, and of course that made him think of Fred Peterson again. "Orders is orders."

"Thanks for understanding. Jack Hoskins is back, and he's going out there."

"No problem." He hung up and started for the short-term parking lot, telling himself it didn't matter; Yune would keep him in the loop.

Probably.

He unlocked his car, got in, and cranked the air conditioning. Quarter past seven. Too late to go home, too early to go to the Maitlands'. Which left cruising aimlessly around town like a self-absorbed teenager. And thinking. About how Terry had called Willow Rainwater ma'am. About how Terry had asked directions to the nearest doc-in-the-box, even though he'd lived in FC all his life. About how Terry had shared a room with Billy Quade, and wasn't that convenient. About how Terry had risen to his feet to ask Mr. Coben his question, which was even more convenient. Thinking about that drop of ink in the glass of water, turning it pale blue, of footprints that just ended, of maggots squirming inside a cantaloupe that had looked fine on the outside. Thinking that if a person *did* begin considering supernatural possibilities, that person would no longer be able to think of himself as a completely *sane* person, and thinking about one's sanity was maybe not a good thing. It was like thinking about your heartbeat: if you had to go there, you might already be in trouble.

He turned on the car radio and hunted for loud music. Eventually he found the Animals belting out "Boom Boom." He cruised, waiting for it to be time to go to the Maitland house on Barnum Court. Finally it was.

18

It was Alec Pelley who answered his knock and led him across the living room and into the kitchen. From upstairs he could hear the Animals again. This time it was their biggest hit. *It's been the ruin of many a poor boy*, Eric Burdon wailed, *and God, I know I'm one.*

Confluence, he thought. Jeannie's word.

Marcy and Howie Gold were sitting at the kitchen table. They had coffee. There was also a cup where Alec had been sitting, but no one offered to pour Ralph a cup. *I have come unto the camp of mine enemies*, he thought, and sat down.

"Thank you for seeing me."

Marcy made no reply, just picked up her cup with a hand that wasn't quite steady.

"This is painful for my client," Howie said, "so let's keep it brief. You told Marcy you wanted to talk to her—"

"Needed," Marcy interrupted. "Needed to talk to me, is what he said."

"So noted. What is it you needed to talk to her about, Detective Anderson? If it's an apology, feel free to make it, but understand that we reserve all our legal options."

In spite of everything, Ralph wasn't quite ready to apologize. None of these three had seen a bloody branch jutting from Frank Peterson's bottom, but Ralph had.

"New information has come to light. It may not be substantive, but it's suggestive of something, although I don't know exactly what. My wife called it a confluence."

"Can you be a little more specific?" Howie asked.

"It turns out that the van used to abduct the Peterson boy was stolen by a kid only a little older than Frank Peterson himself. The kid's name is Merlin Cassidy. He was running away from an abusive stepfather. In the course of his run between New York and south Texas, where he was finally arrested, he stole a number of vehicles. He dumped the van in Dayton, Ohio, in April. Marcy—Mrs. Maitland—you and your family were in Dayton in April."

Marcy had been raising her cup for another sip, but now she set it down with a bang. "Oh, no. You're not putting that on Terry. We flew both ways, and except for when Terry went to visit his dad, we were together the whole time. End of story, and I think it's time for you to leave."

"Whoa," Ralph said. "We knew it was a family trip, and that you went by air, almost from the time Terry became a person of interest. It's just that . . . can't you see how weird it is? The van is there when your family is there, then it turns up here. Terry told me he never saw it, let alone stole it. I want to believe that. We have his fingerprints all over the damn thing, but I still want to. And almost can."

"I doubt it," Howie said. "Stop trying to suck us in."

"Would it help you to believe me, maybe even trust me a little, if I told you we now have physical evidence that Terry was in Cap City? His fingerprints on a book from the hotel newsstand? Testimony that has him leaving those prints at approximately the same time the Peterson boy was abducted?"

"Are you kidding?" Alec Pelley asked. He sounded almost shocked.

"No." Even with the case as effectively dead as Terry himself, Bill Samuels would be furious if he found out Ralph had told Marcy and Marcy's lawyer about *A Pictorial History of Flint County, Douree County, and Canning Township*, but he was determined not to let this meeting end without getting some answers.

Alec whistled. "Holy shit."

"So you *know* he was there!" Marcy cried. Red spots were burning in her cheeks. "You *have* to know it!"

But Ralph didn't want to go there; he had spent too much time there already. "Terry mentioned the Dayton trip the last time I talked to him. He said he wanted to visit his father, but he said *wanted* with a funny kind of grimace. And when I asked him if his dad lived there, he said, 'If you can call what he's doing these days living.' So what's the deal with that?"

"The deal is Peter Maitland is suffering from advanced Alzheimer's disease," Marcy said. "He's in the Heisman Memory Unit. It's part of the Kindred Hospital complex."

"So. Tough for Terry to go see him, I guess."

"Very tough," Marcy agreed. She was warming up a little now. Ralph was glad to discover he hadn't lost all of his skills, but this wasn't like being in an interrogation room with a suspect. Both Howie and Alec Pelley were on high alert, ready to stop her if they sensed her foot coming down on a hidden mine. "But not just because Peter didn't know Terry any longer. They hadn't had much of a relationship for a long time."

"Why not?"

"How is this relevant, Detective?" Howie asked.

"I don't know. Maybe it's not. But since we're not in court, counselor, how about you let her answer the damn question?"

Howie looked at Marcy and shrugged. *Up to you.*

"Terry was Peter and Melinda's only child," Marcy said. "He grew up here in Flint City, as you know, and lived here all his life, except for four years at OSU."

"Where you met him?" Ralph asked.

"That's right. Anyway, Peter Maitland worked for the Cheery Petroleum Company, back in the days when this area was still producing a fair amount of oil. He fell in love with his secretary and divorced his wife. There was a lot of rancor, and Terry took his mother's side. Terry . . . he was all about loyalty, even as a boy. He saw his father as a cheat, which he was, of course, and all of Peter's justifications only made things worse. Long story short, Peter married the secretary—Dolores was her name—and asked for a transfer to the company headquarters."

"Which were in Dayton?"

"Correct. Peter didn't try for joint custody or anything like that. He understood Terry had made his choice. But Melinda insisted that Terry go to see him from time to time, claiming that a boy needed to know his father. Terry went, but only to please his mom. He never stopped seeing his father as the rat who ran away."

Howie said, "That fits the Terry I knew."

"Melinda died in 2006. Heart attack. Peter's second wife died two years later, of lung cancer. Terry kept on going to Dayton once or twice a year, to honor his mother, and kept on reasonably civil terms with his father. For the same reason, I suppose. In 2011—I think it was—Peter began to get forgetful. Shoes in the shower instead of under the bed, car keys in the refrigerator, stuff like that. Because Terry is—*was*—his only close living relative, it was Terry who arranged to get him into the Heisman Memory Unit. That was in 2014."

"Places like that are expensive," Alec said. "Who pays?"

"Insurance. Peter Maitland had very good insurance. Dolores insisted. Peter was a heavy smoker all his life, and she probably thought she'd inherit a bundle when he went. But she went first. Probably from his secondhand smoke."

"You speak as if Peter Maitland is dead," Ralph said. "Is that the case?"

"No, he's still alive." Then, in a deliberate echo of her husband: "If you want to call that living. He's even stopped smoking. It's not allowed in the HMU."

"How long were you in Dayton on your last visit?"

"Five days. Terry visited his father three times while we were there."

"You and the girls never went with him?"

"No. Terry didn't want that, and neither did I. It wasn't as if Peter could have been grandfatherly to Sarah and Grace, and Grace wouldn't have understood."

"What did you do while he was visiting?"

Marcy smiled. "You speak as though Terry spent huge wallops of time with his father, and that wasn't the case. His visits were short, no more than an hour or two. Mostly the four of us were together. When Terry was at the Heisman, we hung out at the hotel, and the girls swam in the indoor pool. One day the three of us went to the Art Institute, and one afternoon I took the girls to a Disney matinee. There was a cinema complex close to the hotel. We hit two or maybe three other movies, but that was the whole family. We went to the air force museum as a family, and to the Boonshoft, which is a science museum. The girls loved that. It was your basic family vacation, Detective Anderson, with Terry taking a few hours away to do his filial duty."

And maybe to steal a van, Ralph thought.

It was possible, Merlin Cassidy and the Maitland family certainly could have been in Dayton at the same time, but it seemed farfetched. Even if that had happened, there was the question of how Terry had gotten the van back to Flint City. Or why he would have bothered. There were plenty of vehicles to be stolen in the FC metro area; Barbara Nearing's Subaru was a case in point.

"Probably ate out a few times, didn't you?" Ralph asked.

Howie sat forward at that, but said nothing for the moment.

"We had a fair amount of room service, Sarah and Grace loved it, but sure, we ate out. Assuming the hotel restaurant counts as *out*."

"Did you happen to eat at a place called Tommy and Tuppence?"

"No. I'd remember a restaurant with a name like that. We ate at IHOP one night, and I think twice at Cracker Barrel. Why?"

"No reason," Ralph said.

Howie gave him a smile that said he knew better, but settled back. Alec sat with his arms crossed over his chest, his face expressionless.

"Is that everything?" Marcy asked. "Because I'm tired of this. And I'm tired of you."

"Did *anything* out of the ordinary happen while you were in Dayton? Anything at all? One of your daughters getting lost for a little while, Terry saying he'd met an old friend, *you* meeting an old friend, maybe a package delivery—"

"A flying saucer?" Howie asked. "How about a man in a trenchcoat with a message in code? Or the Rockettes dancing in the parking lot?"

"Not helpful, counselor. Believe it or not, I'm trying to be part of the solution here."

"There was nothing." Marcy got up and began collecting coffee cups. "Terry visited his father, we had a nice vacation, we flew home. We didn't eat at Tommy and whatever it was, and we didn't steal a van. Now I'd like you to—"

"Daddy got a cut."

They all turned to the door. Sarah Maitland was standing there, looking pale and wan and much too thin in her jeans and Rangers tee-shirt.

"Sarah, what are you doing down here?" Marcy put the cups on the counter and went to the girl. "I told you and your sister to stay upstairs until we were done talking."

"Grace is already asleep," Sarah said. "She was awake last night with more stupid nightmares about the man with straws for eyes. I hope she doesn't have any tonight. If she wakes up, you should give her a shot of Benadryl."

"I'm sure she'll sleep through. Go on, now."

But Sarah stood her ground. She was looking at Ralph, not with her mother's dislike and distrust, but with a kind of concentrated curiosity that made Ralph uncomfortable. He held her gaze, but it was difficult.

"My mother says you got my dad killed," Sarah said. "Is that true?"

"No." Then the apology came at last, and to his surprise, it was almost effortless. "But I played a part, and for that I'm deeply sorry. I made a mistake I'll carry with me for the rest of my life."

"Probably that's good," Sarah said. "Probably you deserve to." And to her mother: "I'll go upstairs now, but if Grace starts yelling in the middle of the night, I'm going to sleep in her room."

"Before you go, Sarah, can you tell me about the cut?" Ralph asked.

"It happened when he visited his father," Sarah said. "A nurse fixed it up right after it happened. She put on that Betadine stuff and a Band-Aid. It was okay. He said it didn't hurt."

"Upstairs, you," Marcy said.

"Okay." They watched her pad to the stairs in her bare feet. When she got there, she turned back. "That Tommy and Tuppence restaurant was right up the street from our hotel. When we went to the art museum in the rent-a-dent, I saw the sign."

19

"Tell me about the cut," Ralph said.

Marcy put her hands on her hips. "Why? So you can make it into some kind of big deal? Because it wasn't."

"He's asking because it's the only thing he's got," Alec said. "But I'm interested, too."

"If you're too tired—" Howie began.

"No, that's all right. It *wasn't* a big deal, just a scrape, really. Was that the second time he visited his father?" She lowered her head, frowning. "No, it was the last time, because we flew home the next morning. When Terry left his father's room, he smacked into an orderly. He said neither of them was looking where he was going. It would have been no more than bump and excuse me, but a janitor had just finished mopping the floor, and it was still wet. The orderly slipped and grabbed Terry's arm, but went down anyway. Terry helped him up, asked if he was all right, and the guy said he was. Ter was halfway down the hall before he saw his wrist was bleeding. One of the orderly's nails must have gotten him when he grabbed Terry, trying to stay on his feet. A nurse disinfected it and put on a Band-Aid, like Sarah said. And that's the whole story. Does it solve the case for you?"

"No," Ralph said. But it wasn't like the yellow bra strap. This was a connection—a confluence, to use Jeannie's word—he thought he could nail down, but he would need Yune Sablo's help. He stood up. "Thanks for your time, Marcy."

She favored him with a cold smile. "That's Mrs. Maitland to you."

"Understood. And Howard, thanks for setting this up." He extended his hand to the lawyer. For a moment it just hung there, but in the end, Howie shook it.

"I'll walk you out," Alec said.

"I think I can find my way."

"I'm sure you can, but since I walked you in, it makes a nice balance."

They crossed the living room and went down the short hall. Alec opened the door. Ralph stepped out, and was surprised when Alec stepped out after him.

"What was it about the cut?"

Ralph eyed him. "I don't know what you're talking about."

"I think you do. Your face changed."

"A little acid indigestion. I'm prone to it, and that was a tough meeting. Although not as tough as the way the girl looked at me. I felt like a bug on a slide."

Alec closed the door behind them. Ralph was two steps down, but because of his height, the two men were still almost eye to eye. "Going to tell you something," Alec said.

"All right." Ralph braced himself.

"That arrest was fucked. Fucked to the sky. I'm sure you know that now."

"I don't think I need another scolding tonight." Ralph started to turn away.

"I'm not done."

Ralph turned back, head lowered, feet slightly spread. It was a fighter's stance.

"I don't have any kids. Marie couldn't. But if I'd had a son your boy's age, and if I had solid proof that a homicidal sexual deviant had been important to him, someone he looked up to, I might have done the same thing, or worse. What I'm saying is that I understand why you lost perspective."

"All right," Ralph said. "It doesn't make things better, but thanks."

"If you change your mind about telling me what it was about the cut, give me a call. Maybe we're all on the same side here."

"Goodnight, Alec."

"Goodnight, Detective. Stay safe."

20

He was telling Jeannie how it went when his phone rang. It was Yune. "Can we talk tomorrow, Ralph? There was something weird in that barn where the kid found the clothes Maitland was wearing in the railway station. More than one thing, actually."

"Tell me now."

"No. I'm going home. I'm tired. And I need to think about this."

"Okay, tomorrow. Where?"

"Someplace quiet and out of the way. I can't afford to be seen talking to you. You're on administrative leave, and I'm off the case. Actually, there *is* no case. Not with Maitland dead."

"What's going to happen with the clothes?"

"They're going to Cap City for forensics examination. After that, they'll be turned over to the Flint County Sheriff's Department."

"Are you kidding? They should be with the rest of the Maitland evidence. Besides which, Dick Doolin can't blow his own nose without an instruction manual."

"That may be true, but Canning Township is county, not city, which makes it the sheriff's jurisdiction. I heard Chief Geller was sending a detective out, but just as a courtesy."

"Hoskins."

"Yeah, that was the name. He's not here yet, and by the time he makes it, everyone will be gone. Maybe he got lost."

More likely stopped somewhere for a few pops, Ralph thought.

Yune said, "Those clothes will end up in an evidence box at the sheriff's department, and they'll still be there when the twenty-second century dawns. No one gives a shit. The feeling is Maitland did it, Maitland's dead, let's move on."

"I'm not ready to do that," Ralph said, and smiled when Jeannie, sitting on the sofa, made fists and popped two thumbs up. "Are you?"

"Would I be talking to you if I was? Where should we meet tomorrow?"

"There's a little coffee shop near the train station in Dubrow. O'Malley's Irish Spoon, it's called. Can you find it?"

"No doubt."

"Ten o'clock?"

"Sounds good. If I have to roll on something, I'll call and reschedule."

"You have all the witness statements, right?"

"On my laptop."

"Make sure you bring it. All my stuff is at the station, and I'm not supposed to be there. Got a lot to tell you."

"Same here," Yune said. "We may crack this yet, Ralph, but I don't know if we'll like what we find. This is a pretty deep forest."

Actually, Ralph thought as he ended the call, *it's a cantaloupe. And the damn thing is full of maggots.*

21

Jack Hoskins stopped at Gentlemen, Please on his way to the Elfman property. He ordered a vodka-tonic, which he felt he deserved after being called back from his vacation early. He gulped it, then ordered another, which he sipped. There were two strippers on stage, both still fully dressed (which in Gentlemen meant they were wearing bras and panties), but humping at each other in a lazy way that gave Jack a moderate boner.

When he took out his wallet to pay, the bartender waved it away. "On the house."

"Thanks." Jack dropped a tip on the bar and left, feeling in a marginally better mood. As he got moving again, he took a roll of breath mints from the glovebox and crunched a couple. People said vodka was odorless, but that was bullshit.

The ranch road had been strung off with yellow police tape—county, not city. Hoskins got out, pulled up one of the stakes the tape was tied to, drove through, and replaced the stake. *Fucking pain in the ass*, he thought, and the ass-pain only deepened when he arrived at a cluster of ramshackle buildings—a barn and three sheds—to discover no one was there. He tried to call in, wanting to share his frustration with someone, even if it was only Sandy McGill, who he regarded as a prissy twat of the first order. All he got was static on the radio, and of course there was no cell service out here in South Jerkoff.

He grabbed his long-barreled flashlight and got out, mostly to stretch his legs; there was nothing to be done here. It was a fool's errand, and he was the fool. A hard wind was blowing, hot breath that would be a brushfire's best friend if one got started. There was a grove of cottonwoods clustered around an old water pump. Their leaves danced and rustled, their shadows racing across the ground in the moonlight.

There was more yellow tape stretched across the entrance to the barn where the clothes had been found. Bagged and on their way to Cap City by now, of course, but it was still creepy to think that Maitland had come here at some point after killing the kid.

In a way, Jack thought, *I'm retracing his path. Past the boat landing where he changed out of his bloody clothes, then to Gentlemen, Please. He went to Dubrow from the titty-bar, but then he must have circled back to . . . here.*

The open barn door was like a gaping mouth. Hoskins didn't want to go near it, not out here in the middle of nowhere and not on his own. Maitland was dead and there were no such things as ghosts, but he still didn't want to go near it. So he made himself do just that, step by slow step, until he could shine his light inside.

Someone was standing at the rear of the barn.

Jack uttered a soft cry, reached for his sidearm, and realized he wasn't wearing it. The Glock was in the small Gardall safe he kept in his truck. He dropped the flashlight. He bent and scooped it up, feeling the vodka surging around in his head, not enough to make him drunk, just enough to make him feel woozy and unsteady on his feet.

He shone the light back into the barn, and laughed. There was no man, just the hame of an old harness, nearly busted into two pieces.

Time to get out of here. Maybe stop at Gentlemen's for one more drink, then home and straight to b—

There was someone behind him, and this was no illusion. He could see the shadow, long and thin. And . . . was that breathing?

In a second, he's going to grab me. I need to drop and roll.

Only he couldn't. He was frozen. Why hadn't he turned around when he saw the scene was deserted? Why hadn't he gotten his gun out of the safe? Why had he ever gotten out of the truck in the first place? Jack suddenly understood that he was going to die at the end of a dirt road in Canning Township.

That was when he was touched. Caressed on the back of his neck by a hand as hot as a hot water bottle. He tried to scream and couldn't. His chest was locked up like the Glock in its safe. Now another hand would join the first and the choking would begin.

Only the hand pulled back. Not the fingers, though. They moved back and forth—lightly, just the tips—playing across his skin and leaving trails of heat.

Jack didn't know how long he stood there, unable to move. It might have been twenty seconds; it might have been two minutes. The wind blew, tousling his hair and caressing his neck like those fingers. The shadows of the cottonwoods schooled across the dirt and weeds like fleeing fish. The person—or the thing—stood behind him, its shadow long and thin. Touching and caressing.

Then both the fingertips and the shadow were gone.

Jack wheeled around, and this time the scream came out, long and loud, when the tail of his sportcoat belled out behind him in the wind and made a flapping sound. He stared at—

Nothing.

Just a few abandoned buildings and an acre or so of dirt.

No one was there. No one had ever been there. No one in the barn; just a busted hame. No fingers on the back of his sweaty neck; just the wind. He returned to his truck in big strides, looking back over his shoulder once, twice, three times. He got in, cringing when a wind-driven shadow raced across the rearview mirror, and started the engine. He drove back down the ranch road at fifty miles an hour, past the old graveyard and the abandoned ranchhouse, not pausing at the yellow tape this time but simply driving through it. He swerved onto Highway 79, tires squalling, and headed back toward FC. By the time he passed the city limits, he had convinced himself nothing had happened out there at that abandoned barn. The throbbing at the nape of his neck also meant nothing.

Nothing at all.

YELLOW

July 21st–July 22nd

1

At ten o'clock on Saturday morning, O'Malley's Irish Spoon was as close to deserted as it ever got. Two geezers sat near the front with mugs of coffee beside them and a chessboard between them. The only waitress was staring, transfixed, at a small TV over the counter, where an infomercial was playing. The item on sale appeared to be some sort of golf club.

Yunel Sablo was sitting at a table toward the rear, dressed in faded jeans and a tee-shirt tight enough to show off his admirable musculature (Ralph had not had admirable musculature since 2007 or so). He was also watching the TV, but when he saw Ralph, he raised a hand and beckoned.

As he sat down, Yune said: "I don't know why the waitress is so interested in that particular club."

"Women don't golf? What kind of male chauvinist world are you living in, amigo?"

"I know women golf, but that particular club is hollow. The idea is if you get caught short on the fourteenth hole, you can piss in it. There's even a little apron included that you can flip over your junk. Thing like that wouldn't work for a woman."

The waitress came over to take their order. Ralph asked for scrambled eggs and rye toast, looking at the menu rather than her, lest he burst into laughter. That was one urge he hadn't expected to struggle against this morning, and a small, strained giggle escaped him, anyway. It was the thought of the apron that did it.

The waitress didn't need to be a mind reader. "Yeah, it might have its funny side," she said. "Unless, that is, your husband's a golf nut with a prostate the size of a grapefruit and you don't know what to get him for his birthday."

Ralph met Yune's eyes, and that tipped them both over. They burst into hearty roars of hilarity that made the chess players look around disapprovingly.

"You going to order anything, honey," the waitress asked Yune, "or just drink coffee and laugh about the Comfort Nine Iron?"

Yune ordered huevos rancheros. When she was gone, he said, "It's a strange world, *ese*, full of strange things. Don't you think so?"

"Given what we're here to talk about, I'd have to agree. What was strange out there in Canning Township?"

"Plenty."

Yune had a leather shoulder-bag, the sort of thing Ralph had heard Jack Hoskins refer to (slightingly) as a man-purse. From it he took an iPad Mini in a battered case that had seen a lot of hard traveling. Ralph had noticed more and more cops carrying these gadgets, and guessed that by 2020, 2025 at the latest, they might entirely replace the traditional cop's notebook. Well, the world moved on. You either moved with it, or got left behind. On the whole, he would rather have one of those for his birthday than a Comfort Nine Iron.

Yune tapped a couple of buttons and brought up his notes. "Kid named Douglas Elfman found the discarded clothes late yesterday afternoon. Recognized the horse's head belt buckle from a news report. Called his dad, who got in touch with the SP right away. I got there with the crime van around quarter to six. The jeans, who knows, bluejeans just about grow on trees, but I recognized the buckle right away. Look for yourself."

He tapped the screen again, and a close-up of the buckle filled the screen. Ralph had no doubt it was the same one that Terry had been wearing in the security cam footage from the Vogel Transportation Center in Dubrow.

Talking to himself as well as to Yune, Ralph said, "Okay, one more link in the chain. He ditches the van behind Shorty's Pub. Takes the Subaru. Ditches that near the Iron Bridge, puts on fresh clothes—"

"501 jeans, Jockey underpants, white athletic socks, and a pretty damn expensive pair of sneakers. Plus the belt with the fancy buckle."

"Uh-huh. Once he's dressed in clothes with no blood on them, he takes a cab from Gentlemen, Please to Dubrow. Only when he gets to the station, he doesn't take the train. Why not?"

"Maybe he was trying to lay a false trail, in which case doubling back was always part of the plan. Or . . . I have a crazy idea. Want to hear?"

"Sure," Ralph said.

"I think Maitland *meant* to run. Meant to take that train to Dallas–Fort Worth, then keep on going. Maybe to Mexico, maybe to California. Why would he want to stay in Flint City after killing the Peterson boy, when he knew people had seen him? Only . . ."

"Only what?"

"Only he couldn't bear to leave with that big game on the line. He wanted to coach his kids to one more win. Get them to the finals."

"That really is crazy."

"Crazier than killing the boy in the first place?"

Yune had him there, but Ralph was spared the need to make a reply when their food came. As soon as the waitress left, Ralph said: "Fingerprints on the buckle?"

Yune swiped his Mini and showed Ralph another close-up of the horse's head. In this shot, the buckle's silver shine had been dulled by white fingerprint powder. Ralph could see an overlay of prints, like footprints in one of those old learn-to-dance diagrams.

"The Forensics Unit had Maitland's dabs in their computer," Yune said, "and the program matched them up right away. But here's the first weird thing, Ralph. The lines and whorls in the buckle prints are faint, and entirely broken up in a few places. Enough for a match that would stand up in court, but the tech who did the work—and he's done thousands of these—said they were like the prints of an old person. Like eighty or even ninety. I asked if it could have been because Maitland was moving fast, wanting to change to yet another set of clothes and just get the hell out of there. The tech said it was possible, but I could tell from his face that it didn't really ring his bell."

"Huh," Ralph said, and dug into his scrambled eggs. His appetite, like his sudden burst of laughter over the dual-purpose golf club, was a welcome surprise. "That *is* weird, but probably not substantive."

And just how long, he wondered, was he going to continue dismissing the anomalies that kept popping up in this business by calling them non-substantive?

"There was another set," Yune said. "They were also blurred—too blurred for the computer tech to even bother sending them out to the FBI's national database—but he had all the stray prints from the van, and those other prints on the buckle . . . see what you think."

He passed the iPad to Ralph. Here were two sets of prints, one labeled VAN UNKNOWN SUB and the other BELT BUCKLE UNKNOWN SUB. They did look alike, but only sort of. No way would they stand up in court as proof of anything, especially if a bulldog defense attorney like Howie Gold challenged them. Ralph was not in court, however, and he thought the same unsub had made them both, because it fit with what he'd learned from Marcy Maitland the night before. Not a perfect fit, no, but close enough for a detective on administrative leave who didn't have to run everything by his superiors . . . or by a district attorney hellbent for election.

THE OUTSIDER

While Yune ate his huevos rancheros, Ralph told him about his meeting with Marcy, holding back one thing for later.

"It's all about the van," he finished. "Forensics may find a few prints from the kid who originally stole it—"

"Already did. We had Merlin Cassidy's prints from the El Paso police. Computer guy matched them to some of the stray prints in the van—mostly on the toolbox, which Cassidy must have opened to see if there was anything valuable inside. They're clear, and they're not these." He swiped back to the blurry UNSUB prints, labeled VAN and BELT BUCKLE.

Ralph leaned forward, pushing his plate aside. "You see how it dovetails, don't you? We know it wasn't Terry who stole the van in Dayton, because the Maitlands flew home. But if the blurry prints from the van and those from the buckle really *are* the same . . ."

"You think he had an accomplice, after all. One who drove the van from Dayton to Flint City."

"Must have," Ralph said. "No other way to explain it."

"One who looked just like him?"

"Back to that," Ralph said, and sighed.

"And both sets of prints were on the buckle," Yune pushed on. "Meaning Maitland and his double wore the same belt, maybe the whole set of clothes. Well, they'd fit, wouldn't they? Twin brothers, separated at birth. Except the records say Terry Maitland was an only child."

"What else have you got? Anything?"

"Yes. We have arrived at the really weird shit." He brought his chair around and sat next to Ralph. The picture now on his iPad showed a close-up of the jeans, socks, underpants, and sneakers, all in an untidy pile, next to a plastic evidence-marker with a 1 on it. "See the stains?"

"Yes. What *is* that crap?"

"I don't know," Yune said. "And the forensics guys don't, either, but one of them said it looked like jizz, and I sort of agree with that. You can't see it in the picture very well, but—"

"*Semen?* Are you kidding?"

The waitress came back. Ralph turned the iPad screen side down.

"Either of you gents want a refill on the coffee?"

They both took one. When she left, Ralph went back to the photo of the clothes, spreading his fingers on the screen to enlarge the image.

"Yune, it's on the crotch of the jeans, all down both legs, on the cuffs . . ."

"Also on the underpants and socks," Yune said. "Not to mention the sneakers, both on em and in em, dried to a nice crack-glaze, like on pottery. Might be enough of the stuff, whatever it is, to fill a hollow nine iron."

Ralph didn't laugh. "It can't be semen. Even John Holmes in his prime—"

"I know. And semen doesn't do this."

He swiped the screen. The new picture was a wide shot of the barn floor. Another evidence tab, this one marked 2, had been placed next to a pile of loose hay. At least Ralph thought it was hay. On the far left side of the photo, evidence tab 3 had been placed atop a softly collapsing bale that looked like it had been there for a long, long time. Much of it was black. The side of the bale was also black, as if some corrosive goo had run down it to the floor.

"Is it the same stuff?" Ralph asked. "You're sure?"

"Ninety per cent. And there's more in the loft. If it's semen, that would be a nocturnal emission worthy of *The Guinness Book of Records.*"

"Can't be," Ralph said, low. "It's something else. For one thing, semen wouldn't turn hay black. It makes no sense."

"Not to me, either, but of course I am just the son of a poor Mexican farming family."

"Forensics is analyzing it, though."

Yune nodded. "As we speak."

"And you'll let me know."

"Yes. You see what I meant when I said this just keeps getting weirder and weirder."

"Jeannie called it inexplicable." Ralph cleared his throat. "She actually used the word *supernatural*."

"My Gabriela has suggested the same," Yune said. "Maybe it's a chick thing. Or a Mexican thing."

Ralph raised his eyebrows.

"*Sí, señor*," Yune said, and laughed. "My wife's mother died young, and she grew up at her *abuela*'s knee. The old lady stuffed her full of legends. When I was talking this mess over with her, Gaby told me one about the Mexican boogeyman. He was supposedly a dude dying of tuberculosis, see, and this old wise man who lived in the desert, an *ermitaño*, told him he could be cured by drinking the blood of children and rubbing their fat on his chest and privates. So that's what this boogeyman did, and now he lives forever. Supposedly he only takes children who misbehave. He pops them in a big black bag he carries. Gaby told me that when she was a little girl, maybe seven, she had a screaming fit one time when the doctor came to the house for her brother, who had scarlet fever."

"Because the doctor had a black bag."

Yune nodded. "What was that boogeyman's name? It's on the tip of my tongue, but I can't pick it off. Don't you hate that?"

"So is that what you think we've got here? The boogeyman?"

"Nope. I may be the son of a poor Mexican farming family, *ese*, or possibly the son of an Amarillo car dealer, but either way, I ain't *atontado*. A man killed Frank Peterson, as mortal as you and me, and that man was almost certainly Terry Maitland. If we could figure out what happened, everything would fall into place and I could go back to sleeping through the night. Because this bugs the shit out of me." He looked at his watch. "Gotta go. Promised my wife I'd take her to a craft fair in Cap City. Any more questions? You ought to have at least one, because yet one more weird thing is staring you right in the face."

"Were there vehicle tracks in the barn?"

"That's not what I was thinking of, but as a matter of fact, there were. Not useful ones, though—you can see the impressions, and there's a little oil, but no tread marks good enough for comparison. My guess is they were made by the van Maitland used to abduct the kid. They weren't close enough together to have been made by the Subaru."

"Uh-huh. Listen, you've got all the witness interviews on your magic gadget, right? Before you split, find the one I did with Claude Bolton. He's a bouncer at Gentlemen, Please. Although he took issue with that word, as I remember."

Yune brought up one file, shook his head, brought up another, and handed the iPad to Ralph. "Scroll down."

Ralph did so, went past what he wanted, and at last centered on it. "Here it is. Bolton said, 'I remember one other thing, no big deal but kind of spooky if he really was the one who killed that kid.' Bolton said the guy cut him. When I asked what he meant, Bolton said he thanked Maitland for working with his friend's nephews, then shook with him. When he did, Maitland's pinky fingernail grazed the back of Bolton's hand. Made a little cut. Bolton said it reminded him of his drug days, because some of the MCs he ran with used to grow out their pinky nails to scoop coke with. Apparently it was a fashion statement."

"And this is important because?" Yune looked at his watch again, rather ostentatiously.

"Probably it's not. Probably it's . . ."

But he wasn't going to say *non-substantive* again. He liked the word less every time it came out of his mouth.

"Probably no big deal, but it's what my wife calls a confluence. Terry got a similar cut when he was visiting his father in a dementia ward in Dayton." Ralph quickly related the story about how the orderly had slipped and grabbed for Terry, cutting him in the process.

Yune thought about it, then shrugged. "I think that one's pure coincidence, *ese*. And I really have to go, if I don't want to incur the Wrath of Gabriela, but there's still that thing you're missing, and I'm not talking about tire tracks. Your pal Bolton even mentions it. Scroll back up and you'll find it."

But Ralph didn't need to. It had been right in front of him. "Pants, underpants, socks, and sneakers . . . but no shirt."

"Correct," Yune said. "Either it was his favorite, or he didn't have another one to change into when he left the barn."

2

Halfway back to Flint City, Ralph finally realized what had been bugging him about the bra strap.

He pulled into the two-acre lot of a Byron's Liquor Warehouse, and hit speed-dial. His call went to Yune's voicemail. Ralph broke the connection without leaving a message. Yune had already gone above and beyond; let him have his weekend. And now that he had time to give it a little thought, Ralph decided this was a confluence he didn't want to share with anyone, except maybe his wife.

The bra strap hadn't been the only bright yellow thing he had seen during those moments of hyper-vigilance before Terry was shot; it was just his brain's stand-in for something that had been part of the larger gallery of grotesques, and overshadowed by Ollie Peterson, who had drawn the old revolver from his newspaper bag only seconds later. No wonder it had gotten lost.

The man with the horrible burns on his face and the tattoos on his hands had been wearing a yellow bandanna on his head, probably to cover more scars. But *had* it been a bandanna? Couldn't it have been something else? The missing shirt, for instance? The one Terry had been wearing in the train station?

I'm reaching, he thought, and maybe he was . . . except his subconscious (those thoughts behind his thoughts) had been yelling at him about it all along.

He closed his eyes and tried to summon up exactly what he'd seen in those last few seconds of Terry's life. The blond anchor's unlovely sneer as she looked at the blood on her fingers. The hypodermic sign reading MAITLAND TAKE YOUR MEDICINE. The boy with the bad lip. The woman leaning forward to give Marcy the finger. And the burned man who'd looked as if God had taken a giant eraser to most of his features, leaving only lumps, raw pink skin, and holes where a nose had been before the fire had put tattoos on his face far fiercer than those on his hands. And what Ralph saw in this moment of recall was not a bandanna on that man's head but something far bigger, something that hung all the way down to his shoulders like a headdress.

Yes, that something could have been a shirt . . . but even if it was, did that mean it was *the* shirt? The one Terry had been wearing in the security footage? Was there a way to find out?

He thought there was, but he needed to enlist Jeannie, who was far more computer-savvy than he was. Also, the time might have come to stop thinking of Howard Gold and Alec Pelley as enemies. *Maybe we're all on the same side here*, Pelley had said last night as he stood on the Maitland stoop, and maybe that was true. Or could be.

Ralph put his car in gear and headed home, pushing the speed limit all the way.

3

Ralph and his wife sat at the kitchen table with Jeannie's laptop in front of them. There were four major TV stations in Cap City, one for each of the networks, plus Channel 81, the public access outlet that ran local news, city council meetings, and various community affairs (such as the Harlan Coben speech where Terry had appeared as an unlikely guest star). All five had been at the courthouse for Terry's arraignment, all five had filmed the shooting, and all had at least some footage of the crowd. Once the gunfire erupted, all the cameras turned to Terry, of course—Terry bleeding down the side of his face and pushing his wife from the line of fire, then collapsing into the street when the killshot struck him. The CBS footage went entirely blank before that happened, because that was the camera Ralph's bullet had struck, shattering it and blinding its operator in one eye.

After they'd looked at each clip twice, Jeannie turned to him, her lips pressed tightly together. She didn't say anything. She didn't have to.

"Run the Channel 81 stuff again," Ralph said. "Their camera was every whichway once the shooting started, but they got the best crowd stuff before."

"Ralph." She touched his arm. "Are you all ri—"

"Fine, I'm fine." He wasn't. He felt as if the world were tilting, and he might soon slide right off the edge. "Run it again, please. And mute it. The reporter's running commentary is distracting."

She did as he asked, and they watched together. Waving signs. People yelling soundlessly, their mouths opening and closing like fish out of water. At one point the camera panned rapidly across and down, not soon enough to show the man who had spit in Terry's face, but in time to show Ralph tripping the troublemaker, making it look like an unprovoked attack. He watched as Terry helped the spitter to his feet (*like something out of the fucking Bible*, Ralph remembered thinking), and then the camera returned to the crowd. He saw the two bailiffs—one plump, the other lean—doing their best to keep the steps clear. He saw the blond anchor from Channel 7 getting to her feet, still looking with disbelief at her bloody fingers. He saw Ollie Peterson with his newspaper sack and a few clumps of red hair sticking out from beneath his watch cap, still a few seconds from being the star of the show. He saw the boy with the cleft lip, the Channel 81 cameraman pausing his shot long enough to register Frank Peterson's face on the boy's tee-shirt before panning further—

"Stop," he said. "Freeze it, freeze it right there."

Jeannie did so, and they looked at the picture—slightly blurred from the cameraman's rapid movement as he tried to get a little bit of everything.

Ralph tapped the screen. "See this guy waving the cowboy hat?"

"Sure."

"The burned man was standing right next to him."

"All right," she said . . . but in a strange, nervous tone of voice Ralph did not remember ever hearing from her before.

"I swear to you he was. I saw him, it was like I was tripping on LSD or mescaline or something, and I saw *everything*. Run the other ones again. This is the best one of the crowd, but the FOX affiliate wasn't too bad, and—"

"No." She hit the power button and closed the laptop. "The man you saw isn't in any of these, Ralph. You know it as well as I do."

"Do you think I'm crazy? Is that it? Do you think I'm having a . . . you know . . ."

"A breakdown?" Her hand was back on his arm again, now squeezing gently. "Of course not. If you say you saw him, you saw him. If you think he was wearing that shirt as a kind of sun protection, or do-rag, or I don't know what, then he probably was. You've had a bad month, probably the worst month of your life, but I trust your powers of observation. It's just that . . . you must see now . . ."

She trailed off. He waited. At last she pushed ahead.

"There is something very wrong with this, and the more you

find, the wronger it gets. It scares me. That story Yune told you scares me. It's basically a vampire story, isn't it? I read *Dracula* in high school, and one thing I remember about it is vampires don't cast reflections in mirrors. And a thing that can't cast a reflection probably wouldn't show up in TV news footage."

"That's nuts. There's no such things as ghosts, or witches, or vam—"

She slapped her open hand down on the table, a flat pistol-shot sound that made him jump. Her eyes were furious, crackling. "Wake up, Ralph! Wake up to what's right in front of you! *Terry Maitland was in two places at the same time!* If you stop trying to find a way to explain that away and just accept it—"

"I can't accept it, honey. It goes against everything I've believed my whole life. If I let something like that in, I really would go crazy."

"The hell you would. You're stronger than that. But you don't have to even consider the idea, that's what I'm trying to tell you. Terry's dead. You can let it go."

"If I do that, and it really wasn't Terry who killed Frankie Peterson? Where does that leave Marcy? Where does it leave her girls?"

Jeannie got up, walked to the window over the sink, and looked out at the backyard. Her hands were clenched into fists. "Derek called again. He still wants to come home."

"What did you tell him?"

"To stick it out until the season ends in the middle of next month. Even though I'd love to have him home. I finally talked him into it, and do you know why?" She turned back. "Because I don't want him in this town while you're still digging around in this mess. Because when it gets dark tonight, I'm going to be frightened. Suppose it really *is* some kind of supernatural creature, Ralph? And what if it finds out you're looking for it?"

Ralph took her in his arms. He could feel her trembling. He thought, *Part of her actually believes this.*

"Yune told me that story, but Yune believes the killer is a natural man. So do I."

With her face against his chest, she said, "Then why isn't the man with the burned face in any of the footage?"

"I don't know."

"I care about Marcy, of course I do." She looked up, and he saw she was crying. "And I care about her girls. I care about *Terry*, for that matter . . . and the Petersons . . . but I care more about you and Derek. You guys are all I have. Can't you let this go now? Finish your leave, see the shrink, and turn the page?"

"I don't know," he said, when in fact he did know. He just didn't want to say so to Jeannie while she was in her current strange state. He couldn't turn the page.

Not yet.

4

That night he sat at the picnic table in the backyard, smoking a Tiparillo and looking up at the sky. There were no stars, but he could still make out the moon behind the clouds that were moving in. The truth was often like that, he thought—a bleary circle of light behind clouds. Sometimes it broke through; sometimes the clouds thickened, and the light disappeared completely.

One thing was sure: when night fell, the skinny, tubercular man from Yune Sablo's fairy tale became more plausible. Not *believable*, Ralph could no more believe in such a creature than he could in Santa Claus, but he could picture him: a darker-skinned version of Slender Man, that bugaboo of pubescent American girls. He'd be tall and grave in his black suit, his face like a lamp, and carrying a bag big enough to hold a small child with his or her knees folded against his or her chest. According to Yune, the Mexican boogeyman prolonged his life by drinking the blood of children and rubbing their fat on his body . . . and while that wasn't exactly what had happened to the Peterson boy, it was in the vicinity. Might it be possible that the killer—maybe Maitland, maybe the unsub of the blurred fingerprints—actually thought he *was* a vampire, or some other supernatural creature? Hadn't Jeffrey Dahmer believed he was creating zombies when he killed all those homeless men?

None of that addresses the question of why the burned man isn't in the news footage.

Jeannie called to him. "Come inside, Ralph. It's going to rain. You can smoke that smelly thing in the kitchen, if you have to have it."

That isn't why you want me to come inside, Ralph thought. *You want me to come in because part of you can't help thinking that Yune's sack-man is lurking out here, just beyond the reach of the yard light.*

Ridiculous, of course, but he could sympathize with her unease. He felt it himself. What had Jeannie said? *The more you find, the wronger it gets.*

Ralph came inside, doused his Tiparillo under the sink tap, then grabbed his phone off the charging stand. When Howie answered, Ralph said, "Can you and Mr. Pelley come over here tomorrow? I have a bunch of stuff to tell you, and some of it's pretty unbelievable. Come to lunch. I'll go out to Rudy's and buy some sandwiches."

Howie agreed at once. Ralph broke the connection and saw Jeannie in the doorway, looking at him with her arms folded over her chest. "Can't let it go?"

"No, honey. I can't. I'm sorry."

She sighed. "Will you be careful?"

"I'll tread with utmost caution."

"You better, or I'll tread on you *without* caution. And no need to get sandwiches from Rudy's. I'll make something."

5

Sunday was rainy, so they convened at the Andersons' seldom-used dining room table: Ralph, Jeannie, Howie, and Alec. Yune Sablo, at home in Cap City, joined them on Howie Gold's laptop, via Skype.

Ralph began by recapping the things all of them knew, then turned it over to Yune, who told Howie and Alec about what they had found in the Elfman barn. When he was finished, Howie said, "None of this makes sense. In fact, it's about four time-zones from making sense."

"This person was sleeping out there in the loft of a deserted barn?" Alec asked Yune. "Hiding out? That's what you're thinking?"

"It's the working assumption," Yune said.

"If so, it couldn't have been Terry," Howie said. "He was in town all day Saturday. He took the girls to the municipal pool that morning, and he was at Estelle Barga Park all that afternoon, getting the field ready—as the home field coach, doing that was his responsibility. There were plenty of witnesses in both places."

"And from Saturday til Monday," Alec put in, "he was jugged in county jail. As you well know, Ralph."

"There are all kinds of witnesses to Terry's whereabouts almost every step of the way," Ralph agreed. "That's always been the root of the problem, but let it go for a minute. I want to show you something. Yune's already seen it; he reviewed the footage this morning. But I asked him something *before* he watched, and now I want to ask you. Did either of you notice a badly disfigured man at the courthouse? He was wearing something on his head, but I'm not going to say what it was just now. Either of you?"

Howie said he hadn't. All his attention had been fixed on his client and his client's wife. Alec Pelley, however, was a different matter.

"Yeah, I saw him. Looked like he got burned in a fire. And what he was wearing on his head . . ." He stopped, eyes widening.

"Go on," Yune said from his living room in Cap City. "Let it out, amigo. You'll feel better."

Alec was rubbing his temples, as if he had a headache. "At the time I thought it was a bandanna or a kerchief. You know, because his hair got burned off in the fire and maybe couldn't grow back because of the scarring and he wanted to keep the sun off his skull. Only it could have been a shirt. The one missing from the barn, is that what you're thinking? The one Terry was wearing in the security footage from the train station?"

"You win the Kewpie doll," Yune said.

Howie was frowning at Ralph. "You're still trying to hang this on Terry?"

Jeannie spoke up for the first time. "He's just trying to get to the truth . . . which I'm not sure is the world's best idea, actually."

"Watch this, Alec," Ralph said. "And point out the burned man."

Ralph ran the Channel 81 footage, then the FOX footage, and then, at Alec's request (he was now leaning so close to Jeannie's laptop that his nose was nearly touching the screen), the Channel 81 footage again. At last he sat back. "He's not there. Which is impossible."

Yune said, "He was standing next to the guy waving his cowboy hat, right?"

"I think so," Alec said. "Next to him and higher up from the blond reporter who got bonked on the noggin with a sign. I see both the reporter and the sign-waver . . . but I don't see him. How can that be?"

None of them answered.

Howie said, "Let's go back to the fingerprints for a minute. How many different sets in the van, Yune?"

"Forensics thinks as many as half a dozen."

Howie groaned.

"Take it easy. We've eliminated at least four of those: the farmer in New York who owned the van, the farmer's oldest son who sometimes drove it, the kid who stole it, and Terry Maitland. That leaves one clear set we haven't identified—could have been one of the farmer's friends or one of his younger kids, playing around inside—and those blurry ones."

"The same blurry ones you found on the belt buckle."

"Probably, but we can't be sure. There are a few visible lines and whorls in those, but nothing like the clear points of identity you'd need to get them admitted into evidence when a case goes to court."

"Uh-huh, okay, understood. So let me ask all three of you gentlemen something. Isn't it possible that a man who had been badly burned—hands as well as face—could leave prints like that? Ones blurred to unrecognizability?"

"Yes." Yune and Alec said it in unison, their voices only overlapping because of the computer's brief transmission lag.

"The problem with that," Ralph said, "is the burned man at the courthouse had tattoos on his hands. If his fingertips burned off, wouldn't the tats have burned off, too?"

Howie shook his head. "Not necessarily. If I'm on fire, maybe I use my hands to try and put myself out, but I don't do it with the backs, do I?" He began slapping at his considerable chest to demonstrate. "I do it with my palms."

There was a moment of silence. Then, in a low, almost inaudible voice, Alec Pelley said, "That burned guy was there. I'd swear to it on a stack of Bibles."

Ralph said, "Presumably the State Police Forensics Unit will analyze the stuff from the barn that turned the hay black, but is there anything we can do in the meantime? I'm open to suggestions."

"Backtrack to Dayton," Alec said. "We know Maitland was there, and we know the van was there, too. At least some of the answers may also be there. I can't fly up myself, too many irons currently in the fire, but I know somebody good. Let me make a call and see if he's available."

That was where they left it.

6

Ten-year-old Grace Maitland had slept poorly ever since her father's murder, and what sleep she had managed was haunted by nightmares. That Sunday afternoon all her weariness came down on her like a soft weight. While her mother and sister were making a cake in the kitchen, Grace crept upstairs and lay on her bed. Although the day was rainy, there was plenty of light, which was good. The dark scared her now. Downstairs she could hear Mom and Sarah talking. That was also good. Grace closed her eyes, and although it only felt like a moment or two before she opened them again, it must have been hours, because the rain was coming down harder now and the light had gone gray. Her room was full of shadows.

A man was sitting on her bed and looking at her. He was wearing jeans and a green tee-shirt. There were tattoos on his hands and crawling up his arms. There were snakes, and a cross, and a dagger, and a skull. His face no longer looked like it had been made out of Play-Doh by an untalented child, but she recognized him, just the same. It was the man who had been outside Sarah's window. At least now he didn't have straws for eyes. Now he had her father's eyes. Grace would have known those eyes anywhere. She wondered if this was happening, or if it was a dream. If so, it was better than the nightmares. A little, anyway.

"Daddy?"

"Sure," said the man. His green tee-shirt changed to her father's Golden Dragons game shirt, and so she knew it was a dream, after all. Next, that shirt turned into a white smocky thing, then back into the green tee-shirt. "I love you, Gracie."

"That doesn't sound like him," Grace said. "You're making him up."

The man leaned close to her. Grace shrank back, eyes fixed on her father's eyes. They were better than the I-love-you voice, but this was still not him.

"I want you to go," she said.

"I'm sure you do, and people in hell want icewater. Are you sad, Grace? Do you miss your daddy?"

"*Yes!*" Grace began to cry. "I want you to *go*! Those aren't my daddy's real eyes, you're just *pretending*!"

"Don't expect any sympathy from me," the man said. "I think it's good that you're sad. I hope you'll be sad for a long time, and cry. Wah-wah-*wah*, just like a baby."

"Please go!"

"Baby want her bottle? Baby pee in her didies, get all *wet*? Baby go wah-wah-wah?"

"*Stop it!*"

He sat back. "I will if you do one thing for me. Will you do something for me, Grace?"

"What is it?"

He told her, and then Sarah was shaking her and telling her to come down and have some cake, so it had just been a dream after all, a bad dream, and she didn't have to do *anything*, but if she did, that dream might never come back.

She made herself eat some cake, although she really didn't want any, and when Mom and Sarah were sitting on the couch and watching some dippy movie, Grace said she didn't like love-movies and was going upstairs to play Angry Birds. Only she didn't. She went into her parents' bedroom (just her mom's now, and how sad that was) and took her mother's cell phone off the dresser. The policeman wasn't in the cell's contact list, but Mr. Gold was. She called him, holding the phone in both hands so it wouldn't shake. She prayed he would answer, and he did.

"Marcy? What's up?"

"No, it's Grace. I'm using my mom's phone."

"Why, hello, Grace. It's nice to hear from you. Why are you calling?"

"Because I didn't know how to call the detective. The one who arrested my father."

"Why do you—"

"I have a message for him. A man gave it to me. I know it was probably just a dream, but I'm playing it safe. I'll tell you and you can tell the detective."

"What man, Grace? Who gave you the message?"

"The first time I saw him, he had straws for eyes. He says he won't come back anymore if I give Detective Anderson the message. He tried to make me believe he had my daddy's eyes, but he didn't, not really. His face is better now, but he's still scary. I don't want him to come back, even if it's only a dream, so will you tell Detective Anderson?"

Mom was in the doorway now, silently watching, and Grace thought she would probably get in trouble, but she didn't care.

"What should I tell him, Grace?"

"To stop. If he doesn't want something bad to happen, tell him he has to stop."

7

Grace and Sarah sat in the living room, on the couch. Marcy was between them, with an arm around each. Howie Gold sat in the easy chair that had been Terry's until the world turned upside down. A hassock went with it. Ralph Anderson drew it in front of the couch and sat on it, his legs so long that his knees almost framed his face. He supposed he looked comical, and if that set Grace Maitland a bit at ease, that was all to the good.

"That must have been a scary dream, Grace. Are you sure it *was* a dream?"

"Of course it was," Marcy said. Her face was tight and pale. "There was no man in this house. There was no way he could have gotten upstairs without us seeing him."

"Or heard him, at least," Sarah put in, but she sounded timid. Afraid. "Our stairs creak like mad."

"You're here for one reason, to ease my daughter's mind," Marcy said. "Would you please do that?"

Ralph said, "Whatever it was, you know there's no man here now, don't you, Grace?"

"Yes." She seemed sure of this. "He's gone. He said he would go if I gave you the message. I don't think he will come back anymore, whether he was a dream or not."

Sarah sighed dramatically and said, "Isn't *that* a relief."

"Hush, munchkin," Marcy said.

Ralph pulled out his notebook. "Tell me what he looked like. This man in your dream. Because I'm a detective, and now I'm sure that's what it was."

Although Marcy Maitland didn't like him and probably never would, her eyes thanked him for this much, at least.

"Better," Grace said. "He looked better. His Play-Doh face was gone."

"That's what he looked like before," Sarah told Ralph. "*She* said."

Marcy said, "Sarah, go into the kitchen with Mr. Gold and get everybody a piece of cake, would you do that?"

Sarah looked at Ralph. "Cake even for him? Do we like him now?"

"Cake for everyone," Marcy said, neatly dodging the question. "It's called hospitality. Go on, now."

Sarah got off the couch and crossed the room to Howie. "I'm getting kicked out."

"Couldn't happen to a nicer person," Howie said. "I will join you in purdah."

"In what?"

"Never mind, kiddo." They went out to the kitchen together.

"Make this brief, please," Marcy said to Ralph. "You're only here because Howie said it was important. That it might have something to do with . . . you know."

Ralph nodded without taking his eyes from Grace. "This man who had the Play-Doh face the first time he showed up . . ."

"And straws for eyes," Grace said. "They stuck out, like in a cartoon, and the black circles people have in their eyes were holes."

"Uh-huh." In his notebook, Ralph wrote, *Straws for eyes?* "When you say his face looked like Play-Doh, could it have been because he was burned?"

She thought about it. "No. More like he wasn't *done*. Not . . . you know . . ."

"Not finished?" Marcy asked.

Grace nodded, and put her thumb in her mouth. Ralph thought, *This ten-year-old thumb sucker with the wounded face . . . she's mine.* True, and the seeming clarity of the evidence upon which he had acted would never change that.

"What did he look like today, Grace? The man in your dream."

"He had short black hair that was sticking up, like a porcupine, and a little beard around his mouth. He had my daddy's eyes, but they weren't really his eyes. He had tattoos on his hands and all up his arms. Some were snakes. At first his shirt was green, then it turned to my daddy's baseball shirt with the golden dragon on it, then it turned into white, like what Mrs. Gerson wears when she does my mom's hair."

Ralph glanced at Marcy, who said, "I think she means a smock top."

"Yes," Grace said. "That. But then it turned back into the green shirt, so I know it was a dream. Only . . ." Her mouth trembled, and her eyes filled with tears that spilled down her flushed cheeks. "Only he said mean things. He said he was glad I was sad. He called me a baby."

She turned her face against her mother's breasts and wept. Marcy looked at Ralph over the top of her head, for a moment not angry at him but only frightened for her daughter. *She knows it was more than a dream*, Ralph thought. *She sees it means something to me.*

When the girl's crying eased, Ralph said, "This is all good, Grace. Thank you for telling me about your dream. All that's over now, okay?"

"Yes," she said in a tear-hoarsened voice. "He's gone. I did what he said, and he's gone."

"We'll have our cake in here," Marcy said. "Go help your sister with the plates."

Grace ran to do it. When they were alone, Marcy said, "It's been hard on both of them, especially Grace. I'd say that's all this is, except Howie doesn't think so, and I don't think you do, either. Do you?"

"Mrs. Maitland . . . Marcy . . . I don't know what to think. Have you checked Grace's room?"

"Of course. As soon as she told me why she called Howie."

"No sign of an intruder?"

"No. The window was shut, the screen was in place, and what Sarah said about the stairs is true. This is an old house, and there's a creak in every step."

"What about her bed? Grace said the man was sitting there."

Marcy gave a distracted laugh. "Who would know, the way she tosses and turns since . . ." She put a hand to her face. "This is just so awful."

He got up and went to the couch, only meaning to comfort, but she stiffened and drew away. "Please don't sit down. And don't touch me. You're here on sufferance, Detective. So just maybe my youngest will sleep tonight without screaming the house down."

Ralph was saved a reply when Howie and the Maitland girls came back in, Grace carefully carrying a plate in each hand. Marcy wiped her eyes, the gesture almost too fast to see, and gave Howie and her daughters a brilliant smile. "Hooray for cake!" she said.

Ralph took his slice and said thank you. He was thinking that he had told Jeannie everything about this fucked-up nightmare of a case, but he wasn't going to tell her about this little girl's dream. No, not this.

8

Alec Pelley thought he had the number he wanted in his contacts, but when he made the call, he got an announcement saying the number had been disconnected. He found his old black address book (once a faithful companion that had gone with him everywhere, in this computer age relegated to a desk drawer, and one of the lower ones, at that) and tried a different number.

"Finders Keepers," said the voice on the other end. Believing that he'd reached an answering machine—a reasonable assumption, considering it was Sunday night—Alec waited for the announcement of office hours, followed by a menu of choices that could be accessed by punching various extensions, and at last the invitation to leave a message after the beep. Instead, sounding a bit querulous, the voice said, "Well? Is anyone there?"

Alec realized that was a voice he knew, although he couldn't place the name. How long had it been since he'd spoken to the owner of that voice? Two years? Three?

"I'm hanging up n—"

"Don't. I'm here. My name is Alec Pelley, and I was trying to reach Bill Hodges. I worked with him on a case a few years back, just after I retired from the State Police. There was a bad actor named Oliver Madden who stole an airplane from a Texas oilman named—"

"Dwight Cramm. I remember. And I remember you, Mr. Pelley, although we've never met. Mr. Cramm did not pay us promptly, I'm sorry to say. I had to invoice him at least half a dozen times, and then threaten legal action. I hope you did better."

"It took a little work," Alec said, smiling at the memory. "The first check he sent me bounced, but the second one went through all right. You're Holly, aren't you? I can't remember the last name, but Bill spoke very highly of you."

"Holly Gibney," she said.

"Well, it's very nice to speak with you again, Ms. Gibney. I tried Bill's number, but I guess he's changed it."

Silence.

"Ms. Gibney? Did I lose you?"

"No," she said. "I'm here. Bill died two years ago."

"Oh, Jesus. I'm very sorry to hear that. Was it his heart?" Although Alec had only met Hodges once—they had done most of their business by phone and email—he had been on the heavy side.

"Cancer. Pancreatic. Now I run the company with Peter Huntley. He was Bill's partner when they were on the force."

"Well, good for you."

"No," she said. "Not good for me. The business is doing quite well, but I would give it up in a minute to have Bill alive and healthy. Cancer is very poopy."

Alec almost thanked her then and ended the call after renewing his condolences. Later on, he wondered how much things would have changed if he had done that. But he remembered something Bill had said about this woman during the business of retrieving Dwight Cramm's King Air: *She's eccentric, a little obsessive-compulsive, and she's not big on personal contact, but she never misses a trick. Holly would have made one hell of a police detective.*

THE OUTSIDER

"I was hoping to hire Bill to do some investigating for me," he said, "but possibly you could take it on. He really did speak highly of you."

"I'm glad to hear it, Mr. Pelley, but I doubt if I'm the right person. Mostly what we do at Finders Keepers is chase bail-jumpers and trace missing persons." She paused, then added, "There is also the fact that we are quite a distance from you, unless you're calling from somewhere in the northeast."

"I'm not, but my interest happens to be in Ohio, and it would be inconvenient for me to fly up myself—there are things going on here that I need to stick with. How far are you from Dayton?"

"One moment," she said, and then, almost immediately: "Two hundred and thirty-two miles, according to MapQuest. Which is a very good program. What is it you need investigated, Mr. Pelley? And before you answer, I need to tell you that if it involves any possibility of violence, I really would have to pass on the case. I abhor violence."

"No violence," he said. "There *was* violence—the murder of a child—but it happened down here, and the man who was arrested for the crime is dead. The question is whether or not he was the doer, and answering that involves back-checking a trip he made to Dayton with his family in April."

"I see, and who would be paying for the company's services? You?"

"No, an attorney named Howard Gold."

"To your knowledge, does Attorney Gold pay more promptly than Dwight Cramm?"

Alec grinned at that. "Absolutely."

And although the retainer *would* come from Howie, the entire Finders Keepers fee—assuming Ms. Holly Gibney agreed to take on the Dayton investigation—would in the end come from Marcy Maitland, who would be able to afford it. The insurance company wouldn't like paying out on an accused murderer, but since

Terry had never been convicted of anything, they would have no recourse. There was also the wrongful death suit against Flint City that Howie would be lodging on Marcy's behalf; he had told Alec that the city would probably settle for an amount in the low seven figures. A fat bank account wouldn't bring her husband back, but it *could* pay for an investigation, and a home relocation if Marcy decided that was best, and the college educations of two girls when the time came. Money was no cure for sorrow, Alec reflected, but it did allow one to grieve in relative comfort.

"Tell me about this case, Mr. Pelley, and I'll tell you if I can take it on."

"Doing that will take some time. I can call tomorrow, during office hours, if that would be better for you."

"Tonight is fine. Just give me a moment to turn off the movie I was watching."

"I'm interrupting your evening."

"Not really. I've seen *Paths of Glory* at least a dozen times. It's one of Mr. Kubrick's finest. Much better than *The Shining* and *Barry Lyndon*, in my opinion, but of course he was much younger when he made it. Young artists are much more likely to be risk-takers, in my opinion."

"I'm not much of a movie buff," Alec replied, remembering what Hodges had said: eccentric and a little obsessive-compulsive.

"They brighten the world, that's what I think. Just one second . . ." In the background, the sound of faint movie music ceased. Then she was back. "Tell me what you need done in Dayton, Mr. Pelley."

"It's not just a very long story, it's a strange one. Let me warn you of that in advance."

She laughed, a sound much richer than her usual careful speech. It made her sound younger. "Yours won't be the first strange story I've heard, believe me. When I was with Bill . . . well, never mind that. But if we're going to be talking for awhile, you might as well call me Holly. I'm going to put you on speaker to free up my hands. Wait . . . okay, now tell me everything."

Thus encouraged, Alec began to talk. Instead of movie music in the background, he heard the steady clitter-clitter-clitter of her keyboard as she took notes. And before the conversation was finished, he was glad he hadn't hung up. She asked good questions, sharp questions. The oddities of the case didn't seem to faze her in the slightest. It was a goddam shame that Bill Hodges was dead, but Alec thought he might have found a perfectly adequate replacement.

When he was finally done, he asked, "Are you intrigued?"

"Yes. Mr. Pelley—"

"Alec. You're Holly and I'm Alec."

"All right, Alec. Finders Keepers will take this case. I will send you regular reports either by phone, email, or FaceTime, which I find is far superior to Skype. When I have gotten everything I can, I will send you a complete summary."

"Thank you. That sounds very—"

"Yes. Now let me give you an account number, so you can transfer the retainer fee to our bank in the amount we discussed."

HOLLY

July 22nd–July 24th

1

She put back the office phone (which she always brought home with her, although Pete kidded her about it) on its stand next to her home phone, and sat quiet in front of her computer for perhaps thirty seconds. Then she pushed the button on her Fitbit to check her pulse. Seventy-five, eight to ten beats faster than normal. She wasn't surprised. Pelley's story of the Maitland affair had excited and engaged her in a way no case had since finishing with the late (and very horrible) Brady Hartsfield.

Except that wasn't exactly right. The truth was she hadn't been really excited about anything since Bill had died. Pete Huntley was fine, but he was—here in the silence of her nice apartment, she could admit it—a bit of a plodder. He was happy to chase the deadbeats, bail-jumpers, stolen cars, lost pets, and daddies delinquent on child support. And while Holly had told Alec Pelley nothing but the truth—she really did abhor violence, except in movies; it made her tummy hurt—chasing after Hartsfield had made her feel alive in a way nothing had since. That was also true of Morris Bellamy, a crazy literature buff who had killed his favorite writer.

There would be no Brady Hartsfield or Morris Bellamy waiting for her in Dayton, which was good, because Pete was on vacation in Minnesota, and her young friend Jerome was on vacation with his family in Ireland.

"I'll kiss the Blarney Stone for ye, darlin," he had said at the airport, employing an Irish brogue every bit as awful as his *Amos 'n Andy* accent, which he still put on occasionally, mostly to offend her.

"You better not," she'd said. "Think of the germs on that thing. Ooogh."

Alec Pelley thought I'd be put off by the strangeness, she thought, smiling a little. *He thought I'd just say, "This is impossible, people can't be in two places at the same time, and people can't disappear from archived news footage. It's either a practical joke, or a hoax." Only what Alec Pelley doesn't know—and I won't tell him—is that people* can *be in two places at the same time. Brady Hartsfield did it, and when Brady finally died, he was in another man's body.*

"Anything is possible," she said to the empty room. "Anything at all. The world is full of strange nooks and crannies."

She booted up Firefox and found the address of the Tommy and Tuppence Pub. The closest lodging was the Fairview Hotel, on Northwoods Boulevard. Was it the same hotel the Maitland family had stayed in? She would ask Alec Pelley via email, but it seemed likely, bearing in mind what the older Maitland daughter had said. Holly checked Trivago and saw she could get an acceptable room for ninety-two dollars per night. She considered upgrading to a small suite, but only for a moment. That would be padding the expense account, a shoddy business practice and a slippery slope.

She called the Fairview (on the office phone, since this was a legitimate expense), made a reservation for three nights starting tomorrow, then opened Math Cruncher on her computer. In her opinion it was the best program for solving everyday problems. Check-in time at the Fairview was three o'clock, and the turnpike speed at which her Prius got optimum gas mileage was 63 MPH. She figured in one stop to top up the tank and get a no doubt substandard meal at a roadside rest . . . added forty-five minutes for the inevitable slowdown due to roadwork . . .

"I'll leave at ten o'clock," she said. "No, better make it nine fifty, just to be safe." And to be even safer, she used her Waze app to suss out an alternate route, should that be necessary.

She showered (so she wouldn't have to do it in the morning), put on her nightie, brushed her teeth, flossed (the latest studies said flossing was not useful in protecting against dental decay, but it was part of Holly's routine, and she would be content to floss until she died), took out her hair clips and put them in a line, then went into the spare bedroom, padding in her bare feet.

The room was her film library. The shelves were lined with DVDs, some in colorful store cases, most homemade courtesy of Holly's state-of-the-art disc burner. There were thousands (4,375, currently), but the one she wanted was easy to find, because the discs were alphabetized. She took it down and placed it on her nightstand, where she would be sure to see it when she packed in the morning.

With that taken care of, she got down on her knees, closed her eyes, and folded her hands. Morning and evening prayers had been her analyst's idea, and when Holly protested that she did not exactly believe in God, her analyst said that a vocalizing of her concerns and plans to a hypothetical higher power would help even if she didn't. And that actually seemed to be the case.

"It's Holly Gibney again, and I am still trying to do my best. If you're there, please bless Pete while he's fishing, because only an idiot goes out in a boat when he doesn't know how to swim. Please bless the Robinsons over there in Ireland, and if Jerome really is thinking about kissing the Blarney Stone, I wish you'd make him think better of it. I am drinking Boost to try and put on a little weight, because Dr. Stonefield says I'm too thin. I don't like it, but each can has two hundred and forty calories, according to the label. I'm taking my Lexapro, and I'm not smoking. Tomorrow I'm going to Dayton. Please help me to stay safe in my car, obey all traffic rules, and help me to do the best I can with the facts at hand. Which are interesting." She considered. "I still miss Bill. I guess that's all for tonight."

She got into bed and was asleep five minutes later.

2

Holly arrived at the Fairview Hotel at 3:17 PM, not quite optimum but not bad. She reckoned it would have been 3:12, had not every fracking traffic light been against her once she left the turnpike. The room was fine. The bath towels on the shower door had been hung a bit crooked, but she set that situation to rights after using the toilet and washing her hands and face. There was no DVD player attached to the television, but at ninety-two dollars a night, she hadn't expected one. If she felt a need to watch the film she had brought, her laptop would be perfectly adequate. Made on the cheap, and shot in probably no more than ten days, it wasn't the sort of movie that required high resolution and Dolby sound.

Tommy and Tuppence was less than a block from the hotel. Holly could see the sign as soon as she stepped from beneath the hotel awning. She walked down and studied the menu posted in the window. In the upper lefthand corner was a pie with steam rising from its crust. Printed below this was **STEAK & KIDNEY PIE IS OUR SPECIALTY**.

She strolled down another block and came to a parking lot, which was about three-quarters full. CITY PARKING, said the sign out front. 6-HOUR LIMIT. She went in, looking for tickets on windshields or a traffic warden's chalk marks on tires. She saw neither, which meant that no one was enforcing the six-hour limit. It was strictly honor system. It wouldn't work in New York, but it probably worked just fine in Ohio. With no monitoring, there was no way to tell how long the van had been here after Merlin Cassidy had abandoned it, but she guessed that with the doors unlocked and the keys dangling invitingly from the ignition, it probably hadn't lasted too long.

She walked back to Tommy and Tuppence, introduced herself to the hostess, and said she was an investigator working a case that had to do with a man who had stayed nearby last spring. It turned out the hostess was also part-owner, and with the evening rush still an hour away, she was perfectly willing to talk. Holly asked if she happened to remember just when the restaurant had leafleted the area with menus.

"What did the guy do?" the hostess asked. Her name was Mary, not Tuppence, and her accent was New Jersey rather than Newcastle.

"I'm not at liberty to say," Holly told her. "It's a legal matter. You understand."

"Well, I do remember," Mary said. "It'd be funny if I didn't."

"Why is that?"

"When we first opened two years ago, this was Fredo's Place. You know, like in *The Godfather*?"

"Yes," Holly said, "although Fredo is best remembered for *Godfather II*, especially for the sequence where his brother Michael kisses him and says 'I know it was you, Fredo, you broke my heart.'"

"I don't know about that, but I do know that there are about two hundred Italian restaurants in Dayton, and we were getting killed. So we decided to try British food, you can't exactly call it cuisine—fish and chips, bangers and mash, even beans on toast—and changed the name to Tommy and Tuppence, like in the Agatha Christie books. We figured we had nothing to lose at that point. And you know what, it worked. I was shocked, but in a good way, believe me. We fill this place for lunch, and most nights for dinner." She leaned forward and Holly could smell gin on her breath, bright and clear. "Want to know a secret?"

"I love secrets," Holly said truthfully.

"The steak and kidney pie comes frozen from a company in Paramus. We just heat it up in the oven. And you know what? The restaurant critic from the *Dayton Daily News* loved it. He gave us five stars! I shit you not!" She leaned forward a little more and whispered, "If you tell anyone that, I'd have to kill you."

Holly zipped a thumb across her thin lips and turned an invisible key, a gesture she'd seen Bill Hodges make on many occasions. "So when you re-opened with the new name and the new menu . . . or maybe just before . . ."

"Johnny, he's my hubby, wanted to paper the neighborhood a week before, but I told him that was no good, people would forget, so we did it the day before. We hired a kid, and printed enough menus for him to cover a nine-block area."

"Including the parking lot up the street."

"Yes. Is that important?"

"Would you check your calendar and tell me what day that was?"

"Don't need to. It's engraven on my memory." She tapped her forehead. "April nineteenth. A Thursday. We opened—*re*-opened, actually—on Friday."

Holly restrained an urge to correct Mary's grammar, thanked her, and turned to go.

"Sure you can't tell me what the guy did?"

"Very sorry, but I'd lose my job."

"Well, at least come in for dinner, if you're staying in town."

"I'll do that," Holly said, but she wouldn't. God knew what else on the menu had been shipped frozen from Paramus.

3

The next step was a visit to the Heisman Memory Unit, and a talk with Terry Maitland's father, if he was having a good day (presuming he *had* good days anymore). Even if he was off in the clouds, she might be able to talk to some of the people who worked there. In the meantime, here she was in her pretty-good hotel room. She powered up her laptop and sent Alec Pelley an email titled **GIBNEY REPORT #1**.

Tommy & Tuppence menus were leafleted in a 9-block area on Thursday, April 19th. Based on interview w/ co-owner MARY HOLLISTER, I am confident this date is correct. Such being the case, we can be sure it was the date MERLIN CASSIDY abandoned the van in nearby parking lot. Note that MAITLAND FAMILY arrived Dayton around noon on Saturday, April 21st. I am almost positive the van was gone by then. I will check w/ local police tomorrow, hoping to close off one more possibility, and will then visit the Heisman Memory Unit. If questions, email or call my cell.

Holly Gibney
Finders Keepers

With that taken care of, Holly went down to the hotel restaurant and ordered a light meal (she never even considered room service, which was always ridiculously expensive). She found a Mel Gibson film she hadn't seen on the in-room movie menu, and ordered it—$9.99, which she would deduct from her report of expenses when she filed it. The picture wasn't great, but Gibson did the best he could with what he had. She noted the title and the running time in her current movie log-book (Holly had already filled over two dozen others), giving it three stars. With that taken care of, she made sure both of the room's door locks were engaged, said her prayers (finishing, as she always did, by telling God that she missed Bill), and went to bed. Where she slept for eight hours, with no dreams. At least none that she remembered.

4

The next morning, after coffee, a brisk three-mile walk, breakfast at a nearby café, and a hot shower, Holly called the Dayton Police Department and asked for Traffic Division. Following a refreshingly brief interval on hold, an Officer Linden came on the line and asked how he could help her. Holly found this delightful. A polite policeman always brightened her day. Although to be fair, most of them were in the Midwest.

She identified herself, said she was interested in a white Econoline van that had been left in a public parking lot on Northwoods Boulevard in April, and asked if DPD regularly checked the city's honor lots.

"Sure," Officer Linden said, "but not to enforce the six-hour limit. They're cops, not meter maids."

"I understand," Holly said, "but they must keep an eye out for possible dump-offs, don't they?"

Linden laughed. "Your company must do a lot of repos and retrievals."

"Along with bail-jumpers, they're our bread and butter."

"Then you know how it works. We're especially interested in expensive cars that have been hanging around those lots for awhile, both in town and in long-term parking at the airport. Your Denalis, your Escalades, your Jags and Beemers. You say this van you're interested in had New York plates?"

"Correct."

"A van like that probably wouldn't have drawn much attention the first day—people from New York *do* come to Dayton, strange as it may seem—but if it was still there on the second day? Probably."

Which still would have been a full day before the Maitlands arrived. "Thank you, Officer."

"I could check the impound yard, if you want."

"That won't be necessary. The van next showed up a thousand miles south of here."

"What's your interest in it, if you don't mind me asking?"

"Not at all," Holly said. This was a police officer, after all. "It was used to abduct a child who was subsequently murdered."

5

Now ninety-nine per cent sure the van had been gone well before Terry Maitland arrived in Dayton with his wife and daughters on April 21st, Holly drove her Prius to the Heisman Memory Unit. It was a long, low sandstone building in the middle of at least four acres of well-kept grounds. A grove of trees separated it from Kindred Hospital, which probably owned it, operated it, and made a tidy profit thereby; it certainly didn't look cheap. *Either Peter Maitland had a large nest egg, good insurance, or both*, Holly thought approvingly. There were plenty of empty guest spaces at this hour of the morning, but Holly chose one at the far end of the lot. Her Fitbit goal was 12,000 steps a day, and every little bit helped.

She paused for a minute to watch three orderlies walking three residents (one of the latter actually looked as if he might know where he was), then went inside. The lobby was high-ceilinged and pleasant, but beneath the smells of floor wax and furniture polish, Holly could detect a faint odor of pee wafting out from deeper in the building. And something else, something heavier. It would have been foolish and melodramatic to call it the smell of lost hope, but that was what it smelled like to Holly, just the same. *Probably because I spent so much of my early life staring at the hole instead of the doughnut*, she thought.

The sign on the main desk read ALL VISITORS MUST CHECK IN. The woman behind the desk (Mrs. Kelly, according to the little plaque on the counter) gave Holly a welcoming smile. "Hello, there. How may I help?"

To this point, all was ordinary and unremarkable. Things only went off the rails when Holly asked if she could visit Peter Maitland. Mrs. Kelly's smile remained on her lips, but disappeared from her eyes. "Are you a member of the family?"

"No," Holly said. "I'm a *friend* of the family."

This, she told herself, was not exactly a lie. She was working for Mrs. Maitland's lawyer, after all, and the lawyer was working for Mrs. Maitland, and that qualified as a kind of friendship, didn't it, if she had been hired to clear the name of the widow's late husband?

"I'm afraid that won't do," said Mrs. Kelly. What remained of her smile was now purely perfunctory. "If you're not family, I'm afraid I'll have to ask you to leave. Mr. Maitland wouldn't know you, anyway. His condition has deteriorated this summer."

"Just this summer, or since Terry came to visit him in the spring?"

Now the smile was gone entirely. "Are you a reporter? If you are, you are required by law to tell me, and I will ask you to leave the premises at once. If you refuse, I'll call security and have you escorted. We've had quite enough of your kind."

This was interesting. It might not have anything to do with the matter she had come here to investigate, but maybe it did. The woman hadn't gone all poopy, after all, until Holly mentioned Peter Maitland's name. "I'm not a reporter."

"I'll take your word for that, but if you're not a relative, I still must ask you to leave."

"All right," Holly said. She took a step or two away from the desk, then had an idea and turned back. "Suppose I had Mr. Maitland's son, Terry, call and vouch for me. Would that help?"

"I suppose," Mrs. Kelly said. She looked grudging about it. "He would have to answer a few questions, though, to satisfy me that it wasn't one of your *colleagues* pretending to be Mr. Maitland. That might sound a trifle paranoid to you, Ms. Gibney, but we have been through a lot here, a *lot*, and I take my responsibilities very seriously."

"I understand."

"Maybe you do and maybe you don't, but it wouldn't do you any good to speak to Peter, in any case. The police found that out. He's in end-stage Alzheimer's. If you talk to the younger Mr. Maitland, he'll tell you."

The younger Mr. Maitland won't tell me anything, Mrs. Kelly, because he's been dead for a week. But you don't know that, do you?

"When was the last time the police tried to talk to Peter Maitland? I'm asking as a friend of the family."

Mrs. Kelly considered this, then said: "I don't believe you, and I'm not answering your questions."

Bill would have gotten all chummy and confidential at this point, he and Mrs. Kelly might even have ended by exchanging email addresses and promising to stay in touch on Facebook, but although Holly was an excellent deductive thinker, she was still working on what her analyst called "people skills." She left, a bit disheartened but not discouraged.

This kept getting more interesting.

6

At eleven o'clock on that bright and sunny Tuesday morning, Holly sat on a shady bench in Andrew Dean Park, sipping a latte from a nearby Starbucks and thinking about her queer interview with Mrs. Kelly.

The woman hadn't known Terry was dead, probably none of the Heisman staff knew, and that didn't surprise Holly very much. The murders of Frank Peterson and Terry Maitland had happened in a small city hundreds of miles away; if it had made the national news at all during a week when an ISIL sympathizer had shot eight people in a Tennessee shopping mall and a tornado had leveled a small Indiana town, it would only have been as a blip far down on *Huffington Post*, there and gone. And it wasn't as if Marcy Maitland would have been in touch with her father-in-law to tell him the sad news—why would she, considering the man's condition?

Are you a reporter? Mrs. Kelly had asked. *We've had quite enough of your kind.*

All right, reporters had come to call, also the police, and Mrs. Kelly, as the out-front person at the Heisman Memory Unit, had had to put up with them. But their questions hadn't been about Terry Maitland, or she would have known he was dead. So what had been the great big fracking deal?

Holly set her coffee aside, took her iPad from her shoulder-bag, powered it up, and verified that she had five bars, which would save her from having to go back to the Starbucks. She paid a small fee to access the archives of the local paper (duly noting it for her expense report), and began her search on April 19th, the day Merlin Cassidy had dumped the van. Also the day it had almost certainly been re-stolen. She went through the local news carefully, and found nothing relating to the Memory Unit. That was true for the following five days, as well, although there was plenty of other news: car crashes, two home invasions, a nightclub fire, an explosion at a gas station, an embezzlement scandal involving a school department official, a manhunt for two missing sisters (white) from nearby Trotwood, a police officer accused of shooting an unarmed teenager (black), a synagogue defaced with a swastika.

Then, on April 25th, the front page headline screamed that Amber and Jolene Howard, the missing Trotwood girls, had been found dead and mutilated in a ravine not far from their home. An unnamed police source said "those little girls were subjected to acts of unbelievable savagery." And yes, both girls had been sexually molested.

Terry Maitland had been in Dayton on April 25th. Of course he had been with his family, but . . .

There were no new developments on the 26th of April, the day Terry Maitland had visited his father for the last time, and nothing on the 27th, the day the Maitland family had flown home to Flint City. Then, on Saturday the 28th, the police announced that they were questioning "a person of interest." Two days later, the person of interest was arrested. His name was Heath Holmes. He was thirty-four years of age, a Dayton resident who was employed as an orderly at the Heisman Memory Unit.

Holly picked up her latte, drank half of it in large gulps, then stared off into the shadowy depths of the park with wide eyes. She checked her Fitbit. Her pulse was galloping along at a hundred and ten beats a minute, and it wasn't just caffeine pushing it.

She went back to the *Daily News* archives, scrolling through May and into June, following the thread of the story. Unlike Terry Maitland, Heath Holmes had survived his arraignment, but very much like Terry (Jeannie Anderson would have called it a *confluence*), he would never be tried for the murders of Amber and Jolene Howard. He had committed suicide in Montgomery County Jail on June 7th.

She checked her Fitbit again and saw her pulse was now up to one-twenty. She chugged down the rest of her latte anyway. Living dangerously.

Bill, I wish you were on this with me. I wish that so much. And Jerome, him, too. The three of us would have grabbed the reins and ridden this pony until it stopped running.

But Bill was dead, Jerome was in Ireland, and she wouldn't get any closer to figuring this out than she already was. At least not on her own. But that didn't mean she was done in Dayton. No, not quite.

She went back to her hotel room, ordered a sandwich from room service (damn the expense) and opened her laptop. She added what she now knew to the notes she had taken during her telephone conversation with Alec Pelley. She stared at the screen, and as she scrolled back and forth, an old saying of her mother's popped into her head: *Macy's doesn't tell Gimbels.* The police in Dayton didn't know about Frank Peterson's murder, and the police in Flint City didn't know about the murders of the Howard sisters. Why would they? The killings had taken place in different regions of the country and months apart. No one knew that Terry Maitland had been in both places, and no one knew about the connection to the Heisman Memory Unit. Every case had an information highway running through it, and this one was washed out in at least two places.

"But *I* know," Holly said. "At least some of it. I do. Only . . ."

The knock at the door made her jump. She let in the room service waiter, signed the check, added a ten per cent tip (after making sure a service gratuity was not included), and hustled him out. Then she paced the room, munching away at a BLT she hardly tasted.

What didn't she know that *could* be known? She was bothered, almost haunted, by the idea that the puzzle she was trying to work had missing pieces. Not because Alec Pelley had purposely held things back, she didn't think that at all, but possibly because there was information—*vital* information—that he considered unimportant.

She supposed she could call Mrs. Maitland, only the woman would cry and be all sad and Holly wouldn't know how to comfort her, she never did. Once not so long ago she had helped Jerome Robinson's sister through a bad patch, but as a rule she was terrible at things like that. Plus, the poor woman's mind would be fogged by her grief, and she also might neglect important facts, those little things that could make a whole picture out of the fragments, like the three or four jigsaw pieces that always seem to fall off the table and onto the floor, and you couldn't see the whole picture until you hunted around and found them.

The person most apt to know all the details, the small ones as well as the big ones, was the detective who had done most of the witness interviews and arrested Maitland. After working with Bill Hodges, Holly believed in police detectives. Not all of them were good, to be sure; she'd had little respect for Isabelle Jaynes, Pete Huntley's partner after Bill had retired from the force, and this one, Ralph Anderson, had made a bad mistake by arresting Maitland in a public place. A bad choice didn't necessarily make him a bad detective, though, and Pelley had explained the crucial mitigating circumstance: Terry Maitland had been in close contact with Anderson's son. Certainly the interviews Anderson had done seemed thorough enough. She thought he was the one most likely to have any missing pieces.

It was something to think about. In the meantime, a return visit to the Heisman Memory Unit was in order.

7

She arrived at two thirty, this time driving around to the left side of the building, where signs announced EMPLOYEE PARKING and KEEP AMBULANCE BAY CLEAR. She chose a space at the far end of the lot, backing in so she could watch the building. By two forty-five, cars began to drift in as those working the three-to-eleven shift arrived. Around three, the day shift employees—mostly orderlies, some nurses, a couple of guys in suits, which probably made them doctors—began to leave. One of the suits drove away in a Cadillac, the other in a Porsche. They were doctors, all right. She evaluated the others carefully, and settled on a target. She was a middle-aged nurse wearing a tunic covered with dancing teddy bears. Her car was an old Honda Civic with rust on the sides, a cracked taillight that had been mended with duct tape, and a fading I'M WITH HILLARY sticker on the bumper. Before getting in, she paused to light a cigarette. The car was old and cigarettes were expensive. Better and better.

Holly followed her out of the parking lot, then three miles west, the city giving way first to a pleasant suburb, then to one not so pleasant. Here the woman turned into the driveway of a tract house on a street where others just like it stood almost hip to hip, many with cheap plastic toys marooned on the little patches of lawn. Holly parked at the curb, said a brief prayer for strength, patience, and wisdom, and got out.

"Ma'am? Nurse? Pardon me?"

The woman turned. She had the creased face and prematurely gray hair of a heavy smoker, so it was hard to tell her age. Maybe forty-five, maybe fifty. No wedding ring.

"Can I help you?"

"Yes, and I'll pay for your help," Holly said. "One hundred dollars in cash, if you'll talk to me about Heath Holmes, and his connection to Peter Maitland."

"Did you follow me from my job?"

"Actually, I did."

The woman's brows contracted. "Are you a reporter? Mrs. Kelly said there'd been a woman reporter around, and promised to fire anyone who talked to her."

"I'm the woman she mentioned, but I'm not a reporter. I'm an investigator, and Mrs. Kelly will never find out you talked to me."

"Let me see some ID."

Holly handed over her driver's license and a Finders Keepers bail bondsman's card. The woman examined them closely, then handed them back. "I'm Candy Wilson."

"It's nice to meet you."

"Uh-huh, that's good, but if I'm going to put my job on the line for you, it will cost two hundred." She paused, then added: "And fifty."

"All right," Holly said. She guessed she could talk the woman down to two hundred, maybe even a hundred and fifty, but she wasn't good at bargaining (which her mother always called *haggling*). Also, this lady looked like she needed it.

"You better come inside," Wilson said. "The neighbors on this street have long noses."

8

The house smelled strongly of cigarettes, which made Holly really crave one for the first time in ages. Wilson plunked down in an easy chair, which, like her taillight, was mended with duct tape. Beside it was a standing ashtray of a type Holly hadn't seen since her grandfather died (of emphysema). Wilson plucked a pack of cigarettes from the pocket of her nylon pants and flicked her Bic. She did not offer the pack to Holly, which was no surprise, given the price of smokes these days, but for which Holly was grateful, anyway. She might have taken one.

"Money first," Candy Wilson said.

Holly, who had not neglected to stop at an ATM on her second trip to the Memory Unit, took her wallet from her purse and counted out the correct amount. Wilson re-counted it, then put it in her pocket with her cigarettes.

"Hope you're telling the truth about keeping your mouth shut, Holly. God knows I need this money, my asshole husband cleaned out our bank account when he left, but Mrs. Kelly doesn't kid around. She's like one of the dragons on that *Thrones* show."

Holly once more zipped a thumbnail across her lips and turned the invisible key. Candy Wilson smiled and seemed to relax. She looked around the living room, which was small and dark and furnished in Early American Yard Sale. "Ugly fucking place, isn't it? We had a nice house over on the west side. No mansion, but better than this pit. My asshole husband sold it right out from under me before he sailed off into the sunset. You know what they say, there are none so blind as those who will not see. I almost wish we'd had kids, so I could turn them against him."

Bill would have known how to reply to this, but Holly didn't, so she took out her notebook and went to the matter at hand. "Heath Holmes worked as an orderly at the Heisman."

"Yes indeed. Handsome Heath, we used to call him. It was sort of a joke and sort of not. He wasn't any Chris Pine or Tom Hiddleston, but he wasn't hard to look at, either. Nice guy, too. Everybody thought so. Which only goes to prove that you never know what's in a man's heart. I found that out with my asshole husband, but at least he never raped and mutilated any little girls. Seen their pictures in the paper?"

Holly nodded. Two cute blondes, wearing identical pretty smiles. Twelve and ten, the exact ages of Terry Maitland's daughters. Another of those things that felt like a connection. Maybe it wasn't, but the whisper that the two cases were actually one had begun to grow louder in Holly's mind. A few more facts of the right kind, and it would become a shout.

"Who does that?" Wilson asked, but the question was rhetorical. "A monster, that's who."

"How long did you work with him, Ms. Wilson?"

"Call me Candy, why don't you? I let people call me by my first name when they pay my utilities for the next month. I worked with him for seven years, and never had a clue."

"The paper said he was on vacation when the girls were killed."

"Yeah, went up to Regis, about thirty miles north of here. To his mother's. Who told the cops he was there the whole time." Wilson rolled her eyes.

"The paper also said he had a record."

"Well, yeah, but nothing gross, just a joyride in a stolen car when he was seventeen." She frowned at her cigarette. "Paper wasn't supposed to have that, you know, he was a juvenile and those records are supposed to be sealed. If they weren't, he probably wouldn't have gotten the job at Heisman, even with all his army training and his five years working at Walter Reed. Maybe, but probably not."

"You speak as if you knew him pretty well."

"I'm not defending him, don't get that idea. I had drinks with him, sure, but it wasn't a date situation, nothing like that. A bunch of us used to go out to the Shamrock sometimes after work—this was back when I still had some money and could buy a round when it was my turn. Those days are gone, honey. Anyway, we used to call ourselves the Forgetful Five, on account of—"

"I think I get it," Holly said.

"Yeah, I bet you do, and we knew all the Alzheimer's jokes. Most of them are kind of mean, and lots of our patients are actually pretty nice, but we told them to kind of . . . I don't know . . ."

"Whistle past the graveyard?" Holly suggested.

"Yes, that's it. You want a beer, Holly?"

"Okay. Thanks." She didn't have much of a taste for beer, and it wasn't really recommended when you were taking Lexapro, but she wanted to keep the conversation rolling.

Wilson brought back a couple of Bud Lights. She offered Holly a glass no more than she had offered one of her cigarettes.

"Yeah, I knew about the joyride bust," she said, once more sitting in the mended easy chair. It gave a tired *woof*. "We all did. You know how people talk when they've had a few. But it was nothing like what he did in April. I still can't believe it. I kissed that guy under the mistletoe at last year's Christmas party." She either shuddered or pretended to.

"So he was on vacation the week of April 23rd . . ."

"If you say so. I just know it was in the spring, because of my allergies." So saying, she lit a fresh cigarette. "Said he was going up to Regis, said he and his mom were going to have a service for his dad, who died a year ago. 'A memory service,' he called it. And maybe he did go, but he came back to kill those girls from Trotwood. No question about it, because people saw him and there was surveillance video from a gas station that showed him filling up."

"Filling what up?" Holly asked. "Was it a van?" This was leading the witness, and Bill wouldn't have approved, but she couldn't help herself.

"I don't know. Not sure the papers said. Probably his truck. He had a Tahoe, all fancied up. Custom tires, lots of chrome. And a camper cap. He could have put them in there. Drugged them, maybe, until he was ready to . . . you know . . . use them."

"Oough," Holly said. She couldn't help it.

Candy Wilson nodded. "Yeah. Kind of thing you don't want to imagine, but you just can't help it. At least I can't. They also found his DNA, as I'm sure you know, because that was in the paper, too."

"Yes."

"And *I* saw him that week, because he came in to work one day. 'Just can't stay away from this place, can you?' I asked him. He didn't say anything, just gave me a creepy smile and kept walking down B Wing. I never saw him smile like that, never. I bet he still had their blood under his fingernails. Maybe even on his cock and balls. Christ, it gives me the willies just thinking about it."

It gave Holly the willies, too, but she didn't say so, only took a sip of her beer and asked what day that had been.

"I don't know off the top of my head, but after those girls disappeared. You know what? I bet I can tell you exactly, because I had a hair appointment that same day after work. To have it colored. Haven't been to the beauty parlor since, as I'm sure you can plainly see. Just a minute."

She went to a little desk in the corner of the room, came up with an appointment book, and flipped back through the pages. "Here it is, Debbie's Hairport. April 26th."

Holly wrote it down, and added an exclamation point. That was the day of Terry's last visit to see his father. He and his family had flown home the following day.

"Did Peter Maitland know Mr. Holmes?"

Wilson laughed. "Peter Maitland doesn't really *know* anybody, hon. He had some clear days last year, and even early this year he remembered enough to get to the caff on his own and ask for chocolate—the things they really like are the things most of them remember the longest. Now he just sits and stares. If I get that shit, I'm going to take a bunch of pills and die while I still have enough working brain cells to remember what the pills are for. But if you're asking if Heath knew Maitland, the answer is sure, you bet. Some of the orderlies switch around, but Heath stuck pretty much to the odd-numbered suites on B Wing. He used to say that some part of them knew him, even when most of their brains were gone. And Maitland is in suite B-5."

"Did he visit Maitland's room on the day you saw him?"

"Must have. I know something that wasn't in the paper, but you can bet your ass it would have been a big deal at Heath's trial, if he'd ever had one."

"What, Candy? What was it, what?"

"When the cops found out he'd been in to the Memory Unit after the murders, they searched all the B Wing suites, paying especially close attention to Maitland's, because Cam Melinsky said he saw Heath coming out of there. Cam's a janitor. He noticed Heath especially because he—Cam, I mean—was washing the hall floor, and Heath took a slip and went on his ass."

"You're sure of this, Candy?"

"I am, and here's the big thing. My best friend on the nursing staff is a woman named Penny Prudhomme, and she heard one of the cops talking on his phone after they searched B-5. He said they found hair in the room, and it was *blond*. What do you think of that?"

"I think they must have run a DNA test on it, to see if it belonged to one of the Howard girls."

"Bet your ass they did. *CSI* stuff."

"Those results were never made public," Holly said. "Were they?"

"No. But you know what the cops found in Mrs. Holmes's basement, don't you?"

Holly nodded. That detail *had* been made public, and reading it must have been like putting an arrow in the parents' hearts. Someone had talked and the paper had printed it. Probably it had been on TV, too.

"A *lot* of sex-killers take trophies," Candy said authoritatively. "I've seen it on *Forensic Files* and *Dateline*. It's common behavior with these whackos."

"Although Heath Holmes never seemed like a whacko to you."

"They hide it," Candy Wilson said ominously.

"But he didn't try very hard to hide this crime, did he? People saw him, and there was even that surveillance video."

"So what? He went crazy, and crazy people don't give a shit."

I'm sure Detective Anderson and the Flint County DA said the exact same thing about Terry Maitland, Holly thought. *Even though some serial killers—*sex-killers, *to use Candy Wilson's term—keep getting away with it for years. Ted Bundy for one, John Wayne Gacy for another.*

Holly got up. "Thank you so much for your time."

"Thank me by making sure Mrs. Kelly doesn't find out I talked to you."

"I'll do that," Holly said.

As she was stepping out the door, Candy said, "You know about his mom, right? What she did after Heath offed himself in jail?"

Holly stopped, keys in hand. "No."

"It was a month later. Guess you didn't get that far in your researches. She hung herself. Just like him, only in her basement instead of a jail cell."

"Holy frack! Did she leave a note?"

"That I don't know," Candy said, "but the basement was where the cops found those bloody underpants. The ones with Winnie and Tigger and Roo on them. If your only son does a thing like that, who needs to leave a note?"

9

When Holly was unsure about what to do next, she almost always sought out either an International House of Pancakes or a Denny's. Both served breakfast all day, comfort food that you could eat slowly without being bothered by things like wine lists and pushy waiters. She found an IHOP close to her hotel.

Once seated at a two-top in the corner, she ordered pancakes (a short stack), a single scrambled egg, and hash browns (the IHOP hash browns were always delicious). While she waited for her food to come, she fired up her laptop and searched for Ralph Anderson's telephone number. She didn't find it, which was no huge surprise; police officers almost always unlisted their phones. She could almost certainly get it, even so—Bill had taught her all the tricks—and she *wanted* to talk to him, because she was sure they both had pieces of the puzzle the other lacked.

"He's Macy's, I'm Gimbels," she said.

"What was that, hon?" It was the waitress, with her evening repast.

"I was just saying how hungry I am," Holly said.

"You better be, because this is a lot of chow." She set the plates down. "But you could use some feeding up, if you don't mind me saying so. You're too skinny."

"I had a friend who used to tell me that all the time," Holly said, and suddenly felt like crying. It was that phrase—*I had a friend.* Time had passed, and time probably did heal all wounds, but God, some of them healed so slowly. And the difference between *I have* and *I had* was such a gulf.

She ate slowly, going heavy on the pancake syrup. It wasn't the real deal, not maple, but it was tasty, just the same, and it was good to eat a meal where you sat down and took your time.

By the time she finished, she had come to a reluctant decision.

Calling Detective Anderson without informing Pelley was apt to get her fired when she wanted—it was Bill's turn of phrase—to chase the case. More importantly, it would be unethical.

The waitress came back to offer more coffee, and Holly agreed. You didn't get free refills at Starbucks. And the IHOP coffee, while not gourmet, was good enough. Like the syrup. *And like me,* Holly thought. Her therapist said these moments of self-validation throughout the day were very important. *I may not be Sherlock Holmes—or Tommy and Tuppence, for that matter—but I am good enough, and I know what I have to do. Mr. Pelley may argue with me, and I hate arguments, but I'll argue back if I have to. I'll channel my inner Bill Hodges.*

She held that thought while she made the call. When Pelley answered, she said: "Terry Maitland didn't kill the Peterson boy."

"What? Did you just say what I think you—"

"Yes. I've discovered some very interesting things here in Dayton, Mr. Pelley, but before I make my report, I need to talk to Detective Anderson. Do you have any objections?"

Pelley didn't give her the argument she had dreaded. "I'd have to talk to Howie Gold about that, and he'd have to clear it with Marcy. But I think it will be okay with both of them."

Holly relaxed and sipped her coffee. "That's good. Clear it with them as fast as you can, please, and get me his number. I'd like to talk to him tonight."

"But why? What have you found out?"

"Let me ask you a question. Do you know if anything unusual happened at the Heisman Memory Unit on the day Terry Maitland visited his father for the last time?"

"Unusual like what?"

This time Holly didn't lead her witness. "Like anything. You may not know, but then again you might. If Terry said something to his wife when he got back to their hotel, for instance. Anything?"

"No . . . unless you mean Terry bumping into an orderly when he went out. The orderly fell down because the floor was wet, but it was just a chance thing. Neither of them was hurt, or anything."

She clutched her phone so hard her knuckles creaked. "You never said anything like that before."

"I didn't think it was important."

"That's why I need to talk to Detective Anderson. There are missing pieces. You just gave me one. He may have more. Also, he can find things out that I can't."

"Are you saying an excuse-me bump as Maitland was going out has relevance? If so, what is it?"

"Let me talk to Detective Anderson first. *Please.*"

There was a long pause, then Pelley said, "Let me see what I can do."

The waitress put down the check as Holly pocketed her phone. "That sounded intense."

Holly gave her a smile. "Thank you for such good service."

The waitress left. The check came to eighteen dollars and twenty cents. Holly left a five-dollar tip under her plate. This was quite a bit more than the recommended amount, but she was excited.

10

She had barely returned to her room when her cell rang. UNKNOWN CALLER, the screen said. "Hello? You've reached Holly Gibney, to whom am I speaking?"

"This is Ralph Anderson. Alec Pelley gave me your number, Ms. Gibney, and told me what you're doing. My first question is, do you *know* what you're doing?"

"Yes." Holly had many worries, and she was a very doubtful person even after years of therapy, but of this much she was sure.

"Uh-huh, uh-huh, well, maybe you do and maybe you don't, I have no way of telling, do I?"

"No," Holly agreed. "At least not as of this moment."

"Alec said you told him Terry Maitland didn't kill Frank Peterson. He said you seemed very sure of it. I'm curious as to how you can make a statement like that when you're in Dayton and the Peterson murder happened here in Flint City."

"Because there was a similar crime here, at the same time Maitland was here. Not a boy killed, but two little girls. Same basic MO: rape and mutilation. The man the police arrested claimed to have been staying with his mother in a town thirty miles away, and she corroborated that, but he was also seen in Trotwood, the suburb where the little girls were abducted. There's surveillance footage of him. Does this sound familiar?"

"Familiar but not surprising. Most killers toss up some kind of alibi once they're caught. You might not know that from your work collaring bail-jumpers, Ms. Gibney—Alec told me what your firm mostly does—but surely you know it from TV."

"This man was an orderly at the Heisman Memory Unit, and although he was supposed to be on vacation, he was there at least once during the same week that Mr. Maitland was there visiting his father. On the occasion of Mr. Maitland's last visit—April 26th, this would have been—these two supposed killers actually bumped into each other. And I mean that literally."

"Are you shitting me?" Anderson nearly shouted.

"I am not. This is what my old partner at Finders Keepers would have called an authentic no-shit situation. Is your interest piqued?"

"Did Pelley tell you the orderly scraped Maitland when he fell down? Reached out and grabbed for him and nicked his arm?"

Holly was silent. She was thinking about the movie she had packed in her carry-on. She wasn't in the habit of self-congratulation—just the opposite—but it now seemed like an act of intuitive genius. Only had she ever doubted there was something far out of the ordinary about the Maitland case? She had not. Mostly because of her association with the monstrous Brady Wilson Hartsfield. A thing like that tended to widen your perspective quite a bit.

"And that wasn't the only cut." He sounded like he was talking to himself. "There was another one. But down here. After Frank Peterson was murdered."

Here was another missing piece.

"Tell me, Detective. Tell me tell me tell me!"

"I think . . . not over the phone. Can you fly down here? We should sit down and talk. You, me, Alec Pelley, Howie Gold, and a State Police detective who's also been working the case. And maybe Marcy. Her, too."

"I think that's a good idea, but I'll have to discuss it with my client, Mr. Pelley."

"Talk to Howie Gold instead. I'll give you his number."

"Protocol—"

"Howie employs Alec, so protocol isn't an issue."

Holly mulled this over. "Can you get in touch with the Dayton Police Department, and the Montgomery County district attorney? I can't find out all I want to know about the murders of the Howard girls and about Heath Holmes—that's the orderly's name—but I think you could."

"Is this guy's trial still pending? If it is, they probably won't want to give out a whole lot of infor—"

"Mr. Holmes is dead." She paused. "Just like Terry Maitland."

"Jesus," he muttered. "How weird can this get?"

"Weirder," she said. Another thing of which she had no doubt.

"Weirder," he repeated. "Maggots in the cantaloupe."

"I beg your pardon?"

"Nothing. Call Mr. Gold, okay?"

"I still think I had better call Mr. Pelley first. Just to be sure."

"If you really think so. And Ms. Gibney . . . I guess maybe you do know your business."

That made her smile.

11

Holly got the green light from Mr. Pelley and called Howie Gold at once, now pacing a worry-track on the cheap hotel carpet and obsessively punching at her Fitbit to read her pulse. Yes, Mr. Gold thought it would be a good idea if she flew down, and no, she didn't need to fly coach. "Book business class," he said. "More legroom."

"All right." She felt giddy. "I will."

"You really don't believe Terry killed the Peterson boy?"

"No more than I think Heath Holmes killed those two girls," she said. "I think it was someone else. I think it was an outsider."

VISITS

July 25th

1

Detective Jack Hoskins of the Flint City PD woke up at two AM on that Wednesday morning in triple misery: he had a hangover, he had a sunburn, and he needed to take a shit. *It's what I get for eating at Los Tres Molinos*, he thought . . . but *had* he eaten there? He was pretty sure he had—enchiladas stuffed with pork and that spicy cheese—but wasn't positive. It might have been Hacienda. Last night was hazy.

Have to cut back on the vodka. Vacation is over.

Yes, and over early. Because their shitty little department currently had just one working detective. Sometimes life was a bitch. Often, even.

He got out of bed, wincing at the single hard thud in his head when his feet hit the floor and rubbing at the burn on the back of his neck. He shucked his shorts, grabbed the newspaper off the nightstand, and plodded to the bathroom to take care of his business. Ensconced on the toilet, waiting for the semi-liquid gush that always came six hours or so after he ate Mexican food (would he never learn?), he opened the *Call* and rattled his way to the comics, the only part of the local paper that was worth a damn.

He was squinting at the tiny dialogue balloons in *Get Fuzzy* when he heard the shower curtain rattle. He looked up and saw a shadow behind the printed daisies. His heart leaped into his throat, walloping. Someone was standing in his tub. An intruder, and not just some stoned junkie thief who'd wriggled through the bathroom window and taken refuge in the only place available when he saw the bedroom light come on. No. This was the same someone who had been standing behind him at that fucking abandoned barn out in Canning Township. He knew it as surely as he knew his own name. That encounter (if it *had* been an encounter) refused to leave his mind, and it was almost as if he had been expecting this . . . *return.*

You know that's bullshit. You thought you saw a man in the barn, but when you put the light on the guy, he turned out to be nothing but a piece of busted farm equipment. Now you think there's a man in your tub, but what looks like his head is just the shower head and what looks like his arm is nothing but your long-handled back-scrubber stuck through the grab handle on the wall. The rattling sound you heard was either a draft or just in your head.

He closed his eyes. Opened them again and stared at the shower curtain with its stupid plastic flowers, the kind of shower curtain only an ex-wife could love. Now that he was fully awake, reality reasserted itself. Just the shower head, just the grab handle with the back-scrubber stuck through it. He was an idiot. A *hungover* idiot, the worst kind. He—

The shower curtain rattled again. It rattled because what he had wanted to believe was his back-scrubber now grew shadowy fingers and reached out to touch the plastic. The shower head turned and seemed to stare at him through the translucent curtain. The newspaper fell from Hoskins's relaxing fingers and landed on the tiles with a soft flap. His head was thudding and thudding. The back of his neck was burning and burning. His bowels relaxed, and the small bathroom was filled with the smell of what Jack was suddenly sure had been his last meal. The hand was reaching for the edge of the curtain. In a second—two, at the most—it would be pulled back and he would be looking at something so horrible it would make his worst nightmare seem like a sweet daydream.

"No," he whispered. "No." He tried to get up from the toilet, but his legs wouldn't support him and his considerable bottom thumped back onto the ring. "Please, no. Don't."

A hand crept around the edge of the curtain, but instead of pulling it back, the fingers only folded around it. Tattooed on those fingers was a word: CANT.

"Jack."

He couldn't reply. He sat naked on the toilet with the last of his shit still dripping and plopping into the bowl, his heart a runaway engine in his chest. He felt that soon it would rip right out of him, and his last sight on earth would be of it lying on the tiles, splattering blood on his ankles and the comics section of the *Flint City Call* with its final twitching beats.

"That's not a sunburn, Jack."

He wanted to faint. To just collapse off the toilet, and if he gave himself a concussion on the tile floor, even fractured his skull, so what? At least he would be out of this. But consciousness stubbornly remained. The shadowy figure in the tub remained. The fingers on the curtain remained: CANT, in fading blue letters.

"Touch the back of your neck, Jack. If you don't want me to pull back this curtain and show myself, do it now."

Hoskins raised a hand and pressed it to the nape of his neck. His body's reaction was immediate: terrifying bolts of pain which ran up to his temples and down to his shoulders. He looked at his hand and saw it was smeared with blood.

"You've got cancer," the figure behind the curtain informed him. "It's in your lymph glands, and your throat, and your sinuses. It's in your *eyes*, Jack. It's eating into your *eyes*. Soon you'll be able to see it, little gray knobs of malignant cancer cells swimming around in your vision. Do you know when you got it?"

Of course he knew. When this creature had touched him out there in Canning Township. When it had *caressed* him.

"I gave it to you, but I can take it back. Would you like me to take it back?"

"Yes," Jack whispered. He began to cry. "Take it back. *Please* take it back."

"Will you do something if I ask you?"

"Yes."

"You won't hesitate?"

"No!"

"I believe you. And you won't give me any reason *not* to believe you, will you?"

"No! *No!*"

"Good. Now clean yourself up. You stink."

The CANT hand withdrew, but the shape behind the shower curtain was still staring at him. Not a man, after all. Something far worse than the worst man who had ever lived. Hoskins reached for the toilet paper, aware as he did so that he was tilting sideways off the seat and that the world was simultaneously dimming and dwindling. And that was good. He fell, but there was no pain. He was unconscious before he hit the floor.

2

Jeannie Anderson woke at four that morning, with her usual wee-hours full bladder. Ordinarily she would have used their bathroom, but Ralph had been sleeping badly ever since Terry Maitland had been shot, and tonight he had been particularly restless. She got out of bed and made her way to the bathroom at the end of the hall, the one past the door to Derek's room. She considered flushing after relieving herself and decided even that might wake him. It could wait until morning.

Two more hours, Lord, she thought as she left the bathroom. *Two more hours of good sleep, that's all I w—*

She stopped halfway down the hall. The downstairs had been

dark when she left the bedroom, hadn't it? She had been more asleep than awake, but surely she would have noticed a light on.

Are you sure of that?

No, not completely, but there certainly was a light on down there now. White light. Muted. The one over the stove.

She went to the stairs and stood at the top, looking down at that light, brow wrinkled, thinking profoundly. Had the burglar alarm been set before they went to bed? Yes. Arming it before bed was a house rule. She set it, and Ralph had double-checked it before they went up. One or the other of them always set the alarm, but the double-checks, like Ralph's poor sleeping, had only begun since the death of Terry Maitland.

She considered waking Ralph and decided against it. He needed his sleep. She considered going back to get his service revolver, in the box on the high shelf in the closet, but the closet door squeaked and that would surely wake him. And wasn't that pretty paranoid? The light probably *had* been on when she went to the bathroom and she just hadn't noticed. Or maybe it had gone on by itself, a malfunction. She descended the steps quietly, moving to the left on the third step and to the right on the ninth to avoid the creaks, not even thinking about it.

She walked to the kitchen door and peeked around the frame, feeling both stupid and not stupid at all. She sighed, blowing back her bangs. The kitchen was empty. She started across the room to turn off the stove light, then stopped. There were supposed to be four chairs at the kitchen table, three for the family and the one they called the guest chair. But now there were only three.

"Don't move," someone said. "If you move, I'll kill you. If you scream, I'll kill you."

She stopped, pulse hammering, the hair on the back of her neck lifting. If she hadn't done her business before coming down, urine would be running down her legs and puddling on the floor. The man, the intruder, was sitting on the guest chair in their living room, just far enough back from the archway that she could only see him from the knees down. He was wearing faded jeans and moccasins with no socks. His ankles were riddled with red blotches that might have been psoriasis. His upper body was just a vague silhouette. All she could tell was that his shoulders were broad and a little slumped—not as if he was tired, but as if they were so crammed with workout muscle that he couldn't square them. It was funny, all you could see at a moment like this. Terror had frozen her brain's usual sorting ability, and everything flowed in without prejudice. This was the man who had killed Frank Peterson. The man who bit into him like a wild animal and raped him with a tree branch. That man was in her house, and here she stood in her shortie pajamas, with her nipples no doubt sticking out like headlights.

"Listen to me," he said. "Are you listening?"

"Yes," Jeannie whispered, but she had begun to sway, on the edge of a faint, and she was afraid she might pass out before he could say what he had come to say. If that happened, he would kill her. After that he might leave, or he might go upstairs to kill Ralph. He'd do it before Ralph's mind cleared enough to know what was going on.

And leave Derek to come home from camp an orphan.

No. No. *No.*

"W-What do you want?"

"Tell your husband it's done here in Flint City. Tell him he has to stop. Tell him that if he does that, things go back to normal. Tell him if he doesn't, I'll kill him. I'll kill them all."

His hand emerged from the shadows of the living room and into the dim light cast by the single-bar fluorescent. It was a big hand. He closed it into a fist.

"What does it say on my fingers? Read it to me."

She stared at the faded blue letters. She tried to speak and couldn't. Her tongue was nothing but a lump clinging to the roof of her mouth.

He leaned forward. She saw eyes under a broad shelf of forehead. Black hair, short enough to bristle. Black eyes, not just on her but *in* her, searching her heart and mind.

"It says MUST," he told her. "You see that, don't you?"

"Y-Y-Y—"

"And what you must do is tell him to stop." Red lips moving inside a black goatee. "Tell him if he or any of them tries to find me, I'll kill them and leave their guts in the desert for the buzzards. Do you understand me?"

Yes, she tried to tell him, but her tongue wouldn't move and her knees were unlocking and she put her arms out to break her fall and she didn't know if she succeeded in that or not because she was gone into darkness before she hit the floor.

3

Jack woke up at seven o'clock with bright summer sun shining through the window and across his bed. Birds were twittering outside. He sat bolt upright, staring wildly around, only faintly aware that his head was throbbing from last night's vodka.

He got out of bed fast, opened the drawer of his bedside table, and took out the .38 Pathfinder he kept there for home protection. He high-stepped across the bedroom with the gun held beside his right cheek and the short barrel pointing at the ceiling. He kicked his boxers aside, and when he got to the door, which stood open, he paused next to it with his back to the wall. The smell wafting out was fading but familiar: the aftermath of last night's enchilada adventures. He *had* gotten up to offload; that much, at least, hadn't been a dream.

"Is anybody in there? If so, answer up. I'm armed and I will shoot."

Nothing. Jack took a deep breath and pivoted around the doorframe, going low, sweeping the room from side to side with the barrel of the .38. He saw the toilet with the lid up and the ring down. He saw the newspaper on the floor, turned to the comics. He saw the tub, with its translucent flowered curtain pulled across. He saw shapes behind it, but those were the shower head, the grab handle, the back-scrubber.

Are you sure?

Before he could lose his nerve, he took a step forward, slid on the bathmat, and grabbed the shower curtain to keep from going ass over teapot. It pulled loose from the rings and covered his face. He screamed, clawed it aside, and pointed the .38 into the tub at nothing. No one there. No boogeyman. He peered at the bottom of the tub. He wasn't exactly conscientious about keeping it clean, and if someone had been standing in there, he would have left footprints. But the dried scum of soap and shampoo was unmarked by tracks. It had all been a dream. A particularly vivid nightmare.

Still, he checked the bathroom window and all three doors leading outside. Everything was buttoned up.

Okay, then. Time to relax. Or almost. He went back to the bathroom for one more look, this time checking the towel cabinet (nothing) and toeing at the fallen shower curtain with disgust. Time to replace that sucker. He'd swing by Home Depot today.

He reached absently to rub the back of his neck, and hissed with pain as soon as his fingers made contact. He went to the sink and turned around, but trying to see the back of your neck by looking over your shoulder was worse than useless. He opened the top drawer under the sink and found nothing but shaving stuff, combs, an unraveling Ace bandage, and the world's oldest tube of Monistat: another little souvenir from the Age of Greta. Like the stupid shower curtain.

In the bottom drawer he found what he was looking for, a mirror with a broken handle. He rubbed the dust from its reflective surface, backed up until his butt was touching the lip of the sink, and held up the mirror. The back of his neck was flaming red, and he could see little seed-pearl blisters forming. How was that possible, when he slathered himself with sunblock as a matter of course, and didn't have a sunburn anywhere else?

That's not a sunburn, Jack.

Hoskins made a little whimpering sound. Surely no one had been in his tub early this morning, no creepy weirdo with CANT tattooed on his fingers—*surely* not—but one thing was certain: skin cancer ran in his family. His mother and one of his uncles had died of it. *It goes with the red hair*, his father had said, after he himself had had skin tags removed from his driver's side arm, precancerous moles from his calves, and a basal cell carcinoma from the back of his neck.

Jack remembered a huge black mole (growing, always growing) on his uncle Jim's cheek; he remembered the raw sores on his mother's breastbone and eating into her left arm. Your skin was the largest organ in your body, and when it went haywire, the results were not pretty.

Would you like me to take it back? the man behind the curtain had asked.

"That was a dream," Hoskins said. "I got a scare out in Canning, and last night I ate a shitload of bad Mexican food, so I had a nightmare. That's all, end of story."

That didn't stop him from feeling for lumps in his armpits, under the angles of his jaw, inside his nose. Nothing. Only a little too much sun on the back of his neck. Except he had no sunburn anywhere else. Just that single throbbing stripe. It wasn't actually bleeding—which sort of proved his early morning encounter had only been a bad dream—but it was already growing that crop of blisters. He should probably see a doctor about it, and he would . . . after he gave it a few days to get better on its own, that was.

Will you do something if I ask you? You won't hesitate?

No one would, Jack thought, looking at the back of his neck in the mirror. If the alternative was getting eaten from the outside in—eaten alive—no one would.

4

Jeannie woke up staring at the bedroom ceiling, at first not able to understand why her mouth was filled with the coppery taste of panic, as if she had narrowly avoided a bad fall, or why her hands were raised, palms splayed out in a warding-off gesture. Then she saw the empty half of the bed on her left, heard the sound of Ralph splashing in the shower, and thought, *It was a dream. The most vivid damn nightmare of all time for sure, but that's all it was.*

Only there was no sense of relief, because she didn't believe that. It wasn't fading as dreams usually did on waking, even the worst ones. She remembered everything, from seeing the light on downstairs to the man sitting in the guest chair just beyond the living room archway. She remembered the hand emerging into the dim light, and closing into a fist so she could read the fading letters tattooed between the knuckles: MUST.

What you must do is tell him to stop.

She threw back the covers and left the room, not quite running. In the kitchen, the light over the stove was off, and all four chairs were in their accustomed places at the table where they ate most of their meals. It should have made a difference.

It didn't.

5

When Ralph came down, tucking his shirt into his jeans with one hand and holding his sneakers in the other, he found his wife sitting at the kitchen table. There was no morning cup of coffee in front of her, no juice, no cereal. He asked her if she was okay.

"No. There was a man here last night."

He stopped where he was, one side of his shirt squared away, the other hanging down over his belt. He dropped his sneakers. "Say *what*?"

"A man. The one who killed Frank Peterson."

He looked around, suddenly wide awake. "When? What are you talking about?"

"Last night. He's gone now, but he had a message for you. Sit down, Ralph."

He did, and she told him what had happened. He listened without saying a word, looking into her eyes. He saw nothing in them but absolute conviction. When she was done, he got up to check the burglar alarm console by the back door.

"It's armed, Jeannie. And the door's locked. At least this one is."

"I know it's armed. And they're all locked. I checked. The windows are, too."

"Then how—"

"I don't know, but he was here."

"Sitting right there." He pointed to the archway.

"Yes. As if he didn't want to get too far into the light."

"And he was big, you say?"

"Yes. Maybe not as big as you—I couldn't tell his height because he was sitting down—but he had broad shoulders and lots of muscle. Like a guy who spends three hours a day in a gym. Or lifting weights in a prison yard."

He left the table and got down on his knees where the kitchen's wooden floor met the living room carpet. She knew what he was looking for, and knew he wouldn't find it. She had checked this, too, and it didn't change her mind. If you weren't crazy, you knew the difference between dreams and reality, even when the reality was far outside the boundaries of normal life. Once she might have doubted that (as she knew Ralph was doubting now), but no more. Now she knew better.

He got up. "That's a new carpet, honey. If a man had sat there, even for a short while, the feet of the chair would have left marks in the nap. There aren't any."

She nodded. "I know. But he was there."

"What are you saying? That he was a ghost?"

"I don't know what he was, but I know he was right. You have to stop. If you don't, something bad is going to happen." She went to him, tilting her head up to look him full in the face. "Something terrible."

He took her hands. "This has been a stressful time, Jeannie. For you as much as for m—"

She pulled away. "Don't go there, Ralph. Don't. He was *here*."

"For the sake of argument, say he was. I've been threatened before. Any cop worth his salt has been threatened."

"You're not the only one being threatened!" She had to struggle not to shout. This was like being caught in one of those ridiculous horror movies where no one believes the heroine when she says Jason or Freddy or Michael Myers has come back yet again. "He was in our *house*!"

He thought about going over it again: locked doors, locked windows, burglar alarm armed but quiet. He thought about reminding her that she had awakened this morning in her own bed, safe and sound. He could see by her face that none of those things would do any good. And an argument with his wife in her current state was the last thing he wanted.

"Was he burned, Jeannie? Like the man I saw at the courthouse?"

She shook her head.

"You're sure? Because you said he was in the shadows."

"He leaned forward at one point, and I saw a little. I saw enough." She shuddered. "Broad forehead, shelving over his eyes. The eyes themselves were dark, maybe black, maybe brown, maybe deep blue, I couldn't tell. His hair was short and bristly. Some gray, but most of it still black. He had a goatee. His lips were very red."

The description struck a chime in his head, but Ralph didn't trust the feeling; it was probably a false positive caused by her intensity. God knew he wanted to believe her. If there had been one single scrap of empirical evidence . . .

"Wait a minute, his feet! He was wearing moccasins without socks and there were these red blotches all over them. I thought it was psoriasis, but I suppose it could have been burns."

He started the coffeemaker. "I don't know what to tell you, Jeannie. You woke up in bed, and there's just no sign anyone was—"

"Once upon a time you cut open a cantaloupe and it was full of maggots," she said. "That happened, you know it did. Why can't you believe *this* happened?"

"Even if I did, I couldn't stop. Don't you see that?"

"What I see is that the man sitting in our living room was right about one thing: *it's over.* Frank Peterson is dead. Terry is dead. You'll get back on active duty, and we . . . we can . . . could . . ."

She trailed off, because what she saw in his face made it clear that going on would be useless. It wasn't disbelief. It was disappointment that she could possibly believe moving on was an option for him. Arresting Terry Maitland at the Estelle Barga ballfield had been the first domino, the one that started a chain reaction of violence and misery. And now he and his wife were having an argument over the man who wasn't there. All his fault, that's what he believed.

"If you won't stop," she said, "you need to start carrying your gun again. I know I'll be carrying the little .22 you gave me three years ago. I thought it was a very stupid present at the time, but I guess you were right. Hey, maybe you were clairvoyant."

"Jeannie—"

"Do you want eggs?"

"I guess so, yeah." He wasn't hungry, but if all he could do for her this morning was eat her cooking, then that was what he would do.

She got the eggs out of the fridge and spoke to him without turning around. "I want us to have police protection at night. It doesn't have to be from dusk to dawn, but I want somebody making regular passes. Can you arrange that?"

Police protection against a ghost won't do much good, he thought . . . but had been married too long to say. "I believe I can."

"You should tell Howie Gold and the others, too. Even if it sounds crazy."

"Honey—"

But she rode over him. "He said you or any of them. He said he'd leave your guts strewn in the desert for the buzzards."

Ralph thought of reminding her that, while they did see the occasional buzzard wheeling in the sky (especially on garbage day), there wasn't much in the way of desert around Flint City. That alone was suggestive that the whole encounter had been a dream, but he kept quiet on this, as well. He had no intention of winding things up again just when they seemed to be winding down.

"I will," he said, and this was a promise he meant to keep. They needed to put it all out on the table. Every bit of the crazy. "You know we're having the meeting at Howie Gold's office, right? With the woman Alec Pelley hired to look into Terry's trip to Dayton."

"The one who stated categorically that Terry was innocent."

This time what Ralph thought of and didn't say (there were oceans of unspoken conversation in long marriages, it seemed) was, *Uri Geller stated categorically that he could bend spoons by concentrating on them.*

"Yes. She's flying in. Maybe it will turn out that she's full of shit, but she worked with a decorated ex-cop in that business of hers, and her procedure seemed sound enough, so maybe she really found something in Dayton. God knows she sounded sure of herself."

Jeannie began to crack eggs. "You'd go on even if I'd come downstairs and found the burglar alarm had been shorted out, the back door was standing open, and his footprints were on the tile. You'd go on even then."

"Yes." She deserved the truth, unvarnished.

She turned to him then, the spatula held high, like a weapon. "May I say that I think you're being sort of a fool?"

"You can say anything you want, but you need to remember two things, honey. Whether Terry was innocent or guilty, I played a part in getting him killed."

"You—"

"Hush," he said, pointing at her. "I'm talking, and you need to understand."

She hushed.

"And if he *was* innocent, there's a child-killer out there, running free."

"I understand that, but you may be opening the door on things far beyond your ability to understand. Or mine."

"Supernatural things? Is that what you're talking about? Because I can't believe that. I will never believe that."

"Believe what you want," she said, turning back to the stove, "but that man was here. I saw his face, and I saw the word on his fingers. MUST. He was . . . dreadful. It's the only word I can think of. Having you not believe me makes me want to cry, or throw this skillet of eggs at your head, or . . . I don't know."

He went to her and encircled her waist. "I believe that *you* believe. That much is true. And here's a promise: if nothing comes of this meeting tonight, you'll find me a lot more open to the idea of letting this go. I understand there are limits. Does that work?"

"I guess it has to, at least for now. I know you made a mistake at the ballfield. I know you're trying to atone for it. But what if you're making a worse mistake by keeping on?"

"Suppose it had been Derek in Figgis Park?" he countered. "Would you want me to let it go then?"

She resented the question, considered it a low blow, but had no answer for it. Because if it had been Derek, she would have wanted Ralph to pursue the man who'd done it—or the *thing*—to the ends of the earth. And she would have been right beside him.

"Okay. You win. But one more thing, and it's non-negotiable."

"What?"

"When you go to that meeting tonight, I'm going to be with you. And don't give me any crap about it being police business, because we both know it's not. Now eat your eggs."

6

Jeannie sent Ralph to Kroger with a grocery list, because no matter who had been in the house last night—human, ghost, or just a character in an extraordinarily vivid dream—Mr. and Mrs. Anderson still had to eat. And halfway to the supermarket, things came together for Ralph. There was nothing dramatic about it, because the salient facts had been there all along, literally right in front of his face, in a police department interview room. Had he interviewed Frank Peterson's real killer as a witness, thanked him for his help, and let him walk free? It seemed impossible, given the wealth of evidence tying Terry to the murder, but . . .

He pulled over and called Yune Sablo.

"I'll be there tonight, don't worry," Yune said. "Wouldn't miss all the news from the Ohio end of this clusterfuck. And I'm already on Heath Holmes. I don't have much yet, but by the time we get together, I should have a fair amount."

"Good, but that's not why I'm calling. Can you pull Claude Bolton's rap sheet? He's the bouncer at Gentlemen, Please. What you're going to find is possession, mostly, maybe one or two busts for possession with intent to sell, pleaded down."

"He's the one who prefers to be called security, right?"

"Yes sir, that's our Claude."

"What's up with him?"

"I'll tell you tonight, if it comes to anything. For now, all I can say is that there seems to be a chain of events that leads from Holmes to Maitland to Bolton. I could be wrong, but I don't think I am."

"You're killin me here, Ralph. Tell!"

"Not yet. Not until I'm sure. And I need something else. Bolton's a tattoo billboard, and I'm pretty sure he had something on his fingers. I should have noticed, but you know how it is when you're interviewing, especially if the guy on the other side of the table has a record."

"You keep your eyes on the face."

"That's right. Always on the face. Because when guys like Bolton start lying, they might as well be holding up a sign reading *I'm full of shit*."

"You think Bolton was lying when he talked about Maitland coming in to use the phone? Because the taxi driver lady sort of corroborated his story."

"I didn't think so at the time, but now I've got a little more. See if you can find out what was on his fingers. If anything."

"What do you *think* might be on them, *ese*?"

"Don't want to say, but if I'm right, it'll be on his sheet. One other thing. Can you email me a picture?"

"Happy to do it. Give me a few minutes."

"Thanks, Yune."

"Any plans to get in touch with Mr. Bolton?"

"Not yet. I don't want him to know I'm interested in him."

"And you really are going to explain all this tonight?"

"As much as I can, yes."

"Will it help?"

"Honest answer? I don't know. Have you got anything back on the stuff you found on the clothes and hay in that barn?"

"Not yet. Let me see what I can find on Bolton."

"Thanks."

"What are you up to right now?"

"Grocery shopping."

"Hope you remembered your wife's coupons."

Ralph smiled and looked at the rubber-banded stack on the seat beside him. "As if she'd let me forget," he said.

7

He came out of Kroger with three bags of groceries, stowed them in the trunk, then looked at his phone. Two messages from Yune Sablo. He opened the one with the photo attachment first. In his mug shot, Claude Bolton looked much younger than the man Ralph had interviewed prior to the Maitland arrest. He also looked stoned to the gills: thousand-yard stare, scraped cheek, and something on his chin that might have been egg or puke. Ralph remembered Bolton saying he went to Narcotics Anonymous these days, and that he'd been clean for five or six years. Maybe so, maybe not.

The attachment on Yune's second email was the arrest record. There were plenty of busts, mostly minor, and plenty of identifying marks. They included a scar on his back, one on his left side below the rib cage, one on his right temple, and about two dozen tattoos. There was an eagle, a knife with a bloody tip, a mermaid, a skull with candles in the eyesockets, and a good many others that didn't interest Ralph. What did were the words on his fingers: CANT on the right hand, MUST on the left.

THE OUTSIDER

The burned man at the courthouse had had tattoos on his fingers, but had they been CANT and MUST? Ralph closed his eyes and tried to see, but got nothing. He knew from experience that finger tattoos weren't uncommon among men who had spent time in jail; they probably saw it in the movies. LOVE and HATE were popular; so were GOOD and EVIL. He remembered Jack Hoskins telling him about a rat-faced little burglar who'd been sporting FUCK and SUCK on his digits, Jack saying it probably wasn't the kind of thing that would get the guy girlfriends.

The one thing Ralph was sure of was there hadn't been any tats on the burned man's arms. There were plenty of them on Claude Bolton's, but of course the fire that had wrecked the burned guy's face might have erased them. Only—

"Only no way was that man at the courthouse Bolton," he said, opening his eyes and staring at the people going in and out of the supermarket. "Impossible. Bolton wasn't burned."

How weird can this get? he had asked the Gibney woman on the phone last night. *Weirder*, she had replied, and how right she had been.

8

He and Jeannie put the groceries away together. When the chore was done, he told her he wanted her to look at something on his phone.

"Why?"

"Just take a look, okay? And remember that the person in the photo is quite a bit older now."

He handed her his phone. She stared at the mug shot for ten seconds, then handed it back. Her cheeks had lost all their color.

"It's him. His hair is shorter now, and he's got a full goatee instead of that little mustache, but that's the man who was in our house last night. The one who said he'd kill you if you didn't stop. What's his name?"

"Claude Bolton."

"Are you going to arrest him?"

"Not yet. Not sure I could, even if I wanted to, being on administrative leave and all."

"Then what are you going to do?"

"Right now? Find out where he is."

His first thought was to call Yune back, but Yune was digging away on the Dayton killer, Holmes. His second idea, quickly rejected, was Jack Hoskins. The man was a drunk and a blabbermouth. But there was a third choice.

He called the hospital, was informed that Betsy Riggins had gone home with her little bundle of joy, and reached her there. After asking how the new baby was doing (thus provoking a ten-minute rundown on everything from breast feeding to the high cost of Pampers), he asked her if she would mind helping a brother out by making a call or maybe two in her official capacity. He told her what he wanted.

"Is this about Maitland?" she asked.

"Well, Betsy, considering my current situation, that's sort of a don't ask, don't tell kind of deal."

"If it is, you could get in trouble. And *I* could get in trouble for helping you."

"If it's Chief Geller you're worried about, he won't hear it from me."

There was a long pause. He waited her out. Finally she said, "I felt bad for Maitland's wife, you know. Really bad. She made me think of those TV news stories about the aftermath of suicide bombings, survivors walking around with blood in their hair and no idea of what just happened. Could this maybe help her out?"

"It's possible," he said. "I don't want to go any further than that."

"Let me see what I can do. John Zellman isn't a total asshole, and that town line titty-bar of his needs a new license to operate every year. That might incline him to be helpful. I'll call you back if I strike out. If it goes the way I think it will, he'll call you."

"Thanks, Betsy."

"This stays between us, Ralph. I'm counting on having a job to come back to when my maternity leave is over. Tell me you hear that."

"Loud and clear."

9

John Zellman, owner and operator of Gentlemen, Please, called Ralph fifteen minutes later. He sounded curious rather than irritated, and was willing to help. Yes, he was sure Claude Bolton had been at the club when that poor kid had been grabbed and killed.

"Why so positive, Mr. Zellman? I thought he didn't go on duty until four PM."

"Yeah, but he came in early that day. Around two. He wanted time off to go to the big city with one of the strippers. He said she had a personal problem." Zellman snorted. "He was the one with the personal problem. Right under his zipper."

"Gal named Carla Jeppeson?" Ralph asked, scrolling through the transcript of Bolton's interview on his iPad. "Also known as Pixie Dreamboat?"

"That's her," Zellman said, and laughed. "If no tits count for shit, that ole girl's gonna be around for a long time. But some men kind of like that, don't ask me why. Her and Claude have got a thing, but it won't last long. Her husband's in McAlester now—bad checks, I think—but he'll be out by Christmas. She's just passing the time with Claude. I told him that, but you know what they say—a foreskin just wants to *get* in."

"You're sure that was that day he came in early. July 10th."

"Sure I am. Made a note of it, because no way was Claude gonna get paid for two days in Cap City when he had his vacation coming right up—*with* pay, mind you—less than two weeks later."

"Kind of outrageous. Did you consider firing him?"

"No. At least he was honest about it, you know? And listen. Claude's one of the good ones, and they're scarcer than hen's teeth. Mostly security guys are either pussies who look tough but don't want anything to do with a brawl if one breaks out in front of the runway, as they sometimes do, or guys who want to go all Incredible Hulk every time some customer gives them a little lip. Claude can throw somebody out with the best of them when he has to, but most times he doesn't. He's good at quieting them down. He's got a touch. I think it's on account of all those meetings he goes to."

"Narcotics Anonymous. He told me."

"Yeah, he's up-front about it. Proud, actually, and I guess he's got a right to be. A lot of guys never get that monkey off their backs once it climbs on. It's a tough monkey. Long claws."

"Staying clean, is he?"

"If he wasn't, I could tell. I know from junkies, Detective Anderson, believe me. Gentlemen is a clean place."

Ralph had his doubts, but let it pass. "No slips?"

Zellman laughed. "They all slip, at least in the beginning, but not since he's been working for me. He doesn't drink, either. I asked him why not once, if drugs were his problem. He said both things were the same. Said if he took a drink, even an O'Doul's, he'd be off looking for blow or something even stronger." Zellman paused, then said, "Maybe he was a douche when he was using, but he isn't now. He's decent. In a business where your trade comes to drink margaritas and stare at shaved pussies, that's kind of rare."

"I hear you. Is Bolton on vacation now?"

"Yup. As of Sunday. Ten days."

"Is it what you might call a stay-cation?"

"You mean is he here in FC? No. He's down in Texas, somewhere near Austin. It's where he's from. Hold on a second, I pulled his file before I called you." There was the sound of shuffling papers, then Zellman was back. "Marysville, that's the name of the town. Just a wide spot in the road, from the way he talks about it. I got the address because I send part of his paycheck down there every other week. It goes to his mother. She's old and pretty feeble. Got the emphysema, too. Claude went down to see if he could get her into one of those assisted living places, but he wasn't too hopeful. Says she's one stubborn old nanny goat. I don't see how he can afford it, anyway, on what he makes up here. When it comes to taking care of old people, the government should help regular guys like Claude, but does it? Bullshit it does."

Says the man who probably voted for Donald Trump, Ralph thought. "Well, thank you, Mr. Zellman."

"Can I ask why you want to talk to him?"

"Just a couple of follow-up questions," Ralph said. "Small stuff."

"Dotting *i*'s and crossing *t*'s, huh?"

"That's right. Do you have an address?"

"Sure, to send the money. Got a pencil?"

What he had was his trusty iPad, open to the Quick Notes app. "Shoot."

"Box 397, Rural Star Route 2, Marysville, Texas."

"And what's Mom's name?"

Zellman laughed cheerfully. "Lovie. Ain't that a good one? Lovie Ann Bolton."

Ralph thanked him and hung up.

"Well?" Jeannie asked.

"Hang on," Ralph said. "Notice I've got my think-face on."

"Ah, so you do. Could you use an iced tea while you think?" She was smiling. It looked good on her, that smile. It looked like a step in the right direction.

"No doubt."

He returned to his iPad (wondering how he had ever gotten along without the damn thing), and found Marysville about seventy miles west of Austin. It was little more than a dot on the map, its single claim to fame something called the Marysville Hole.

Ralph considered his next move while he drank his iced tea, then called Horace Kinney of the Texas Highway Patrol. Kinney was now a captain, mostly riding a desk, but Ralph had worked with him several times on interstate cases when the man had been a trooper, logging ninety thousand miles a year in north and west Texas.

"Horace," he said after they had finished with the pleasantries, "I need a favor."

"Big or small?"

"Medium, and it requires a bit of delicacy."

Kinney laughed. "Oh, you need to go to New York or Connecticut for delicacy, hoss. This is Texas. What do you need?"

Ralph told him. Kinney said he had just the man, and he happened to be in the area.

10

Around three o'clock that afternoon, Flint City PD dispatcher Sandy McGill looked up to see Jack Hoskins standing in front of her desk with his back turned.

"Jack? Did you need something?"

"Take a look at the back of my neck and tell me what you see."

Puzzled but willing, she stood up and looked. "Turn to the light a little more." And when he did so: "Ow, that's one hell of a sunburn. You should go down to the Walgreens and get some aloe vera cream."

"Will that fix it?"

"Only time will fix it, but it will take some of the sting out."

"But a sunburn is all it is, right?"

She frowned. "Sure, but bad enough to have blistered in places. Don't you know enough to put on sunblock when you're out fishing? Do you want to get skin cancer?"

Just hearing her say those words out loud made the back of his neck feel hotter. "I guess I forgot."

"How bad is it on your arms?"

"Not quite so bad." No burn on them at all, in fact; it was just on the back of his neck. Where someone had touched him out at that abandoned barn. Caressed him with just his fingertips. "Thanks, Sandy."

"Blonds and redheads get it the worst. If it doesn't get better, you should get it looked at."

He left without replying, thinking of the man in his dream. The one lurking behind the shower curtain.

I gave it to you, but I can take it back. Would you like me to take it back?

He thought, *It will go away on its own, like any other sunburn.*

Maybe so, but maybe not, and it really did hurt worse now. He could hardly bear to touch it, and he kept thinking of the open sores eating into his mother's flesh. At first the cancer had crawled, but once it really took hold, it galloped. By the end it was eating into her throat and vocal cords, turning her screams into growls, but listening through the closed door of her sickroom, eleven-year-old Jack Hoskins had still been able to hear what she was telling his father: to put her out of her misery. *You'd do it for a dog*, she'd croaked. *Why won't you do it for me?*

"Just a sunburn," he said, starting his car. "That's all it is. A fucking *sunburn*."

He needed a drink.

11

It was five that afternoon when a Texas Highway Patrol car drove up Rural Star Route 2 and turned into the driveway at Box 397. Lovie Bolton was on her front porch with a cigarette in her hand and her oxygen tank in its rubber-wheeled carrier beside her rocking chair.

"Claude!" she rasped. "We got a visitor! It's the State Patrol! Better come on around here and see what he wants!"

Claude was in the weedy backyard of the little shotgun house, taking in wash off the line and folding it neatly into a wicker basket. Ma's washing machine was all right, but the dryer had shit the bed shortly before he arrived, and these days she was too short of breath to hang out the clothes herself. He meant to buy her a new dryer before he left, but kept putting it off. And now the THP, unless Ma was wrong, and she probably wasn't. She had plenty of problems, but her eyes were fine.

He walked around the house and saw a tall cop getting out of a black-and-white SUV. At the sight of the gold Texas logo on the driver's side door, Claude felt his gut tighten. He hadn't done anything for which he could be arrested in a long, long time, but that tightening was a reflex. Claude reached into his pocket and gripped his six-year NA medallion, as he often did in moments of stress, hardly aware he was doing it.

The trooper tucked his sunglasses into his breast pocket as Ma struggled to rise from her rocker.

"No, ma'am, don't get up," he said. "I'm not worth it."

She cackled rustily and settled back. "Ain't you some big one. What's your name, Officer?"

"Sipe, ma'am. Corporal Owen Sipe. I'm pleased to meet you." He shook the hand not holding the cigarette, minding the old lady's swollen joints.

"Same goes right back, sir. This is my son, Claude. He's down from Flint City, kind of heppin me out."

Sipe turned to Claude, who let go of his chip and held out his own hand. "Pleased to meet you, Mr. Bolton." He held onto Claude's hand for a moment, studying it. "Got a little ink on your fingers, I see."

"Got to see both to get the whole message," Claude said. He held out the other hand. "I did em myself, in jail. But if you're here to see me, you probably know that."

"CANT and MUST," Trooper Sipe said, ignoring the question. "I've seen finger tattoos before, but never those."

"Well, they tell a story," Claude said, "and I pass it on when I can. It's how I make amends. I'm clean these days, but it was a hard struggle. Went to a lot of AA and NA meetings while I was locked up. At first it was just because they had doughnuts from Krispy Kreme, but eventually what they were saying took hold. I learned that every addict knows two things: he *can't* use and he *must* use. That's the knot in your head, see? You can't cut it and you can't untie it, so you have to learn to rise above it. It can be done, but you have to remember the basic situation. You *must* but you *can't*."

"Huh," Sipe said. "Sort of a parable, isn't it?"

"These days he don't drink nor drug," Lovie said from her rocker. "He don't even use this shit." She cast the stub of her cigarette into the dirt. "He's a good boy."

"I'm not here because anyone thinks he's done something bad," Sipe said mildly, and Claude relaxed. A little. You never wanted to relax too much when the State Patrol swung by for an unexpected visit. "Got a call from Flint City, closing out a case would be my best guess, and they need you to verify something about a man named Terry Maitland."

Sipe brought out his phone, diddled with it, and showed Claude a picture.

"Is this the belt buckle the Maitland fella was wearing the night you saw him? And don't ask me what that means, because I sure don't know. They just sent me out here to ask the question."

This was not why Sipe had been sent out, but the message from Ralph Anderson, relayed to Sipe by Captain Horace Kinney, was to make sure everything stayed friendly, with no suspicions aroused.

Claude examined the phone, then handed it back. "Can't be positive—that was a while ago—but it sure looks like it."

"Well, thank you. Thank you both." Sipe pocketed his phone and turned to go.

"That's it?" Claude asked. "You drove all the way out here to ask one question?"

"That's the long and short of it. I guess someone really wants to know. Thank you for your time. I'll pass this along on my way back to Austin."

"That's a long drive, Officer," Lovie said. "Why don't you come in first, and have a glass of sweet tea? It's only from a mix, but it ain't bad."

"Well, I can't come in and sit, want to get home before dark if I can, but I'd take a taste out here, if you don't mind."

"We don't mind a bit. Claude, go in and get this nice man a glass of tea."

"*Small* glass," Sipe said, holding his thumb and finger a smidge apart. "Two swallows and I'm down the road."

Claude went in. Sipe leaned a shoulder against the side of the porch, looking up at Lovie Bolton, whose good-natured face was a river of wrinkles.

"Your boy treats you pretty good, I guess?"

"I'd be lost without him," Lovie declared. "He sends me a 'lotment every other week, and comes down when he can. Wants to get me in an old folks' home in Austin, and I might go one of these days if he could afford it, which right now he can't. He's the best kind of son, Trooper Sipes: hellraiser early, trustworthy later on."

"I heard that," Sipe said. "Say, he ever take you out to the Big 7, down the road there? They make one hell of a breakfast."

"I don't trust roadside cafés," she said, taking her cigarettes from the pocket of her housedress and clamping one between her dentures. "Got ptomaine in one over Abilene way back in '74, and like to die. My boy takes over the cookin when he's here. He ain't no Emeril, but he ain't bad. Knows his way around a skillet. Don't burn the bacon." She dropped him a wink as she lit up, Sipe smiling and hoping there was a tight seal on her tank and she wasn't going to blow them both to hell.

"I bet he made you breakfast this morning," Sipe said.

"You bet he did. Coffee, raisin toast, and scrambled eggs with plenty of butter, just the way I like em."

"Are you an early riser, ma'am? I only ask because, with the oxygen and all—"

"Him and me both," she said. "Up with the sun."

Claude came back out with three glasses of iced tea on a tray, two tall ones and a shortie. Owen Sipe drank his in two gulps, smacked his lips, and said he had to be off. The Boltons watched him go, Lovie in her rocker, Claude sitting on the steps, frowning at the rooster-tail of dust marking the trooper's progress back to the main road.

"See how much nicer the cops are when you ain't been doin nothin bad?" Lovie asked.

"Yeah," Claude said.

"Drove all the way out here just to ask about some belt buckle. Think of that!"

"That wasn't why he came, Ma."

"No? Then why?"

"Not sure, but that wasn't it." Claude put his glass down on the step and looked at his fingers. At CANT and MUST, the knot he had finally risen above. He stood up. "I better get the rest of those clothes off the line. Then I want to go over to Jorge's and ask if I can help him out tomorrow. He's roofin."

"You're a good boy, Claude." He saw tears standing in her eyes, and was moved by them. "You come here and give your ma a big old hug."

"Yes, ma'am," Claude said, and did just that.

12

Ralph and Jeannie Anderson were getting ready to go to the meeting at Howie Gold's office when Ralph's cell phone rang. It was Horace Kinney. Ralph spoke to him while Jeannie put on her earrings and slipped into her shoes.

"Thank you, Horace. I owe you one." He ended the call.

Jeannie was looking at him expectantly. "Well?"

"Horace sent a THP trooper out to the Bolton place in Marysville. He had a cover story, but what he was really there for—"

"I know what he was there for."

"Uh-huh. According to Mrs. Bolton, Claude cooked them breakfast around six o'clock this morning. If you saw Bolton downstairs at four—"

"I saw the clock when I got up to pee," Jeannie said. "It was 4:06."

"MapQuest says the distance between Flint City and Marysville is four hundred and thirty miles. He never could have made it from here to there in time to make breakfast at six, honey."

"The mother could have been lying." She said it without much conviction.

"Sipe—the trooper Horace sent—said he didn't pick that up on his radar, and thinks he would've."

"So it's Terry all over again," she said. "A man in two places at the same time. Because he was here, Ralph. He *was*."

THE OUTSIDER

Before he could answer, the doorbell rang. Ralph shrugged on a sportcoat to cover the Glock on his belt and went downstairs. District Attorney Bill Samuels stood on the front stoop, looking strangely unlike himself in jeans and a plain blue tee-shirt.

"Howard called me. Said there was going to be a meeting—'an informal get-together about the Maitland business,' is how he put it—at his office, and suggested I might like to come. I thought we could go together, if that's all right."

"I guess so," Ralph said, "but listen, Bill—who else have you told? Chief Geller? Sheriff Doolin?"

"Nobody. I'm no genius, but I didn't hit my head falling out of the dumb-tree, either."

Jeannie joined Ralph at the door, checking her purse. "Hello, Bill. I'm surprised to see you here."

Samuels's smile was without humor. "To tell you the truth, I'm surprised to be here. This case is like a zombie that won't stay dead."

"What does your ex think about all this?" Ralph asked, and when Jeannie gave him a frown: "Just tell me if I'm stepping out of line."

"Oh, we've discussed it," Samuels said. "Except that's not quite right. *She* discussed and I listened. She thinks I played a part in getting Maitland killed, and she's not entirely wrong." He tried to smile and couldn't quite make it. "But how were we to know, Ralph? Tell me that. It was a slam-dunk, wasn't it? Looking back . . . knowing all we did . . . can you honestly say you would have done anything different?"

"Yes," Ralph said. "I wouldn't have arrested him in front of the whole fucking town, and I would have made sure he went into the courthouse by the back door. Come on, let's go. We're going to be late."

MACY'S TELLS GIMBELS

July 25th

1

As it turned out, Holly did not fly business class, although she could have if she had opted for the 10:15 Delta flight, which would have put her in Cap City at 12:30. Because she wanted some extra time in Ohio, however, she booked an arduous three-stage trip on puddle-jumpers that would probably bounce her all over the uneasy July air. Cramped and not particularly pleasant, but bearable. What she found less bearable was the knowledge that she wouldn't arrive in Flint City until six PM, and that was if all her arrangements worked out perfectly. The meeting at Attorney Gold's office was scheduled for seven, and if there was one thing Holly hated above all others, it was being late for a scheduled appointment. Being late was the wrong way to get off on the right foot.

She packed her few things, checked out of the hotel, and drove the thirty miles to Regis. She went first to the house where Heath Holmes had been staying with his mother on his vacation. It was closed up, the windows boarded across, likely because vandals had been using them for target practice. On the lawn, which badly needed mowing, was a sign that read FOR SALE CONTACT FIRST NATIONAL BANK OF DAYTON.

Holly looked at the house, knew that the local kids would soon be whispering that it was haunted (if they weren't already), and mused on the nature of tragedy. Like measles, mumps, or rubella, tragedy was contagious. Unlike those diseases, there was no vaccine. The death of Frank Peterson in Flint City had infected his unfortunate family and spread through the entire town. She doubted if that was quite the case in this suburban community, where fewer people had long-term ties, but the Holmes family was certainly gone; nothing left of them but this empty house.

She debated taking a photo of the boarded-up house with the FOR SALE sign in the foreground—a picture of sorrow and loss if there ever was one—and decided not to. Some of the people she was going to meet might understand, might feel those things, but most of them probably would not. To them it would just be a picture.

She drove from the Holmes residence to the Peaceful Rest Cemetery, on the outskirts of town. Here she found the family reunited: father, mother, and only son. There were no flowers, and the stone marking the resting place of Heath Holmes had been pushed over. She imagined the same thing might have happened to Terry Maitland's stone. Sorrow was catching; so was anger. His was a small marker, nothing on it but the name, the dates, and a bit of dried scum that might have been the residue of a thrown egg. With some effort, she set it up again. She had no illusions that it would stay that way, but a person did what a person could.

"You didn't kill anyone, Mr. Holmes, did you? You were just in the wrong place at the wrong time." She found some posies on a nearby grave, and borrowed a few to scatter on Heath's. Picked flowers were a poor remembrance—they died—but better than nothing. "You're stuck with it, though. Nobody here would ever believe the truth. I don't think the people I'm going to meet tonight will believe it, either."

She would try to convince them, just the same. A person did what a person could, whether it was setting up gravestones or trying to convince twenty-first-century men and women that there were monsters in the world, and their greatest advantage was the unwillingness of rational people to believe.

Holly looked around and saw a vault on a nearby low hill (in this part of Ohio, all the hills were low). She walked to it, gazed at the name chiseled in the granite over the lintel—GRAVES, how appropriate—and walked down the three stone steps. She peered inside at the stone benches, where one could sit and meditate on the Graves of yesteryear here entombed. Had the outsider hidden here after his filthy work was done? She didn't believe so, because anyone—maybe even one of the vandals who had pushed over Heath Holmes's stone—might wander over for a peek inside. Also, the sun would shine into the meditation area for an hour or two in the afternoons, giving it a bit of fugitive warmth. If the outsider was what she believed he was, he would prefer darkness. Not always, no, but for certain periods of time. Certain crucial periods. She hadn't finished her research yet, but she was almost sure of that much. And something else: murder might be its life's work, but sorrow was its food. Sorrow and anger.

No, it hadn't taken its rest in this vault, but she believed it had been in this cemetery, perhaps even before the deaths of Mavis Holmes and her son. Holly thought (she knew it might only be a fancy) she could smell its presence. Brady Hartsfield had had that same smell about him, the stink of the unnatural. Bill had known it; the nurses who had cared for Hartsfield had known it, too, even though he was supposedly in a state of semi-catatonia.

She walked slowly to the little parking lot outside the cemetery gates with her bag banging against her hip. Her Prius waited alone in the sizzling summer heat. She walked past it, then turned a slow three-sixty, studying every aspect of the surrounding area. She was close to farm country—she could smell the fertilizer—but this was a transitional belt of industrial abandonment, ugly and barren. There would be no pictures of it in the Chamber of Commerce promotional brochures (assuming Regis had a Chamber of Commerce). There were no points of interest. There was nothing to attract the eye; it was repelled instead, as if the very earth was saying *go away, there is nothing for you here, goodbye, don't come again.* Well, there was the cemetery, but few people would visit Peaceful Rest once winter came, and the north wind would freeze those few away after the briefest of visits to make their manners to the dead.

Yonder to the north were train tracks, but the rails were rusty and there were weeds growing up between the crossties. There was a long-deserted train station, its windows boarded up like those of the Holmes house. Beyond it, on a spur, stood two lonely boxcars, their wheels buried in vines. They looked as if they had been there since the Vietnam era. Near the deserted station were long-abandoned storage facilities and what she assumed were obsolete repair sheds. Beyond those, a broken factory stood hip-deep in sunflowers and bushes. A swastika had been spray-painted on crumbling pink bricks that had been red a long, long time ago. On one side of the highway that would take her back to town, a leaning billboard proclaimed ABORTION STOPS A BEATING HEART! **CHOOSE LIFE!** On the other side was a long low building with a sign on its roof reading SPE DY ROBO CAR WASH. In its empty parking lot was another sign, one she'd seen once already today: FOR SALE CONTACT FIRST NATIONAL BANK OF DAYTON.

I think you were here. Not in the vault, but close by. Where you could smell tears when the wind was right. Where you could hear the laughter of the men or boys who pushed over Heath Holmes's stone and then likely urinated on his grave.

In spite of the day's heat, Holly felt cold. Given more time, she might have investigated those empty places. There was no danger; the outsider was long gone from Ohio. Very likely gone from Flint City, too.

She snapped four pictures: the train station, the boxcars, the factory, the deserted car wash. She reviewed them and decided they would do. They'd have to. She had a plane to catch.

Yes, and people to convince.

If she could, that was. She felt very small and lonely just now. It was easy to imagine laughter and ridicule; thinking of such things came naturally to her. But she would try. She had to. For the murdered children, yes—Frank Peterson and the Howard girls and all the ones who had come before them—but also for Terry Maitland and Heath Holmes. A person did what a person could.

She had one more stop to make. Luckily, it was on her way.

2

An old man sitting on a bench in Trotwood Community Park was happy to give her directions to the place where the bodies of "those poor gals" had been found. It wasn't far, he said, and she would know it when she got there.

She did.

Holly pulled over, got out, and gazed at a ravine which mourners—and thrill-seekers masquerading as mourners—had attempted to turn into a shrine. There were glittery cards upon which words like SORROW and HEAVEN predominated. There were balloons, some deflating, some fresh and new, even though Amber and Jolene Howard had been discovered here three months earlier. There was a statue of Mary, which some wag had decorated with a mustache. There was a teddy bear that made Holly shudder. Its plump brown body was covered with mold.

She raised her iPad, took a picture.

There was no whiff of that smell she had gotten (or imagined she'd gotten) at the cemetery, but she had no doubt the outsider would have visited this place at some point after the bodies of Amber and Jolene had been discovered, sampling the grief of the pilgrims to this makeshift shrine like a fine old Burgundy. Also the excitement of those—not many, but a few, there were always a few—who came to meditate on what it might be like to do such things as had been done to the Howard girls, and listen to their screams.

Yes, you came, but not too soon. Not until you could do so without attracting unwanted attention, the way you did on the day Frank Peterson's brother shot Terry Maitland.

"Only that time you couldn't resist, could you?" Holly murmured. "It would have been like a starving man trying to resist a Thanksgiving dinner with all the trimmings."

A minivan pulled in ahead of Holly's Prius. On one side of the bumper was a sticker reading MOM'S TAXI. The one on the other side read I BELIEVE IN THE 2ND AMENDMENT, AND I VOTE. The woman who got out was well-dressed, plump, pretty, in her thirties. She was holding a bouquet of flowers. She knelt, put them beside a wooden cross with LITTLE GIRLS on one arm and WITH JESUS on the other. Then she stood up.

"So sad, isn't it?" she said to Holly.

"Yes."

"I'm a Christian, but I'm glad the man who did it is dead. *Glad.* And I'm glad he's in hell. Is that awful of me?"

"He's not in hell," Holly said.

The woman recoiled as if she had been slapped.

"He *brings* hell."

Holly drove to the Dayton Airport. She was running a bit behind, but resisted the urge to exceed the speed limit. Laws were laws for a reason.

3

Having to fly on the commuter planes (Tin Can Airways was what Bill had called them) had its advantages. For one, the final leg put her down at Kiowa Airfield in Flint County, saving her a seventy-mile drive from Cap City. Leapfrog travel also gave her a chance to continue her researches. During her brief layovers between flights, she used airport Wi-Fi to download as much information as she could, and as fast as she could. During the flights themselves she read what she had downloaded, scrolling fast and concentrating fiercely, barely hearing the dismayed yelps when her second flight, a thirty-seat turboprop, hit an air pocket and dropped like an elevator.

She arrived at her destination only five minutes late, and by putting on a burst of speed, was first to Hertz, earning a dirty look from the overburdened salesman type she beat out with a final sprint. On the way into town, seeing how close she was shaving it, she gave in to temptation and broke the speed limit. But only by five miles an hour.

4

"That's her. Got to be."

Howie Gold and Alec Pelley were standing outside the building where Howie kept his offices. Howie was pointing to a slim woman in a gray business suit and white blouse trotting up the sidewalk, a big totebag banging against one slim hip. Her hair was cut close to her small face, with graying bangs that stopped just short of her eyebrows. There was a touch of fading lipstick on her mouth, but she wore no other makeup. The sun was sinking, but what remained of the day was still hot, and a trickle of sweat ran down one of her cheeks.

"Ms. Gibney?" Howie asked, stepping forward.

"Yes," she panted. "Am I late?"

"Two minutes early, actually," Alec said. "May I take your bag? It looks heavy."

"I'm fine," she said, looking from the stocky, balding lawyer to the investigator who had hired her. Pelley was at least six inches taller than his boss, with graying hair combed straight back, tonight dressed in tan slacks and a white shirt open at the neck. "Are the others here?"

"Most," Alec said. "Detective Anderson—ah, speak of the devil."

Holly turned and saw three people approaching. One was a woman, holding the remains of her youthful good looks quite well into her middle age, although the circles under her eyes, only partially concealed by foundation and a bit of powder, suggested she might not have been sleeping well lately. To her left was a skinny, nervous-looking man with a cowlick coming loose from the back of his otherwise rigidly controlled hair. And on her right . . .

Detective Anderson was a tall man with sloping shoulders and the beginnings of what would probably become a paunch if he didn't start exercising more and watching what he ate. His head was slightly thrust forward, his eyes, bright blue, taking her in from top to bottom and stem to stern. It wasn't Bill, of course it wasn't, Bill was two years dead and never coming back. Also, this man was much younger than Bill had been when Holly first met him. It was the eager curiosity in his face that was the same. He was holding the woman's hand, which suggested she was Mrs. Anderson. Interesting that she should have come with him.

There were introductions all around. The slender man with the cowlick, it turned out, was Flint County district attorney William ("Please call me Bill") Samuels.

"Let's go upstairs and get out of this heat," Howie said.

Mrs. Anderson—Jeanette—asked Holly if she had had a good flight, and Holly made the appropriate response. Then she turned to Howie and asked if there was perhaps audio-visual capability in the room they would be using. He told her there certainly was, and she was welcome to use it if she had material to present. When they stepped out of the elevator, Holly enquired about the women's room. "I could use a minute or two. I came directly from the airport."

"Absolutely. End of the hall, turn left. Should be unlocked."

Holly was afraid Mrs. Anderson would volunteer to go with her, but Jeanette didn't. Which was good. Holly did have to pee ("spend a penny," was how her mother always put it), but she had something more important in mind, a matter that could only be attended to in complete private.

In the stall, with her skirt up and her bag between her sensible loafers, she closed her eyes. Mindful that tiled rooms like this were natural amplifiers, she prayed silently.

This is Holly Gibney again, and I need help. You know I'm not good with strangers even one at a time, and tonight I have six of them to deal with. Seven, if Mr. Maitland's widow is here. I'm not terrified, but I'd be lying if I didn't say I was scared. Bill could do things like this, but I'm not him. Just help me to do it the way he would. Help me to understand their natural disbelief and not be afraid of it.

She finished aloud, but in a whisper. "Please God, help me not to frack up." She paused, then added, "I'm not smoking."

5

The meeting took place in Howard Gold's conference room, and while it was smaller than the one on *The Good Wife* (Holly had watched all seven seasons, and had now moved on to the sequel), it was very nice. Tasteful pictures, polished mahogany table, leather chairs. Mrs. Maitland had indeed come. She was sitting at Mr. Gold's right as Howie took his place at the head of the table and asked who was watching her girls.

Marcy gave him a wan smile. "Lukesh and Chandra Patel volunteered. Their son was on Terry's team. In fact, Baibir was on third base when . . ." She looked at Detective Anderson. "When your men arrested him. Baibir was heartbroken. He didn't understand."

Anderson crossed his arms and said nothing. His wife put a

hand on his shoulder and murmured something no one else was meant to hear. Anderson nodded.

"I'm going to call this meeting to order," Mr. Gold said. "I have no agenda, but perhaps our visitor would like to begin. This is Holly Gibney, a private detective Alec hired to investigate the Dayton end of this business, assuming the two cases really are connected. That's one of the things we're here to determine, if possible."

"I'm not a private detective," Holly demurred. "My partner, Peter Huntley, is the one with the private investigator's license. What our company mostly does is repo work and skip-tracing. We do take on an occasional criminal investigation where we're unlikely to be scolded by the police. We've had good luck with missing pets, for instance."

That sounded lame, and she felt blood heating her face.

"Ms. Gibney is being a trifle too modest," Alec said. "I believe you were involved with running a violent fugitive named Morris Bellamy to earth."

"That was my partner's case," Holly said. "My *first* partner. Bill Hodges. He's since passed away, Mr. Pelley—Alec—as you know."

"Yes," Alec said. "I'm sorry for your loss."

The Latino man Detective Anderson had introduced as Yunel Sablo of the State Police now cleared his throat. "I believe," he said, "that you and Mr. Hodges were also involved in a case of mass vehicular homicide and intended terrorism. A young man named Hartsfield. And that you, Ms. Gibney, were personally responsible for stopping him before he could cause an explosion in a crowded auditorium. One that might have killed thousands of young people."

A murmur went around the table. Holly felt her face growing hotter. She would have liked to tell them that she had failed, that she had only halted Brady's homicidal ambitions for awhile, that he had come back to cause yet more deaths before being stopped for good, but this was neither the time nor the place.

Lieutenant Sablo wasn't finished. "I think you received a commendation from the city?"

"There were actually three of us who got commendations, but all it amounted to was a gold key and a bus pass good for ten years." She looked around at them, unhappily aware that she was still blushing like a sixteen-year-old. "That was a long time ago. As for this case, I'd rather save my report for last. And my conclusions."

"Like the final chapter in one of those old British drawing-room mysteries," Mr. Gold said, smiling. "We all tell what we know, then you stand up and astound us with an explanation of who done it, and how."

"Good luck with that," Bill Samuels said. "Just thinking about the Peterson case makes my head hurt."

"I believe we have most of the pieces," Holly said, "but I don't believe they're all out on the table, even now. What I keep remembering—I'm sure you'll think it's silly—is that old saying about how Macy's doesn't tell Gimbels. But now Macy's and Gimbels are both here—"

"Not to mention Saks, Nordstrom's, and Needless Markup," Howie said. Then, seeing Holly's expression: "I'm not joshing you, Ms. Gibney, I'm agreeing with you. Everything on the table. Who starts?"

"Yune should," Anderson said. "Since I'm on administrative leave."

Yune put a briefcase on the table and took out his laptop. "Mr. Gold, can you show me how to use the projection gadget?"

Howie obliged, and Holly watched closely, so she would know how to do it herself when her turn came. Once the right cords were connected, Howie dimmed the lights a bit.

"Okay," Yune said. "Apologies to you, Ms. Gibney, if I'm beating you to some of the stuff you found out while you were in Dayton."

"Perfectly all right," Holly said.

"I spoke with Captain Bill Darwin of the Dayton Police Department, and Sergeant George Highsmith of the Trotwood PD. When I told them we had a similar case, possibly connected by a stolen van that had been near both their crime scene and ours, they were willing to help, and thanks to the magic of telecommunication, I should have it all right here. If this gadget works, that is."

Yune's desktop appeared on the screen. He clicked on a file marked HOLMES. The first image was that of a man in an orange county jail jumpsuit. He had short-cropped auburn hair and beard stubble on his cheeks. His eyes were slightly squinted, giving him a look that could have been sinister or simply stunned at the sudden turn his life had taken. Holly had seen the mug shot on the front page of the *Dayton Daily News*, April 30th issue.

"This is Heath James Holmes," Yune said. "Thirty-four. Arrested for the murders of Amber and Jolene Howard. I have crime scene pictures of the girls, but won't show them to you. You wouldn't sleep. The mutilations are the worst I've ever seen."

Silence from the seven people watching. Jeannie was clutching her husband's arm. Marcy was staring at Holmes's photo as if mesmerized, with a hand over her mouth.

"Other than a minor juvenile bust for joyriding in a stolen car and a couple of speeding tickets, Holmes's record is squeaky clean. His twice-yearly work evaluations, first at Kindred Hospital and then at the Heisman Memory Unit, are excellent. Co-workers and patients spoke highly of him. There are comments like *always friendly* and *genuinely caring* and *goes the extra mile*."

"People said all those things about Terry," Marcy murmured.

"Means nothing," Samuels protested. "People said the same things about Ted Bundy."

Yune continued. "Holmes told co-workers he planned to spend his one-week vacation with his mother in Regis, a small town thirty miles north of Dayton and Trotwood. Midway through his vacation week, the bodies of the Howard girls were discovered by a postman on his delivery rounds. The guy saw a huge flock of crows congregated at a ravine about a mile from the Howard home, and stopped to investigate. Given what he found, he probably wishes he hadn't."

He clicked, and two little blond girls replaced Heath Holmes's squint and stubble. The photo had been taken at a carnival or an amusement park; Holly could see a Tilt-a-Whirl in the background. Amber and Jolene were smiling and holding up cones of cotton candy like prizes.

"No victim-blaming here, but the Howard girls were a handful. Alcoholic mother, father not in the picture, low-income home in a lousy neighborhood. The school had them tabbed as 'at-risk students,' and they had skipped out on several occasions. Which they did on Monday, April 23rd, at about ten in the morning. It was Amber's free period, and Jolene said she had to use the bathroom, so they probably planned it in advance."

"Escape from Alcatraz," Bill Samuels said.

Nobody laughed.

Yune continued. "They were seen shortly before noon in a little beer-and-grocery about five blocks from the school. This is a still, taken from the store's surveillance camera."

The black-and-white image was crisp and clear—like something out of an old film noir, Holly thought. She stared at the two towheads, one with a couple of sodas and the other with a couple of candybars. They were dressed in jeans and tees. Neither looked pleased; the girl with the candybars was pointing, her mouth wide open and her brow furrowed.

"The clerk knew they were supposed to be in school and wouldn't sell to them," Yune said.

"No kidding," Howie said. "You can almost hear the older one giving him hell."

"True," Yune said, "but that's not the interesting part. Check out the upper right corner of the picture. On the sidewalk and looking in the window. Here, I'll zoom it a little."

Marcy murmured something very softly. It might have been *Christ*.

"It's him, isn't it?" Samuels said. "It's Holmes. Watching them."

Yune nodded. "That clerk was the last person to report seeing Amber and Jolene alive. But at least one more camera picked them up."

He clicked, and another photo from another surveillance camera came up on the screen at the front of the conference room. This one had its electronic eye trained on an island of gas pumps. The time-code in the corner said 12:19 PM, April 23rd. Holly thought this must be the photo her nurse informant had mentioned. Candy Wilson had guessed that the vehicle in it was probably Holmes's truck, a Chevy Tahoe that was "all fancied up," but she had been wrong. The picture showed Heath Holmes in mid-stride, returning to a panel truck with DAYTON LANDSCAPING & POOLS printed on the side. His gas presumably paid for, he was returning to the vehicle with a soda in each hand. Leaning out the driver's side window to take them was Amber, the older of the two Howard girls.

"When was that truck stolen?" Ralph asked.

"April 14th," Yune said.

"He stashed it until he was ready. Which means this was a planned crime."

"It would seem so, yes."

Jeannie said, "And those girls just . . . got in with him?"

Yune shrugged. "Again, no victim-blaming—you can't blame a couple of kids this young for making bad choices—but this picture does suggest they were with him willingly, at least to start with. Mrs. Howard told Sergeant Highsmith that the older girl made a habit of 'hooking rides' when she wanted to go someplace, even though she was told repeatedly it was dangerous behavior."

Holly thought the two surveillance photos told a simple story. The outsider had seen the girls refused service at the beer-and-grocery, and offered to get them their sodas and candy a little bit further along, when he gassed up. After that, he might have told them he'd take them home or wherever else they might want to go. Just a nice guy helping out a couple of girls playing hooky—hell, he'd been young once himself.

"Holmes was next seen a little after six PM," Yune resumed. "This was in a Waffle House on the outskirts of Dayton. He had blood on his face, hands, and shirt. He told the waitress and the short-order cook that he'd had a bloody nose, and washed up in the men's. When he came out, he ordered some food to go. As he left, the cook and the waitress saw he also had spots of blood on the back of his shirt and the seat of his pants, which made his story seem a little less likely, being as how most people have their noses on in front. The waitress took down his plate number and called the police. They both later picked Holmes out of a six-pack. Hard to mistake that auburn hair."

"Still driving the panel truck when he stopped at the Waffle House?" Ralph asked.

"Uh-huh. It was found abandoned in the Regis municipal parking lot shortly after the girls were found. There was a lot of blood in the back, his fingerprints and the girls' fingerprints all over everything. Some in blood. Again, the resemblance to the Frank Peterson killing is very strong. Striking, in fact."

"How close to his house in Regis was this panel truck found?" Holly asked.

"Less than half a mile. Police theorize he dumped it, strolled home, changed out of his bloody clothes, and cooked Mama a nice supper. The police got a hit on the fingerprints almost right away, but it took them a couple of days to cut through the red tape and get a name."

"Because Holmes's one bust, the joyriding thing, happened when he was still legally a minor," Ralph said.

"*Sí, señor.* On April 26th, Holmes went in to the Heisman

Memory Unit. When the lady in charge—Mrs. June Kelly—asked him what he was doing there during his vacation, he said he had to get something out of his locker, and he thought he'd check on a couple of patients while he was there. This struck her a bit odd, because while the nurses do have lockers, the orderlies only have these plastic cubby things in the break room. Also, orderlies are told from the jump that the correct word when referring to the paying clientele is *residents*, and Holmes usually just called them his guys and gals. All friendly-like. Anyway, one of the guys he checked on that day was Terry Maitland's father, and the police found blond hairs in the man's bathroom. Hairs that forensics matched to Jolene Howard's."

"Pretty goddam convenient," Ralph said. "Did nobody suggest it might be a plant?"

"The way the evidence kept stacking up, they just assumed he was careless or wanted to be caught," Yune said. "The panel truck, the fingerprints, the surveillance photos . . . girls' underpants found in the basement . . . and finally the icing on the cake, a DNA match. Cheek swabs taken in custody matched semen the perp left at the scene."

"My God," Bill Samuels said. "It really is *déjà vu* all over again."

"With one big exception," Yune said. "Heath Holmes wasn't lucky enough to get filmed at a lecture that happened to be going on at the same time the Howard girls were being abducted and murdered. His mother swore he had been in Regis the whole time, said he'd never gone in to the Heisman, and he certainly hadn't gone to Trotwood. 'Why would he?' she said. 'It's a shitty town full of shitty people.'"

"Her testimony would have cut zero ice with a jury," Samuels said. "Hey, if your mom won't lie for you, who will?"

"Other people in the neighborhood saw him during his vacation week," Yune went on. "He cut his mother's grass, he fixed her gutters, he painted the stoop, and he helped the lady across the street plant some flowers. This was on the same day the Howard girls were taken. Also, that tricked-out truck of his was kind of hard to miss when he was driving around and doing errands."

Howie asked, "The lady across the street, could she place him with her anywhere near the time those two girls were killed?"

"She said around ten in the morning. Close to an alibi, but no cigar. Regis is a lot nearer to Trotwood than Flint is to Cap City. Cops theorized that as soon as he finished helping the neighbor with her petunias or whatever, he drove to the municipal lot, swapped his Tahoe for the panel truck, and went hunting."

"Terry *was* luckier than Mr. Holmes," Marcy said, looking first at Ralph and then at Bill Samuels. Ralph met her gaze; Samuels either could not or would not. "Just not lucky enough."

Yune said, "I've got one more thing—another piece of the puzzle, Ms. Gibney would say—but I'm going to save it until Ralph recaps the Maitland investigation, both pro and con."

Ralph made short work of this, speaking in concise sentences, as if testifying in court. He made a point of telling them what Claude Bolton had told him—that Terry had nicked him with a fingernail while shaking his hand. After telling them about the discovery of the clothes out in Canning Township—pants, underwear, socks, sneakers, but no shirt—he circled back to the man he'd seen on the courthouse steps. He said he wasn't certain that the man had been using the shirt Terry had been wearing at the Dubrow train station to cover his presumably scarred and hairless head, but he believed that it could have been.

"There must have been TV coverage at the courthouse," Holly said. "Have you checked it?"

Ralph and Lieutenant Sablo exchanged a look.

"We did," Ralph said, "but that man's not there. Not in any of the footage."

There was a general stirring, and Jeannie was holding his arm again—clutching it, really. Ralph gave her hand a reassuring pat, but he was looking at the woman who had flown here from Dayton. Holly didn't look puzzled. She looked satisfied.

6

"The man who killed the Howard girls used a panel truck," Yune said, "and when he was done with it, he dumped it in an easily discoverable location. The man who killed Frank Peterson did the same with the van he used to abduct the boy; actually drew attention to it by leaving it behind Shorty's Pub and speaking to a couple of witnesses—the way Holmes spoke to the cook and the waitress in the Waffle House. The Ohio cops found plenty of fingerprints in the panel truck, both the killer's and his victims'; we found plenty in the van. But the van prints included at least one set that went unidentified. Until late today, that is."

Ralph leaned forward, intent.

"Let me show you some stuff." Yune fiddled with his laptop. Two fingerprints appeared on the screen. "These are from the kid who stole the van in upstate New York. One from the van, one from his intake when he was arrested in El Paso. Now check this out."

He fiddled some more, and the two prints came together perfectly.

"That takes care of Merlin Cassidy. Now here's Frank Peterson—one print from the ME, and one from the van."

The overlay again showed a perfect match.

"Next, Maitland. One print from the van—one of many, I might add—and the other from his intake at the Flint City PD."

He brought them together, and again the match was perfect. Marcy made a sighing sound.

"Okay, now prepare to have your mind boggled. On the left, an unsub print from the van; on the right, a Heath Holmes print from *his* intake in Montgomery County, Ohio."

He brought them together. This time the fit was not perfect, but it was very close. Holly believed a jury would have accepted it as a match. She certainly did.

"You'll notice a few minor differences," Yune said. "That's because the Holmes print from the van is a bit degraded, maybe from the passage of time. But there are enough points of identity to satisfy me. Heath Holmes was in that van at some point. This is new information."

The room was silent.

Yune put up two more prints. The one on the left was sharp and clear. Holly realized they had already seen it. Ralph did, too. "Terry's," he said. "From the van."

"Correct. And on the right, here's one from the buckle left in the barn."

The whorls were the same, but oddly faded in places. When Yune brought them together, the van print filled in the blanks on the buckle print.

"No doubt they're the same," Yune said. "Both Terry Maitland's. Only the one on the buckle looks like it came from a much older finger."

"How is that possible?" Jeannie asked.

"It's not," Samuels said. "I saw a set of Maitland's prints on his intake card . . . which were made days *after* he last touched that buckle. They were firm and clear. Every line and whorl intact."

"We also took an unsub print from that buckle," Yune said. "Here it is."

This one no jury would accept; there were a few lines and whorls, but they were faint, barely there at all. Most of the print was no more than a blur.

Yune said, "It's impossible to be sure, given the poor quality, but I don't believe that's Mr. Maitland's fingerprint, and it *can't* be Holmes's, because he was dead long before that buckle first showed up in the train station video. And yet . . . Heath Holmes *was* in the van that was used to abduct the Peterson boy. I'm at a loss to explain the when, the how, or the why, but I'm not exaggerating when I say I'd give a thousand dollars to know who left that blurry fingerprint on the belt buckle, and at least five hundred to know how come the Maitland fingerprint on it looks so old."

He unplugged his laptop and sat down.

"Plenty of pieces on the table," Howie said, "but I'll be damned if they make a picture. Does anyone have any more?"

Ralph turned to his wife. "Tell them," he said. "Tell them who you dreamed was in our house."

"It was no dream," she said. "Dreams fade. Reality doesn't."

Speaking slowly at first, but picking up speed, she told them about seeing the light on downstairs, and finding the man sitting beyond the archway, on one of the chairs from their kitchen table. She finished with the warning he had given her, emphasizing it with the fading blue letters inked on his fingers. *You MUST tell him to stop.* "I fainted. I've never done that before in my life."

"She woke up in bed," Ralph said. "No sign of entry. Burglar alarm was set."

"A dream," Samuels said flatly.

Jeannie shook her head hard enough to make her hair fly. "He was *there*."

"*Something* happened," Ralph said. "That much I'm sure of. The man with the burned face had tats on his fingers—"

"The man who wasn't there in the films," Howie said.

"I know how it sounds—crazy. But someone else in this case had finger-tats, and I finally remembered who it was. I had Yune send me a picture, and Jeannie ID'd it. The man Jeannie saw in her dream—or in our house—is Claude Bolton, the bouncer at Gentlemen, Please. The one who got a cut while shaking Maitland's hand."

"The way Terry got cut when he bumped into the orderly," Marcy said. "That orderly was Heath Holmes, wasn't it?"

"Oh, sure," Holly said, almost absently. She was looking at one of the pictures on the wall. "Who else would it be?"

Alec Pelley spoke up. "Have either of you checked on Bolton's whereabouts?"

"I did," Ralph said, and explained. "He's in a west Texas town called Marysville, four hundred miles from here, and unless he had a private jet stashed somewhere, he was there at the time Jeannie saw him in our house."

"Unless *his* mom was lying," Samuels said. "As previously noted, mothers are often willing to do that when their sons are under suspicion."

"Jeannie had the same thought, but it seems unlikely in this case. The cop was there on a pretext, and he says they both seemed relaxed and open. Zero perp-sweat."

Samuels folded his arms across his chest. "I'm not convinced."

"Marcy?" Howard said. "I think it's your turn to add to the puzzle."

"I . . . I really don't want to. Let the detective do it. Grace talked to him."

Howie took her hand. "It's for Terry."

Marcy sighed. "All right. Grace saw a man, too. Twice. The second time in the house. I thought she was having bad dreams because she was upset by her father dying . . . as any child would be . . ." She stopped, chewing at her lower lip.

"Please," Holly said. "It's very important, Mrs. Maitland."

"Yes," Ralph agreed. "It is."

"I was so sure it wasn't real! Positive!"

"Did she describe him?" Jeannie asked.

"Sort of. The first time was about a week ago. She and Sarah were sleeping together in Sarah's room, and Grace said he was floating outside the window. She said he had a Play-Doh face and straws for eyes. *Anybody* would think that was just a nightmare, wouldn't they?"

Nobody said anything.

"The second time was on Sunday. She said she woke up from a nap and he was sitting on her bed. She said he didn't have straws for eyes anymore, that he had her father's eyes, but he still scared her. He had tattoos on his arms. And on his hands."

Ralph spoke up. "She told me his Play-Doh face was gone. That he had short black hair, all sticky-uppy. And a little beard around his mouth."

"A goatee," Jeannie said. She looked sick. "It was the same man. The first time she might have been having a dream, but the second time . . . that was Bolton. It must have been."

Marcy put her palms against her temples and pressed, as if she had a headache. "I know it sounds that way, but it *had* to have been a dream. She said his shirt changed colors while he was talking to her, and that's the kind of thing that happens in dreams. Detective Anderson, do you want to tell the rest?"

He shook his head. "You're doing fine."

Marcy swiped at her eyes. "She said he made fun of her. He called her a baby, and when she started to cry, he said it was good that she was sad. Then he told her he had a message for Detective Anderson. That he had to stop, or something bad would happen."

"According to Grace," Ralph said, "the first time the man showed up, he looked like he wasn't done. Not finished. The second time he appeared, she described a man who sure sounds like Claude Bolton. Only he's in Texas. Make of it what you will."

"If Bolton's *there*, he couldn't have been *here*," Bill Samuels said, sounding exasperated. "That seems pretty obvious."

"It seemed obvious with Terry Maitland," Howie said. "And now, we have discovered, with Heath Holmes." He turned his attention to Holly. "We don't have Miss Marple tonight, but we do have Ms. Gibney. Can you put these pieces together for us?"

Holly didn't seem to hear him. She was still staring at a painting on the wall. "Straws for eyes," she said. "Yes. Sure. Straws . . ." She trailed off.

"Ms. Gibney?" Howie said. "Do you have something for us, or not?"

Holly came back from wherever she had been. "Yes. I can explain what's going on. All I ask is that you keep an open mind. It will be quicker, I think, if I show you part of a movie I brought. I have it in my bag, on a DVD."

With another brief prayer for strength (and to channel Bill Hodges when they voiced their disbelief and—perhaps—outrage), she stood up and placed her laptop at the end of the table where Yune's had been. Then she took out her DVD external drive and hooked it up.

7

Jack Hoskins had considered asking for sick time for his sunburn, emphasizing that skin cancer ran in his family, and decided it was a bad idea. Terrible, in fact. Chief Geller would almost certainly tell him to get out of his office, and when word got around (Rodney Geller wasn't the close-mouthed sort), Detective Hoskins would become a laughingstock in the department. In the unlikely event that the chief agreed, he would be expected to go to the doctor, and Jack wasn't ready for that.

He had been called back in three days early, however, which wasn't fair when his damn vacation had been on the roster board since May. Feeling this made it his right (his *perfect* right) to turn those three days into what Ralph Anderson would have called a stay-cation, he spent that Wednesday afternoon bar-hopping. By his third stop, he had managed to mostly forget about the spooky interlude out in Canning Township, and by the fourth, he had stopped worrying quite so much about the sunburn, and the peculiar fact that he seemed to have come by it at night.

His fifth stop was at Shorty's Pub. There he asked the bartender—a very pretty lady whose name now slipped his mind, although not the entrancing length of her legs in tight Wrangler jeans—to look at the back of his neck and tell him what she saw. She obliged.

"It's a sunburn," she said.

"*Just* a sunburn, right?"

"Yeah, just a sunburn." Then, after a pause: "But a pretty bad one. Got a few little blisters there. You should put some—"

"Aloe on it, yeah. I heard."

After five vodka-tonics (or maybe it had been six), he drove home at exactly the speed limit, bolt upright and peering over the wheel. Wouldn't be good to get stopped. The legal limit in this state was .08.

He arrived at the old hacienda about the same time Holly Gibney was beginning her presentation in Howard Gold's conference room. He stripped to his undershorts, remembered to lock all the doors, and went in the bathroom to tap a kidney that badly needed tapping. With that chore accomplished, he once more used the hand-mirror to check out the back of his neck. Surely the sunburn was getting better by now, probably starting to flake. But no. The burn had turned black. Deep fissures crisscrossed the nape of his neck. Pearly rivulets of pus dribbled from two of them. He moaned, closed his eyes, then opened them again and breathed a sigh of relief. No black skin. No fissures. No pus. But the nape *was* bright red, and yes, there were some blisters. It didn't hurt as much to touch it as it had earlier, but why would it, when he had a skinful of Russian anesthetic?

I have to stop drinking so much, he thought. *Seeing shit that's not there is a pretty clear signal. You could even call it a warning.*

He had no aloe vera ointment, so he slathered the burn with some arnica gel. That stung, but the pain soon went away (or at least subsided to a dull throb). That was good, right? He took a hand towel to drape over his pillow so it wouldn't get all stained, lay down, and turned out the light. But the dark was no good. It seemed he could feel the pain more in the dark, and it was all too easy to imagine something in the room with him. The something that had been behind him out there at that abandoned barn.

The only thing out there was my imagination. The way that black skin was my imagination. And the cracks. And the pus.

All true, but it was also true that when he turned on the bedside lamp, he felt better. His final thought was that a good night's sleep would put everything right.

8

"Do you want me to dim the lights a bit more?" Howie asked.

"No," Holly said. "This is information, not entertainment, and although the movie is short—only eighty-seven minutes—we won't need to watch all of it, or even most of it." She wasn't as nervous as she had feared she would be. At least not so far. "But before I show it to you, I need to make something very clear, something I think you all must know by now, although you may not be quite ready to admit the truth into your conscious minds."

They looked at her, silent. All those eyes. She could hardly believe she was doing this—surely not Holly Gibney, the mouse who had sat at the back of all her classrooms, who never raised her hand, who wore her gym clothes under her skirts and blouses on phys ed days. Holly Gibney who even in her twenties hadn't dared speak back to her mother. Holly Gibney who had actually lost her mind on two occasions.

But all that was before Bill. He trusted me to be better, and for him I was. And I will be now, for these people.

"Terry Maitland didn't murder Frank Peterson and Heath Holmes didn't murder the Howard girls. Those murders were committed by an outsider. He uses our modern science—our modern forensics—against us, but his real weapon is our refusal to believe. We're trained to follow the facts, and sometimes we scent him when the facts are conflicting, but we refuse to follow that scent. He knows it. He uses it."

"Ms. Gibney," Jeannie Anderson said, "are you saying the murders were committed by a supernatural creature? Something like a vampire?"

Holly considered the question, biting at her lips. At last she said, "I don't want to answer that. Not yet. I want to show you some of the movie I brought first. It's a Mexican film, dubbed in English and released as part of drive-in double features in this country fifty years ago. The English title is *Mexican Wrestling Women Meet the Monster*, but in Spanish—"

"Oh, come on," Ralph said. "This is ridiculous."

"Shut up," Jeannie said. She kept her voice low, but they all heard the anger in it. "Give her a chance."

"But—"

"You weren't there last night. I was. *You need to give this a chance.*"

Ralph crossed his arms over his chest, just as Samuels had. It was a gesture Holly knew well. A warding-off gesture. An *I won't listen* gesture. She pushed on.

"The Mexican title is *Rosita Luchadora e Amigas Conocen El Cuco*. In Spanish it means—"

"That's it!" Yune shouted, making them all jump. "That's the name I couldn't get when we were eating at that restaurant on Saturday! Do you remember the story, Ralph? The one my wife's *abuela* told her when she was just *pequeña*?"

"How could I forget?" Ralph said. "The guy with the black bag who kills little kids and rubs their fat . . ." He stopped, thinking—in spite of himself—of Frank Peterson and the Howard girls.

"Does what?" Marcy Maitland asked.

"Drinks their blood and rubs their fat on him," Yune said. "It supposedly keeps him young. *El Cuco*."

"Yes," Holly said. "He's known in Spain as *El Hombre con Saco*. The Man with the Sack. In Portugal he's Pumpkinhead. When American children carve pumpkins for Halloween, they're carving the likeness of *El Cuco*, just as children did hundreds of years ago in Iberia."

"There was a rhyme about *El Cuco*," Yune said. "*Abuela* used to sing it sometimes, at night. *Duérmete, niño, duérmete ya* . . . can't remember the rest."

"Sleep, child, sleep," Holly said. "*El Cuco*'s on the ceiling, he's come to eat you."

"Good bedtime rhyme," Alec commented. "Must have given the kids sweet dreams."

"Jesus," Marcy whispered. "You think something like that was in our *house*? Sitting on my daughter's *bed*?"

"Yes and no," Holly said. "Let me put on the movie. The first ten minutes or so should be enough."

9

Jack dreamed he was driving a deserted two-lane highway with nothing but empty on both sides and a thousand miles of blue sky above. He was at the wheel of a big truck, maybe a tanker, because he could smell gasoline. Sitting beside him was a man with short black hair and a goatee. Tattoos covered his arms. Hoskins knew him, because Jack visited Gentlemen, Please frequently (although rarely in his official capacity), and had had many pleasant conversations with Claude Bolton, who had a record but was not a bad fellow at all since he'd cleaned up his act. Except this version of Claude was a *very* bad fellow. It was this Claude who had pulled back the shower curtain enough for Hoskins to be able to read the word on his fingers: CANT.

The truck passed a sign reading MARYSVILLE, POP. 1280.

"That cancer's spreading fast," Claude said, and yes, it was the voice that had come from behind the shower curtain. "Look at your hands, Jack."

He looked down. His hands on the wheel had turned black. As he stared at them, they fell off. The tanker truck ran off the road, tilted, started to go over. Jack understood that it was going to explode, and he hauled himself out of the dream before that could happen, gasping for breath and staring up at the ceiling.

"Jesus," he whispered, checking to make sure his hands were still there. They were, and so was his watch. He had been asleep less than an hour. "Jesus Chri—"

Someone moved on his left. For a moment he wondered if he had brought the pretty bartender with the long legs home with him, but no, he'd been alone. A fine young woman like that wouldn't want to have anything to do with him, anyway. To her he would just be an overweight, fortysomething drunk who was losing his h—

He looked around. The woman in bed with him was his mother. He only knew it was her because of the tortoiseshell clip dangling from the few remaining strings of her hair. She had been wearing that clip at her funeral. Her face had been made up by the mortician, kind of waxy and doll-like, but on the whole not too bad. This face was mostly gone, the flesh putrefying off the bone. Her nightgown clung to her because it was drenched with pus. There was the stench of rotting meat. He tried to scream, couldn't.

"This cancer is waiting for you, Jack," she said. He could see her teeth clacking, because her lips were gone. "It's eating into you. He can take it back now, but soon it will be too late even for him. Will you do what he wants?"

"Yes," Hoskins whispered. "Yes, anything."

"Then listen."

Jack Hoskins listened.

10

There was no FBI warning at the front of Holly's film, which didn't surprise Ralph. Who would bother to copyright such an elderly artifact, when it was trash to begin with? The music was a hokey mixture of wavering violins and jarringly cheerful *norteño* accordion riffs. The print was scratchy, as if it had been run many times by long-dead projectionists who hadn't given much of a shit.

I can't believe I'm sitting here, Ralph thought. *This is loonybin stuff.*

Yet both his wife and Marcy Maitland were watching with the concentration of students preparing for a final exam, and the others, although clearly not so invested, were paying close attention. Yune Sablo had a faint smile on his lips. Not the smile of a person who feels what he's seeing is ridiculous, Ralph thought, but of a man glimpsing a bit of the past; a childhood legend brought to life.

The movie opened on a nighttime street where all the businesses seemed to be either bars or whorehouses or both. The camera followed a pretty woman in a low-cut dress, walking hand in hand with her daughter, who looked to be about four. This evening stroll through a bad part of town with a kid who should have been in bed might have been explained later in the film, but not in the part Ralph and the others saw.

A drunk wavered up to the woman, and while his mouth said one thing, the voice actor dubbing his voice said, "Hey, baybee, want a date?" in a Mexican accent that made him sound like Speedy Gonzales. She brushed him off and walked on. Then, in a shadowy area between two streetlights, a dude in a long black cloak straight out of a Dracula film swooped from an alley. He had a black bag in one hand. With the other, he snatched up the kiddo. Mom screamed and gave chase, catching him under the next streetlight and grabbing at his bag. He whirled around, the convenient streetlight illuminating the face of a middle-aged man with a scar on his forehead.

Mr. Cloak snarled, revealing a mouthful of fake fangs. The woman drew back, hands raised, looking less like a mother in terror than an opera singer about to belt her way into an aria from *Carmen*. The child-stealer flipped his cloak over the little girl and fled, but not before a fellow emerging from one of the street's many bars hailed him in another hideous Speedy Gonzales accent: "Hey Professor Espinoza, where you go'een? Let me buy you a dreenk!"

In the next scene, the mother was brought to the town's morgue (EL DEPOSITO DE CADAVERES on the frosted glass door), and did the predictable histrionic screaming when the sheet was lifted to reveal her presumably mutilated child. Next came the arrest of the man with the scar, who turned out to be a well-respected educator at a nearby university.

What followed was one of cinema's shorter trials. The mother testified; so did a couple of guys with Speedy Gonzales accents, including the one who had offered to buy the professor a dreenk; the jury filed out to consider its verdict. Adding a surreal touch to these otherwise predictable proceedings was the appearance of five women in the back row, all dressed in what appeared to be superhero costumes complete with fancy masks. Nobody in the courtroom, including the judge, seemed to find them out of place.

The jury filed back in; Professor Espinoza was convicted of murder most foul; he hung his head and looked guilty. One of the masked women jumped to her feet and declared, "Thees ees a miscarritch of justice! Professor Espinoza would never harm a child!"

"But I saw heem!" the mother screamed. "Thees time you are wrong, Rosita!"

The masked women in the superhero costumes trooped out of the courtroom in their cool boots, and the movie cross-faded to a close-up of a hangman's noose. The camera drew back to show a scaffold surrounded by a crowd of onlookers. Professor Espinoza was led up the steps. As the rope was placed around his neck, his gaze fixed on a man in a hooded monk's robe at the back of the crowd. There was a black bag between the monk's sandaled feet.

This was a stupid and poorly made movie, but Ralph still felt a prickle run down his arms and covered Jeannie's hand with his own when she reached for him. He knew exactly what they were going to see next. The monk pushed back his hood to reveal Professor Espinoza's face, convenient forehead scar and all. He grinned, showing those ridiculous plastic fangs . . . pointed at his black bag . . . and laughed.

"*There!*" the real professor screamed from the gallows. "*There he is, there!*"

The crowd turned, but the man with the black bag was gone. Espinoza got his own black bag: a death-hood that was pulled over his head. From beneath it he screamed, "The monster, the monster, the mon—" The trap opened, and he plummeted through.

The next sequence was of the masked superhero women chasing the fake monk over some rooftops, and it was here that Holly pushed pause. "Twenty-five years ago, I saw a version with subtitles instead of dubbing," she said. "What the professor is screaming at the end is *El Cuco, El Cuco.*"

"What else?" Yune murmured. "Jesus, I haven't seen one of those *luchadora* movies since I was a kid. There must have been a dozen of them." He looked around at the others, as if coming out of a dream. "*Las luchadoras*—lady wrestlers. And the star of this one, Rosita, she was famous. You should see her with her mask off, *ay caramba.*" He shook his hand, as if he had touched something hot.

"There weren't just a dozen, there were at least fifty," Holly said quietly. "Everyone in Mexico loved *las luchadoras.* The films were like today's superhero movies. On a much smaller budget, of course."

She would like to lecture them on this fascinating (to her, it was) bit of film history, but this was not the time, not with Detective Anderson looking as though he had just taken a big bite of something nasty. Nor would she tell them that she had also loved the *luchadora* films. They had been played for laughs on the local Cleveland TV station that broadcast *Shlock Theater* every Saturday night. Holly supposed the local college kids got drunk and tuned in to yuk it up about the poor dubbing and the costumes they no doubt considered hokey, but there had been nothing funny about *las luchadoras* to the frightened and unhappy high school girl that she had been. Carlotta, Maria, and Rosita were strong, and brave, always helping the poor and downtrodden. Rosita Muñoz, the most famous, even proudly called herself a *cholita*, which was how that unhappy high school girl had felt about herself most of the time: a halfbreed. A freak.

"Most of the Mexican wrestling women movies were retellings of ancient legends. This one is no different. Do you see how it fits what we know about these murders?"

"Perfectly," Bill Samuels said. "I'll give you that. The only problem is that it's nuts. Out to lunch. If you actually believe in *El Cuco*, Ms. Gibney, then you are *el cuckoo*."

Says the man who told me about the disappearing footprints, Ralph thought. He did not believe in *El Cuco*, but he thought the woman had displayed a lot of guts in showing them the film when she must have known what their reaction would be. He was interested to see how Ms. Gibney of Finders Keepers would respond.

"*El Cuco* is said to live on the blood and fat of children," Holly said, "but in the world—our *real* world—he would survive not just on those things, but on people who think as you do, Mr. Samuels. As I suppose you all do. Let me show you one more thing. Just a snippet, I promise."

She went to chapter nine of the DVD, the second-to-last. The action picked up with one of the *luchadoras*—Carlotta—cornering the hooded monk in a deserted warehouse. He tried to escape by way of a convenient ladder. Carlotta grabbed him by the back of his billowing robe and tossed him over her shoulder. He did a midair flip and landed on his backside. The hood flew back, revealing a face that was not a face at all, but a lumpy blank. Carlotta screamed as two glowing prongs emerged from where the eyes should have been. They must have had some kind of mystic repelling power, because Carlotta staggered against the wall and held one hand up in front of her *luchadora* mask, trying to shield herself.

"Stop it," Marcy said. "Oh God, please."

Holly poked her laptop. The image on the screen disappeared, but Ralph could still see it: an optical effect that was prehistoric compared to the CGI stuff you could view in any Cineplex these days, but effective enough if you had heard a certain little girl's story of the intruder in her bedroom.

"Do you think that's what your daughter saw, Mrs. Maitland?" Holly asked. "Not exactly, I don't mean that, but—"

"Yes. Of course. Straws for eyes. That's what she said. Straws for eyes."

11

Ralph stood up. His voice was calm and level. "With all due respect, Ms. Gibney, and considering your past . . . uh, exploits . . . I have no doubt that respect is due, there is no supernatural monster named *El Cuco* who lives on the blood of children. I'd be the first to admit that this case—the two cases, if they're linked, and it seems more and more certain that they are—has some very strange elements, but this is a false trail you're leading us down."

"Let her finish," Jeannie said. "Before you close your mind entirely, for God's sake let her have her say."

He saw that his wife's anger was now on the edge of fury. He understood why, could even sympathize. By refusing to entertain

Gibney's ridiculous story of *El Cuco*, Jeannie felt he was also refusing to believe what she herself had seen in their kitchen early this morning. And he wanted to believe her, not just because he loved and respected her, but because the man she described fitted Claude Bolton to a T, and he couldn't explain that. Still, he said the rest, to all of them and especially to Jeannie. He had to. It was the bedrock truth upon which his whole life stood. Yes, there had been maggots in the cantaloupe, but they had gotten in there by some natural means. Not knowing what it was didn't change that, or negate it.

He said, "If we believe in monsters, in the supernatural, how do we believe in anything?"

Ralph sat down and tried to take Jeannie's hand. She pulled it away.

"I understand how you feel," Holly said. "I get it, believe me, I do. But I've seen things, Detective Anderson, that allow me to believe in this. Oh, not the movie, not even the legend behind the movie, exactly. But in every legend there's a grain of truth. Leave it for now. I would like to show you a timeline I drew up before I left Dayton. May I do that? It won't take long."

"You have the floor," Howie said. He sounded bemused.

Holly opened a file and projected it on the wall. Her printing was small but clear. Ralph thought what she had drawn up would pass muster in any courtroom. That much he had to give her.

"Thursday, April 19th. Merlin Cassidy leaves the van in a Dayton parking lot. I believe it was stolen the same day. We won't call the thief *El Cuco*, we'll just call him the outsider. Detective Anderson will feel more comfortable with that."

Ralph kept silent, and this time when he tried for Jeannie's hand, she let him take it, although she did not fold her fingers over his.

"Where did he stash it?" Alec asked. "Any idea?"

"We'll get to that, but for now, may I stick with the Dayton chronology?"

Alec lifted a hand for her to go on.

"Saturday, April 21st. The Maitlands fly to Dayton and check into their hotel. Heath Holmes—the real one—is in Regis, staying with his mother.

"Monday, April 23rd. Amber and Jolene Howard are killed. The outsider eats of their flesh and drinks of their blood." She looked at Ralph. "No, I don't know it. Not for sure. But reading between the lines of the newspaper stories, I'm sure that body parts were missing, and the bodies were bled mostly white. Is that similar to what happened to the Peterson boy?"

Bill Samuels spoke up. "Since the Maitland case is closed and we're having an informal discussion here, I have no problem telling you that it is. Flesh was missing from Frank Peterson's neck, right shoulder, right buttock, and left thigh."

Marcy made a strangled sound. When Jeannie started to go to her, Marcy waved her off. "I'm all right. I mean . . . no, I'm not, but I'm not going to throw up or faint or anything."

Observing her ashy skin, Ralph was not so sure.

Holly said, "The outsider dumps the panel truck he used to abduct the girls near the Holmes home—" She smiled at that. "—where he can be sure it will be found, and become another part of the evidence against his chosen scapegoat. He leaves the girls' underwear in the Holmes basement—another brick in the wall.

"Wednesday, April 25th. The bodies of the Howard girls are found in Trotwood, between Dayton and Regis.

"Thursday, April 26th. While Heath Holmes is in Regis, helping his mother around the house and running errands, the outsider shows up at the Heisman Memory Unit. Was he looking for Mr. Maitland specifically, or could it have been anyone? I don't know for sure, but I think he had Terry Maitland in his sights, because he knew the Maitlands were visiting from another state, far away. The outsider, whether you call him natural or unnatural or supernatural, is like many serial killers in one way. He likes to move around. Mrs. Maitland, *could* Heath Holmes have known that your husband was planning to visit his father?"

"I guess so," Marcy said. "The Heisman likes to know in advance when relatives are coming from other parts of the country. They make a special effort in those cases, get the residents haircuts or perms, and arrange off-unit visits, when possible. That wasn't, in the case of Terry's dad. His mental problems were too far advanced." She leaned forward, eyes fixed on Holly. "But if this outsider wasn't Holmes, even if he *looked* like Holmes, how could *he* know?"

"Oh, that's easy if you accept the basic premise," Ralph said. "If the guy is *replicating* Holmes, so to speak, he'd probably have access to all of Holmes's memories. Have I got it right, Ms. Gibney? Is that how the story goes?"

"Let's say it is, at least to a degree, but let's not get hung up on it. I'm sure we're all tired, and Mrs. Maitland would probably like to get home to her children."

Hopefully before she passes out, Ralph thought.

Holly went on. "The outsider knows he'll be seen and noticed at the Heisman Memory Unit. It's what he wants. And he's sure to leave more evidence that will incriminate the real Mr. Holmes: hair from one of the murdered girls. But I believe his most important reason for going there on April 26th was to spill Terry Maitland's blood, exactly as he later spilled blood from Mr. Claude Bolton. It's always the same pattern. First come the murders. Then he marks his next victim. His next self, you could say. After that, he goes into hiding. Except it's really a kind of hibernation. Like a bear, he may move around from time to time, but mostly he stays in a pre-selected den for a certain length of time, resting, while the change takes place."

"In the legends, the transformation takes years," Yune said. "Whole generations, maybe. But that's legend. You don't think it takes that long, do you, Ms. Gibney?"

"I think only weeks, months at the very most. For awhile during the transformative process from Terry Maitland to Claude Bolton, his face might look like it was made out of Play-Doh." She turned to look at Ralph directly. She found this difficult, but sometimes it was necessary. "Or as if he had been badly burned."

"Don't buy it," Ralph said. "And that's an understatement."

"Then why wasn't the burned man in any of the footage?" Jeannie asked.

Ralph sighed. "I don't know."

Holly said, "Most legends hold a grain of truth, but they're not *the* truth, if you see what I mean. In the stories, *El Cuco* lives on blood and flesh, like a vampire, but I think this creature also feeds on bad feelings. *Psychic* blood, you could say." She turned to Marcy. "He told your daughter he was glad she was unhappy and sad. I believe that was the truth. I believe he was *eating* her sadness."

"And mine," Marcy said. "And Sarah's."

Howie spoke up. "Not saying any of this is true, not saying that at all, but the Peterson family fits the scenario, doesn't it? All of them wiped out except for the father, and he's in a persistent vegetative state. A creature who lives on unhappiness—a grief-eater instead of a sin-eater—would have loved the Petersons."

"And how about that shit-show at the courthouse?" Yune put in. "If there really was a monster that eats negative emotions, that would have been Thanksgiving dinner for it."

"Do you people hear yourselves?" Ralph asked. "I mean, do you?"

"Wake up," Yune said harshly, and Ralph blinked as if he had been slapped. "I know how far out it is, we all do, you don't need to keep telling us, like you're the only sane man in the lunatic asylum. But there is something here that's way out of our experience. The man at the courthouse, the one who wasn't in any of the news footage, is only part of it."

Ralph felt his face growing warm, but kept silent and took his scolding.

"You need to stop fighting this every step of the way, *ese*. I know you don't like the puzzle, I don't like it, either, but at least admit that the pieces fit. There's a chain here. It leads from Heath Holmes to Terry Maitland to Claude Bolton."

"We know where Claude Bolton is," Alec said. "I think a trip down to Texas to interview him would be the logical next move."

"Why, in God's name?" Jeannie asked. "I saw the man who looks like him *here*, just this morning!"

"We should discuss that," Holly said, "but I want to ask Mrs. Maitland a question first. Where was your husband buried?"

Marcy looked startled. "Where . . . ? Why, here. In town. Memorial Park Cemetery. We hadn't . . . you know . . . made plans for that, or anything. Why would we? Terry wouldn't have turned forty until December . . . we thought we had years . . . that we deserved years, like anyone leading good lives . . ."

Jeannie got a handkerchief from her purse and handed it to Marcy, who began to wipe at her eyes with trance-like slowness.

"I didn't know what I should . . . I was just . . . you know, stunned . . . trying to get my head around the idea that he was gone. The funeral director, Mr. Donelli, suggested Memorial because Hillview is almost full . . . and on the other side of town, besides . . ."

Stop her, Ralph wanted to say to Howie. *It's painful and pointless. It doesn't matter where he's buried, except to Marcy and her daughters.*

But once more he kept silent and took it, because it was another kind of scolding, wasn't it? Even if Marcy Maitland might not mean it that way. He told himself this would be over eventually, leaving him free to discover a life beyond Terry fucking Maitland. He had to believe there would be one.

"I knew about the other place," Marcy went on, "of course I did, but I never thought of mentioning it to Mr. Donelli. Terry took me there once, but it's so far out of town . . . and so lonely . . ."

"What other place would that have been?" Holly asked.

A picture rose unbidden in Ralph's mind—six cowboy pallbearers carrying a plank coffin. He sensed the arrival of another confluence.

"The old graveyard in Canning Township," Marcy said. "Terry took me out once, and it looked like nobody had been buried there for a long time, or even visited. There were no flowers or memorial flags. Just some crumbling grave markers. You couldn't read the names on most of them."

Startled, Ralph glanced at Yune, who nodded slightly.

"That's why he was interested in that book in the newsstand," Bill Samuels said in a low voice. "*A Pictorial History of Flint County, Douree County, and Canning Township.*"

Marcy continued to wipe her eyes with Jeannie's handkerchief. "Of course he would have been interested in a book like that. There have been Maitlands in this part of the state ever since the Land Rush of 1889. Terry's great-great-grandparents—or maybe even a generation greater than that, I don't know for sure—settled in Canning."

"Not in Flint City?" Alec asked.

"There *was* no Flint City back then. Just a little village called Flint, a wide spot in the road. Until statehood, in the early twentieth century, Canning was the biggest town in the area. Named after the biggest landowner, of course. When it came to acreage, the Maitlands were second or third. Canning was an important town until the big dust storms came in the twenties and thirties, when most of the good topsoil blew away. These days there's nothing out there but a store and a church hardly anyone goes to."

"And the graveyard," Alec said. "Where people did their burying until the town dried up. Including a bunch of Terry's ancestors."

Marcy smiled wanly. "That graveyard . . . I thought it was awful. Like an empty house nobody cares about."

Yune said, "If this outsider was absorbing Terry's thoughts and memories as the transformation progressed, then he would have known about the graveyard." He was looking at one of the pictures on the wall now, but Ralph had a good idea what was going through his mind. It was going through his, as well. The barn. The discarded clothes.

"According to the legends—there are dozens about *El Cuco* online—these creatures like places of death," Holly said. "It's where they feel most at home."

"If there are creatures who eat sadness," Jeannie mused, "a graveyard would make a nice cafeteria, wouldn't it?"

Ralph wished mightily that his wife hadn't come. If not for her, he would have been out the door ten minutes ago. Yes, the barn where the clothes had been found was near that dusty old boneyard. Yes, the goo that had turned the hay black was puzzling, and yes, perhaps there had been an outsider. That was a theory he was willing to accept, at least for the time being. It explained a lot. An outsider who was consciously re-creating a Mexican legend would explain even more . . . but it didn't explain the disappearing man at the courthouse, or how Terry Maitland could have been in two places at the same time. He kept coming up against those things; they were like pebbles lodged in his throat.

Holly said, "Let me show you some pictures I took at another graveyard. They may open a line of more normal investigation. If either Detective Anderson or Lieutenant Sablo is willing to talk to the police in Montgomery County, Ohio, that is."

Yune said, "At this point I'd talk to the pope, if it would help to clear this up."

One by one, Holly projected the photos on the screen: the train station, the factory with the swastika spray-painted on the side, the deserted car wash.

"I took these from the parking lot of the Peaceful Rest Cemetery in Regis. It's where Heath Holmes is buried with his parents."

She cycled through the pictures again: train station, factory, car wash.

"I think the outsider took the van he stole from the lot in Dayton to one of these places, and I think if you could persuade the Montgomery County police to search them, some trace of it might still be there. The police might even find some trace of *him.* There, or maybe here."

This time she projected the photograph of the boxcars, sitting lonely and deserted on their siding. "He couldn't have hidden the van in either of those, but he might have stayed in one of them. They're even closer to the cemetery."

Here at last was something Ralph could take hold of. Something real. "Sheltered places. There *could* be traces. Even after three months."

"Tire tracks," Yune said. "Maybe more discarded clothes."

"Or other stuff," Holly said. "Will you check? And they should be prepared to do an acid phosphate test."

Semen stains, Ralph thought, and remembered the goo in the barn. What had Yune said about those? A nocturnal emission worthy of *The Guinness Book of Records*, wasn't that it?

Yune sounded admiring. "You know your stuff, ma'am."

Color rose in her cheeks, and she looked down. "Bill Hodges was very good at his job. He taught me a lot."

"I can call the Montgomery County prosecutor, if you want," Samuels said. "Get somebody from whatever police department has jurisdiction in that town—Regis?—to coordinate with the Staties. Given what that Elfman kid found in that barn in Canning Township, it's worth looking into."

"What?" Holly asked, immediately alight. "What did he find, beside the belt buckle with the prints on it?"

"A pile of clothes," Samuels said, "Pants, underwear shorts, sneakers. There was some kind of goo on them, also on the hay. It turned the hay black." He paused. "No shirt, though. The shirt was missing."

Yune said, "That shirt might have been what the burned man

was wearing on his head like a do-rag when we saw him at the courthouse."

"How far is this barn from the graveyard?" Holly asked.

"Less than half a mile," Yune said. "The residue on the clothes looked like semen. Is that what you're thinking, Ms. Gibney? Is that why you want the Ohio cops to do an acid phosphate test?"

"Can't have been semen," Ralph said. "There was too much of it."

Yune ignored this. He was staring at Holly, as if fascinated with her. "Are you thinking the stuff in the barn is a kind of residue from the change? We're having samples checked, but the results haven't come back yet."

"I don't know what I'm thinking," Holly said. "My research about *El Cuco* so far amounts to a few legends I read while I was flying down here, and they're not reliable. They were passed down orally, generation to generation, long before forensic science existed. I'm just saying that the police in Ohio should check the places in my photographs. They might not find anything . . . but I think they will. I hope they will. Traces, as Detective Anderson said."

"Are you done, Ms. Gibney?" Howie asked.

"Yes, I think so." She sat down. Ralph thought she looked exhausted, and why not? She'd had a busy few days. In addition to that, being crazy had to wear a person out.

Howie said, "Ladies and gentlemen, are there ideas on how we proceed from here? The floor is open for suggestions."

"The next step seems obvious," Ralph said. "This outsider might be here in FC—the testimony from my wife and Grace Maitland seems to suggest that—but somebody needs to go down to Texas and interview Claude Bolton, see what he knows. If anything. I nominate me."

Alec said, "I want to go with you."

"I think that's a trip I'd also like to make," Howie said. "Lieutenant Sablo?"

"I'd like to, but I have two cases in court. If I don't testify, a couple of very bad boys could walk. I'll call the ADA in Cap City, see if there's any chance of a postponement, but I'm not hopeful. It's not like I can tell him I'm on the trail of a shape-shifting Mexican monster."

Howie smiled. "I should think not. What about you, Ms. Gibney? Want to go a little further south? You'd continue to be compensated, of course."

"Yes, I'll go. Mr. Bolton may know things we need to find out. If, that is, we can ask the right questions."

Howie said, "What about you, Bill? Want to see this thing through?"

Samuels smiled thinly, shook his head, then stood up. "All this has been interesting, in a mad sort of way, but as far as I'm concerned, the case is closed. I'll make some calls to the police in Ohio, but that's where my participation ends. Mrs. Maitland, I'm sorry for your loss."

"You ought to be," Marcy said.

He winced at that, but pressed on. "Ms. Gibney, it's been fascinating. I appreciate your hard work and due diligence. You also make a surprisingly persuasive case for the fantastic, I say that without a trace of irony, but I'm going to go home, grab a beer out of the fridge, and start forgetting this whole thing."

They watched him gather up his briefcase and leave, the cowlick wagging at them like an admonitory finger as he went out the door.

When he was gone, Howie said he would make their travel arrangements. "I'll charter the King Air I sometimes use. The pilots will know the closest landing strip. I'll also arrange for a car. If it's just the four of us, a sedan or a small SUV should do."

"Leave a seat for me," Yune said. "Just in case I can wiggle out of court."

"Happy to."

Alec Pelley said, "Someone needs to reach out to Mr. Bolton tonight, and tell him to expect visitors."

Yune lifted a hand. "That much I can do."

"Make him understand no one is after him for doing something illegal," Howie said. "The last thing we want is for him to jack-rabbit somewhere."

"Call me after you talk to him," Ralph said to Yune. "Even if it's late. I want to know how he reacts."

"So do I," Jeannie said.

"You should tell him something else," Holly said. "You should tell him to be careful. Because if I'm right about this, he's the next in line."

12

Full dark had come when Ralph and the others stepped out of Howie Gold's building. Howie himself was still upstairs, making arrangements, and his investigator was with him. Ralph wondered what they would talk about with everyone else gone.

"Ms. Gibney, where are you staying?" Jeannie asked.

"The Flint Luxury Motel. I reserved a room."

"Oh no, you can't," Jeannie said. "The only luxury there is on the sign out front. The place is a pit."

Holly looked disconcerted. "Well, there must be a Holiday Inn—"

"Stay with us," Ralph said, beating Jeannie to it and hoping it would earn him some points later on. God knew he could use them.

Holly hesitated. She didn't do well in the houses of other people. She didn't do well even in the one where she had grown up, when on her quarterly duty visits to her mother. She knew that in the home of these strangers she would lie awake long and wake early, hearing every unfamiliar creak of the walls and the floors, listening to the murmured voices of the Andersons and wondering if they were talking about her . . . which they almost certainly would be. Hoping that if she had to get up in the night to spend a penny, they wouldn't hear her. She needed her sleep. The meeting had been stressful enough, and the steady pushback of Detective Anderson's disbelief had been understandable but exhausting.

But, as Bill Hodges would have said. But.

Anderson's disbelief was the but. It was the reason she *had* to accept the invitation, and she did.

"Thank you, that's very kind, but I have to run an errand first. It won't take long. Give me your address, and my iPad will take me right to you."

"Is it anything I can help you with?" Ralph asked. "I'd be happy to—"

"No. Really. I'll be fine." She shook hands with Yune. "Come with us if you can, Lieutenant Sablo. I'm sure you want to."

He smiled. "I do, believe me, but it's like that poem says—I have promises to keep."

Marcy Maitland was standing by herself, holding her purse against her stomach and looking shell-shocked. Jeannie went to her without hesitation. Ralph watched with interest as Marcy initially drew back, as if in alarm, then allowed herself to be hugged. After a moment she even put her head on Jeannie Anderson's shoulder and hugged back. She looked like a tired child. When the two women drew apart, both of them were crying.

"I'm so sorry for your loss," Jeannie said.

"Thank you."

"If there's anything I can do for you or your girls, anything at all—"

"You can't, but *he* can." She turned her attention to Ralph, and although her eyes were still wet with tears, they were cold. Assessing. "This outsider, I want you to find him. Don't let him get away just because you don't believe in him. Can you do that?"

"I don't know," Ralph said, "but I'll try."

Marcy said no more, only took Yune Sablo's offered arm and let him lead her to her car.

13

Half a block down, parked in front of the long-abandoned Woolworth's, Jack sat in his truck, sipping from a flask and watching the group on the sidewalk. The only one he couldn't identify was a slender woman in the kind of suit a businesswoman might wear on a trip. Her hair was short, the graying bangs a little ragged, as if she had cut them herself. The case slung over her shoulder looked big enough to hold a shortwave radio. This woman watched as Sablo, the taco-bender state cop, squired Mrs. Maitland away. The stranger then walked to her car, which was too nondescript to be anything but an airport rental. Hoskins thought briefly of following her, but decided to stick with the Andersons. It had been Ralph who brought him here, after all, and wasn't there some saying about going home with the girl you took to the dance?

Besides, Anderson bore watching. Hoskins had never liked him, and since that snotty two-word evaluation a year ago (*No opinion*, he'd written . . . as if his shit didn't stink), Jack had detested him. He had been delighted when Anderson tripped over his dick with the Maitland arrest, and it didn't surprise him to discover the self-righteous sonofabitch was now meddling in things better left alone. A closed case, for instance.

Jack touched the back of his neck, winced, then started his truck. He supposed he could go home after he saw the Andersons inside, but he thought maybe he'd just park up the street and keep an eye on their house. See what happened. He had a Gatorade bottle he could piss in, and he might even be able to sleep a little, if the steady hot throb from the back of his neck would allow that.

It wouldn't be the first time he'd slept in this truck; he'd done it on several occasions since the day the old ball and chain had walked out.

Jack wasn't sure what came next, but he had a clear fix on the basic task: to stop the meddling. The meddling in exactly *what* he didn't know, only that it had something to do with the Peterson boy. And the barn in Canning Township. That was enough for now, and—sunburn aside, possible skin cancer aside—he was getting interested.

He felt that when the time came for the next step, he would be told.

14

With the help of her navigation app, Holly made a quick and easy drive to the Flint City Walmart. She loved Walmarts, the size of them, the anonymity of them. Shoppers didn't seem to look at other shoppers as they did in other stores; it was as if they were all in their own private capsules, buying clothes or video games or toilet paper in bulk. It wasn't even necessary to speak to a cashier, if you used the self-checkout. Which Holly always did. Her shopping was quick, because she knew exactly what she wanted. She went first to OFFICE SUPPLIES, then to MENS AND BOYS WEAR, finally to AUTOMOTIVE. She took her basket to the self-checkout and tucked the receipt into her wallet. These were business expenses, for which she expected to be reimbursed. If she lived, that was. She had an idea (*one of Holly's famous intuitions*, she heard Bill Hodges saying) that was more likely to happen if Ralph Anderson—so like Bill in some ways, so very different from him in others—could get past the divide in his mind.

She returned to her car and drove to the Anderson house. But before leaving the parking lot, she said a brief prayer. For all of them.

15

Ralph's cell phone rang just as he and Jeannie were entering the kitchen. It was Yune. He had gotten the Marysville number of Lovie Bolton from John Zellman, the owner of Gentlemen, Please, and had reached Claude with no trouble.

"What did you tell him?" Ralph asked.

"Pretty much what we decided on in Howie's office. That we wanted to interview him, because we're having doubts about Terry Maitland's guilt. Emphasized that we didn't think Bolton himself was guilty of anything, and that the people who'd be coming to see him were acting strictly as private citizens. He asked if you'd be one of them. I said you would. Hope that's okay with you. It seemed to be with him."

"That's fine." Jeannie had gone directly upstairs, and now he heard the start-up chime of the desktop computer they shared. "What else?"

"I said that if Maitland *was* framed, then Bolton might be at risk for the same treatment, especially since he was a man with a record."

"How did he react to that?"

"Okay. He didn't get defensive or anything. But then he said something interesting. Asked me if I was sure it really had been Terry Maitland he saw in the club the night the Peterson boy was murdered."

"He said that? Why?"

"Because Maitland acted like he'd never seen him before, and when Bolton asked how the baseball team was doing, Maitland passed it off with some kind of generality. No details, even though the team was in the playoffs. He also told me Maitland was wearing fancy sneakers. 'Like the ones the kids save up for so they can look like gangbangers,' he said. According to Bolton, he never saw Maitland in anything like that."

"Those were the sneakers we found in that barn."

"No way to prove it, but I'm sure you're right."

Upstairs, Ralph now heard the moaning, grinding sound of their old Hewlett-Packard printer coming to life, and wondered what the hell Jeannie was up to.

Yune said, "Remember the Gibney woman telling us about the hair they found in Maitland's father's room at the assisted living place? From one of the murdered girls?"

"Sure."

"What do you want to bet that if we go through Maitland's credit purchases, we'll find a record of him buying those sneakers? And a slip with a signature on it that matches Maitland's exactly?"

"I guess this hypothetical outsider could do that," Ralph said, "but only if he snitched one of Terry's credit cards."

"He wouldn't even need to do that. Remember, the Maitlands have lived in Flint City like forever. They've probably got charge accounts at half a dozen downtown stores. All this guy would have to do is walk into the sporting goods department, pick out those fancy kicks, and sign his name. Who'd question him? Everyone in town knows him. It's the same thing as the hair and the girls' underthings, don't you see? He takes their faces and does his dirt, but that isn't enough for him. He also weaves the rope that hangs them. Because he eats sadness. *He eats sadness!*"

Ralph paused, put a hand over his eyes, pressed his fingers to one temple and his thumb to the other.

"Ralph? Are you there?"

"Yes. But Yune... you're making leaps I'm not ready to make."

"I understand. I'm not a hundred per cent on board with this myself. But you need to at least keep the possibility in mind."

But it's not a possibility, Ralph thought. *It's an impossibility.*

He asked Yune if he had told Bolton to be careful.

Yune laughed. "I did. He laughed. Said there were three guns in the house, two rifles and a pistol, and that his mother is a better shot than he is, even with emphysema. Man, I wish I was going down there with you."

"Try to make it happen."

"I will."

As he ended the call, Jeannie came down with a thin sheaf of paper. "I've been researching Holly Gibney. Tell you what, for a soft-spoken lady with absolutely no clothes sense, she's been up to a lot."

As Ralph took the pages, headlights spilled up the driveway. Jeannie grabbed the pages back before he could do more than look at the newspaper headline on the first sheet: **RETIRED COP, TWO OTHERS SAVE THOUSANDS AT MINGO AUDITORIUM CONCERT**. He assumed Ms. Holly Gibney was one of the two others.

"Go help her in with her luggage," Jeannie said. "You can read these in bed."

16

Holly's luggage consisted of the shoulder-bag that held her laptop, a hold-all small enough to fit in an airplane's overhead compartment, and a plastic Walmart bag. She let Ralph take the hold-all, but insisted on keeping custody of the shoulder-bag and whatever she'd purchased at Wally World.

"You're very good to have me," she said to Jeannie.

"It's our pleasure. Can I call you Holly?"

"Yes, please. That would be good."

"Our spare room is at the end of the upstairs hall. The sheets are fresh, and it has its own bathroom. Just don't stumble over my sewing machine table if you have to use the facility in the middle of the night."

An unmistakable expression of relief crossed Holly's face at this, and she smiled. "I'll try not to."

"Would you like cocoa? I could make some. Or maybe something stronger?"

"Just bed, I think. I don't mean to be impolite, but I've had a very long day."

"Of course you have. I'll show you the way."

But Holly lingered for a moment, looking through the archway and into the Andersons' living room. "Your intruder was sitting just there when you came downstairs?"

"Yes. In one of our kitchen chairs." She pointed, then crossed her arms and cupped her elbows. "At first I could only see him from the knees down. Then the word on his fingers. MUST. Then he leaned forward and I could see his face."

"Bolton's face."

"Yes."

Holly considered this, then broke into a radiant smile that surprised both Ralph and his wife. It made her look years younger. "If you'll excuse me, I'm off to dreamland."

Jeannie led her upstairs, chatting away. *Setting her at ease in a way I never could*, Ralph thought. *It's a talent, and it will probably work even on this extremely peculiar woman.*

Peculiar she might be, but she was strangely likeable, in spite of her mad ideas about Terry Maitland and Heath Holmes.

Mad ideas that just happen to fit the facts.

But it was impossible.

That fit them like a glove.

"Still impossible," he murmured.

Upstairs, the two women laughed. Hearing that made Ralph smile. He waited where he was until he heard Jeannie's steps heading back to their room, then he went up himself. The door to the guest room at the end of the hall was firmly closed. The sheaf of papers—the fruits of Jeannie's hurried research—was lying on his pillow. He undressed, lay down, and began to read about Ms. Holly Gibney, co-owner of a skip-tracing firm called Finders Keepers.

17

Outside and down the block, Jack watched as the woman in the suit turned into Anderson's driveway. Anderson came out and helped her with her things. She didn't have much, traveling light. One of her bags was from Walmart. So that was where she'd gone. Maybe to get a nightie and a toothbrush. Judging from the look of her, the nightie would be ugly and the bristles of the toothbrush would be hard enough to draw blood from her gums.

He took a nip from his flask, and as he was screwing on the cap and thinking about going home (why not, since all the good little children were in for the night), he realized he was no longer alone in the truck. Someone was sitting on the passenger side. He had just appeared in the corner of Hoskins's eye. That was impossible, of course, but he couldn't have been there all along. Could he?

Hoskins looked straight ahead. The sunburn on his neck, which had been relatively quiet, began to throb again, and very painfully.

A hand came into his peripheral vision, floating. It seemed he could almost see the seat through it. Written on the fingers in faded blue ink was the word MUST. Hoskins closed his eyes, praying that his visitor would not touch him.

"You need to take a drive," the visitor said. "Unless you want to die the way your mother died, that is. Do you remember how she screamed?"

Yes, Jack remembered. Until she couldn't scream anymore.

"Until she couldn't scream anymore," said the passenger. The hand touched his thigh, very lightly, and Jack knew the skin there would soon begin to burn, just like the back of his neck. The pants he was wearing would be no protection; the poison would seep right through. "Yes, you remember. How could you forget?"

"Where do you want me to go?"

The passenger told him, and then the touch of that awful hand disappeared. Jack opened his eyes and looked around. The other side of the bench seat was empty. The lights in the Anderson house were out. He looked at his watch and saw it was fifteen minutes to eleven. He had fallen asleep. He could almost believe he'd just had a dream. A very bad one. Except for one thing.

He started the truck and put it in gear. He would stop to gas up at the Hi station on Route 17 outside of town. That was the right place, because the guy who worked the night shift—Cody, his name was—always had a good supply of little white pills. Cody sold them to the truckers either highballing north to Chicago or down south to Texas. For Jack Hoskins of the Flint City PD, there would be no charge.

The truck's dashboard was dusty. At the first stop sign, he leaned over to his right and wiped it clean, getting rid of the word his passenger's finger had left there.

MUST.

NO END TO THE UNIVERSE

July 26th

1

What sleep Ralph got was thin and broken by bad dreams. In one of them, he held the dying Terry Maitland in his arms, and Terry said, "You robbed my children."

Ralph woke at four thirty and knew there would be no more sleep. He felt as if he had entered some heretofore unsuspected plane of existence, and told himself everyone felt that way in the small hours. That was good enough to get him into the bathroom, where he brushed his teeth.

Jeannie was sleeping as she always did, with the coverlet pulled up so high that she was nothing but a hump with a fluff of hair showing over the top. There was gray in that hair now, as there was in his. Not much, but more would be coming right along. That was all right. Time's passage was a mystery, but it was a *normal* mystery.

The breeze from the air conditioner had spilled some of the pages Jeannie had printed onto the floor. He put them back on the night table, picked up his jeans, decided they would do for another day (especially in dusty south Texas), and went to the window with them in his hand. The first gray light was creeping into the day. It would be a hot one here, and hotter still where they were going.

He observed—without much surprise, although he couldn't have said why—that Holly Gibney was down there, dressed in her own pair of jeans and sitting in the lawn chair where Ralph himself had been sitting little more than a week ago, when Bill

Samuels had come calling. The evening Bill had told him the story of the disappearing footprints and Ralph had matched him with the one about the infested cantaloupe.

He pulled on his pants and an Oklahoma Thunder tee-shirt, checked Jeannie again, and left the room with the old scuffed moccasins he wore as bedroom slippers dangling from two fingers of his left hand.

2

He stepped out the back door five minutes later. Holly turned at the sound of his approach, her small face cautious and alert but not (or so he hoped) unfriendly. Then she saw the mugs on the old Coca-Cola tray and her face lit up with that radiant smile. "Is that what I hope it is?"

"It is if you were hoping for coffee. I take mine straight, but I brought the other stuff in case you want it. My wife takes it white and sweet. Like me, she says." He smiled.

"Black is fine. Thank you so much."

He put the tray on the picnic table. She sat across from him, took one of the mugs, sipped. "Oh, this is good. Nice and strong. There's nothing better than strong black coffee in the morning. That's what I think, anyway."

"How long have you been up?"

"I don't sleep much," she said, neatly dodging the question. "It's very pleasant here. The air is so fresh."

"Not so fresh when the wind comes from the west, believe me. Then you smell the refineries in Cap City. Gives me a headache."

He paused, looking at her. Holly looked away, holding her cup to her face, as if to shield it. Ralph thought back to last night, and how she had seemed to steel herself for every handshake. He had an idea that this woman found many of the world's ordinary gestures and interactions quite difficult. And yet she had done some amazing things.

"I read up on you last night. Alec Pelley was right. You have quite a resume."

She made no reply.

"In addition to stopping that guy Hartsfield from bombing a bunch of kids, you and your partner, Mr. Hodges—"

"*Detective* Hodges," she corrected. "Retired."

Ralph nodded. "In addition to that, you and Detective Hodges saved a girl who was kidnapped by a crazy guy named Morris Bellamy. Bellamy was killed during the rescue. You were also involved in a shootout with a doctor who went off the rails and killed his wife, and last year you nailed a bunch of guys who were stealing rare-breed dogs, either ransoming them back to their owners or selling them on if the owners wouldn't pay. When you said part of your business was finding lost pets, you weren't kidding."

She was blushing again, all the way up from the base of her neck to her forehead. It was pretty clear that this enumeration of her past exploits made her more than uncomfortable; she found it actively painful.

"It was mostly Bill Hodges who did those things."

"Not the dognappers. He passed on a year before that case."

"Yes, but by then I had Pete Huntley. Ex-*Detective* Huntley." She looked directly at him. Made herself do it. Her eyes were clear and blue. "Pete's good, I couldn't keep the business going without him, but Bill was better. Whatever I am, Bill made me. I owe him everything. I owe him my life. I wish he were here now."

"Instead of me, you mean?"

Holly didn't reply. Which *was* a reply, of course.

"Would he have believed in this *El Cuco* shape-shifter?"

"Oh yes." She said it without hesitation. "Because he . . . and I . . . and our friend Jerome Robinson, who was with us . . . have the benefit of certain experiences that you don't have. Although you may, depending on how the next few days go. You may before the sun goes down tonight."

"Can I join you?"

It was Jeannie, with her own cup of coffee.

Ralph gestured for her to sit down.

"If we woke you, I'm very sorry," Holly said. "You were so kind to let me stay."

"Ralph woke me, tiptoeing out like an elephant," Jeannie said. "I might have gone back to sleep, but then I smelled coffee. Can't resist that. Oh good, you brought out the half and half."

Holly said, "It wasn't the doctor."

Ralph raised his eyebrows. "Beg pardon?"

"His name was Babineau, and he went off the rails, all right, but he was forced off them, and he didn't kill Mrs. Babineau. Brady Hartsfield did that."

"According to what I read in the news stories my wife found online, Hartsfield died in the hospital before you and Hodges tracked Babineau down."

"I know what the news stories said, but they're wrong. May I tell you the real story? I don't like to tell it, I don't even like to remember those things, but you might need to hear it. Because we're going into danger, and if you keep believing that it's a man we're going after—twisted, perverse, murderous, but still just a man—you're going to be putting yourself into greater danger."

"The danger is here," Jeannie protested. "This outsider, the one who looks like Claude Bolton . . . I saw him *here*. I said that last night, at the meeting!"

Holly nodded. "I think the outsider was here, I might even be able to prove it to you, but I don't think he was *completely* here. And I don't think he's here now. He's *there*, in Texas, because Bolton is there, and the outsider will be close to him. He'll have to be close, because he's been . . ." She paused, chewing her lip. "I think he's been exhausting himself. He's not used to people coming after him. Of knowing what he is."

"I don't understand," Jeannie said.

"May I tell you the story of Brady Hartsfield? That might help." She looked at Ralph, again making an effort to meet his eyes. "It may not make you believe, but it will make you understand why I *can*."

"Go ahead," Ralph said.

Holly began to speak. By the time she finished, the sun was rising red in the east.

3

"Wow," Ralph said. It was all he could think of.

"This is true?" Jeannie asked. "Brady Hartsfield . . . what? Somehow jumped his consciousness into this doctor of his?"

"Yes. It might have been the experimental drugs Babineau was feeding him, but I never thought that was the only reason he was able to do it. There was something in Hartsfield already, and the knock on the head I gave him brought it out. That's what I believe." She turned to Ralph. "*You* don't believe it, though, do you? I could probably get Jerome on the phone, and he'd tell you the same thing . . . but you wouldn't believe him, either."

"I don't know what to believe," he said. "This rash of suicides brought on by subliminal messages in video games . . . the newspapers reported it?"

"Newspapers, TV, the Internet. It's all there."

Holly paused, looking down at her hands. The nails were unpolished, but quite neat; she had quit chewing them, just as she had quit smoking. Broken herself of the habit. She sometimes thought that her pilgrimage to something at least approximating mental stability (if not genuine mental health) had been marked by the ritual casting off of bad habits. It had been hard to let them go. They were friends.

She spoke without looking at either of them now, looking off into the distance instead. "Bill was diagnosed with pancreatic cancer at the same time the business with Babineau and Hartsfield happened. He was in the hospital for awhile afterwards, but then he came home. By that time all of us knew how it was going to end . . . including him, although he never said so, and he fought that fracking cancer right to the finish. I used to go over almost every night, partly to make sure he was eating something, partly just to sit with him. To keep him company, but also to . . . I don't know . . ."

"Fill yourself up with him?" Jeannie said. "While you still had him?"

The smile again, the radiant one that made her look young. "Yes, that's it. Exactly. One night—this wasn't long before he went back into the hospital—the power went out in his part of town. A tree fell on a line, or something. When I got to Bill's house, he was sitting on the front step and looking up at the stars. 'You never see them like this when the streetlights are on,' he said. 'Look at how many there are, and how bright!'

"It seemed like you could see the whole Milky Way that night. We sat there for a little while—five minutes, I guess—not talking, just looking. Then he said, 'Scientists are starting to believe that there's no end to the universe. I read that in the *New York Times* last week. And when you can see all the stars there are to see, and know there's even more beyond them, that's easy to believe.' We never talked much about Brady Hartsfield and what he did to Babineau after Bill got really sick, but I think he was talking about it then."

"More things in heaven and earth than are dreamed of in your philosophy," Jeannie said.

Holly smiled. "I guess Shakespeare said it best. He said pretty much everything best, I think."

"Maybe it wasn't Hartsfield and Babineau he was talking about," Ralph said. "Maybe he was trying to come to terms with his own . . . situation."

"Of course he was," Holly said. "That, and all the mysteries. Which is what we need to—"

Her cell phone tweeted. She took it from her back pocket, glanced at the screen, and read the text.

"That was from Alec Pelley," she said. "The plane Mr. Gold chartered will be ready to take off at nine thirty. Are you still planning on making the trip, Mr. Anderson?"

"Absolutely. And since we're in this together—whatever *it* is— you better start calling me Ralph." He finished his coffee in two swallows and stood up. "I want to arrange for a couple of unis to keep an eye on the house while I'm gone, Jeannie. Any problem with that?"

She batted her eyelashes. "Just make sure they're good-looking."

"I'll try for Troy Ramage and Tom Yates. Neither of them looks like a movie star, but they're the two who actually arrested Terry Maitland at the ballfield. It feels right for them to have at least some role in this."

Holly said, "There's something I need to check, and I'd like to do it now, before it's full daylight. Can we go back to the house?"

4

At Holly's request, Ralph pulled the shades in the kitchen and Jeannie closed the drapes in the living room. Holly herself sat at the kitchen table with the markers and the roll of Scotch Magic Tape she'd bought in the office supplies department at Walmart. She tore off two short lengths of tape and placed them over her iPhone's embedded flash. These she colored blue. She tore off a third length, put it over the blue strips, and colored it purple.

She stood up and pointed to the chair nearest the archway. "That's the one he was sitting in?"

"Yes."

Holly took two flash pictures of the seat, moved to the archway, and pointed again. "And this is where he sat."

"Yes. Right there. But there were no marks on the carpet in the morning. Ralph looked."

Holly dropped to one knee, took four more pictures of the carpet, then stood up. "Okay. That should be good."

"Ralph?" Jeannie asked. "Do you know what she's doing?"

"She's turned her phone into a makeshift black light." *Something I could have done myself, if I had actually believed my wife—I've known about this particular trick for at least five years.* "You're looking for stains, aren't you? Residue, like the stuff in the barn."

"Yes, but if there is any, there's much less of it, or you would have seen it with your naked eye. You can buy a kit online to do this kind of testing—it's called CheckMate—but this should work. Bill taught me. Let's see what we've got. If anything."

They gathered around her, one on either side, and for once Holly didn't mind the physical closeness. She was too absorbed, and too hopeful. *I have Holly hope*, she told herself.

The stains were there. A faint yellowish spatter on the seat of the chair, where Jeannie's intruder had sat, and several more—like small drips of paint—on the carpet at the edge of the archway.

"Holy shit," Ralph murmured.

"Look at this one," Holly said. She spread her fingers to enlarge a splotch on the carpet. "See how it makes a right angle? That's from one of the chair legs."

She went back to the chair and took another flash photo of it, only this time down low. Once more they gathered around the iPhone. Holly spread her fingers again, and one of the chair legs leaped forward. "That's where it dribbled down. You can raise the shades and open the drapes, if you want."

When the kitchen was once more filled with morning light, Ralph took Holly's phone and went through the pictures again, swiping from one to the next, then going back. He felt the wall of his disbelief beginning to crumble, and in the end all it had taken was a bunch of photos on a small iPhone screen.

"What does it mean?" Jeannie asked. "I mean, in practical terms? Was he here, or wasn't he?"

"I told you, I haven't had the chance to do anything like the amount of research I'd need to give an answer I felt sure of. But if I was forced to guess, I'd say . . . both."

Jeannie shook her head, as if to clear it. "I don't understand."

Ralph was thinking about the locked doors and the burglar alarm that hadn't gone off. "Are you saying this guy was a . . ." *Ghost* was the word that first came to mind, but it wasn't the right one.

"I'm not saying anything," Holly said, and Ralph thought, *No, you're not. Because you want me to say it.*

"That he was a projection? Or an avatar, like in the video games our son plays?"

"Interesting idea," Holly said. Her eyes were sparkling. Ralph had an idea (sort of an infuriating one) that she might be holding back a smile.

"There's residue, but the chair didn't leave marks in the carpet," Jeannie said. "If he was here in any physical sense, he was . . . light. Maybe no heavier than a feather pillow. And you say doing this . . . this projection . . . exhausts him?"

"It seems logical—to me, at least," Holly said. "The one thing we can be sure of is that *something* was here when you came downstairs yesterday morning. Would you agree with that, Detective Anderson?"

"Yes. And if you don't start calling me Ralph, Holly, I'll have to arrest you."

"How did I get back upstairs?" Jeannie asked. "Did he . . . please tell me he didn't carry me after I passed out."

"I doubt it," Holly said.

Ralph said, "Maybe some sort of . . . just guessing here . . . hypnotic suggestion?"

"I don't know. There's a great deal we may never know. I'd like a quick shower, if that's all right?"

"Of course," Jeannie said. "I'll scramble us some eggs." Then, as Holly started out: "Oh my God."

Holly turned back.

"The stove light. It was on. The one over the burners. There's a button." When looking at the pictures, Jeannie had seemed excited. Now she only looked scared. "You need to push it to turn the light on. There was enough of him here to do that, at least."

Holly said nothing to this. Neither did Ralph.

5

After breakfast, Holly returned to the guest room, supposedly to pack her things. Ralph suspected she was actually giving him time and privacy to say goodbye to his wife. She had her odd quirks, did Holly Gibney, but stupid she was not.

"Ramage and Yates will be keeping a close eye out," he told Jeannie. "They both took personal days."

"They did that for you?"

"And I think for Terry. They feel almost as badly as I do about how that went down."

"Have you got your gun?"

"In my carry-on for now. Once we land, I'll have it holstered on my belt. And Alec will have his. I want you to get yours out of the gun safe. Keep it close."

"Do you really think—"

"I don't know what to think, I'm with Holly on that. Just keep it close. And don't shoot the mailman."

"Listen, maybe I should come."

"I don't think that's a good idea."

He didn't want them in the same place today, but didn't want to say why and worry her even more. They had a son to think about, one who was currently playing baseball or shooting arrows at targets backed with bales of hay or making beaded belts. Derek, who wasn't much older than Frank Peterson had been. Derek, who simply assumed, as most kids did, that his parents were immortal.

"You could be right," she said. "Somebody ought to be here if D calls, don't you think?"

He nodded and kissed her. "That's just what I was thinking."

"Be careful." She was looking up at him, eyes wide, and he had a sudden piercing memory of those eyes looking up at him in that same loving, hopeful, anxious way. That had been at their wedding, as they stood before their friends and relatives, swapping vows.

"I will. I always am."

He started to pull away from her. She pulled him back. Her grip on his forearms was strong.

"Yes, but this isn't like any other case you've ever worked. We both know that now. If you can get him, get him. If you can't . . . if you run into something you can't handle . . . back off. Back off and come home to me, do you understand?"

"I hear you."

"Don't say you hear me, say you will."

"I will." Again he thought of the day they'd made their vows.

"I hope you mean that." Still with that piercing gaze, so full of love and anxiety. The one that said *I've cast my lot with you, please don't ever let me regret it.* "I need to tell you something, and it's important. Are you listening?"

"Yes."

"You're a good man, Ralph. A good man who made a bad mistake. You're not the first to do that, and you won't be the last. You have to live with it, and I'll help you. Make it better if you can, but please don't make it worse. *Please.*"

Holly was coming rather ostentatiously downstairs, making sure they heard her approach. Ralph stood where he was a moment longer, looking down into his wife's wide eyes—as beautiful now as they had been those years ago. Then he kissed her and stood back. She gave his hands a squeeze, a good hard one, and let him go.

6

Ralph and Holly drove to the airport in Ralph's car. Holly sat with her shoulder-bag in her lap, back straight, knees primly together. "Does your wife have a firearm?" she asked.

"Yes. And she's been to the department qualifying range. Wives and daughters are allowed to do that here. What about you, Holly?"

"Of course not. I flew down here, and it wasn't on a charter."

"I'm sure we could get you something. We're going to Texas, after all, not New York."

She shook her head. "I haven't fired a gun since Bill was alive. That was on the last case we worked together. And I didn't hit what I was aiming at."

He didn't speak again until they had merged with the heavy flow of turnpike traffic headed for the airport and Cap City. Once that dangerous feat was accomplished, he said, "Those samples from the barn are at the State Police forensics lab. What do you think they're going to find when they finally get around to running them through all their fancy equipment? Any ideas?"

"Based on what showed up on the chair and the carpet, I'd guess it will be mostly water, but with a high pH. I'd guess there would be traces of a mucus-like fluid of the type produced by the bulbourethral glands, also known as Cowper's glands, named after the anatomist William Cowper who—"

"So you *do* think it's semen."

"More like pre-ejaculate." A faint tinge of color had come into her cheeks.

"You know your stuff."

"I took a course in forensic pathology after Bill died. I took several courses, in fact. Taking courses . . . it passed the time."

"There was semen on the backs of Frank Peterson's thighs. Quite a lot of it, but not an abnormal amount. The DNA matched Terry Maitland's."

"The residue from the barn and the residue in your house isn't semen, and not pre-ejaculate, no matter how similar. When the lab tests the stuff from Canning Township, I think they will find unknown components and dismiss them as contamination. They'll just be glad they don't have to use the samples in court. They won't consider the idea that they're dealing with a completely unknown substance: the stuff he exudes—or sluffs off—when he changes. As for the semen found on the Peterson boy . . . I'm sure the outsider left semen when he killed the Howard girls, too. Either on their clothes or on their bodies. Just another calling card, like the lock of hair in Mr. Maitland's bathroom and all the fingerprints you found."

"Don't forget the eye-wits."

"Yes," she agreed. "This creature likes witnesses. Why wouldn't he, if he can wear another man's face?"

Ralph followed the signs to the charter company Howard Gold used. "So you don't think these were actually sex crimes? They were just arranged to look that way?"

"I wouldn't make that assumption, but . . ." She turned to him. "Sperm on the back of the boy's legs, but none . . . you know . . . in him?"

"No. He was penetrated—raped—with a branch."

"Oough." Holly grimaced. "I doubt if the postmortem on the girls revealed any semen inside them, either. I think there might be a sexual element to his killings, but he might be incapable of actual intercourse."

"That's the case with a good many normal serial killers." He laughed at this—as much of an oxymoron as jumbo shrimp—but didn't take it back, because the only substitute he could think of was *human* serial killers.

"If he eats sadness, he also must eat the pain of his victims as they're dying." The flush in her cheeks was gone, leaving her pale. "It's probably extremely rich, like gourmet food or some fine old Scotch. And yes, that could excite him sexually. I don't like to think of these things, but I believe in knowing your enemy. We . . . I think you should turn left there, Detective Anderson." She pointed.

"Ralph."

"Yes. Turn left, Ralph. That's the road that goes to Regal Air."

7

Howie and Alec were already there, and Howie was smiling. "Takeoff's been pushed back a bit," he said. "Sablo's on his way."

"How did he manage that?" Ralph asked.

"He didn't. I did. Well, I managed half of it. Judge Martinez is in the hospital with a perforated ulcer, and that was God's doing. Or maybe just too much hot sauce. I'm a fan of Texas Pete myself, but the way that guy poured it on used to give me the shivers. As for the other case Lieutenant Sablo was supposed to testify in, the ADA owed me a favor."

"Should I ask why?" Ralph asked.

"No," Howie said, now smiling widely enough to show his back teeth.

With time to kill, the four of them sat in the small waiting room—nothing so grand as a departure lounge—and watched the planes take off and land. Howie said, "When I got home last night, I went on the Internet and read up on doppelgangers. Because that's what this outsider is, wouldn't you say?"

Holly shrugged. "It's as good a word as any."

"The most famous fictional one is in a story by Edgar Allan Poe. 'William Wilson,' it's called."

"Jeannie knew about that one," Ralph said. "We talked about it."

"But there have been plenty in real life. Hundreds, it seems like. Including one on the *Lusitania*. There was a passenger named Rachel Withers, in first class, and several people saw another woman who looked just like her, right down to the streak of white in her hair, during the voyage. Some said the double was traveling in steerage. Some said she was part of the staff. Miss Withers and a gentleman friend went looking for her, and supposedly spotted her only seconds before a torpedo from a German U-boat hit on the starboard side. Miss Withers died, but her gentleman friend survived. He called her doppelganger 'a harbinger of doom.' The French writer, Guy de Maupassant, met his doppelganger one day while walking on a street in Paris—same height, same hair, same eyes, same mustache, same accent."

"Well, the French," Alec said, shrugging. "What do you expect? De Maupassant probably bought him a glass of wine."

"The most famous case happened in 1845, at a girls' school in Latvia. The teacher was writing on the blackboard when her exact double walked into the room, stood beside the teacher, and mimicked her every move, only without the chalk. Then she walked out. Nineteen students saw it happen. Isn't that amazing?"

No one replied. Ralph was thinking of an infested cantaloupe, and disappearing footprints, and something Holly's dead friend had said: *No end to the universe.* He supposed it was a concept some people might find uplifting, even beautiful. Ralph, a just-the-facts man for his entire working life, found it terrifying.

"Well, *I* think it's amazing," Howie said, a bit sulkily.

Alec said, "Tell me something, Holly. If this guy absorbs his victims' thoughts and memories when he takes their faces—through some sort of mystic blood transfusion, I guess—how come he didn't know where to find the nearest walk-in clinic? And then there's Willow Rainwater, the cab driver. Maitland knew her from the kids' basketball program at the Y, but the man she drove to Dubrow acted like he'd never met her. Didn't call her Willow, or Ms. Rainwater. Called her *ma'am*."

"I don't *know*," Holly said, rather crossly. "All I do know I picked up on the fly, and I mean that literally, because I was on airplanes when I did my reading. The only thing I can do is make guesses, and I'm tired of that."

"Maybe it's like speed-reading," Ralph said. "Speed readers are very proud of being able to go through long books cover to cover in a single sitting, but what they mostly pick up is the general gist. If you question them on the details, they usually come up blank." He paused. "At least that's what my wife says. She's in a book club, and there's this one lady who's a little boasty about her reading skills. Drives Jeannie crazy."

They watched as the ground crew fueled the King Air and the two pilots did their pre-flight walk-around. Holly dragged out her iPad and began to read (Ralph thought she was moving along pretty speedily herself). At quarter to ten, a Subaru Forester pulled into the tiny Regal parking lot and Yune Sablo got out, shrugging a camo knapsack over one shoulder as he talked on his cell phone. He ended his call as he came in.

"Amigos! *Cómo están?*"

"Fine," Ralph said, standing. "Let's get this show on the road."

"That was Claude Bolton I was talking to. He's going to meet us at the Plainville airport. It's about sixty miles from Marysville, where he lives."

Alec raised his eyebrows. "Why would he do that?"

"He's worried. Says he didn't sleep much last night, was up and down half a dozen times, felt like someone was watching the house. He said it reminded him of days in prison when everyone knew something was going to go down, but no one knew exactly what, only that it was going to be bad. Said his mother started to get the willies, too. He asked me exactly what was going on, and I told him we'd fill him in when we got there."

Ralph turned to Holly. "If this outsider exists, and if he was close to Bolton, could Bolton feel his presence?"

Instead of protesting again about being asked to guess, she answered in a voice that was soft but very firm. "I'm sure of it."

BIENVENIDOS A TEJAS

July 26th

1

Jack Hoskins crossed into Texas around 2 AM on July 26th, and checked into a fleapit called the Indian Motel just as the day's first light was showing in the east. He paid the sleepy-eyed clerk for a week, using his MasterCard—the only one that wasn't maxed out—and asked for a room at the far end of the ramshackle building.

The room smelled of used booze and old cigarette smoke. The coverlet was threadbare, and the case of the pillow on the swaybacked bed was yellow with age, sweat, or both. He sat down in the room's only chair and ran quickly and without much interest through the text messages and voicemails on his phone (these latter had ceased around 4 AM, when the mailbox reached its capacity). All from the station, many from Chief Geller himself. There had been a double murder on the West Side. With both Ralph Anderson and Betsy Riggins out of service, he was the only detective on duty, where was he, he was needed on the scene immediately, blah-blah-blah.

He lay down on the bed, first on his back, but that hurt the sunburn too much. He turned onto his side, the springs squalling a protest under his considerable weight. *I'll weigh less if the cancer takes hold*, he thought. *Ma was nothing but a skeleton wrapped in skin by the end. A skeleton that screamed.*

"Not going to happen," he told the empty room. "I just need some goddam sleep. This is going to work out."

Four hours would be enough. Five, if he was lucky. But his brain wouldn't turn off; it was like an engine racing in neutral. Cody, the little dope-pushing rat at the Hi station, had had the little white pills, all right, and he'd also had a good supply of coke, which he claimed was almost pure. From the way Jack felt now, lying on this crappy excuse for a bed (he didn't even consider getting into it, God knew what might be crawling around on the sheets), the claim had been true. A few short snorts were all he'd had, in the hours after midnight when it seemed like the drive would never end, and now he felt like he might never sleep again—felt, in fact, as if he could shingle a roof and then run five miles. Yet eventually sleep did come, although it was thin and haunted by dreams of his mother.

When he woke up it was after noon, and the room was stinking hot in spite of the poor excuse for an air conditioner. He went into the bathroom, peed, and tried to look at the nape of his throbbing neck. He couldn't, and maybe that was for the best. He went back into the room and sat on the bed to put on his shoes, but he could only find one of them. He groped for the other, and it was pushed into his hand.

"Jack."

He froze, his arms pebbling with gooseflesh and the short hairs on the back of his neck lifting. The man who had been in his shower back in Flint City was now under his bed, just like the monsters he had feared as a little boy.

"Listen to me, Jack. I'm going to tell you exactly what you need to do."

When the voice finally ceased giving him instructions, Jack realized the pain in his neck (sort of funny, that's what he'd always called the old ball and chain) was gone. Well . . . almost. And what he was supposed to do seemed straightforward, if kind of drastic. Which was all right, because he was pretty sure he could get away with it, and stopping Anderson's clock would be an absolute pleasure. Anderson was the chief meddler, after all; old Mr. No Opinion had brought this on himself. It was too bad about the others, but they weren't on Jack. It was Anderson who had dragged them along.

"Tough titty said the kitty," he murmured.

Once his shoes were on, Jack got down on his knees and looked beneath the bed. There was plenty of dust under there, and some of it looked disturbed, but there was nothing else. Which was good. Which was a relief. That his visitor *had* been there, Jack had no doubt, and he had no doubt about what had been tattooed on the fingers that had pushed the shoe into his hand: CANT.

With the sunburn pain down to a low mutter and his head relatively clear, he thought he could eat something. Steak and eggs, maybe. He had a piece of work ahead of him, and he had to keep his energy up. Man did not live by blow and pep-pills alone. Without food, he might faint in the hot sun, and then he would burn.

Speaking of sun, it hit him like a punch in the face when he went out, and his neck gave a warning throb. He realized with dismay that he was out of sunblock and had forgotten his aloe cream. It was possible they sold something like that in the café attached to the motel, along with the rest of the rickrack they always kept by the cash register in places like this: tee-shirts and ball caps and country CDs and Navajo souvenirs made in Cambodia. They had to sell a few of the necessities along with that crap, because the nearest town was—

He came to a dead halt, one hand reaching for the café's door, peering through the dusty glass. They were in there. Anderson and his merry band of assholes, including the skinny woman with the gray bangs. There was also an old bag in a wheelchair and a muscular man with short black hair and a goatee. The old bag started laughing about something, then she started coughing. Jack could hear it even outside, like a damn backhoe in low gear. The man with the goatee whacked her on the back a few times, and then they were all laughing.

You'll be laughing on the other side of your damn faces when I get done with you, Jack thought, but actually it was good that they were laughing. Otherwise they might have spotted him.

He turned away, trying to understand what he had seen. Not the bunch of them hee-hawing, he didn't care about that, but when Goatee Man reached to thump Wheelchair Woman on the back, Jack had seen tats on his fingers. The glass was dusty and the blue ink was faded, but he knew what they said: CANT. How the man had gotten from under his bed and into the diner so fast was a mystery that Jack Hoskins didn't care to contemplate. He had a job to do, that was enough, and getting rid of the cancer that was growing in his skin was only half of it. Getting rid of Ralph Anderson was the other half, and it would be a pleasure.

Old Mr. No Opinion.

2

Plainville Airfield sat in scrubland on the outskirts of the tired little city it served. There was a single runway, which Ralph thought horribly short. The pilot applied full braking as soon as the wheels touched down, and unsecured objects went flying. They came to a stop on a yellow line at the end of the narrow strip of tar, no more than thirty feet from a gully filled with weeds, stagnant water, and Shiner cans.

"Welcome to nowhere in particular," Alec remarked as the King Air lumbered toward a prefab terminal building that looked as if it might blow away in the next high wind. There was a road-dusty Dodge van waiting for them. Ralph recognized it as the wheelchair-accessible Companion model even before he saw the handicap plate. Claude Bolton, tall and muscular in faded jeans, blue work shirt, battered cowboy boots, and a Texas Rangers gimme cap, stood beside it.

Ralph was first off the plane, and he extended a hand. After a second of hesitation, Claude shook it. Ralph found it impossible not to look at the faded letters on the man's fingers: CANT.

"Thank you for making this easy," Ralph said. "You didn't have to, and I appreciate it." He introduced the others.

Holly shook his hand last, and said, "Those tattoos on your fingers . . . are they about drinking?"

Right, Ralph thought. *That's one piece of the puzzle I forgot to take out of the box.*

"Yes'm, that's right." Bolton spoke like someone teaching a well-learned and well-loved lesson. "The big paradox is what they call it in AA meetings down here. I first heard about it in prison. You *must* drink, but you *can't* drink."

"I feel that way about cigarettes," Holly said.

Bolton grinned, and Ralph thought how odd it was that the least socially adept person in their little party was the one who had put Bolton at ease. Not that Bolton had seemed really worried; more on watch. "Yes ma'am, cigarettes is a hard one. How you doing with it?"

"Haven't had one in almost a year," Holly said, "but I take it a day at a time. *Can't* and *must*. I like that."

Had she actually known all along what the finger tattoos meant? Ralph couldn't tell.

"Only way to break the *can't-must* paradox is with the help of a higher power, so I got me one. And I keep my sobriety medallion handy. What I was taught is that if you get wantin a drink, stick that medallion in your mouth. If it melts, you can take one."

Holly smiled—the radiant one Ralph was coming to like so well.

The side door of the van opened, and a rusty ramp squalled out. A large lady with an extravagant corona of white hair rolled down it in a wheelchair. She had a short green oxygen bottle in her lap with a plastic tube leading from it to the cannula in her nose. "Claude! Why are you standin around with these people in the heat? If we're gonna roll, we should roll. It's getting on for noon."

"This is my mother," Claude said. "Ma, this is Detective Anderson, who questioned me on the thing I told you about. These other ones are new to me."

Howie, Alec, and Yune introduced themselves to the old lady. Holly came last. "It's very nice to meet you, Mrs. Bolton."

Lovie laughed. "Well, we'll see how you feel about that when you get to know me."

"I'd better go see about our rental," Howie said. "I think it's that one parked by the door." He pointed at a mid-size dark blue SUV.

"I'll lead the way in the van," Claude said. "You won't have any problem followin along; not much in the way of traffic on the Marysville road."

"Why don't you ride with us, honey?" Lovie Bolton asked Holly. "Keep a old lady company."

Ralph expected Holly to refuse, but she agreed at once. "Just give me a minute."

She beckoned Ralph with her eyes, and he followed her toward the King Air as Claude watched his mother turn her chair and roll back up the ramp. A small plane was taking off, and at first Ralph couldn't hear what Holly was asking him. He bent closer.

"What do I tell them, Ralph? They're sure to ask what we're doing here."

He considered, then said: "Why don't you just hit the high spots?"

"They won't believe me!"

That made him grin. "Holly, I think you handle disbelief pretty well."

•

3

Like many ex-cons (at least those that didn't want to risk going back inside), Claude Bolton drove the Dodge Companion van at exactly five miles an hour under the speed limit. Half an hour into the trip, he turned in at the Indian Motel & Café. He got out and spoke almost apologetically to Howie, who was behind the wheel of the rental. "Hope you don't mind if we have a bite," he said. "My ma sometimes has problems if she don't eat regular, and she didn't have any time to make sammitches. I was afraid we might miss you." He lowered his voice, as if confiding a shameful secret. "It's her blood sugar. When it goes low, she gets fainty."

"I'm sure we could all use a bite," Howie said.

"This story the lady told—"

"Why don't we talk about it when we get to your house, Claude," Ralph said.

Claude nodded. "Yeah, that might be better."

The café smelled—not unpleasantly—of grease and beans and frying meat. Neil Diamond was on the jukebox, singing "I Am, I Said" in Spanish. The specials (which weren't very) were posted behind the counter. Above the kitchen pass-through was a defaced photograph of Donald Trump. His blond hair had been colored black; he had been given a forelock and a mustache. Below it someone had printed *Yanqui vete a casa*: Yankee go home. At first Ralph was surprised—Texas was a red state, after all, as red as they came—but then he remembered that if whites weren't the actual minority this near to the border, it was a close-run thing.

They sat at the far end of the room, Alec and Howie at a two-top, the others at a bigger table nearby. Ralph ordered a burger; Holly ordered a salad, which turned out to be mostly wilted iceberg lettuce; Yune and the Boltons went for the full Mexican, which consisted of a taco, a burrito, and an empanada. The waitress banged a pitcher of sweet tea down on the table without being asked.

Lovie Bolton was studying Yune, her eyes bright as a bird's. "Sablo, you said your name was? That's a funny one."

"Yes, not many of us around," Yune said.

"You come from the other side, or are you natural-born?"

"Natural-born, ma'am," Yune said. Half of his well-stuffed taco disappeared at a single bite. "Second generation."

"Well, good for you! Made in the USA! I used to know an Augustin Sablo when I lived way down south, before I was married. He drove a bread truck in Laredo and Nuevo Laredo. When he came by t'house, my sisters and I used to clamor for *churro éclairs*. No relation to him, I suppose?"

Yune's olive complexion darkened a bit—not quite a blush—but the look he shot Ralph was amused. "Yes, ma'am, that would have been my *papi*."

"Well, ain't it a small world?" Lovie said, and began to laugh. Her laughter turned to coughing, and her coughing turned to choking. Claude thumped her on the back so hard the cannula flew from her nose and fell into her plate. "Oh, son, lookit that," she said when she had her breath back. "Now I got snot on my burrito." She resettled the cannula. "Well, what the hey. It came from inside me, it can go right back. No harm done." She chomped.

Ralph began to laugh, and the others joined him. Even Howie and Alec joined in, although they had missed most of the interplay. Ralph had a moment to think how laughter drew people together, and was glad Claude had brought his mother along. She was a hot ticket.

"Small world," she repeated. "Yes it is." She leaned forward so that her considerable bosom pushed her plate forward. She was still looking at Yune with those bright bird eyes. "You know the story she told us?" She cut her eyes to Holly, who was picking at her salad with a small frown.

"Yes, ma'am."

"You believe it?"

"I don't know. I . . ." Yune lowered his voice. "I tend to."

Lovie nodded and lowered her own voice. "Did you ever see the parade in Nuevo? *Processo dos Passos?* Maybe when you were a boy?"

"*Sí, señora.*"

She lowered her voice further. "What about *him*? The *farnicoco*? You see him?"

"*Sí*," Yune said, and although Lovie Bolton was as white as she could be, Ralph thought Yune had fallen into Spanish without even thinking of it.

She lowered her voice further still. "Give you nightmares?"

Yune hesitated, then said, "*Sí. Muchas pesadillas.*"

She leaned back, satisfied but grave. She looked at Claude. "You listen to these folks, sonny. You've got a big problem, I think." She winked at Yune, but not as a joke; her face was grave. "*Muchos.*"

4

As the little caravan pulled back out onto the highway, Ralph asked Yune about the *processo dos Passos*.

"A parade during Holy Week," Yune said. "Not exactly approved by the church, but winked at."

"*Farnicoco?* That's the same as Holly's *El Cuco?*"

"Worse," Yune said. He looked grim. "Worse even than the Man with the Sack. *Farnicoco* is the Hooded Man. He's Mr. Death."

5

By the time they got to the Bolton home in Marysville, it was almost three o'clock and the heat was like a hammer. They crowded into the small living room, where the air conditioner—a noisy window-shaker that looked to Ralph old enough for Social Security—did its best to keep up with so many warm bodies. Claude went out to the kitchen and brought back cans of Coke in a Styrofoam cooler. "If you were hoping for beer, you're out of luck," he said. "I don't keep it."

"This is fine," Howie said. "I don't think any of us will be drinking alcohol until we settle this matter to the best of our ability. Tell us about last night."

Bolton glanced at his mother. She folded her arms and nodded.

"Well," he said, "the way it turned out, there really wasn't nothing to it. I went to bed after the late news, like always, and I felt all right then—"

"Bullpucky," Lovie broke in. "You ain't been yourself since you got here. Restless . . ." She looked around at the others. ". . . off his feed . . . talking in his sleep—"

"Do you want me to tell it, Ma, or do you?"

She flapped a hand for him to go on and sipped from her can of Coke.

"Well, she's not wrong," Bolton admitted, "although I wouldn't want the guys back at work to know it. Security staff in a place like Gentlemen, Please ain't supposed to get all spooked, you know. But I have been, kind of. Only nothing like last night. Last night was different. I woke up around two, out of a nasty dream, and got up to lock the doors. I never lock em when I'm here, although I make Ma do it when she's here alone, after her Home Helpers from Plainville leave at six."

"What was your dream?" Holly asked. "Can you remember?"

"Somebody under the bed, lying there and looking up. That's all I can remember."

She nodded for him to go on.

"Before I locked the front door, I stepped out on the porch to have a look around, and I noticed all the coyotes had stopped howling. Usually they howl like everything, once the moon's up in the sky."

"They do unless someone's around," Alec said. "Then they stop. Like the crickets."

"Come to think of it, I couldn't hear them, either. And Ma's garden out back is usually full of em. I went back to bed, but couldn't sleep. I remembered I hadn't locked the windows and got up to do that. The catches squeak, and that woke Ma up. She asked me what I was doing, and I told her to go on back to sleep. I climbed into bed and almost drifted off myself—by then it had to be going on three—when I remembered I hadn't locked the window in the bathroom, the one over the tub. I got the idea that someone was climbing in through it, so I got out of bed and ran to see. I know it sounds stupid now, but . . ."

He looked at them and saw none of them smiling or looking skeptical.

"All right. All right. I guess if you've come all the way down here, you probably *don't* think it sounds stupid. Anyway, I tripped over Ma's damn hassock, and that time she did get up. She asked me if someone was trying to get in the house, and I said no, but for her to stay in her room."

"I didn't, though," Lovie said complacently. "I never minded any man except my husband, and he's been gone a long time."

"There was no one in the bathroom or trying to get in there through the window, but I had a feeling—I can't tell you how strong it was—that he was still out there, hiding and waiting for his chance."

"Not under your bed?" Ralph asked.

"No, I checked under there first thing. Crazy, sure, but . . ." He paused. "I didn't go to sleep until daybreak. Ma woke me up and said we had to go to the airport so we could meet you."

"Let him sleep as long as I could," Lovie said. "That's why I never made any sammitches. The bread's on top of the fridge, and if I try to reach up there, I lose my breath."

"And how do you feel now?" Holly asked Claude.

He sighed, and when he ran a hand up the side of his face, they could hear the rasp of his beard. "Not right. I stopped believing in the boogeyman right around the same time I stopped believing in Santa Claus, but I feel all upset and paranoid, the way I did when I was on the coke. Is this guy after me? Do you really believe that?"

He looked from face to face. It was Holly who answered him. "*I* do," she said.

6

They were silent for a bit, thinking. Then Lovie spoke up. "*El Cuco*, you called him," she said to Holly.

"Yes."

The old woman nodded, tapping her arthritis-swollen fingers on her oxygen bottle. "When I was a little girl, the Mex kids called him *Cucuy* and the Anglos called him Kookie, or Chookie, or just the Chook. I even had a pitcher book about that sucker."

"I bet I had the same one," Yune said. "My *abuela* gave it to me. A giant with one big red ear?"

"*Sí, mi amigo.*" Lovie took out her cigarettes and lit one. She chuffed out smoke, coughed, and went on. "In the story, there were three sisters. The youngest one cooked and cleaned and did all the other chores. The two older girls were lazy and made fun of her. *El Cucuy* came. The house was locked, but he looked like their *papi*, so they let him in. He took the bad sisters to teach them a lesson. He left the good one who worked so hard for the daddy who was raising the girls on his own. Do you remember?"

"Sure," Yune said. "You don't forget the stories you hear when you're just a kid. That storybook version of *El Cucuy* was supposed to be a good guy, but all I remember is how scared I was when he dragged the girls up the mountain to his cave. *Las niñas lloraban y le rogaban que las soltara.* The little girls cried and begged him to let them go."

"Yes," Lovie said. "And in the end, he did and those bad girls changed their ways. That's the storybook version. But the real *cucuy* don't let the children go, no matter how much they cry and beg. You all know that, don't you? You've seen his work."

"So you believe it, too," Howie said.

Lovie shrugged. "Like they say, *quien sabe*? Did I ever believe in *el chupacabra*? What the old *los indios* call the goat-sucker?" She snorted. "No more than I believe in Bigfoot. But there are strange things, just the same. Once—it was on Good Friday, at Blessed Sacrament on Galveston Street—I saw a statue of the Virgin Mary cry tears of blood. We all saw it. Later, Father Joaquim said it was just wet rust from under the eaves running down her face, but we all knew better. Father did, too. You could see it in his eyes." She swung her gaze back to Holly. "You said you'd seen things yourself."

"Yes," Holly said quietly. "I believe there's something. It may not be the traditional *El Cuco*, but is it the thing the legends are based on? I think so."

"The boy and those girls you told about, he drank their blood and ate their flesh? This outsider?"

"He might have," Alec said. "Based on the crime scenes, it's possible."

"And now he's me," Bolton said. "That's what you think. All he needed was some of my blood. Did he drink it?"

No one answered him, but Ralph could actually see the thing that looked like Terry Maitland doing just that. He could see it with dreadful clarity. That was how far this insanity had gotten into his head.

"Was that him here last night, skulking around?"

"Maybe not physically here," Holly said, "and he may not be you just yet. He might still be *becoming* you."

"Maybe he was checking the place out," Yune said.

Maybe he was trying to find out about us, Ralph thought. *And if he was, he did. Claude knew we were coming.*

"So what is going to happen now?" Lovie demanded. "Is he gonna kill another kid or two in Plainville or in Austin, and try to get my boy blamed for it?"

"I don't think so," Holly said. "I doubt if he's strong enough yet. It was months between Heath Holmes and Terry Maitland. And he's been . . . active."

"There's something else, too," Yune said. "A practical aspect. This part of the country's gotten hot for him. If he's smart—and he must be, to have survived this long—he'll want to move on."

That felt right. Ralph could see Holly's outsider putting his Claude Bolton face and muscular Claude Bolton body on a bus or a train in Austin and heading into the golden west. Las Vegas, maybe. Or Los Angeles. Where there might be another accidental encounter with a man (or even a woman—who knew), and a little more blood spilled. Another link in the chain.

The opening bars of Selena's "Baila Esta Cumbia" came from Yune's breast pocket. He looked startled.

Claude grinned. "Oh yeah. We got coverage even out here. Twenty-first century, man."

Yune took out his phone, looked at the screen, and said, "Montgomery County PD. I better answer this. Excuse me."

Holly looked startled, even alarmed, as he took the call and walked out on the porch with "Hello, this is Lieutenant Sablo" trailing after him. Holly excused herself as well, and followed him.

Howie said, "Maybe it's about—"

Ralph shook his head without knowing why. At least not on the surface of his mind.

"Where's Montgomery County?" Claude asked.

"Arizona," Ralph said, before either Howie or Alec could reply. "Another matter. Nothing to do with this."

"What exactly are we going to do about *this*?" Lovie asked. "Do you have any idea how to catch this fella? My son is all I got, you know."

Holly came back in. She went to Lovie, bent, whispered in her ear. When Claude leaned over to eavesdrop, Lovie made a shooing gesture. "Go on in the kitchen, son, and bring back those chocolate pinwheel cookies, if they ain't melted in the heat."

Claude, obviously trained to mind, went out to the kitchen. Holly continued to whisper, and Lovie's eyes widened. She nodded. Claude came back with the bag of cookies at the same time Yune came in from the porch, stowing his phone back in his pocket.

"That was—" he began, then stopped. Holly had turned slightly, so her back was to Claude. She raised a finger to her lips and shook her head.

"That was nothing," he said. "They picked up a guy, but not the one we've been looking for."

Claude put the cookies (which did look sadly melted in their cellophane bag) on the table and glanced around suspiciously. "I don't think that's what you started to say. What's going on here?"

Ralph thought that was a good question. Outside on the rural route, a pickup truck trundled by, the lockbox in the bed reflecting bright spears of sun that made him wince.

"Son," Lovie said, "I want you to get in your car and drive to Tippit and get us some chicken dinners at Highway Heaven. That's a pretty good place. We'll feed these folks, then they can go back t'other way and spend the night at the Indian. It ain't much, but it's a roof."

"Tippit's forty miles!" Claude protested. "Dinners for seven people will cost a fortune, and be dead cold when I get back!"

"I'll heat everything up on the stove," she said calmly, "and those dinners'll be good as new. Go on, now."

Ralph liked the way Claude put his hands on his hips and looked at her with humor and exasperation. "You're tryin to get rid of me!"

"That's it," she agreed, butting her cigarette in a tin ashtray heaped with dead soldiers. "Because if Miss Holly here is right, what *you* know, *he* knows. Maybe that don't matter, maybe all the cats are out of the bag, but maybe it does. So you be a good son and go get those dinners."

Howie took out his wallet. "Allow me to pay, Claude."

"That's all right," Claude said, a trifle sullenly. "I can pay. I ain't broke."

Howie smiled his big lawyer's smile. "But I insist!"

Claude took the money and tucked it into the wallet chained to his belt. He looked around at his guests, still trying to be sullen, but then he laughed. "My ma usually gets what she wants," he said. "I guess you figured that out by now."

7

The Boltons' byroad, Rural Star Route 2, eventually led to an actual highway: 190 out of Austin. Before it got that far, a dirt road—four lanes wide but now falling into disrepair—branched off to the right. It was marked by a billboard which was also falling into disrepair. It depicted a happy family descending a spiral staircase. They were holding up gas lanterns that showed their expressions of awe as they peered at the stalactites suspended high above them. The come-on line below the family read VISIT THE MARYSVILLE HOLE, ONE OF NATURE'S GREATEST WONDERS. Claude knew what it said from the old days, when he'd been a restless teenager stuck in Marysville, but in these new days all you could read was VISIT THE MARYSV and ATEST WONDERS. A wide strip, reading CLOSED UNTIL FURTHER NOTICE (itself faded), had been pasted over the rest.

A feeling of lightheadedness came over him as he drove by what local kids called (with knowing sniggers) the Road to the Hole, but it passed when he kicked the AC up a notch. Although he had protested, he was actually glad to be out of the house. That sense of being watched had faded away. He turned on the radio, tuned to Outlaw Country, got Waylon Jennings (the best!), and began to sing along.

Chicken dinners from Highway Heaven was maybe not such a bad idea. He could have a whole order of onion rings to himself, eating them on the way home while they were still hot and greasy.

8

Jack waited in his room at the Indian Motel, peering out between the drawn drapes, until he saw a van with a handicap plate pulling out onto the road. That had to be the old bag's ride. A blue SUV followed it, undoubtedly full of the meddlers down from Flint City.

When they were out of sight, Jack went up to the café, where he ate a meal and then inspected the items for sale. There was no aloe cream, and no sunblock, either, so he bought two bottles of water and a couple of outrageously overpriced bandannas. They wouldn't be much protection from the hot Texas sun, but better than nothing. He got in his truck and drove southwest, in the direction the meddlers had gone, until he came to the billboard and the road leading to the Marysville Hole. Here he turned in.

About four miles up, he came to a weather-worn little cabin standing in the middle of the road. It must have been a ticket booth when the Hole was a going concern, he supposed. The paint, once bright red, was now the faded pink of blood diluted in water. On the front was a sign reading ATTRACTION CLOSED, TURN BACK HERE. The road had been chained off beyond the ticket booth. Jack went around the chain, jouncing along the dirt hardpan, crunching tumbleweeds, swerving around sagebrush. The truck took a final bounce and then he was back on the road . . . if you could call it that. On this side of the chain it was your basic mess of weed-choked potholes and washouts that had never been filled in. His Ram—high-sprung and equipped with four-wheel drive—took the washouts easily, spitting dirt and stones from beneath its oversized tires.

Two slow miles and ten minutes later, he came to an acre or so of empty parking lot, the yellow lines of the spaces faded to ghosts, the asphalt cracked and heaved into plates. To the left, backed up against a steep brush-covered hill, was an abandoned gift shop with a fallen sign he had to read upside down: SOUVENIRS AND AUTHENTIC INDIAN CRAFTS. Straight ahead was the ruin of a wide cement walk leading to an opening in the hill. Well, once upon a time it had been an opening; now it was boarded over and plastered with signs reading KEEP OUT, NO TRESPASSING, PRIVATE PROPERTY, and COUNTY SHERIFF PATROLS THIS AREA.

Right, Jack thought. *They maybe take a swing-through once every February 29th.*

Another crumbling road led away from the parking lot, past the gift shop. It went up one side of a slope and down the other. It took him first to a bunch of decrepit tourist cabins (also boarded up) and then on to some kind of service shed, where company vehicles and equipment had probably once been stored. There were more KEEP OUT signs on this, plus a cheery one that read WATCH FOR RATTLESNAKES.

Jack parked his truck in the scant shade of this building. Before getting out, he tied one of the bandannas over his head (giving him a weird resemblance to the man Ralph had seen at the courthouse on the day Terry Maitland was shot). The other he fluffed around his neck to keep that fucking burn from getting worse. He keyed open the lockbox in the truckbed and reverently lifted out the gun case that contained his pride and joy: a Winchester .300 bolt-action, the same gun Chris Kyle had used to shoot all those ragheads (Jack had seen *American Sniper* eight times). With the Leupold VX-1 riflescope, he could hit a target at two thousand yards. Well, four out of six tries on a good day, and with no wind, and he didn't expect to be shooting at anywhere near that distance when the time came. If it came.

He spotted a few forgotten tools lying in the weeds, and appropriated a rusty pitchfork in case of rattlers. Behind the building, a path led up the back of the hill in which the entrance to the Hole was located. This side was rockier, not really a hill at all but an eroded bluff. There were a few beercans along the way, and several rocks had been tagged with things like SPANKY 11 and DOO-DAD WAS HERE.

Halfway up, another path split off, apparently circling back to the defunct gift shop and the parking lot. Here was a weather-worn, bullet-pocked wooden sign showing an Indian chief in full headdress. Below him was an arrow, the accompanying message so faded it was barely legible: BEST PICTOGRAPHS THIS WAY. More recently, some wit had drawn a Magic Marker word balloon coming from the big chief's mouth. It read CAROLYN ALLEN SUCKS MY REDSKIN COCK.

This path was broader, but Jack had not come here to admire Native American art, so he continued upward. The climb was not particularly dangerous, but Jack's exercise over the last few years had mostly consisted of bending his elbow in various bars. By the time he was three-quarters of the way up, he was short of breath. His shirt and both bandannas were dark with sweat. He set the gun case and pitchfork down, then bent and gripped his knees until the dark specks dancing in front of his eyes disappeared and his heart rate returned to something like normal. He had come here to avoid a terrible death from the sort of ravenous, skin-eating cancer that had taken his mother. Dying of a myocardial infarction while trying to do that would be a bitter joke.

He started to straighten up, then paused, squinting. In the shade beneath an overhanging ledge, safe from the worst of the elements, there was more graffiti. But if these had been left by kids, they were long dead, and for many hundreds of years. One showed stick men with stick spears surrounding what might have been an antelope—something with horns, anyway. In another, stick men were standing in front of what looked like a tepee. In a third—almost too faded to make out—a stick man was standing over the prone body of another stick man, his spear raised in triumph.

Pictographs, Jack thought, *and not even the best ones, according to the big chief back there. Kindergarten kids could do better, but they'll be here long after I'm gone. Especially if the cancer gets me.*

The idea made him angry. He picked up a chunk of sharp rock and hammered at the pictographs until they were obliterated.

There, he thought. *There, you dead fuckers. You're gone and I win.*

It occurred to him that he might be going crazy . . . or had already gone. He pushed that away and resumed his climb. When he reached the top of the bluff, he found he had a fine view of the parking lot, the gift shop, and the boarded-up entrance to the Marysville Hole. His visitor with the tats on his fingers wasn't sure the meddlers would come here, but if they did, Jack was to handle them. Which he could do with the Winchester, he had no doubt of that. If they didn't come—if they just returned to Flint City after talking to the man they'd come to talk to—Jack's work would be done. Either way, the visitor assured him, Jack would be as good as new. No cancer.

What if he's lying? What if he can give it, but not take it away? Or what if it's not really there at all? What if he's not there? What if you're just crazy?

These thoughts he also pushed away. He opened the gun case,

took out the Winchester, and mounted the sight. It put the parking lot and the entrance to the cave right in front of him. If they came, they would be as big as the ticket booth he'd gone around.

Jack crawled into the shade of an overhanging rock (first checking for snakes, scorpions, or other wildlife) and had a drink of water, swallowing a couple of pep-pills with it. He added a toot from the four-gram bottle Cody had sold him (no freebies when it came to Colombian marching powder). Now it was just a stakeout, like dozens he'd been on during his career as a cop. He waited, dozing intermittently with the Winchester laid across his lap but always alert enough to detect movement, until the sun was low in the sky. Then he got to his feet, wincing at the stiffness in his muscles.

"Not coming," he said. "At least not today."

No, the man with the finger tattoos agreed. (Or Jack imagined he agreed.) *But you'll be back here tomorrow, won't you?*

Indeed he would. For a week, if that was what it took. A month, even.

He headed back down, moving carefully; the last thing he needed after hours in the hot sun was a busted ankle. He stowed his rifle in the lockbox, drank some more water from the bottle he'd left in the truck's cab (it was now tepid going on hot) and drove back to the highway, this time turning toward Tippit, where he might be able to buy some supplies: sunblock for sure. And vodka. Not too much, he had a responsibility to fulfil, but maybe enough so he could lie down on his crappy swaybacked bed without thinking about how that shoe had been pushed into his hand. Jesus, why had he ever gone out to that fucking barn in Canning Township?

He passed Claude Bolton's car going back the other way. Neither noticed the other.

9

"All right," Lovie Bolton said when Claude was down the road and out of sight. "What's this all about? What is it you didn't want my boy to hear?"

Yune ignored her for the moment, turning to the others. "The Montgomery County Sheriff's Office sent a couple of deputies out to look at the places Holly photographed. They found a pile of bloody clothes in that abandoned factory with the swastika spray-painted on the side. One of the items was an orderly's jacket with a tag reading PROPERTY OF HMU sewn into it."

"Heisman Memory Unit," Howie said. "When they analyze the blood on the clothes, what do you want to bet it turns out to be from one or both of the Howard girls?"

"Plus any fingerprints they find will belong to Heath Holmes," Alec added. "They may be blurry, if he'd started his change."

"Or not," Holly said. "We don't know how long the change takes, or even if it's the same every time."

"The sheriff up there has questions," Yune said. "I put him off. Considering what we might be dealing with, I hope I can put him off forever."

"You folks need to stop talking amongst yourselves and fill me in," Lovie said. "Please. I'm worried about my boy. He's as innocent as those other two men, and they are both dead."

"I understand your concern," Ralph said. "One minute. Holly, when you were filling the Boltons in on the ride from the airport, did you tell them about the graveyards? You didn't, did you?"

"No. Just hit the high spots, you said. So that's what I did."

"Oh, hold it," Lovie said. "Just hold the phone. There was a movie I saw when I was a girl in Laredo, one of those wrestling women movies—"

"*Mexican Wrestling Women Meet the Monster*," Howie said. "We saw it. Ms. Gibney brought a copy. Not Academy Award material, but interesting, just the same."

"That was one of the ones Rosita Muñoz was in," Lovie said. "The *cholita luchadora*. We all wanted to be her, me and my friends. I even dressed up like her one Halloween. My mother made my costume. That movie about the *cuco* was a scary one. There was a professor . . . or a scientist . . . I don't remember which, but *El Cuco* took his face, and when the *luchadoras* finally tracked him down, he was living in a crypt or a vault in the local graveyard. Isn't that how the story went?"

"Yes," Holly said, "because that's part of the legend, at least the Spanish version of it. The *cuco* sleeps with the dead. Like vampires are supposed to do."

"If this thing actually exists," Alec said, "it *is* a vampire, at least sort of. It needs blood to make the next link in the chain. To perpetuate itself."

Once again Ralph thought, *Do you people hear yourselves?* He liked Holly Gibney a lot, but he also wished he'd never met her. Thanks to her there was a war going on in his head, and he wished mightily for a truce.

Holly turned to Lovie. "That empty factory where the Ohio police found the bloody clothes is close to the graveyard where Heath Holmes and his parents are buried. More clothes were found in a barn not far from an old graveyard where some of Terry Maitland's ancestors are buried. So here's the question: Is there a graveyard close to here?"

Lovie considered. They waited. At last she said, "There's a boneyard in Plainville, but nothing in Marysville. Hell, we don't even have a church. There used to be one, Our Lady of Forgiveness, but it burned down twenty years ago."

"Shit," Howie muttered.

"How about a family plot?" Holly asked. "Sometimes people bury on their property, don't they?"

"Well, I don't know about other folks," the old lady said, "but *we* never had one. My momma and daddy are buried back in Laredo, and their momma and daddy, too. Way back it'd be Indiana, which is where my people migrated down from after the Civil War."

"What about your husband?" Howie asked.

"George? All his people were from Austin, and that's where he's buried, right next to his parents. I used to take the bus once in a while to visit him, usually on his birthday, took flowers and all, but since I got this goddam COPD, I haven't been."

"Well, I guess that's that," Yune said.

Lovie seemed not to hear. "I could sing, you know, back when I still had my wind. And I played guitar. I came to Austin from Laredo after high school, because of the music. Nashville South, they call it. I got a job in the paper factory on Brazos Street while I was waitin for my big break at the Carousel or the Broken Spoke or wherever. Makin envelopes. I never did get my big break, but I married the foreman. That was George. Never regretted it until he retired."

"I think we're drifting off the subject," Howie said.

"Let her talk," Ralph said. He had that little tingle, the feel of something coming. Still over the horizon, but yes, coming. "Go on, Mrs. Bolton."

She looked doubtfully at Howie, but when Holly nodded and smiled, Lovie smiled back, lit another cigarette, and went on.

"Well, after he got his thirty in and had his pension, George moved us out here to the back of beyond. Claude was just twelve—we had him late, long after we decided God wasn't going to give us no children. Claude never liked Marysville, missed the bright lights and his worthless friends—bad company was always my boy's downfall—and I didn't care for it much either at first, although I have come to enjoy the peace of it. When you get old, peace is about all you want. You folks might not believe that now, but you'll find out. And that idea of a family plot ain't such a bad one, now I think of it. I could do worse than going into the ground out back, but I s'pose Claude will end up dragging my meat and bones to Austin, so I can lay with my husband, like I did in life. Won't be long now, neither."

She coughed, looked at her cigarette with distaste, and buried it with the others in the overfilled ashtray, where it smoldered balefully.

"You know why we happened to end up in Marysville? George had the idea he was going to raise alpacas. After they died, which didn't take long, it was going to be goldendoodles. If you don't know, goldendoodles are a cross between golden retrievers and poodles. You think eeva-lution ever approved of a mix like that? I goddam doubt it. His brother put the notion in his head. No greater fool than Roger Bolton ever walked the earth, but George thought their fortunes was made. Roger moved down here with his family and the two of em went partners. Anyway, the goldendoodle pups died, just like the alpacas. George and me were a little tight for money after that, but we had enough to get by. Roger, though, he poured his whole savings into that damn fool scheme. So he looked around for work and . . ."

She stopped, an expression of amazement dawning on her face.

"What about Roger?" Ralph asked.

"Damn," Lovie Bolton said. "I'm old, but that's no excuse. It was right in front of my face."

Ralph leaned forward and took one of her hands. "What are you talking about, Lovie?" Going to her first name, as he always eventually did in the interrogation room.

"Roger Bolton and his two sons—Claude's cousins—are buried not four miles from here, along with four other men. Or maybe 'twas five. And those children, of course, them twins." She shook her head slowly back and forth. "I was so mad when Claude got six months in Gatesville for stealing. And ashamed. That's when he started using drugs, you know. But I saw later it was God's mercy. Because if he'd been here, he would have been with them. Not his dad, by then George had already had two heart attacks and couldn't go, but Claude . . . yes, he would have been with them."

"Where?" Alec asked. He was leaning forward now, staring intently.

"The Marysville Hole," she said. "That's where those men died, and that's where they remain."

10

She told them it had been like the part in *Tom Sawyer* when Tom and Becky get lost in the cave, only Tom and Becky eventually got out. The Jamieson twins, just eleven years old, never did. Nor did those who tried to rescue them. The Marysville Hole took them all.

"That's where your brother-in-law got work after the dog business failed?" Ralph asked.

She nodded. "He'd done some explorin there—not in the public part, but on the Ahiga side—so when he applied, they hired him on as a guide quick as winkin. Him and the other guides used to take tourists down in groups of a dozen or so. It's the biggest cave in all of Texas, but the most popular part, what folks really wanted to see, was the main chamber. It was quite a place, all right. Like a cathedral. They called it the Chamber of Sound, because of the what-do-you-call-em, acoustics. One of the guides would stand at the bottom, four or five hundred feet down, and whisper the Pledge of Allegiance, and the people at the top would hear every word. Echoes seemed to go on forever. Also, the walls were covered with Indian drawings, I forget the word for em—"

"Pictographs," Yune said.

"That's it. You got a Coleman gas lamp when you went in, so

you could look at em, or up at the stalactites hangin down from the ceiling. There was an iron spiral staircase that went all the way to the bottom, four hundred steps or more, around and around and around. It's still there, I shouldn't wonder, although I wouldn't trust it these days. It's damp down there, and iron rusts. Only time I took them stairs, it made me dizzy as hell, and I wasn't even lookin up at the stalactites, like most of em. You want to believe I took the elevator back to the top. Goin down is one thing, but only a pure-d fool climbs up four hundred steps if she don't have to.

"The bottom was two, maybe three hundred yards across. There were colored lights set up to show off all the mineral streaks in the rocks, there was a snack bar, and there were six or eight passageways to explore. They had names. Can't recall all of them, but there was the Navajo Art Gallery—where there were more pictographs—and the Devil's Slide, and Snake's Belly, where you had to bend over and even crawl in places. Can you imagine?"

"Yes," Holly said. "Oough."

"Those were the main ones. There were even more leadin off from *them*, but they were closed off, because the Hole isn't just one cave but dozens of em, goin down and down, some never explored."

"Easy to get lost," Alec said.

"You bet. Now here's what happened. There were two or three openins leadin away from the Snake's Belly passageway that *weren't* boarded over or barred up, because they were considered too small to bother with."

"Only they weren't too small for the twins," Ralph guessed.

"That's the nail, sir, and you hit it on the head. Carl and Calvin Jamieson. Couple of pint-sizers lookin for trouble, and they sure found it. They were with the party that went into Snake's Belly, right behind their ma and pa at the end of the line, but not with em when they came out. The parents . . . well, I don't have to tell you how they took on, do I? My brother-in-law wasn't the one leadin the group the Jamieson family was a part of, but he was in the search party that went after em. Headed it up would be my guess, although I have no way of knowin."

"His sons were also part of it?" Howie asked. "Claude's cousins?"

"Yessir. The boys worked part-time at the Hole themselves, and came on the run as soon as they heard. Lots of folks came, because the news spread like wildfire. At first it looked like it wasn't going to be no problem. They could hear the boys callin from all the openins leadin off from the Snake's Belly, and they knew exactly which one they went into, because when one of the guides shone his flashlight, they could see a little plastic Chief Ahiga Mr. Jamieson bought one of the boys in the gift shop. Musta fallen out of his pocket while he was crawlin. As I say, they could hear em yellin, but couldn't none of the grown-ups fit in that hole. Couldn't even reach the toy. They hollered for the boys to come to the sound of their voices, and if there wasn't room to turn around to just back up. They shone their lights in and waved em around, and at first it sounded like the kids were gettin closer, but then their voices started to fade, and faded some more, until finally they were gone. You ask me, they were never close to begin with."

"Tricky acoustics," Yune said.

"*Sí, señor.* So then Roger said they should go around to the Ahiga side, which he knew pretty well from his explorin, what they call *spee*-lunkin. Once they got there, they heard those boys again, clear as day, cryin and yellin, so they got rope and lights from the equipment buildin and went in to fetch em out. Seemed like the right thing, but it was the end of em, instead."

"What happened?" Yune asked. "Do you know? Does anybody?"

"Well, like I told you, that place is a goddam maze. They left one man behind to pay out rope and tie on more in case they needed it. That was Ev Brinkley. He left town shortly after. Went to Austin. Brokenhearted, he was . . . but at least alive, and able to walk in the sunlight. Those others . . ." Lovie sighed. "No more sunlight for them."

Ralph thought about that—the horror of it—and saw what he felt on the faces of the others.

"Ev was down to his last hundred feet of free-rope when he heard somethin he said sounded like a cherry-bomb a kid set off in a tawlit bowl with the lid shut. What musta happened is some goddam fool fired a pistol, hopin to lead the boys to the rescue party, and there was a cave-in. It wasn't Roger done that, I'd bet a thousand dollars it wasn't. Old Rog was a fool about many things, especially those dogs, but never fool enough to fire a gun in a cave, where the ricochet could go anywhere."

"Or where the sound could bring down a piece of ceiling," Alec said. "It must have been like firing a shotgun to start an avalanche up in the high country."

"So they were crushed," Ralph said.

Lovie sighed and resettled her cannula, which had come askew. "Nawp. Might've been better if they were. At least it woulda been quick. But people in the big cavern—the Chamber of Sound—could hear em callin for help, just like those lost lads. By then there were sixty or seventy men and women out there, eager to do whatever they could. My George had to be there—his brother and his nephews were among those trapped, after all—and finally I gave up on keepin him home. I went with him, to make sure he didn't try to do some damn fool thing like tryin to pitch in. That would've killed him for sure."

"And when this accident happened," Ralph said, "Claude was in the reformatory?"

"Gatesville Trainin School is what I believe they called it, but yes, a reformatory's what it was."

Holly had produced a yellow legal pad from her carry-bag, and was bent over it, taking notes.

"By the time I got to the Hole with George, it was dark. The parkin lot's a good size, but it was damn near full. They'd set up big lights on posts, and with all the trucks and people scurryin around, it was like they were makin a Hollywood movie. They went in through the Ahiga entrance carryin ten-cell flashlights, wearin hardhats and puffy coats like flak jackets. They followed the rope to the cave-in. A long way, some of it through standin water. The rockfall was pretty bad. Took em all that night and half the next morning to clear it enough to get past. By then, people in the big cave couldn't hear the lost ones callin no more."

"Your brother-in-law's bunch wasn't waiting for rescue on the other side, I take it," Yune said.

"No, they were gone. Roger or one of the others might have thought he knew a way back to the big cave, or they might've been afraid more of the ceiling was gonna cave in. No way to tell. But they left a trail, at least to start with; marks on the walls and litter on the floor, coins and screws of paper. One man even left his bowling card from the Tippit Lanes. One more punch and he'd've got himself a free string. That was in the paper."

"Like Hansel and Gretel, leaving breadcrumbs behind," Alec mused.

"Then everything just stopped," Lovie said. "Right in the middle of a gallery. The marks, the dropped coins, the balls of paper. Just stopped."

Like the footprints in Bill Samuels's story, Ralph thought.

"The second rescue party kept goin for awhile, callin and wavin their flashlights, but no one called back. The fella who wrote it up for the Austin paper interviewed a bunch of those guys from the second rescue party later on, and they all said the same thing—there were just too many paths to choose from, all of em goin down, some leadin to dead ends and some to chimneys as dark as wells. They weren't supposed to holler for fear of starting another cave-in, but then one of them yelled anyway, and sure enough, a piece of the roof come down. That's when they decided they better get the hell out."

"Surely they didn't abandon the search after one try," Howie said.

"No, course not." She fished another Coke out of the cooler, cracked it, and swallowed half at a go. "Not used to talkin s'much, and I'm parched." She checked her oxygen bottle. "Almost out of this stuff, too, but there's another one in the bathroom there, with the rest of my goddam medical supplies, if someone wants to fetch it."

Alec Pelley took charge of this task, and Ralph was relieved when the woman didn't attempt to light up as he swapped them out. Once the oxygen was flowing again, she resumed her story.

"There was a *dozen* search parties went in there over the years, right up until the ground-shaker in '07. After that it was considered too dangerous. It was only a three or four on the Richter, but caves are fragile, you know. The Chamber of Sound stood up to it pretty well, although a bunch of the stalactites fell off the ceilin. Some of the other passages, though, collapsed. I know the one they called the Art Gallery did. Since the shaker, Marysville Hole has been closed. The main entrance is stopped up, and I believe Ahiga is, too."

For a moment no one spoke. Ralph didn't know about the others, but he was thinking of what it must have been like to die a slow death deep underground, in the dark. He didn't want to think about it and couldn't help it.

Lovie said, "You know what Roger said to me once? Couldn't have been six months before he died. He said the Marysville Hole might go all the way down to hell. And that makes it a place where this outsider of yours would feel right at home, don't you think?"

"Not a word about this when Claude comes back," Holly said.

"Oh, he knows," Lovie said. "Those were his people. He didn't care for his cousins much—they were older and used to bullyrag him something awful—but they were still his people."

Holly smiled, but not the radiant one; it didn't touch her eyes. "I'm sure he does, but he doesn't know *we* know. And that's the way it has to stay."

11

Lovie, now looking tired going on exhausted, said the kitchen was too small for seven people to eat in comfortably, so they'd have to take their meal out back, in what she called the gaze-bo. She told them (proudly) that Claude had built it for her himself, with a kit he got at the Home Depot.

"It might be a little hot at first, but a breeze usually sets in this time of day, and it's screened against the bugs."

Holly suggested that the old lady should take a lie-down, and let the company set up for supper outside.

"But you won't know where anything is!"

"Don't worry about that," Holly said. "Finding things is what I do for a living, you know. And these gentlemen will help out, I'm sure."

Lovie gave in and wheeled along to her bedroom, where they heard her grunting effortfully, followed by the squall of bedsprings.

Ralph stepped out on the front porch to call Jeannie, who answered on the first ring. "E.T. phone home," she said cheerfully.

"Everything quiet there?"

"Except for the TV. Officers Ramage and Yates have been watching NASCAR. I only surmise bets were made, but know for sure they ate all the brownies."

"Sorry to hear that."

"Oh, and Betsy Riggins came by to show off her new baby. I'd never say this to her, but he looks quite a bit like Winston Churchill."

"Uh-huh. Listen, I think either Troy or Tom should stay the night."

"I was thinking both. In with me. We can cuddle. Perhaps even canoodle."

"What a good idea. Be sure to take some pictures." A car was approaching; Claude Bolton, back from Tippit with their chicken dinners. "Don't forget to lock up and set the burglar alarm."

"The locks and alarm didn't help the other night."

"Humor me and do it anyway." The man who looked exactly like his wife's nighttime visitor was at that moment getting out of his car, and seeing him gave Ralph a queer feeling of double vision.

"All right. Have you found anything out?"

"Hard to tell." This was skirting the truth; Ralph thought they had found out a great deal, none of it good. "I'll try to call you later on, but right now I have to go."

"Okay. Stay safe."

"I will. Love you."

"Love you, too. And I mean it: *stay safe.*"

He went down the porch steps to help Claude with half a dozen plastic bags from Highway Heaven.

"Food's cold, just like I said. But does she listen? Never did, never will."

"We'll be fine."

"Reheated chicken's always tough. I got the mashed potatoes, because reheated French fries, forget it."

They started toward the house. Claude stopped at the foot of the porch steps.

"Did you guys have a good talk with my ma?"

"We did," Ralph said, wondering exactly how to handle this. As it turned out, Claude handled it for him.

"Don't tell me. That guy might be able to read my mind."

"So you believe in him?" Ralph was honestly curious.

"I believe that gal believes. That Holly. And I believe there might have been someone around last night. So whatever you talked about, I don't want to hear."

"Maybe that's for the best. But Claude? I think one of us should stay here with you and your mother tonight. I was thinking Lieutenant Sablo could do that."

"You expecting trouble? Because I don't feel anything just now except hungry."

"Not trouble, exactly," Ralph said. "I was just thinking that if something bad happened around here, and if there happened to be a witness who said the person who did it looked a lot like Claude Bolton, you might like to have a cop handy who could testify that you never left your momma's house."

Claude considered. "That might not be such a bad idea. Only we don't have a guest room, or anything. The couch makes into a bed, but sometimes Ma gets up when she can't get back to sleep and goes out to the living room to watch TV. She likes those worthless preachers that are always yelling for love-offerins." He brightened. "But there's a spare mattress out in the back entry, and it's gonna be a warm night. I guess he could camp out."

"In the gaze-bo?"

Claude grinned. "Right! I built that sucker myself."

12

Holly put the chicken under the broiler for five minutes, and it crisped up nicely. The seven of them ate in the gazebo—there was a ramp for Lovie's wheelchair—and the conversation was both pleasant and lively. Claude turned out to be quite the raconteur, telling tales about his colorful career as a "security official" at Gentlemen, Please. The stories were funny, but neither mean nor off-color, and no one laughed harder at them than Claude's mother. She laughed herself into another coughing fit when Howie told the story of how one of his clients, in an effort to prove he was mentally unfit to stand trial, had taken his pants off in court and waved them at the judge.

The reason for their trip to Marysville was never touched upon. Lovie's lie-down before dinner had been a short one, and when the meal was done, she announced that she was going back to bed. "Not many dishes with take-out," she said, "and what there is I can warsh in the morning. I can do it right from my chair, you know, although I have to be careful of the goddam oxygen tank." She turned to Yune. "You sure you're gonna be all right out here, Officer Sablo? What if someone comes stirrin around, like last night?"

"I'm fully armed, ma'am," Yune said, "and this is a very nice place out here."

"Well . . . you come on in anytime. Wind might kick up strong after midnight. Back door'll be locked, but the key's under that *olla de barro*." She pointed at the old clay pot, then crossed her hands above her admirable bosom and did a little bow. "You are fine folks, and I thank you for coming here and trying to do right by my boy." With that, she rolled away. The six of them sat a little longer.

"That's a good woman," Alec said.

"Yes," Holly said. "She is."

Claude lit a Tiparillo. "Cops on my side," he said. "That's a new experience. I like it."

Holly said, "Is there a Walmart in Plainville, Mr. Bolton? I need to do some shopping, and I love Walmarts."

"Nope, and a good thing, because Ma does, too, and I'd never get her out of it. Closest thing to it we got in these parts is the Home Depot in Tippit."

"That should do," she said, and stood up. "We'll clean those dishes so Lovie doesn't have to in the morning, and then we'll be on our way. We'll be back tomorrow to pick up Lieutenant Sablo, then leave for home. I think we've done all we can do here. Do you agree, Ralph?"

Her eyes told him what to say, and he said it. "Sure."

"Mr. Gold? Mr. Pelley?"

"I think we're fine," Howie said.

Alec went along. "Pretty well done here."

13

Although they returned to the house only fifteen minutes or so after Lovie had taken her leave, they could already hear rough snores coming from her bedroom. Yune filled the sink with suds, rolled up his sleeves, and began to wash the few things they had used. Ralph dried; Holly put away. The evening light was still strong, and Claude was out back with Howie and Alec, touring the property and looking for any signs of the previous night's intruder . . . if there had been one.

"I'd've been all right even if I'd left my sidearm home," Yune said. "I had to go through Mrs. Bolton's bedroom to get into her bathroom where she keeps her oxygen, and she's well gunned up. Got a Ruger American ten-plus-one on the dresser, extra clip right beside it, and a Remington twelve-gauge leaning in the corner, right next to her Electrolux. Don't know what old Claudie's got, but I'm sure he's got something."

"Isn't he a convicted felon?" Holly asked.

"He is," Ralph agreed, "but this is Texas. And he seems rehabilitated to me."

"Yes," she said. "He does, doesn't he?"

"I think so, too," Yune said. "Seems like he's turned his life around. I've seen it before when people get into AA or NA. When it works, it's like a miracle. Still, this outsider couldn't have picked a better face to hide behind, wouldn't you say? Given his history of drug sales and service, not to mention a gang background with Satan's Seven, who'd believe him if he said he was being framed for something?"

"No one believed Terry Maitland," Ralph said heavily, "and Terry was immaculate."

14

It was dusk when they got to the Home Depot, and after nine o'clock when they arrived back at the Indian Motel (observed by Jack Hoskins, once more peering through the drapes in his room and rubbing obsessively at the back of his neck).

They carried their purchases into Ralph's room and laid them out on the bed: five short-barreled UV flashlights (with extra batteries) and five yellow hardhats.

Howie picked up one of the flashlights and winced at the bright purple glare. "This thing will really pick up his trail? His *spoor*?"

"It will if it's there," Holly said.

"Huh." Howie dropped the flashlight back on the bed, put on one of the hardhats, and went to the mirror over the dresser to inspect himself. "I look ridiculous," he said.

No one disagreed.

"We're really going to do this? *Try* to, at least? That's not a rhetorical question, by the way. It's me trying to get my head around it as an actual fact."

"I think we'd have a hard job convincing the Texas Highway Patrol to pitch in," Alec said mildly. "What exactly would we tell them? That we think there's a monster hiding in the Marysville Hole?"

"If we don't do it," Holly said, "he'll kill more children. It's how he lives."

Howie turned to her, almost accusingly. "How are we going to get in? The old lady said it's buttoned up tighter than a nun's underwear. And even if we do, where's the rope? Doesn't Home Depot sell rope? They must sell rope."

"We shouldn't need any," she said quietly. "If he's in there—and I'm almost sure he is—he won't have gone deep. For one thing, he'd be afraid of getting lost himself, or of being caught in a cave-in. For another, I think he's weak. He should be in the hibernation part of his cycle, but instead he's been exerting himself."

"By projecting?" Ralph asked. "That's what you believe."

"Yes. What Grace Maitland saw, what your wife saw . . . I believe those were projections. I think a small part of his physical self *was* there, that's why there were traces in your living room, why he could move the chair and turn on the stove light, but not even enough to leave impressions on the new carpet. Doing that has to tire him out. I think he might have shown up wholly in the flesh only a single time, at the courthouse on the day Terry Maitland was shot. Because he was hungry, and knew there would be a lot to eat."

"He was there in the flesh but didn't show up on any of the TV videotape?" Howie asked. "Like a vampire who doesn't cast a reflection in mirrors?"

He spoke as if expecting her to deny this, but she didn't. "Exactly."

"Then you think he's supernatural. A supernatural being."

"I don't know what he is."

Howie took off the hardhat and tossed it onto the bed. "Guesswork. That's all you've got."

Holly looked wounded by this, and at a loss for how to reply. Nor did she seem to realize what Ralph saw, and was sure Alec saw, as well: Howard Gold was frightened. If this thing went sideways, there was no judge to whom he could object. He could not ask for a mistrial.

Ralph said, "It's still hard for me to accept all this stuff about *El Cuco* or shape-shifters, but there *was* an outsider, that I do accept now. Because of the Ohio connection, and because Terry Maitland simply couldn't have been in two places at the same time."

"The outsider screwed up there," Alec said. "He didn't know Terry was going to be at that convention in Cap City. Most of his chosen scapegoats would be like Heath Holmes, with alibis like cheesecloth."

"That doesn't follow," Ralph said.

Alec raised his eyebrows.

"If he got Terry's . . . I don't know how to say it. Memories, sure, but not *just* memories. A sort of . . ."

"A sort of terrain map of his consciousness," Holly said quietly.

"Okay, call it that," Ralph said. "I can accept that there's stuff he could have missed, the way speed readers miss stuff while they're zipping along, but that convention would have been a big deal to Terry."

"Then why would the *cuco* still—" Alec began.

"Maybe he had to." Holly had picked up one of the UV flashlights and was shining it on the wall, where it picked up a ghostly handprint from some previous resident. It was a thing Ralph could have done without seeing. "Maybe he was too hungry to wait for a better time."

"Or maybe he didn't care," Ralph said. "Serials often get to that point, usually just before they get caught. Bundy, Speck, Gacy . . . eventually they all started to believe they were a law unto themselves. Godlike. They got arrogant and overreached. And this outsider didn't overreach by all that much, did he? Think about it. We were going to arraign Terry and see him put on trial for the murder of Frank Peterson in spite of everything we knew. We were sure his alibi had to be bogus, no matter how strong it was."

And part of me still wants to believe that. The alternative turns everything I thought I understood about the world I live in upside down.

He felt feverish and a little sick to his stomach. How could a normal man in the twenty-first century accept a shape-shifting monster? If you believed in Holly Gibney's outsider, her *El Cuco*, then everything was on the table. No end to the universe.

"He's not arrogant anymore," Holly said quietly. "He's used to staying in one place for months after he kills and while he makes his change. He only moves on when that change is complete, or nearly complete. That's what I believe, based on what I've read and what I learned in Ohio. But his usual pattern has been disrupted. He had to run from Flint City once that boy discovered he'd been staying in that barn. He knew the police would come. So he came down here early, to be near Claude Bolton, and he found a perfect home."

"The Marysville Hole," Alec said.

Holly nodded. "But he doesn't know we know. That's our advantage. Claude knows his uncle and cousins are buried there, yes. What Claude doesn't know is how the outsider hibernates in or near places of the dead, preferably those associated with the bloodline of the person he's changing into or out of. I'm sure it works that way. It must."

Because you want it to, Ralph thought. Yet he couldn't find any holes in her logic. If, that was, you accepted the basic postulate of a supernatural being that had to follow certain rules, possibly out of tradition, possibly out of some unknown imperative none of them would ever be able to understand.

"Can we be sure Lovie won't tell him?" Alec asked.

"I think so," Ralph said. "She'll keep quiet for his own good."

Howie took one of the flashlights and shone it at the rattling air conditioner, this time picking up a litter of spectrally glowing fingerprints. He snapped it off and said, "What if he has a helper? Tell me that. Count Dracula had that guy Renfield. Dr. Frankenstein had a hunchback guy, Igor—"

Holly said, "That's a popular misconception. In the original *Frankenstein* movie, the doctor's assistant was actually named Fritz, played by Dwight Frye. Later, Bela Lugosi—"

"I stand corrected," Howie said, "but the question remains: What if our outsider has an accomplice? Somebody with orders to keep tabs on us? Doesn't that make sense? Even if the outsider doesn't know we found out about the Marysville Hole, he knows we're too close for comfort."

"I see your point, Howie," Alec said, "but serials are usually loners, and the ones who stay free the longest are drifters. There are exceptions, but I don't think our guy is one of them. He hopped down to Flint City from Dayton. If you backtrailed him from Ohio, you might find murdered children in Tampa, Florida, or Portland, Maine. There's an African proverb: *he travels fastest who travels alone.* And practically speaking, who could he hire for a job like that?"

"A nut," Howie said.

"Okay," Ralph said, "but from where? Did he just stop by Nuts R Us and pick one up?"

"Fine," Howie said. "He's on his own, just cowering in the Marysville Hole and waiting for us to come and get him. Drag him into the sun or put a stake in his heart or both."

"In Stoker's novel," Holly said, "they cut off Dracula's head when they caught him, and stuffed his mouth full of garlic."

Howie tossed the flashlight on the bed and threw up his hands. "Also fine. We'll stop by Shopwell and buy some garlic. Also a meat cleaver, since we neglected to buy a hacksaw while we were in Home Depot."

Ralph said, "I think a bullet in the head should do the trick nicely."

They considered this in silence for a moment, and then Howie said he was going to bed. "But before I do, I'd like to know what the plan is for tomorrow."

Ralph waited for Holly to enlighten Howie on this point, but she looked at Ralph, instead. He was startled and moved by the hollows under her eyes and the lines that had appeared at the corners of her mouth. Ralph himself was tired, he supposed they all were, but Holly Gibney was exhausted, at this point running on nothing but nerves. And given her tightly wrapped persona, he guessed that for her that would be like running on thorns. Or broken glass.

"Nothing before nine o'clock," Ralph said. "We all need at least eight hours of sleep, more if we can get it. Then we pack up, check out, go to the Boltons', and pick up Yune. From there to the Marysville Hole."

"Wrong direction, if we want Claude to think we're flying home," Alec said. "He'll wonder why we aren't headed back to Plainville."

"Okay, we tell Claude and Lovie we have to go to Tippit first because . . . mmm, I don't know, we have some more shopping to do at Home Depot?"

"Pretty thin," Howie said.

Alec asked, "Who was the state cop who came out to talk to Claude? Do you remember?"

Ralph didn't offhand, but he had kept case-notes on his iPad. Routine was routine, even when chasing the boogeyman. "His name was Owen Sipe. Corporal Owen Sipe."

"Okay. You tell Claude and his momma—which is the same thing as telling the outsider, if he really can get inside Claude's head—that you got a call from Corporal Sipe saying that a man roughly matching Claude's description is wanted in Tippit for questioning in a robbery or a car theft or maybe a home invasion. Yune can verify that Claude was at home all night—"

"Not if he was out sleeping in the gaze-bo," Ralph said.

"You're telling me he wouldn't have heard Claude start his car? That thing needed a new muffler two years ago."

Ralph smiled. "Point taken."

"Okay, so you say we're going to Tippit to check it out, and if it leads nowhere, we're going to fly back to Flint City. Sound okay?"

"Sounds fine," Ralph said. "Just let's be damn sure Claude doesn't see the flashlights and hardhats."

15

As eleven o'clock came and went, Ralph was lying on the sway-backed bed in his room, knowing he should turn out the light and not doing it. He had called Jeannie and gabbed with her for almost half an hour, some of it about the case, some of it about Derek, most of it inconsequential shit. After that he tried the TV, thinking one of Lovie Bolton's late-night preachers might work as a sleeping pill—or at least quiet the constant rat-run of his thoughts—but all he got when he turned it on was a message saying OUR SATELLITE IS CURRENTLY DOWN, THANK YOU FOR YOUR PATIENCE.

He was reaching for the lamp when a light knock came at the door. He crossed the room, reached for the knob, thought better of it, and tried the peephole. It turned out to be useless, clogged with dirt or something.

"Who is it?"

"Me," Holly said. Her voice was as small as her knock.

He opened the door. Her tee-shirt was untucked and the coat of her suit, which she had put on against the late-night chill, hung down comically on one side. Her short gray hair flew in the rising wind. She was holding her iPad. Ralph suddenly realized he was in his boxers, with the buttonless fly no doubt gaping slightly. He remembered something they used to say when they were kids: *Who gave you a license to sell hotdogs?*

"I woke you up," she said.

"You didn't. Come in."

She hesitated, then stepped into the room and sat in the single chair while he put on his pants.

"You need to get some sleep, Holly. You look very tired."

"I am. But sometimes it seems as if the more tired I am, the harder it is to go to sleep. Especially if I'm worried and anxious."

"Tried Ambien?"

"It's not recommended for people taking antidepressants."

"I see."

"I did some research. Sometimes that puts me to sleep. I started by looking up the newspaper stories concerning the tragedy

Claude's mother told us about. There was a lot of coverage, and a lot of background. I thought you might like to hear."

"Will it help us?"

"I think it will."

"Then I want to hear."

He moved to the bed, and Holly perched on the edge of the chair, knees together.

"All right. Lovie kept talking about the Ahiga side, and she said one of the Jamieson twins dropped a plastic Chief Ahiga out of his pocket." She opened her iPad. "This was taken in 1888."

The sepia-toned photograph showed a noble-looking Native American man in profile. He was wearing a headdress that flowed halfway down his back.

"For awhile the chief lived with a small contingent of Navajos on the Tigua reservation near El Paso, then married a Caucasian woman and moved first to Austin, where he was treated badly, and then to Marysville, where he was accepted as a member of the community after cutting his hair and professing his Christian faith. His wife had a little money, and they opened the Marysville Trading Post. Which eventually became the Indian Motel and Café."

"Home sweet home," Ralph said, looking around at the shabby room.

"Yes. Here is Chief Ahiga in 1926, two years before he died. By then he'd changed his name to Thomas Higgins." She showed him a second picture.

"Holy shit!" Ralph exclaimed. "I'd say he went native, but this is more like the opposite."

It was the same noble profile, but now the cheek facing the camera was deeply scored with wrinkles and the headdress was gone. The former Navajo chieftain was wearing rimless spectacles, a white shirt, and a tie.

Holly said, "In addition to running Marysville's only successful business, it was Chief Ahiga, aka Thomas Higgins, who discovered the Hole and ran the first tours. They were quite popular."

"But the cave was named for the town instead of for him," Ralph said. "Which figures. He may have been a Christian and a successful businessman, but he remained a redskin to the community. Still, I guess the locals treated him better than the Christians in Austin. Got to give them some credit for that. Go on."

She showed him another picture. This one was of a wooden sign with a painted version of Chief Ahiga in his headdress, and a legend beneath reading BEST PICTOGRAPHS THIS WAY. She used her fingers to zoom out, and Ralph could see a path leading through the rocks.

"The cave has the town's name," she said, "but at least the chief got something—the Ahiga entrance, much less glamorous than the Chamber of Sound, but with a direct connection to it. Ahiga's where the staff brought in supplies, and it was a way out in case of an emergency."

"That's where the rescue parties went in, hoping to find an alternate route that would take them to the kids?"

"Correct." She leaned forward, eyes shining. "The main entrance isn't just boarded up, Ralph, it's cemented over. They didn't want to lose any more kids. The Ahiga entrance—the back door—was also boarded up, but none of the articles I read said anything about it being plugged with cement."

"That doesn't mean it wasn't."

She gave her head an impatient toss. "I know, but *if* it wasn't . . ."

"Then that's how he got in. The outsider. That's what you believe."

"We should go there first, and if there are signs of a break-in . . ."

"I get it," he said, "and it sounds like a plan. Good going. You're a hell of a detective, Holly."

She thanked him with her eyes lowered, and in the tentative

voice of a woman who doesn't know quite what to do with compliments. "You're kind to say that."

"It's not kindness. You're better than Betsy Riggins, and *much* better than the waste of space known as Jack Hoskins. He'll be retiring soon, and if the job was mine to give, you'd get it."

Holly shook her head, but she was smiling. "Bail-jumpers, repos, and lost dogs are enough for me. I never want to be part of another murder investigation."

He stood up. "Time for you to go back to your room and get some shut-eye. If you're right about any of this, tomorrow's going to be a John Wayne day."

"In a minute. I had another reason for coming here. You better sit down."

16

Even though she was a much stronger person than she had been on the day she'd had the great good fortune to meet Bill Hodges, Holly was not used to telling people they had to change their behavior, or that they were flat-out wrong. That younger woman had been a terrified, scurrying mouse who sometimes thought suicide might be the best solution for her feelings of terror, inadequacy, and free-floating shame. What she felt most of all on the day when Bill had sat down next to her behind a funeral parlor she could not bring herself to enter, was the sense that she had lost something vital; not just a purse or a credit card, but the life she could have led if things had been just a little different, or if God had seen fit to put just a little more of some important chemical in her system.

I think you lost this, Bill had said, without ever actually saying it. *Here, better put it back in your pocket.*

Now Bill was dead and here was this man, so like Bill in many ways: his intelligence, his occasional flashes of good humor, and most of all, his doggedness. She was sure Bill would have liked him, because Detective Ralph Anderson also believed in chasing the case.

But there were differences, too, and not just that he was thirty years younger than Bill had been when he died. That Ralph had made a terrible mistake in arresting Terry Maitland in public, before he understood the true dimensions of the case, was only one of those differences, and probably not the most important, no matter how it haunted him.

God, help me tell him what I need to tell him, because this is the only chance I'll have. And let him hear me. Please God, let him hear me.

She said, "Every time you and the others talk about the outsider, it's conditional."

"I'm not sure I understand you, Holly."

"I think you do. '*If* he exists. *Supposing* he exists. *Assuming* he exists.'"

Ralph was silent.

"I don't care about the others, but I need you to believe, Ralph. *I need you to believe.* I do, but I'm not enough."

"Holly—"

"No," she said fiercely. "*No.* Listen to me. I know it's crazy. But is the idea of *El Cuco* any more inexplicable than some of the terrible things that happen in the world? Not natural disasters or accidents, I'm talking about the things some people do to others. Wasn't Ted Bundy just a version of *El Cuco*, a shape-shifter with one face for the people he knew and another for the women he killed? The last thing those women saw was his other face, his inside face, the face of *El Cuco*. There are others. They walk among us. You know they do. They're aliens. Monsters beyond our understanding. Yet you believe in *them*. You've put some of them away, maybe seen them executed."

He was silent, thinking about this.

"Let me ask you a question," she said. "Suppose it *had* been

Terry Maitland who killed that child, and tore off his flesh, and put a branch up inside him? Would he be any less inexplicable than the thing that might be hiding in that cave? Would you be able to say, 'I understand the darkness and evil that was hiding behind the mask of the boys' athletic coach and good community citizen. I know exactly what made him do it'?"

"No. I've arrested men who have done terrible things—and a woman who drowned her baby daughter in the bathtub—and I've *never* understood. Most times they don't understand themselves."

"No more than I understood why Brady Hartsfield set out to kill himself at a concert and take a thousand or more innocent children with him. What I'm asking is simple. Believe in this. If only for the next twenty-four hours. Can you do that?"

"Will you be able to get some sleep if I say yes?"

She nodded, her eyes never leaving him.

"Then I believe. For the next twenty-four hours, at least, *El Cuco* exists. Whether or not he's in the Marysville Hole remains to be seen, but he exists."

Holly exhaled and stood up, hair windblown, suit coat hanging down on one side, shirt untucked. Ralph thought she looked both adorable and horribly fragile. "Good. I'm going to bed."

He saw her to the door and opened it. As she stepped out, he said, "No end to the universe."

She looked at him solemnly. "That's right. No end to the fracking thing. Goodnight, Ralph."

THE MARYSVILLE HOLE

July 27th

1

Jack awoke at four in the morning.

The wind was blowing outside, blowing hard, and he hurt all over. Not just his neck, but his arms, his legs, his belly, his butt. It felt like a sunburn. He threw back the covers, sat on the edge of the bed, and turned on the bedside lamp, which cast a sallow sixty-watt glow. He looked down at himself and saw nothing on his skin, but the pain was there. It was *inside*.

"I'll do what you want," he told the visitor. "I'll stop them. I promise."

There was no answer. The visitor either wasn't replying or wasn't there. Not now, at least. But he had been. Out at that goddam barn. Just one light ticklish touch, almost a caress, but it had been enough. Now he was full of poison. *Cancer* poison. And sitting here in this shitty motel room, long before dawn, he was no longer sure the visitor could take back what he had given him, but what choice did he have? He had to try. If that didn't work . . .

"I'll shoot myself?" The idea made him feel a little better. It was an option his mother hadn't had. He said it again, more decisively. "I'll shoot myself."

No more hangovers. No more driving home at exactly the speed limit, stopping at every light, not wanting to get pulled over when he knew he'd blow at least a 1, maybe even a 1.2. No more calls from his ex, reminding him that he was once more late with her monthly check. As if he didn't know. What would she do if those checks stopped coming? She'd have to go to work, see how the other half lived, oh boo-hoo. No more sitting home all day, watching Ellen and Judge Judy. What a shame.

He dressed and went out. The wind wasn't exactly cold, but it was chilly, and seemed to go right through him. It had been hot when he left Flint City, and he'd never thought of bringing a jacket. Or a change of clothes. Or even a toothbrush.

That's you, honey, he could hear the old ball and chain saying. *That's you all over. A day late and a buck short.*

Cars, pickup trucks, and a few campers were drawn up to the motel building like nursing puppies. Jack went down the covered walkway far enough to make sure the blue SUV belonging to the meddlers was still there. It was. They were all tucked up in their rooms, no doubt dreaming pleasant pain-free dreams. He entertained a brief fantasy of going room to room and shooting them all. The idea was attractive but ridiculous. He didn't know which rooms they were in, and eventually someone—not necessarily the Chief Meddler—would start shooting back. This was Texas, after all, where people liked to believe they were still living in the days of cattle drives and gunfighters.

Better to wait for them where the visitor said they might come. He could shoot them there and be pretty sure of getting away with it; no one around for miles. If the visitor could take away the poison once the job was done, all would end well. If he couldn't, Jack would suck the end of his service Glock and pull the trigger. Fantasies of his ex waitressing or working in the glove factory for the next twenty years were entertaining, but not the most important consideration. He wasn't going the way his mother had gone, with her skin splitting open every time she tried to move. That was the important consideration.

He got in his truck, shivering, and headed for the Marysville Hole. The moon sat near the horizon, looking like a cold stone. The shivering became shaking, so bad that he swerved across the broken white line a couple of times. That was okay; all the big rigs either used Highway 190 or the interstate. There was no one on the Rural Star at this ungodly hour except for him.

Once the Ram's engine was warm, he turned the heater on high and that was better. The pain in his lower body began to subside. The back of his neck still throbbed like a very bitch, though, and when he rubbed it, his palm came away covered with snowflakes of dead skin. The idea occurred to him that maybe the pain in his neck was just a real, ordinary sunburn, and everything else was in his mind. Psychosomatic, like the old ball and chain's bullshit migraines. Could psychosomatic pain actually wake you up out of a sound sleep? He didn't know, but he knew that the visitor who'd been hiding behind the shower curtain in his bedroom had been real, and you didn't want to screw around with someone like that. What you wanted to do with someone like that was exactly what he said.

Plus there was Ralph Fucking Anderson, who had always been on his case. Mr. No Opinion, who got him hauled back from his fishing vacation by getting suspended . . . which is what Ralphie-boy *was*, and fuck that administrative leave shit. Ralph Fucking Anderson was the reason that he, Jack Hoskins, had been out in Canning Township instead of sitting in his little cabin, watching DVDs and drinking vodka-tonics.

As he turned in at the billboard (CLOSED UNTIL FURTHER NOTICE), a sudden insight electrified him: Ralph Fucking Anderson *might have sent him out there on purpose*! He could have known the visitor would be waiting, and what the visitor would do. Ralphie-boy had wanted to get rid of him for years, and once you factored that in, all the pieces fell into place. The logic was undeniable. The only thing Ralphie-boy hadn't counted on was being double-crossed by the man with the tattoos.

As to how this fuckaree would turn out, Jack saw three possibilities. Maybe the visitor could get rid of the poison now coursing through Jack's system. That was number one. If it was psychosomatic, it would eventually go away on its own. That was number two. Or maybe it was real and the visitor *couldn't* take it away. That was number three.

Mr. No Fucking Opinion was going to be history no matter which possibility turned out to be the right one. That was a promise Jack made not to the visitor but to himself. Anderson was going *down*, and the others would go with him. Clean sweep. Jack Hoskins, American Sniper.

He came to the abandoned ticket booth and detoured around the chain. The wind would probably die away once the sun was up and the temperature really started to climb again, but it was still blowing now, sending sheets of dusty grit flying, and that was good. He wouldn't have to worry about the meddlers seeing his tracks. If they came at all, that was.

"If they don't, can you still fix me up?" he asked. Not expecting an answer, but one came.

Oh yes, you'll be good to go.

Was that a real voice or only his own?

What did it matter?

2

Jack drove past the falling-down tourist cabins, wondering why anyone would want to spend good money to stay near what was essentially just a hole in the ground (at least the name of the place was truthful). Did no one have any better places to go? Yosemite? The Grand Canyon? Even the World's Largest Ball of String would be better than a hole in the ground out here in Dry 'n Dusty Asshole, Texas.

He parked beside the service shed as he had on his previous trip, grabbed his flashlight from the glove compartment, then got the Winchester and a box of ammo out of the lockbox. He stuffed his pockets with shells, started for the path, then turned back and shone his light through one of the dusty windows of the shed's garage-type roll-up door, thinking there might be something he could use inside. There wasn't, but what he saw still made him smile: a dust-covered compact car, probably a Honda or a Toyota. On the back window was a decal reading MY SON IS A FLINT CITY HIGH SCHOOL HONOR STUDENT! Poisoned or not, Jack's rudimentary detective skills were intact. His visitor was here, all right; he had driven down from FC in this stolen car.

Feeling better—and actually hungry for the first time since the tattooed hand had come creeping around the shower curtain—Jack returned to the truck and rummaged in the glove compartment some more. He eventually unearthed a package of peanut butter crackers and half a roll of Tums. Not exactly the breakfast of champions, but better than nothing. He started up the trail, munching one of the Nabs and carrying the Winnie in his left hand. There was a strap, but if he slung it over his shoulder, it would chafe his neck. Maybe make it bleed. His pockets, heavy with cartridges, swung and bumped against his legs.

He halted at the faded Indian sign (old Chief Wahoo testifying that Carolyn Allen sucked his redskin cock), struck by a sudden thought. Anyone coming down the byroad leading to the tourist cabins would see his Ram parked beside the service shed and wonder what was up with that. He considered going back to move it, then decided he was worrying needlessly. If the meddlers came, they'd park near the main entrance. As soon as they got out to look around, he would open fire from his shooter's perch on top of the bluff, knocking two or maybe even three of them down before they realized what was happening. The others would go scurrying around like chickens in a thunderstorm. He'd get them before they could find cover. There was no need to worry about what they might see from the tourist cabins, because Mr. No Opinion and his friends were never going to get out of the parking lot.

3

The path up the bluff was treacherous in the dark, even with the help of the flashlight, and Jack took his time. He had enough problems without falling and breaking something. By the time he got to his lookout point, the first hesitant light was starting to seep into the sky. He shone his flash on the pitchfork he'd left behind the day before, started to reach for it, then recoiled. He hoped this wasn't an omen of how the rest of his day was going to go, but the situation had its irony, and even in his current situation, Jack could appreciate it.

He had brought the pitchfork to guard against snakes, and now one was lying beside and partly on top of it. It was a rattlesnake, and not a little one; this was a real monster. He couldn't shoot it, a bullet might only wound the goddam thing, in which case it would probably strike at him, and he was wearing sneakers, having neglected to buy boots in Tippit. Also, there was the potential for a ricochet that might do him serious damage.

He held his rifle by the end of its stock, slowly extending the barrel as far as he could. He got it under the dozing rattler and flipped it high over his shoulder before it could slither away. The ugly bastard landed on the path twenty feet behind him, coiled, and began sounding off, a noise like beads being shaken in a dry gourd. Jack snatched up the pitchfork, took a step forward, and jabbed at it. That rattler slithered into a crack between two leaning boulders and was gone.

"That's right," Jack said. "And don't come back. This is *my* place."

He lay down and peered through the scope. There was the parking lot with its ghostly yellow lines; there was the decaying gift shop; there was the boarded-up cave entrance, the sign over it faded but still legible: WELCOME TO THE MARYSVILLE HOLE.

Nothing to do now but wait. Jack settled in to do it.

4

Nothing before nine o'clock, Ralph had said, but they were all in the Indian Motel's café by quarter past eight. Ralph, Howie, and Alec ordered steak and eggs. Holly passed on the steak but ordered a three-egg omelet with ranch fries, and Ralph was gratified to see she ate every bite. She was once more wearing the jacket of her suit over her tee-shirt and jeans.

"That's going to be hot later on," Ralph said.

"Yes, and it's very wrinkled, but it's got nice big pockets for my stuff. I'm also taking my shoulder-bag, although I'll leave it in the car if we have to hike." She leaned forward and dropped her voice. "Sometimes the maids steal in places like this."

Howie covered his mouth, perhaps to stifle a belch, perhaps to hide a smile.

5

They drove to the Bolton place, where they found Yune and Claude sitting on the front porch steps and drinking coffee. Lovie was in her little side garden, weeding from her wheelchair with her oxygen bottle in her lap, a cigarette in her mouth, and a big straw sunhat clapped on her head.

"All good last night?" Ralph asked.

"Fine," Yune said. "Wind was a little noisy out back, but once I went to sleep, I slept like a baby."

"What about you, Claude? Everything okay?"

"If you mean did I feel like there was someone creeping around again, I didn't. Ma, either."

"Well, there might be a reason for that," Alec said. "Cops in Tippit had a home invasion last night. Man of the house heard breaking glass, grabbed his shotgun, scared the guy off. Told the police the intruder had black hair, a goatee, and plenty of tattoos."

Claude was outraged. "I never budged out of my bedroom last night!"

"We don't doubt that," Ralph said. "It could be the guy we've been looking for. We're going to Tippit to check it out. If he's gone—and he probably is—we'll fly back to Flint City and try to figure out what to do next."

"Although I don't know what more we *can* do," Howie added. "If he's not hanging around here and if he's not in Tippit, he could be anywhere."

"No other leads?" Claude asked.

"Not a one," Alec said.

Lovie rolled over to them. "If you-all decide to go home, stop in and see us on your way to the airport. I'll make up some sammitches from the leftover chicken. Long as you don't mind eatin it twice, that is."

"We'll do that," Howie said. "Thank you both."

"It's me should be thanking you," Claude said.

He shook hands with them all around, and Lovie opened her arms to give Holly a hug. Holly looked startled, but allowed it. "You come back, now," Lovie whispered in her ear.

"I will," Holly replied, hoping it was a promise she would be able to keep.

6

Howie drove with Ralph riding shotgun and the other three in the backseat. The sun was up, and it was going to be another hot one.

"Just wondering how the cops in Tippit got in touch with you," Yune said. "I didn't think anyone in authority knew we were down here."

"They don't," Alec replied. "If this outsider actually exists, we didn't want to raise any suspicions with the Boltons about why we're going in the wrong direction."

Ralph didn't need to be a mind reader to know what Holly was thinking at this moment: *Every time you and the others talk about the outsider, it's conditional.*

Ralph turned around in his seat. "Listen to me now. No more ifs or maybes. For today, the outsider *does* exist. For today, he can read Claude Bolton's mind any time he wants to, and unless we know differently, he's in the Marysville Hole. No more assumptions, just belief. Can you do that?"

For a moment, no one replied. Then Howie said, "I'm a defense lawyer, son. I can believe anything."

7

They came to the billboard showing the awestruck family holding up their gas lanterns. Howie drove slowly up the cracked asphalt entry road, avoiding the potholes as best he could. The temperature, which had been in the mid-fifties when they set out, was now edging into the seventies. It would go higher.

"See that knoll up there?" Holly pointed. "The main cave entrance is in the base of it. Or was, until they plugged it. We should check there first. If he tried to get in that way, there might be some sign."

"Fine with me," Yune said, looking around. "Jesus, this is desolate country."

"The loss of those boys and the rescue party that went after them was terrible for their families," Holly said, "but it was also a disaster for Marysville. The Hole was the town's only job provider. A lot of locals left after it closed down."

Howie braked. "That must have been the ticket booth, and I spy a chain across the road."

"Go around it," Yune said. "Give this baby's suspension a workout."

Howie drove around the chain, his seatbelted passengers bouncing up and down. "Okay, folks, we are now officially trespassing on private property."

A coyote broke from cover at their approach and sprinted away, his lean shadow racing beside him. Ralph spotted the remains of wind-eroded tire tracks and assumed that local kids—there had to be at least a few of them left in Marysville—brought their ATVs out here. He was mostly focused on the rocky bluff ahead, site of what had been Marysville's one and only tourist attraction. Its *raison d'etre*, if you wanted to be fancy about it.

"We're all carrying," Yune said. He was sitting upright in his seat, eyes fixed straight ahead, on alert. "Is that correct?"

The men answered in the affirmative. Holly Gibney said nothing.

8

From his perch atop the bluff, Jack saw them coming long before they reached the acre of parking lot. He checked his weapon—fully loaded, with one in the pipe. He had placed a flat stone at the edge of the drop. Now he lay at full length with the barrel resting on it. He sighted through the scope, putting the crosshairs on the driver's side of the windshield. A sunflash momentarily blinded him. He winced, drew back, rubbed his eye until the floating spot was gone, then peered into the scope again.

Come on, he thought. *Stop in the middle of the parking lot. That would be perfect. Stop there and get out.*

The SUV instead trundled diagonally across the parking lot and stopped in front of the cave's boarded-over entrance. All the doors opened and five people got out, four men and one woman. Five little meddlers, all in a row, lovely. Unfortunately, it was a shit shot. The sun in its current position cast the cave's entrance in shadow. Jack might have chanced that—the Leupold scope was damned good—but there was the problem of the SUV, now blocking at least three of the five, including Mr. No Opinion.

Jack lay with his cheek against the rifle stock and his pulse beating slow and steady in his chest and throat. He was no longer aware of his throbbing neck; the only thing he cared about was the cluster of meddlers standing below the sign reading WELCOME TO THE MARYSVILLE HOLE.

"Come on out of there," he whispered. "Come out and look around a little. You know you want to."

He waited for them to do it.

9

The Hole's arched entryway was blocked by two dozen wooden planks, attached by huge rusty bolts to the cement plug beyond. With such double coverage against unauthorized explorers, there was hardly any need of No Trespassing signs, but there were a couple, anyway. Plus a few fading spraypaint tags—left, Ralph presumed, by the same kids who brought their ATVs out here.

"Anyone think this looks tampered with?" Yune asked.

"Nope," Alec said. "Why they even bothered with the boards is beyond me. You'd need a good charge of dynamite to put a hole in that cement plug."

"Which would probably finish the job the quake started," Howie added.

Holly turned around and pointed over the hood of the SUV. "See that road on the other side of the gift shop? That goes to the Ahiga entrance. Tourists weren't allowed to go into the cave that way, but there are many interesting pictographs."

"And you know this how?" Yune asked.

"The map they gave out to tourists is still online. *Everything* is online these days."

"It's called research, amigo," Ralph said. "You should try it some time."

They got back into the SUV, Howie once more behind the wheel with Ralph riding shotgun. Howie started slowly across the parking lot. "That road looks pretty crappy," he said.

"You should be okay," Holly said. "There are tourist cabins on the other side of the rise. According to the newspaper stories, the second rescue party used them as a staging area. Plus there would have been lots of media people and worried relatives once the news got out."

"Not to mention your ordinary garden variety rubberneckers," Yune said. "They probably—"

"Stop, Howie," Alec said. "Whoa." They were a little more than halfway across the parking lot now, the SUV's stubby nose pointing toward the road that went to the cabins. And, presumably, to the Hole's back door.

Howie braked. "What?"

"Maybe we're making this tougher than it has to be. The outsider doesn't necessarily have to be in the cave—he was hiding in a barn out there in Canning Township."

"Meaning?"

"Meaning we should check the gift shop. See if there's signs of a break-in."

"I'll do it," Yune said.

Howie opened the driver's door. "Why don't we all go?"

10

The meddlers left the boarded-up entrance and returned to the SUV, the stocky balding guy walking around the hood to get back to the wheel. That gave Jack a clear shot. He laid the crosshairs on the guy's face, took a breath, held it, and tightened down on the trigger. It didn't move. There was a nightmarish moment when he thought something was wrong with the Winchester, then he realized he'd forgotten to release the safety. How stupid could you get? He tried to push it without taking his eye from the scope. His thumb, greasy with sweat, slid off, and by the time he released the safety, the stocky man was in the driver's seat and slamming the door. The others were back in, as well.

"Shit!" Jack whispered. "Shit, shit, *shit!*"

He watched with increasing panic as the SUV started across the parking lot and toward the service road that would take it out of his line of fire. They would crest the first hill, they would see the cabins, they would see the service shed, and they would see his truck parked beside it. Would Ralph Anderson know to whom that truck belonged? Of course he would. If not from the leaping fish decals on the side, then from the bumper sticker—MY OTHER RIDE IS YOUR MOM—on the back.

You can't let them get up that road.

He didn't know if that was the visitor's voice or his own, and didn't care, because it was right either way. He had to stop the SUV, and two or three high-powered slugs in the engine block would do the job. Then he could start shooting through the windows. He probably wouldn't get them all, not with the sun glaring on the glass, but the ones who were left would come spilling out into the empty parking lot, maybe wounded, dazed for sure.

His finger curled on the trigger, but before he could fire the first shot, the SUV stopped on its own near the abandoned gift shop with its fallen sign. The doors opened.

"Thank you, God," Jack murmured. He applied his eye to the scope again, waiting for Mr. No Opinion to emerge. They all had to go, but the chief meddler was going first.

11

The diamondback emerged from the crack where it had taken refuge. It slithered toward Jack's splayed feet, stopped, tasted the warming air with its flickering tongue, then slithered forward again. It had no intention of attacking, its purpose was only investigatory, but when Jack fired the first shot, it raised its tail and began to rattle. Jack—who had forgotten shooter's plugs or cotton for his ears as well as his toothbrush—never heard it.

12

Howie was the first out of the SUV. He stood with his hands on his hips, surveying the fallen sign reading SOUVENIRS AND AUTHENTIC INDIAN CRAFTS. Alec and Yune exited the backseat on the driver's side. Ralph got out of the shotgun seat to open the rear door for Holly, who was having trouble with the handle. As he did this, something lying on the cracked pavement caught his eye.

"Damn," he said. "Look at that."

"What is it?" Holly asked as he bent down. "What, what?"

"I think it's an arrowhe—"

A gunshot rang out, the almost liquid whipcrack of a high-powered rifle. Ralph felt the passage of the slug, which meant it had missed the top of his head by no more than an inch or two. The SUV's passenger side mirror shattered and flew away, hitting the cracked asphalt and tumbling across it in a series of brilliant flashes.

"*Gun!*" Ralph shouted, grabbing Holly around the shoulders and dragging her to her knees. "*Gun, gun, gun!*"

Howie looked around at him. His expression was both startled and bemused. "Say what? Did you—"

The second shot came, and the top of Howie Gold's head disappeared. For a moment he stood where he was, blood coursing down his cheeks and brow. Then he toppled. Alec ran toward him and the third shot came, throwing Alec back against the hood of the SUV. Blood burst through his shirt above the belt line. Yune started toward him. There was a fourth shot. Ralph saw it tear away the side of Alec's neck, and then Howie's investigator dropped out of sight behind the car.

"*Get down!*" Ralph shouted at Yune. "*Get down, he's up on that bluff!*"

Yune dropped to his knees and scrambled. Three more shots came in rapid succession. One of the SUV's tires began to hiss. The windshield cracked into a milk-glaze and sagged in around a hole above the steering wheel. The third shot punched through the rear quarter-panel on the driver's side and blew an exit hole as big as a tennis ball on the passenger side, close to where Ralph and Yune now crouched, flanking Holly. There was a pause, then another fusillade: four shots this time. The rear windows broke, spraying nuggets of safety glass. Another of those ragged holes appeared in the rear deck.

"We can't stay here," Holly said. She sounded perfectly calm. "Even if he doesn't hit us, he'll hit the gas tank."

"She's right," Yune said. "Alec and Gold, what do you think? Any chance?"

"No," Ralph said. "They're—"

Another of those liquid whipcracks. They all flinched, and another tire began to hiss.

"They're gone," Ralph finished. "We have to run for that souvenir shop. You two go first. I'll cover you."

"I'll do the covering," Yune said. "You and Holly do the running."

A scream came from the shooter's position. Of pain or rage, Ralph couldn't tell.

Yune stood up, legs spread, pistol held in both hands, and began to fire spaced shots at the top of the knoll. "*Go!*" he shouted. "*Right now! Go, go, go!*"

Ralph stood up. Holly stood up beside him. As on the day when Terry Maitland was shot, it seemed to Ralph that he could see everything. His arm was around Holly's waist. There was a bird circling in the sky, wings outstretched. The tires were hissing. The SUV was settling on the driver's side. At the top of the knoll he could see a stuttery, moving flash that had to be the scope of the bastard's rifle. Ralph had no idea why it was moving around like that and didn't care. There was a second scream, then a third, the last one almost a shriek. Holly grabbed Yune's arm and jerked him. He gave her an amazed look, like a man rudely yanked out of a dream, and Ralph knew he had been ready to die. Expected to die. The three of them sprinted for the shelter of the gift shop, and although it had to be less than two hundred feet from the mortally wounded SUV, they seemed to be running in slow motion, like a trio of best friends at the end of some stupid romantic comedy. Only in those movies, no one ran past the mangled bodies of two men who had been alive and healthy only ninety seconds before. In those movies, no one stepped in a puddle of fresh blood and left bright red tracks behind. Another shot rang out, and Yune shouted.

"I'm hit! Fucker hit me!" He went down.

13

Jack was reloading, his ears ringing, when the rattlesnake decided it had had enough of this bothersome intruder in its territory. It struck him high on the right calf. Its fangs penetrated Jack's chino pants with no trouble at all, and its poison sacs were full. Jack rolled over, holding his rifle high in his right hand, screaming—not at the pain, which was just beginning, but at the sight of the rattler slithering up his leg, its forked tongue flicking, its beady black eyes intent. The slippery weight of it was hideous. It struck him again, this time in the thigh, and continued its sinuous upward trek, still rattling away. The next strike might be into his balls.

"*Get off! GET THE FUCK OFF ME!*"

Trying to get rid of it with the rifle would do no good, it could evade that, so Jack dropped the gun and seized it in both hands. It struck at his right wrist, missing the first time but hitting on its second try, leaving holes the size of colons in a newspaper headline, but its poison sacs were exhausted. Jack neither knew nor cared. He twisted it in his hands like a man wringing out a washcloth, and saw its skin split. Down below, someone was firing repeatedly—a pistol, by the sound—but the range was long and nothing came close. Jack flung the rattlesnake, saw it thump to the rocky scree, and slither away once more.

Get rid of them, Jack.

"Yes, okay, right."

Was he speaking, or only thinking? He couldn't tell. The ringing in his ears had become a high hum, like a steel wire being stroked until it vibrated.

He grabbed the rifle, rolled onto his belly, placed the barrel back on the flat rock, peered into the scope. The remaining three were running for the shelter of the gift shop, the woman in the middle.

He tried to put the crosshairs on Anderson, but his hands—one of them repeatedly snakebitten—were trembling, and he got the olive-skinned guy on the end instead. It took two tries, but he got him. The guy's arm flew back over his head like a pitcher getting ready to throw his best fastball, and he fell on his side. The other two stopped to help him. This was his best chance, and maybe the last. If he didn't take them now, they'd get behind the building.

Pain was flowing up his leg from the initial bite, and he could feel the flesh of his calf swelling, but that wasn't the worst part. The worst part was the heat that was now spreading like a flash fever. Or the sunburn from hell. He fired again and thought at first he'd hit the woman, but it was only a flinch. She grabbed the olive-skinned man by his unwounded arm. Anderson got him around the waist and yanked him to his feet. Jack pulled the trigger again, and got nothing but a dry click. He fumbled in his pocket for more shells, loaded two, dropped the rest. His hands were going numb. The leg that had been bitten was going numb. His tongue seemed to be swelling in his mouth. He screamed again, this time in frustration. By the time he applied his eye to the scope again, they were gone. He could see their shadows for a moment, then those were gone, too.

14

With Holly on one side and Ralph on the other, Yune was able to make it to the splintered side of the gift shop, where he collapsed with his back against the building, panting. His face was ashy, his forehead dotted with pearls of sweat. The left sleeve of his shirt was bloody down to the wrist.

He groaned. "Fuck, doesn't that fucking *smart*." From the knoll, the shooter fired again. The bullet whined off the asphalt.

"How bad?" Ralph said. "Let me see."

He unbuttoned Yune's cuff, and although he pulled the sleeve up gently, Yune yelped and bared his teeth. Holly was on her cell phone.

When the wound was revealed, it didn't look as bad as Ralph had feared; the bullet had probably done little more than crease him. In a movie, that would have left Yune ready to rejoin the fray, but this was real life, and real life was different. The high-powered slug had gotten enough of him to do a job on his elbow. The flesh around it was already swelling, turning purple, as if it had been smashed with a club.

"Tell me the elbow's only dislocated," Yune said.

"That would be good, but I think it's broken," Ralph said. "You still lucked out, man. If it had gotten any more of you, I think it would have torn your lower arm right off. I don't know what he's shooting, but it's big."

"My shoulder's dislocated for sure," Yune said. "Happened when my arm whipped back. *Fuck!* What are we going to do, amigo? We're pinned."

"Holly?" Ralph asked. "Anything?"

She shook her head. "I had four bars at the Boltons', but not even one here. 'Get off me,' is that what he shouted? Did either of you h—"

The rifleman fired again. Alec Pelley's body jumped, then lay still. "*I'll get you, Anderson!*" came floating down from the top of the knoll. "*I'll get you, Ralphie-boy! I'll get all of you!*"

Yune looked at Ralph, startled.

"We messed up," Holly said. "The outsider had a Renfield after all. And whoever he is, he knows you, Ralph. Do you know him?"

Ralph shook his head. The shooter had been yelling at the top of his voice, almost howling, and there were echoes. It could have been anyone.

Yune studied his wounded arm. The bleeding had slowed, but the swelling hadn't. Soon he would have no appreciable elbow joint at all. "This hurts worse than when my wisdom teeth went to hell. Tell me you have an idea, Ralph."

Ralph scooted to the far end of the building, cupped his hands around his mouth, and shouted. *"The police are on their way, asshole! The Highway Patrol! Those guys won't bother asking you to surrender, they'll shoot you like a rabid dog! If you want to live, you better run for it!"*

There was a pause, then another scream. It might have been pain, laughter, or both. It was followed by two more shots. One thumped into the building above Ralph's head, knocking a board loose and sending up a flurry of splinters.

Ralph pulled back and looked at the other two ambush survivors. "I think that was a no."

"He sounds hysterical," Holly said.

"Out of his mind," Yune agreed. He put his head back against the wall. "Christ, it's hot on this asphalt. And it'll be a lot hotter by noon. *Muy caliente.* If we're still here, we'll bake."

Holly said, "Do you shoot with your right hand, Lieutenant Sablo?"

"Yes. And since we're pinned down by a lunatic with a rifle, why don't you just go on and call me Yune, like *el jefe* here?"

"You need to get over to the end of the building, where Ralph is. And Ralph, you need to get over here with me. When Lieutenant Sablo starts shooting, we'll run for the road that goes to the tourist cabins and the Ahiga entrance. I estimate we'll be in the open for no more than fifty yards. We can cover that in fifteen seconds. Maybe twelve."

"Twelve seconds could be enough for him to get one of us, Holly."

"I think we can make it." Still as cool as the breeze from a fan blowing over a bowl of ice cubes. It was amazing. When she'd come into Howie's conference room two nights ago, she'd been so tightly wrapped that a loud cough might have had her leaping for the ceiling.

She's been in situations like this before, Ralph thought. *And maybe it's in situations like this where the real Holly Gibney comes out.*

Another gunshot, followed by a spang of metal. Then another.

"He's shooting for the SUV's gas tank," Yune said. "The rental people won't like that."

"We have to go, Ralph." Holly was staring directly into his eyes—another thing she'd had trouble with before, but not now. No, not now. "Think of all the Frank Petersons he'll murder if we let him get away. They'll go with him because they think they know him. Or because he seems friendly, the way he must have seemed friendly to the Howard girls. Not the one up there, I mean the one he's protecting."

Three more shots in rapid succession. Ralph saw holes appear low on the SUV's rear quarter-panel. Yes, he was aiming for the gas tank.

"And what are we supposed to do if Mr. Renfield comes down to meet us?" Ralph asked.

"Maybe he won't. Maybe he'll stay where he is, on the high ground. We only have to go as far as the path that leads to the Ahiga entrance. If he comes down before we can get there, you can shoot him."

"Happy to, if he doesn't shoot me first."

"I think there might be something wrong with him," Holly said. "Those screams."

Yune nodded. "'Get off me.' I heard it, too."

The next gunshot ruptured the SUV's tank, and gasoline began to pour onto the asphalt. There was no immediate explosion, but if the guy on the knoll hit the tank again, the SUV would almost certainly blow.

"Okay," Ralph said. The only alternative he could see was crouching here and waiting for the outsider's accomplice to start pumping high-velocity slugs directly through the gift shop, trying to take out one or more of them that way. "Yune? Give us as much cover as you can."

Yune edged to the corner of the building, hissing with pain at each sliding movement. He held his Glock against his chest with his right hand. Holly and Ralph moved to the other end. Ralph could see the service road leading up the hill and to the tourist cabins. It was flanked by a pair of large boulders. An American flag was painted on one, the Texas Lone Star flag on the other.

Once we get behind the one with the American flag on it, we should be safe.

Almost certainly true, but fifty yards had never looked so much like five hundred. He thought of Jeannie at home doing her yoga, or downtown running errands. He thought of Derek at camp, maybe in the craft room with his new buds, talking about TV shows, video games, or girls. He even had time to wonder who Holly was thinking about.

Him, apparently. "Are you ready?"

Before he could reply, the shooter fired again and the SUV's gas tank exploded in a ball of orange fire. Yune leaned out from his corner and began shooting at the top of the knoll.

Holly sprinted. Ralph followed.

15

Jack saw the SUV burst into flame and screamed in triumph, although it made no sense to do so; it wasn't as though there was anyone in it. Then movement caught his eye and he saw two of the meddlers running for the service road. The woman was in the lead, Anderson right behind her. Jack swung his rifle toward them and sighted through the scope. Before he could pull the trigger, there was the *zzzz* of an incoming round. Rock chips struck his shoulder. The one they'd left behind was shooting, and although the range was far too long for accuracy with whatever handgun the guy was using, that last one had been too close for comfort. Jack ducked, and as his chin pressed down on his neck, he felt the glands there bulge and throb, as if they were loaded with pus. His head was aching, his skin was sizzling, and his eyes seemed too big for their sockets.

He peered through the scope just in time to glimpse Anderson disappearing behind one of those big boulders. He had lost them. Nor was that all. Black smoke was rising from the burning SUV, and now that it was full day, there was no wind to disperse it. What if someone saw that and called whatever excuse for a volunteer fire department they had in this poor-ass town?

Go down.

No need to question whose voice it was this time.

You need to get to them before they can get to the Ahiga path.

Jack had no idea what an Ahiga was, but he had no doubt what the visitor inside his head was talking about: the path marked by the sign showing Chief Wahoo. He cringed as another bullet from the asshole down there spanked rock chips from a nearby outcropping, took the first step back the way he had come, and fell down. For a moment pain obliterated all thought. Then he grabbed at a bush sticking out between two rocks and pulled himself up. He looked down at himself, at first unable to believe what had become of him. The leg the snake had bitten now looked two times as big as the other one. The cloth of his pants was pulled tight. Worse, his crotch was bulging. It was as if he had stuffed a small pillow in there.

Go down, Jack. Get them and I'll take the cancer away.

Oh, but right now he had more immediate concerns, didn't he? He was swelling up like a waterlogged sponge.

The snakebite poison, too. I can make you well.

Jack wasn't sure he could believe Tat-Man, but he understood he had no choice. Also, there was Anderson. Mr. No Opinion didn't get to walk away from this. It was all his fault, and he didn't get to walk away.

He started down the path at a shambling trot, clutching the

barrel of the Winchester and using the stock as a cane. His second fall came when the rocky scree slid away under his left foot and his swollen, throbbing right leg wasn't able to compensate. The leg of his pants split open the next time he went down, disclosing flesh that was turning purplish-black and necrotic. He clawed at the rocks and got to his feet again, his face puffing and running with sweat. He was pretty sure he was going to die on this godforsaken chunk of rock and weeds, but he was goddamned if he was going to do it alone.

16

Ralph and Holly ran up the spur road bent double, heads tucked. At the top of the first hill, they stopped to catch their breath. Below and to the left, they could see the circle of decaying tourist cabins. To the right was a long building, probably storage for equipment and supplies back when the Marysville Hole had been a going concern. A truck was parked beside it. Ralph looked at it, looked away, then snapped back.

"Oh my Christ."

"What? *What?*"

"No wonder he knew me. That's Jack Hoskins's truck."

"Hoskins? The other detective from Flint City?"

"Yes, him."

"Why would he—" Then she shook her head hard enough to make her bangs fly. "It doesn't matter. He's stopped shooting and that means he's probably coming. We need to go."

"Maybe Yune hit him," Ralph said, and when she gave him a disbelieving look: "Yeah, okay."

They hurried past the equipment building. There was another path on the far side, leading up the back side of the knoll. "I go first," Ralph said. "I'm the one with the gun."

Holly didn't argue.

They trotted up the incline, the narrow path twisting and turning. Loose scree slid and grated under their shoes, threatening to spill them. Two or three minutes into the climb, Ralph began to hear the clatter and bounce of rocks somewhere higher up. Hoskins was indeed coming to meet them.

They rounded an outcropping, Ralph with his Glock leveled, Holly behind him and on his right. The next stretch of the path ran straight for fifty feet or so. The sound of Hoskins's descent was louder now, but the maze of rocks made it impossible to tell just how close he was.

"Where's the goddam spur path that goes to the back entrance?" Ralph asked. "He's getting closer. This is too much like playing chicken in that James Dean movie."

"Yes, *Rebel Without a Cause*. I don't know, but it can't be far."

"If we run into him before we get off Main Street here, there's going to be shooting. And ricochets. The minute you see him, I want you to drop—"

She thumped him on the back. "If we beat him to the path, there won't be any shooting and I won't have to. *Go!*"

Ralph ran up the straight stretch, telling himself he'd caught his second wind. It wasn't true, but it was good to stay positive. Holly was behind him and whapping him on the shoulder, either to hurry him along or to assure him that she was still there. They reached the next turning in the path. Ralph peered around it, expecting to look into the muzzle of Hoskins's rifle. He didn't see that, but he did see a wooden sign with Chief Ahiga's fading portrait on it.

"Come on," he said. "Fast."

They ran for the sign, and now Ralph could hear the oncoming shooter gasping for breath. Almost sobbing for it. There was a rattle of stones and a cry of pain. It sounded like Hoskins had fallen down.

Good! Stay down!

But then the clattery, slip-sliding footsteps resumed. Very near. Closing in. Ralph grabbed Holly and pushed her onto the Ahiga path. Her small pale face was running with sweat. Her lips were pressed tightly together and her hands were buried in the pockets of her suit coat, which was now powdered with rock dust and splattered with blood.

Ralph raised a finger to his lips. She nodded. He stepped behind the sign. The dry Texas heat had caused the boards to shrink a bit, and he was able to peer through one of the cracks. He saw Hoskins as he staggered into view. His first thought was that Yune had gotten lucky and put a bullet in him after all, but that didn't explain Hoskins's split pants and grotesquely swollen right leg. *No wonder he fell*, Ralph thought. It was amazing that he'd gotten this far down the steep path on that leg. He still had the rifle he'd used to kill Gold and Pelley, but was using it as a cane, and his fingers were nowhere near the trigger. Ralph didn't know if he would be able to hit anything anyway, even at close range. Not the way his hands were trembling. His bloodshot eyes were deep in their sockets. Rock dust had turned his face into a kabuki mask, but where perspiration had cut trails through it, the skin was red, as if with a terrible rash.

Ralph stepped out from behind the sign, Glock held in both hands. "Stop right there, Jack, and let go of the rifle."

Jack skidded and stumbled to a halt thirty feet away, but he continued to hold the rifle by the barrel. That wasn't okay, but Ralph could live with it. If Hoskins started to raise it, however, his life was going to end.

"You shouldn't be here," Jack said. "Like my old granddad used to say, was you born dumb or did you just grow that way?"

"I have no appetite for your bullshit. You killed two men and wounded another one. Shot them from ambush."

"They never should have come here," Jack said, "but since they did, they got what they deserved for messing in with what didn't concern them."

"And what would that be, Mr. Hoskins?" Holly asked.

Hoskins's lips cracked and oozed tiny beads of blood when he smiled. "Tat-Man. As I think you know. Meddling bitch."

"Okay, now that you've got that out of your system," Ralph said, "put the rifle down. You've done enough damage with it. Just drop it. If you bend over, you'll fall on your face. Was it a snake that got you?"

"The snake was just a little extra. You need to leave, Ralph. Both of you need to leave. Or else he'll poison you like he poisoned me. A word to the wise."

Holly took a step closer to Jack. "How did he poison you?" Ralph put a warning hand on her arm.

"Just touched me. Back of the neck. That was all it took." He shook his head in tired wonder. "Out at that barn in Canning Township." His voice rose, trembling with outrage. "Where *you* sent me!"

Ralph shook his head. "It must have been the chief, Jack. I didn't know anything about it. I'm not going to tell you again to put the gun down. You're done with this."

Jack considered . . . or seemed to. Then he lifted the rifle very slowly, going hand over hand down the barrel toward the trigger housing. "I'm not going the way my mother did. Nosir, I am not. I'll shoot your friend there first, Ralph, then you. Unless you stop me."

"Jack, don't. Last warning."

"Stick your warning up your—"

He was trying to point the gun at Holly. She didn't move. Ralph stepped in front of her and fired three times, the reports deafening in the tight space. One for Howie, one for Alec, one for Yune. The distance was a trifle long for a pistol, but the Glock was a good gun and he'd never had any trouble qualifying on the range. Jack

Hoskins went down, and to Ralph, the expression on his dying face looked like relief.

17

Ralph sat down on a jutting lip of rock across from the sign, breathing hard. Holly went to Hoskins, knelt, and rolled him over. She had a look, then came back. "He was bitten more than once."

"Must have been a rattler, and a big one."

"Something else poisoned him first. Something worse than any snake. He called it Tat-Man, we call it the outsider. *El Cuco*. We need to finish this."

Ralph thought of Howie and Alec, lying dead on the other side of this godforsaken chunk of rock. They had families. And Yune—still alive but wounded, suffering, probably in shock by now—also had a family.

"I suppose you're right. Want this pistol? I can take his rifle, if you do."

Holly shook her head.

"All right. Let's do this."

18

Past the first turning, the Ahiga path widened and began to descend. There were pictographs on both sides. Some of the ancient images had been embellished or entirely covered with spraypaint tags.

"He'll know we're coming," Holly said.

"I know. We should have brought one of those flashes."

She reached into one of her voluminous side pockets—the one that had been sagging—and pulled out one of the stubby Home Depot UV flashlights.

"You're sort of amazing," Ralph said. "I don't suppose you've got a couple of hardhats in there, do you?"

"No offense, but your sense of humor is a little weak, Ralph. You should work on that."

Around the next turning of the path, they came to a natural hollow in the rock about four feet off the ground. Above it, fading letters in black paint read WE WILL NEVER FORGET. Inside the niche was a dusty vase with thin branches jutting from it like skeletal fingers. The petals that had once adorned those branches were long gone, but something else remained. Scattered around the bottom of the vase were half a dozen toy versions of Chief Ahiga, like the one that had been left behind when the Jamieson twins had crawled into the bowels of the earth, never to be found. The toys were yellow with age, and the sun had cracked the plastic.

"People have been here," Holly said. "Kids I'd say, based on the spraypaint tags. But they never vandalized this."

"Never even touched it, from the look," Ralph said. "Come on. Yune's on the other side with a bullet wound and a busted elbow."

"Yes, and I'm sure he's in great pain. But we need to be careful. That means moving slowly."

Ralph took her by the elbow. "If this guy gets both of us, that leaves Yune on his own. Maybe you should go back."

She pointed to the sky, where black smoke from the burning SUV was rising. "Someone will see that, and they'll come. And if something happens to us, Yune's the only one who will know why."

She shook his hand loose and began walking up the path. Ralph spared one more look for the little shrine, undisturbed all these years, and then followed her.

19

Just when Ralph thought the Ahiga path was going to lead them to nowhere but the back of the gift shop, it took an acute lefthand turn, almost doubling back on itself, and ended at what looked for all the world like the entrance to some suburbanite's toolshed. Only the green paint was flaked and fading, and the windowless door in the center of it stood ajar. The door was flanked by warning signs. The plastic that encased them had bleared over time, but they were still readable: ABSOLUTELY NO TRESPASSING on the left, and THIS PROPERTY CONDEMNED BY ORDER OF MARYSVILLE TOWN COUNCIL on the right.

Ralph went to the door, Glock ready. He motioned Holly to stand against the path's rocky side, then swung the door open, bending at the knees and bringing his gun to bear as he did so. Inside was a small entryway, empty except for the litter of boards that had been torn away from a six-foot fissure leading into darkness. The splintered ends were still attached to the rock by more of those huge, time-rusted bolts.

"Ralph, look at this. It's interesting."

She was holding the door and bending to examine the lock, which had been pretty well destroyed. It didn't look like the work of a crowbar or tire iron to Ralph; he thought someone had hammered it with a rock until it finally gave.

"What, Holly?"

"It's a one-way, do you see? Only locked if you're on the outside. Somebody was hoping the Jamieson twins, or some of the first rescue party, were still alive. If they found their way here, they wanted to make sure they weren't locked in."

"But no one ever did."

"No." She crossed the entryway to the fissure in the rock. "Can you smell that?"

Ralph could, and knew they were standing at the entrance to a different world. He could smell stale dampness, and something else—the high, sweet aroma of rotting flesh. It was faint, but it was there. He thought of that long-ago cantaloupe, and the insects that had been squirming around inside it.

They stepped into the dark. Ralph was tall, but the fissure was taller, and he didn't have to duck his head. Holly turned on the flashlight, at first shining it straight ahead into a rocky corridor leading downward, then at their feet. They both saw a series of glowing droplets leading into the dark. Holly did him the courtesy of not pointing out that it was the same stuff her makeshift black light had picked up in his living room.

They were only able to walk side by side for the first sixty feet or so. After that the passage narrowed and Holly handed him the flashlight. He held it in his left hand, the pistol in his right. The walls sparkled with eerie streaks of mineral, some red, some lavender, some a greenish-yellow. He occasionally shone the light upward, just to make sure *El Cuco* wasn't up there, crawling along the ragged ceiling among the stubs of stalactites. The air wasn't cold—he had read somewhere that caves maintained a temperature roughly equal to the average temperature of the region in which they were located—but it felt cold after being outside, and of course both of them were still coated in fear-sweat. A draft was coming from deeper in, blowing in their faces and bringing that faint rotten smell.

He stopped, and Holly ran into him, making him jump. "What?" she whispered.

Instead of answering, he shone the light on a rift in the rock to their left. Spray-painted beside it were two words: CHECKED and NOTHING.

They moved on, slowly, slowly. Ralph didn't know about Holly, but he felt an increasing sense of dread, a growing certainty that he was never going to see his wife and son again. Or daylight. It was amazing how fast a person could miss the daylight. He felt that if they did get out of here, he could drink daylight like water.

Holly whispered, "This is a horrible place, isn't it?"

"Yes. You should go back."

Her only answer was a slight push in the center of his back.

They passed several more breaks in the downward passage, each one marked with those same two words. How long ago had they been sprayed there? If Claude Bolton had been a teenager, it had to be at least fifteen years, maybe twenty. And who had been in here since then—other than their outsider, that was? Anyone? Why would they come? Holly was right, it was horrible. With each step he felt more like a man being buried alive. He forced himself to remember the clearing in Figgis Park. And Frank Peterson. And a jutting branch marked with bloody fingerprints where the bark had been stripped from it by repeated plunging blows. And Terry Maitland, asking how Ralph was going to clear his own conscience. Asking that as he lay dying.

He kept going.

The passage abruptly narrowed even further, not because the walls were closer but because there was rubble on both sides. Ralph shone the flashlight upward and saw a deep cavity in the rock roof. It made him think of an empty socket after a tooth has been pulled.

"Holly—this is where the roof caved in. The second rescue party probably carted the biggest pieces out. This stuff . . ." He swept the light across the heaps of rubble, picking out another couple of those spectrally glowing spots.

"This is the stuff they didn't bother with," Holly finished. "Just pushed it out of the way."

"Yes."

They started moving again, at first only edging along. Ralph, something of a widebody, had to turn sideways. He handed Holly the flashlight and raised his gun hand to the side of his face. "Shine the light under my arm. Keep it pointed straight ahead. No surprises."

"O-Okay."

"You sound cold."

"I *am* cold. You should be quiet. He could hear us."

"So what? He knows we're coming. You *do* think a bullet will kill him, right? You—"

"*Stop, Ralph, stop!* You'll step in it!"

He stopped at once, heart hammering. She shone the light a bit past his feet. Draped over the last pile of rubble before the passage widened again was the body of a dog or a coyote. A coyote seemed more likely, but it was impossible to tell for sure, because the animal's head was gone. Its belly had been opened and the viscera had been scooped out.

"That's what we were smelling," she said.

Ralph stepped over it carefully. Ten feet further on, he halted again. It had been a coyote, all right; here was the head. It seemed to be staring at them with exaggerated surprise, and at first he couldn't understand just why.

Holly was a little quicker on the uptake. "Its eyes are gone," she said. "Eating the insides wasn't enough. It ate the eyes right out of that poor creature's head. Oough."

"So the outsider doesn't just eat human flesh and blood." He paused. "Or sadness."

Holly spoke quietly. "Thanks to us—mostly thanks to you and Lieutenant Sablo—it's been very active in what's usually its time of hibernation. And it's been denied the food it likes. It must be very hungry."

"And weak. You said it must be weak."

"Let us hope so," Holly said. "This is extremely frightening. I hate closed-in places."

"You can always—"

She gave him another of those light thumps. "Keep going. And watch your step."

20

The trail of faintly luminous droplets continued. Ralph had come to think of them as the thing's sweat. Fear-sweat, like theirs? He hoped so. He hoped the fucker had been terrified, and still was.

There were more fissures, but no more spraypaint; these were little more than cracks, too small even for a child to fit into. Or escape from. Holly was able to walk beside him again, although it was a tight fit. They could hear water dripping somewhere far away, and once Ralph felt a new breeze, this one against his left cheek. It was like being caressed with ghost fingers. It was coming from one of those cracks, producing a hollow, almost glassy moan, like the sound of breath blown over the top of a beer bottle. A horrible place, all right. He found it all but impossible to believe people had paid money to explore this stone crypt, but of course they didn't know what he knew, and now believed. It was sort of amazing how being in the guts of the ground helped a person to believe what had previously seemed not just impossible but downright laughable.

"Careful," Holly said. "There's more."

This time it was a couple of gophers that had been torn to pieces. Beyond them was the remains of another rattler, all of it gone except for tatters of its diamondback skin.

A little further on, they came to the top of a steep downward slope, its surface polished as smooth as a dancefloor. Ralph thought it had probably been created by some ancient underground river that had flowed during the age of the dinosaurs and dried up before Jesus walked the earth. To one side was a steel railing, now spotted with florets of rust. Holly ran the light along it, and they saw not just scattered droplets of luminescence, but palm prints and fingerprints. Prints that would match Claude Bolton's, Ralph had no doubt.

"Sonofabitch was careful, wasn't he? Didn't want to take a spill."

Holly nodded. "I think this is the passageway Lovie called the Devil's Slide. Watch your ste—"

From somewhere behind and below them came a brief squall of rock, followed by a barely perceptible thud that went through their feet. It reminded Ralph of how even solid ice could sometimes shift. Holly looked at him, wide-eyed.

"I think we're okay. This old cave's been talking to itself for a long time."

"Yes, but I bet the conversation's been livelier since the groundshaker Lovie told us about. The one that happened in '07."

"You can always—"

"Don't ask me again. I have to see this through."

He supposed she did.

They went down the incline, holding the railing but being careful to avoid the handprints left by the one who had gone before them. At the bottom there was a sign:

WELCOME TO THE DEVIL'S SLIDE
BE SAFE USE HANDRAIL

Beyond the Slide, the passage widened still more. There was another of those arched entryways, but part of the wooden facing had fallen away, disclosing what nature had left here: nothing but a ragged maw.

Holly cupped her hands around her mouth and called softly, "Hello?"

Her voice came back to them perfectly, in a series of overlapping echoes: *Hello . . . ello . . . ello . . .*

"I thought so," she said. "It's the Chamber of Sound. It's the big one that Lovie—"

"Hello."

Ello . . . lo . . . lo . . .

Spoken quietly, but stopping Ralph in the middle of drawing a breath. He felt Holly seize his forearm with a hand that felt like a claw.

"Now that you're here . . ."

You're . . . you . . . here . . . ere . . .

". . . and gone to so much trouble to find me, why don't you come in?"

21

They stepped through the arch side by side, Holly holding onto Ralph's arm like a bride with stage fright. She had the light; Ralph had his Glock, and intended to use it as soon as he had a target. One shot. Only there was no target, not at first.

Beyond the arch was a jutting lip of stone that made a sort of balcony seventy feet above the main cave's floor. A metal stairway spiraled down. Holly glanced up and felt dizzy. The stairs rose another two hundred feet or more, past an opening that had probably been the main entrance, all the way to the stalactite-hung roof. She realized the entire bluff was hollow, like a fake bakery shop cake. Going down, the stairway looked okay. Above them, part of it had come loose from the fist-sized bolts that held it, and hung drunkenly over the drop.

Waiting for them at the bottom, in the light of an ordinary standing lamp—the kind you might see in any reasonably well-appointed living room—was the outsider. The lamp's cord snaked away to a softly humming red box with HONDA printed on the side. At the extreme outer edge of the circle of radiance was a cot with a blanket bunched at the bottom.

Ralph had caught up with many fugitives in his time, and the thing they had come looking for could have been any of them: hollow-eyed, too thin, used hard. He was wearing jeans, a rawhide vest over a dirty white shirt, and scuffed cowboy boots. He appeared unarmed. He was looking up at them with Claude Bolton's face: the black hair, the high cheekbones suggesting some Native American blood a few generations back, the goatee. Ralph couldn't see the ink on his fingers from where he was, but he knew it was there.

Tat-Man, Hoskins had called him.

"If you really mean to talk to me, you'll have to chance the stairs. They held me, but I have to tell you the truth—they're not all that steady." His words, although spoken in a conversational voice, overlapped each other, doubling and tripling, as if there were not just one outsider but many, a cabal of them hiding in the shadows and the fissures where the light of that single floor lamp could not reach.

Holly started for the stairs. Ralph stopped her. "I'll go first."

"I should. I'm lighter."

"I'll go first," he repeated. "When I get down—if I get down—you come." He spoke quietly, but guessed that, given the acoustics, the outsider could hear every word. *At least I hope so*, Ralph thought. "But stop at least a dozen steps up. I have to talk to him."

He was looking at her as he said this, and looking hard. She glanced at the Glock, and he gave the barest nod. No, there would be no talking, no long-winded Q-and-A. All that was over. One shot to the head, and then they were out of here. Assuming the roof didn't fall in on them, that was.

"All right," she said. "Be careful."

There was no way to do that—either the old spiral staircase would hold or it wouldn't—but he tried to think himself lighter as he went down. The stairs groaned and squalled and shuddered.

"Doing well so far," the outsider said. "Walk close to the wall, that might be safest."

Afest . . . est . . . est . . .

Ralph reached the bottom. The outsider stood motionless near his strangely domestic lamp. Had he bought it—and the generator, and the cot—at the Home Depot in Tippit? Ralph thought it likely. It seemed to be the go-to place in this godforsaken part of the Lone Star State. Not that it mattered. Behind him, the stairs began to squall and groan again as Holly descended.

Now that Ralph was on the same level, he stared at the outsider with what was almost scientific curiosity. He looked human, but was oddly hard to grasp, even so. It was like looking at a picture with your eyes slightly crossed. You knew what it was you were seeing, but everything was skewed and slightly out of true. It was Claude Bolton's face, but the chin was wrong, not rounded but square, and slightly cleft. The jawline on the right was longer than the one on the left, giving the face as a whole a slanted aspect that stopped just short of grotesque. The hair was Claude's, as black and shiny as a crow's wing, but there were streaks of a lighter reddish-brown shade. Most striking of all were the eyes. One was brown, as Claude's were brown, but the other was blue.

Ralph knew the cleft chin, the long jaw, the reddish-brown hair. And the blue eye, that most of all. He had seen the light go out of it as Terry Maitland died in the street on a hot July morning not long ago.

"You're still changing, aren't you? The projection my wife saw may have looked exactly like Claude, but the real you hasn't caught up yet. Has it? You're not quite there."

He meant these to be the last words the outsider would hear. The protesting groans from the stairs had stopped, which meant Holly was standing high up enough to be safe. He raised the Glock, gripping his right wrist in his left hand.

The outsider lifted his arms to either side, presenting himself.

"Kill me if you want, Detective, but you'll be killing yourself and your lady friend, too. I don't have access to your thoughts, as I do Claude's, but I have a good idea of what's in your mind, just the same: you're thinking that one shot is an acceptable risk. Am I right?"

Ralph said nothing.

"I'm sure I am, and I must tell you it would be a *great* risk." He raised his voice and shouted, *"CLAUDE BOLTON IS MY NAME!"*

The echoes seemed even louder than the shout. Holly gave a cry of surprise as a piece of stalactite high above, perhaps cracked almost through already, detached from the ceiling and fell like a rock dagger. It posed no danger to any of them, hitting bottom well outside the feeble circle of lamplight, but Ralph took the point.

"Since you knew enough to find me here, you may already know this," the outsider said, lowering his arms, "but in case you don't, two boys were lost in the caves and passages below this one, and when a rescue party tried to find them—"

"Someone fired a gun and brought down a piece of the roof," Holly said from the stairs. "Yes, we know."

"That happened in the Devil's Slide passage, where the sound of the gunshot would have been dampened." Smiling. "Who knows what will happen if Detective Anderson fires his gun in here? Surely a few of the bigger stalactites will come raining down. Even so, you might avoid them. Of course if you don't, you'll be crushed. Then there's the possibility you might cause the entire top of the bluff to collapse, burying us all in a landslide. Want to risk it, Detective? I'm sure you meant to when you came down the stairs, but I have to tell you that the odds would not be in your favor."

Those stairs creaked briefly as Holly came down another step. Maybe two.

Keep your distance, Ralph thought, but there was no way he could make her do that. This lady had a mind of her own.

"We also know why you're here," she said. "Claude's uncle and cousins are here. In the ground."

"Indeed they are." He—it—was smiling more widely now. The gold tooth in that smile was Claude's, like the letters on his fingers. "Along with many others, including the two children they hoped to save. I feel them in the earth. Some are close. Roger Bolton and his sons are over there, not twenty feet below Snake's Belly." He pointed. "I feel them the most strongly, not just because they're close, but because they are the blood I'm becoming."

"Not good to eat, though, I guess," Ralph said. He was looking at the cot. Barely visible on the stone floor beside it, next to a Styrofoam cooler, was another untidy litter of bones and skin.

"No, of course not." The outsider looked at him impatiently. "But their remains give off a glow. A kind of . . . I don't know, these are not things I ordinarily talk about . . . a kind of emanation. Even those foolish boys give off that glow, although it's faint. They're very far down. You might say they died exploring uncharted regions of the Marysville Hole." At this, his smile reappeared, showing not just the gold tooth but almost all of them. Ralph wondered if he had been smiling like that as he murdered Frank Peterson, eating his flesh and drinking the child's dying agony along with his blood.

"A glow like a nightlight?" Holly asked. She sounded genuinely curious. The stairs squalled as she descended another step or two. Ralph wished mightily that she was going the other way: up and out, back into the hot Texas sunshine.

The outsider only shrugged.

Go back, he thought at Holly. *Turn around and go back. When I'm sure you've had time enough to make it out the Ahiga back door, I'll take the shot. Even if it makes my wife a widow and my son fatherless, I'll take the shot. I owe it to Terry and all the others who came before him.*

"A nightlight," she repeated, coming down another step. "You know, for comfort. I had one when I was a girl."

The outsider was looking up at her over Ralph's shoulder. With his back to the standing lamp and his face in the shadows, Ralph could see a strange shine in those mismatched eyes. Except that wasn't quite right. It wasn't *in* them but coming *from* them, and now Ralph understood what Grace Maitland had meant when she said the thing she'd seen had straws for eyes.

"Comfort?" The outsider seemed to consider the word. "Yes, I suppose so, although I've never thought of it that way. But also information. Even dead, they're full of *Bolton*-ness."

"Do you mean memories?" Another step closer. Ralph took his left hand off his wrist and motioned her back, knowing she wouldn't go.

"No, not those." He looked impatient with her again, but there was something else there, too. A certain eagerness Ralph knew from many interrogation rooms. Not every suspect wanted to talk, but most of them did, because they had been alone in the closed room of their thoughts. And this thing must have been alone with its thoughts for a very long time. Alone, period. You only had to look at him to know it.

"Then what is it?" She was still in the same place, and thank God for small blessings, Ralph thought.

"Bloodline. There's something in bloodline that goes beyond memory or the physical similarities that are carried down through the generations. It's a way of being. A way of seeing. It's not food, but it *is* strength. Their souls are gone, their ka, but something is left, even in their dead brains and bodies."

"A kind of DNA," she said. "Maybe tribal, maybe racial."

"I suppose. If you like." He took a step toward Ralph, holding out the hand with MUST written on the fingers. "It's like these tattoos. They aren't alive, but they hold certain infor—"

"*Stop!*" she shouted, and Ralph thought, *Christ, she's even closer. How could she do that without me hearing?*

The echoes rose, seeming to expand, and something else fell. Not a stalactite this time, but a chunk of rock from one of the rough walls.

"Don't do that," the outsider said. "Unless you want to risk bringing the whole thing down on our heads, don't raise your voice like that."

When Holly spoke again, her voice was lower but still urgent. "Remember what he did to Detective Hoskins, Ralph. His touch is poisonous."

"Only when I'm in this transformative state," the outsider said mildly. "It's a form of natural protection, and rarely fatal. More like poison ivy than some sort of radiation. Of course, Detective Hoskins was . . . susceptible, shall we say. And once I've touched someone, I can often—not always, but often— get into their minds. Or the minds of their loved ones. I did that with Frank Peterson's family. Only a little, enough to push them in directions they were already going."

"You should stay where you are," Ralph said.

The outsider raised his tattooed hands. "Certainly. As I've said, you're the man with the gun. But I can't let you leave. I'm too tired to relocate, you see. I had to make the drive down here far too soon, and I had to buy a few supplies, which drained me even more. It seems we're at a standoff."

"You put yourself in this position," Ralph said. "I mean, you know that, right?"

The outsider looked at him out of a face that still held the fading remains of Terry Maitland and said nothing.

"Heath Holmes, okay. The others before Holmes, also okay. But Maitland was a mistake."

"I suppose that's so." The outsider looked puzzled, but still complacent. "Yet I've taken others who had strong alibis and immaculate reputations. With evidence and eyewitness testimony, the alibis and reputations make no difference. People are blind to explanations that lie outside their perception of reality. You should never have come looking for me. You never should have even *sensed* me, no matter how strong his alibi was. Yet you did. Was it because I came to the courthouse?"

Ralph said nothing. Holly had come down the last step and was now standing beside him.

The outsider sighed. "That was a mistake, I should have thought more seriously about the presence of TV cameras, but I was still hungry. Yet I *could* have stayed away. I was gluttonous."

"Add overconfident, while you're at it," Ralph said. "And overconfidence breeds carelessness. Cops see a lot of that."

"Well, perhaps I was all three. But I think I might have gotten away even with that." He was looking speculatively at the pale, gray-haired woman next to Ralph. "It's you I have to thank for being in this current situation, isn't it? Holly. Claude says your name is Holly. What made you able to believe? How were you able to convince a party of modern men who probably don't believe in anything beyond the range of their five senses to come down here? Have you seen another one like me somewhere?" The eagerness in his voice was unmistakable.

"We didn't come here to answer your questions," Holly said. One of her hands was stuffed into the pocket of her wrinkled suit jacket. In the other, she held the UV flashlight, which was not turned on at the moment; the only light came from the standing lamp. "We came here to kill you."

"I'm not sure how you hope to do that . . . Holly. Your friend might chance firing his gun if it was just the two of us, but I don't think he wants to risk your life, as well. And while one or both of you might try to attack me physically, I think you'd find me surprisingly strong as well as a bit poisonous. Yes, even in my current depleted state."

"It's a standoff for now," Ralph said, "but not for long. Hoskins wounded State Police Lieutenant Yunel Sablo but didn't kill him. By now he will have called this in."

"A good try, but not out here," the outsider said. "There is no cell reception for six miles going east and a dozen going west. Did you think I wouldn't check?"

Ralph had been hoping for just that, but it had been a thin hope. As it happened, however, he had another card in his hand. "Hoskins also blew up the vehicle we came in. There's smoke. Plenty of it."

For the first time he saw real alarm in the outsider's face.

"That changes things. I'll have to run. In my current state, that will be difficult and painful. If you wanted to make me angry, Detective, you've succeed—"

"You asked me if I'd seen one of your kind before," Holly interrupted. "I haven't—well, not exactly—but I'm sure Ralph has. Strip away the shape-changing, the memory-sucking, and the glowing eyes, and you're just a sexual sadist and common pedophile."

The outsider recoiled as if she had struck him. For a moment he seemed to forget all about the burning SUV sending up smoke signals from the abandoned parking lot. "That's offensive, ridiculous, and untrue. I eat to live, that's all. Your kind does the same thing when you slaughter pigs and cows. That's all you are to me—cattle."

"You're lying." Holly took a step forward, and when Ralph tried to take her by the arm, she shook him off. Red roses had begun to bloom in her pale cheeks. "Your ability to look like someone you're not—some*thing* you're not—guarantees trust. You could have taken any of Mr. Maitland's friends. You could have taken his *wife*. But instead of that, you took a child. You *always* take children."

"They're the strongest, sweetest food! Have you never eaten veal? Or calves' liver?"

"You don't just eat them, you ejaculate on them." Her mouth twisted in disgust. "You *splooge* on them. Oough!"

"To leave DNA!" he shouted.

"You could leave it other ways!" she shouted back, and something else fell from the eggshell ceiling above them. "But you don't put your thing in, do you? Is it because you're impotent?" She raised a finger, then let it curl. "Is it is it *is it*?"

"Shut up!"

"You take children because you're a child rapist who can't even do it with his penis, you have to use a—"

He ran at her, his face twisting into an expression of hate that had nothing of Claude Bolton or Terry Maitland in it; this was its own thing, as black and awful as the lower depths where the Jamieson twins had finally surrendered their lives. Ralph raised his gun, but Holly stepped into his line of fire before he could get off a round.

"*Don't shoot, Ralph, don't shoot!*"

Something else fell, this time something big, smashing the outsider's cot and cooler and sending shards of mineral-sparkling stones spinning across the polished floor.

Holly pulled something from a pocket of her suit coat on the side that always sagged. The thing was long and white and stretched, as if it contained something heavy. At the same time, she turned on the UV flashlight and shined it full in the outsider's face. He winced, made a snarling sound, and turned his head, still reaching for her with Claude Bolton's tattooed hands. She drew the white thing cross-body above her small breasts, all the way to her shoulder, and swung it with all her strength. The loaded end connected with the outsider's head just below the hairline, at the temple.

What Ralph saw then would haunt his dreams for years to come. The left half of the outsider's head caved in as if it had been made of papier-mâché rather than bone. The brown eye jumped in its socket. The thing went to its knees, and its face seemed to liquefy. Ralph saw a hundred features slide across it in mere seconds, there and gone: high foreheads followed low ones, bushy eyebrows and ones so blond they were hardly there, deepset eyes and ones that bulged, lips both wide and thin. Buck teeth protruded, then disappeared; chins jutted and sank. Yet the last face, the one that lingered longest, almost certainly the outsider's *true* face, was utterly nondescript. It was the face of anyone you might pass on the street, seen at one moment and forgotten the next.

Holly swung again, striking the cheekbone this time and driving the forgettable face into a hideous crescent. It looked like something out of an insane children's book.

In the end, it's nothing, Ralph thought. *Nobody. What looked like Claude, what looked like Terry, what looked like Heath Holmes . . . nothing. Only false fronts. Only stage dressing.*

Reddish wormlike things began to pour from the hole in the outsider's head, from its nose, from the cramped teardrop which was all that remained of its unsteady mouth. The worms fell to the stone floor of the Chamber of Sound in a squirming flood. Claude Bolton's body first began to tremble, then to buck, then to shrivel inside its clothes.

Holly dropped the flashlight and raised the white thing over her head (it was a sock, Ralph saw, a man's long white athletic sock), now holding it in both hands. She brought it down one final time, crashing it into the top of the thing's head. Its face split down the middle like a rotted gourd. There was no brain in the cavity thus revealed, only a writhing nest of those worms, inescapably reminding Ralph of the maggots he had discovered in that long-ago cantaloupe. Those already released were squirming across the floor toward Holly's feet.

She backed away from them, ran into Ralph, then buckled at the knees. He grabbed her and held her up. All the color had left her face. Tears spilled down her cheeks.

"Drop the sock," he said in her ear.

She looked at him, dazed.

"Some of those things are on it."

When she still did nothing but look at him with a kind of dazed wonder, Ralph attempted to pull it from her fist. At first he couldn't. She had it in a death grip. He pried at her fingers, hoping he wouldn't have to break them to make her let go, but he would if he had to. If that was what it took. Those things would be a lot worse than poison ivy if they touched her. And if they got under her skin . . .

She seemed to come back to herself—a little, anyway—and opened her hand. The sock dropped, the toe making a clunking sound when it hit the stone floor. He backed away from the worms, which were still blindly seeking (or maybe not blind at all; they were coming right for the two of them), pulling Holly by the hand, which was still curled from the fierce grip she'd had on the sock. She looked down, saw the danger, and drew in a breath.

"Don't scream," he told her. "Can't risk anything else falling down. Just *climb.*"

He began to pull her up the stairs. After the first four or five she was able to climb on her own, but they were going backward in order to keep an eye on the worms, which were still spilling from the outsider's cloven head. Also from the teardrop mouth.

"Stop," she whispered. "Stop, look at them, they're just milling around. They can't get up the steps. And they're starting to die."

She was right. They were slowing down, and a great heap of them near the outsider wasn't moving at all. But the body was; somewhere inside it, the animating force was still trying to live. The Bolton-thing humped and jerked, arms waving in a kind of semaphore. As they watched, the neck shortened. The remains of the head began to draw into the collar of the shirt. Claude Bolton's black hair at first stuck up, then was gone.

"What is it?" Holly whispered. "What are *they?*"

"I don't know and I don't care," Ralph said. "I only know that you'll never have to buy a drink for the rest of your life, at least when you're with me."

"I rarely drink alcohol," she said. "It goes badly with my medicine. I think I told you tha—"

She abruptly leaned over the rail and vomited. He held her while she did it.

"I'm sorry," she said.

"Don't be. Let's—"

"Get the frack *out* of here," she finished for him.

22

Sunlight had never felt so good.

They got as far as the Chief Ahiga sign before Holly said she felt lightheaded and had to sit down. Ralph found a flat rock that was big enough for both of them, and sat beside her. She glanced at the sprawled body of Jack Hoskins, made a desolate squeaking sound, and began to cry. At first it came out in a series of choked, reluctant sobs, as if someone had told her it was terribly wrong to weep in front of another person. Ralph put an arm around her shoulders, which felt sadly thin. She buried her face against the front of his shirt and began to sob in earnest. They had to get back to Yune, who might have been more badly hurt than it had seemed—they had been under fire, after all, hardly the time to make an accurate diagnosis. Even at best, the man had a broken elbow and a dislocated shoulder. But she needed at least a little time, and she had earned it by doing what he, the big detective, had been unable to do.

Within forty-five seconds, the storm had begun to lessen. In a minute, it was over. She was good. Strong. Holly looked up at him, eyes red and swimming, but Ralph wasn't entirely sure she knew at first where she was. Or who he was, for that matter.

"I can't do it again, Bill. Not ever. Ever ever *ever*! And if this one comes back the way Brady did, I'll kill myself. Do you hear me?"

He shook her gently. "He's not coming back, Holly. I promise you."

She blinked. "Ralph. I meant to say Ralph. Did you see what came out of his . . . did you see those worms?"

"Yes."

"Oough! *Oough!*" She made a retching noise, and covered her mouth.

"Who told you how to make a blackjack out of a sock? And how hard it can hit if the sock is one of the long ones? Was it Bill Hodges?"

Holly nodded.

"What was it loaded with?"

"Ball bearings, just like Bill's. I bought them in the Walmart automotive department, back in Flint City. Because I can't use guns. I didn't think I'd have to use the Happy Slapper, either, it was only an impulse."

"Or an intuition." He smiled, although he was hardly aware of it; he still felt numb all over, and kept looking around to make sure none of those worms were squirming after them, desperate to survive in a new host. "Is that what you call it? The Happy Slapper?"

"It's what Bill called it. Ralph, we have to go. Yune—"

"I know. But I have to do something first. Sit where you are."

He went to Hoskins's body and made himself hunt through the dead man's pockets. He found the keys to the pickup truck and returned to Holly. "Okay."

They started down the path. Holly stumbled once and he grabbed her. Then it was his turn to almost go down, and it was she grabbing him.

Like a couple of damn cripples, he thought. *But after what we saw—*

"There's so much we don't know," she said. "Where he came from. If those bugs were a disease or maybe even some kind of alien lifeform. Who his victims were—not just the children he killed, but the ones who got blamed for the killings. There must have been a lot of them. A *lot*. Did you see his face at the end? How it changed?"

"Yes," Ralph said. He would never forget it.

"We don't know how long he lived. How he could project himself. What he *was*."

"That much we do know," Ralph said. "He—*it*—was *El Cuco*. Oh, and something else: the sonofabitch is dead."

23

They were most of the way down the path when a horn began to beep in short blasts. Holly stopped, biting at lips which had already taken a lot of abuse.

"Relax," Ralph said. "I think that's Yune."

The path was wider now, and less steep, so they were able to move faster. When they came around the storage shed, they saw it was indeed Yune, sitting half in and half out of Hoskins's pickup, beeping the horn with his right hand. His swollen and bloody left arm lay in his lap like a log.

"You can quit that now," Ralph said. "Mother and Father are here. How are you?"

"My arm hurts like blue fuck, but otherwise I'm okay. Did you get him? *El Cuco?*"

"We got him," Ralph said. "*Holly* got him. He wasn't human, but he died, just the same. His days of killing children are over."

"*Holly* got him?" He looked at her. "How?"

"We can talk about that later," she said. "Right now I'm more concerned about you. Have you passed out? Are you lightheaded?"

"I got a little dizzy walking over here. Seemed to take forever, and I had to rest a couple of times. I was hoping I'd meet you coming out. Praying, more like it. Then I saw this truck. Must belong to the shooter. John P. Hoskins, according to the registration. Is he who I think he is?"

Ralph nodded. "Of the Flint City police. And it's *was*. He's dead, too. I shot him."

Yune's eyes widened. "What the hell was he doing here?"

"The outsider sent him. How he managed that I have no idea."

"I thought he might have left the keys, but no joy on that. And nothing for pain relief in the glove compartment, either. Just the registration, his insurance card, and a bunch of crap."

"I've got the keys," Ralph said. "They were in his pocket."

"And I've got something for pain," Holly said. She reached into one of the voluminous side pockets of her beat-up suit coat and brought out a large brown prescription bottle. It was unlabeled.

"What else have you got in there?" Ralph asked. "A camp stove? Coffee pot? Shortwave radio?"

"Work on that sense of humor, Ralph."

"That's not me being funny, that's true admiration."

"I concur most heartily," Yune said.

She opened her traveling pharmacy, dumped an assortment of pills into her palm, and put the bottle carefully down on the truck's dashboard. "These are Zoloft . . . Paxil . . . Valium, which I rarely take anymore . . . and these." She carefully slid the rest of the pills back into the bottle, saving out two orange ones. "Motrin. I take it for tension headaches. Also for TMJ pain, although that's better since I started using a night guard. I have the hybrid model. It's expensive but it's the best one on the . . ." She saw them looking at her. "What?"

Yune said, "Just more admiration, *querida*. I love a woman who comes prepared for all eventualities." He took the pills, swallowed them dry, and closed his eyes. "Thank you. So much. May your night guard never fail you."

She looked at him doubtfully as she stored the bottle back in her pocket. "I have two more when you need them. Have you heard any fire sirens?"

"No," Yune said. "I'm starting to think they're not coming."

"They will," Ralph said, "but you won't be here when they arrive. You need to go to the hospital. Plainville's a little closer than Tippit, plus the Bolton place is on the way. You'll need to stop there. Holly, will you be okay driving if I stay here?"

"Yes, but why . . ." Then she hit her forehead lightly with the palm of her hand. "Mr. Gold and Mr. Pelley."

"Yes. I have no intention of leaving them where they fell."

"Messing up a crime scene is generally frowned on," Yune said. "As I think you know."

"I do, but won't allow two good men to cook in the hot sun and next to a burning vehicle. Do you have a problem with that?"

Yune shook his head. Droplets of sweat shone in the bristles of his Marine-style haircut. *"Por supuesto no."*

"I'll drive us around to the parking lot, and then Holly can take over. Are you getting any relief from that Motrin, amigo?"

"I am, actually. It ain't great, but it's better."

"Good. Because before we get rolling, we have to talk."

"About?"

"About how we're going to explain this," Holly said.

24

Once they were in the parking lot, Ralph got out. He met Holly coming around the hood of the truck, and this time it was she who hugged him. It was brief but strong. The rental SUV had mostly burned itself out, and the smoke was thinning.

Yune moved—carefully, with several winces and hisses of pain—into the passenger seat. When Ralph leaned in, he said, "You're sure he's dead?" Ralph knew it wasn't Hoskins he was asking about. "You're *sure?*"

"Yes. He didn't exactly melt like the Wicked Witch of the West, but close. When the shit hits the fan out here, they're going to find nothing but his clothes and maybe a bunch of dead worms."

"Worms?" Yune frowned.

"Based on how fast they were dying," Holly said, "I think the worms will decay very rapidly. But there will be DNA on the clothes, and if they should happen to run it against Claude's, they could get a match."

"Or a mix of Claude's and Terry's, because his change-over wasn't complete. You saw that, right?"

Holly nodded.

"Which would make it worthless. I think Claude is going to be all right." Ralph took his cell phone from his pocket and put it in Yune's good hand. "You'll be okay to make the calls as soon as you start getting some bars?"

"*Claro.*"

"And you know the order of the calls?"

As Yune ticked them off, they heard faint sirens coming from the direction of Tippit. Someone had noticed the smoke after all, it seemed, but the person who saw it hadn't bothered to come and investigate himself. Which was probably good. "DA Bill Samuels. Then your wife. Chief Geller after that. Finishing up with Captain Horace Kinney of the Texas Highway Patrol. All the numbers are in your contacts. The Boltons we talk to in person."

"*I'll* talk to them," Holly said. "You're going to sit still and rest your arm."

"Very important Claude and Lovie get on board with the story," Ralph said. "Now go on. If you're still here when the fire trucks arrive, you'll be stuck."

With the seat and the mirror adjusted to her satisfaction, Holly turned to Yune and to Ralph, still leaning in the passenger door. She looked tired but not exhausted. Her tears had passed. He saw nothing on her face but concentration and purpose.

"We need to keep this simple," she said. "As simple and as close to the truth as we can get."

"You've been through this before," Yune said. "Or something like it. Haven't you?"

"Yes. And they *will* believe us, even if they're left with questions that can never be answered. You both know why. Ralph, those sirens are getting closer and we have to go."

Ralph closed the passenger door and watched them drive away in the dead Flint City detective's pickup. He considered the hardpan Holly would have to cross in order to avoid the chain, and thought she'd manage it just fine, skirting the worst of the holes and washes in order to spare Yune's arm. Just when he thought he couldn't admire her more . . . he did.

He went to Alec's body first, because it was the harder one to retrieve. The vehicle fire was almost out, but the heat radiating from it was fierce. Alec's face and arms had blackened, his head had been burned bald, and as Ralph grabbed him by the belt and began hauling him toward the gift shop, he tried not to think of the crispy bits and melted gobbets that were being left behind. And of how much Alec now looked like the man who had been at the courthouse that day. *All he needs is the yellow shirt over his head*, Ralph thought, and that was too much. He let go of the belt and managed to stagger twenty paces before bending over, grasping his knees, and throwing up everything in his stomach. When that part was done, he went back and finished what he had started, dragging first Alec and then Howie Gold into the shade of the gift shop.

He rested, getting his breath back, then examined the shop's door. It was padlocked, but the door itself looked weather-worn and flimsy. The second time he hit it, the hinges gave way. The interior was shadowy and explosively hot. The shelves were not entirely empty; a few souvenir tee-shirts emblazoned with I EXPLORED THE MARYSVILLE HOLE still remained. He took two and shook off the dust as best he could. Outside, the sirens were very close. Ralph thought they wouldn't want to drive their expensive equipment across the hardpan; they'd stop to cut the chain, instead. He still had a little time.

He knelt and covered the faces of the two men. Good men who

had fully expected to have years of life left in front of them. Men with families who would grieve. The only good thing (if there was anything good about it) was that their grief would not become a monster's meal.

He sat beside them, forearms resting on his knees, chin on his chest. Was he responsible for these deaths, too? Partly, perhaps, because the chain always led back to that catastrophically unwise public arrest of Terry Maitland. But even in his exhaustion, he felt he did not need to own all of what had happened.

They will believe us, Holly had said. *And you both know why.*

Ralph did. They would believe even a shaky story, because footsteps didn't just end and there was no way maggots could hatch inside a ripe cantaloupe with its tough skin intact. They would believe because to admit any other possibility was to call reality itself into question. The irony was inescapable: the very thing that had protected the outsider during its long life of murder would now protect them.

No end to the universe, Ralph thought, and waited in the shade of the gift shop for the fire trucks to arrive.

25

Holly drove to the Boltons' sitting upright, hands on the wheel at ten and two, listening as Yune made the calls. Bill Samuels was horrified to learn that Howie Gold and Alec Pelley were dead, but Yune cut off his questions. There would be time for questions and answers later, but that time was not now. Samuels was to re-interview all the witnesses who had been previously questioned, beginning with Willow Rainwater. He was to tell her straight out that serious questions had been raised about the identity of the man she had taken from the strip club to the train station in Dubrow. Was she still sure that person had been Terry Maitland?

"Try to question her in a way that plants doubts," Yune said. "Can you do that?"

"Sure," Samuels said. "I've been doing it in front of juries for the last five years. And based on her statement, Ms. Rainwater already has a few. So do the other witnesses, especially since that tape of Terry at the convention in Cap City went public. It's got half a million hits just on YouTube. Now tell me about Howie and Alec."

"Later. Time is tight, Mr. Samuels. Talk to the wits, starting with Rainwater. And something else: the meeting we had two nights ago. This is *muy importante*, so listen up."

Samuels listened, Samuels agreed, and Yune moved on to Jeannie Anderson. That call was longer, because she both needed and deserved a fuller explanation. When he finished, there were tears, but perhaps mostly of relief. It was awful that men had died, that Yune himself had been injured, but her man—and her son's father—was okay. Yune told her what she needed to do, and Jeannie agreed to do it immediately.

He was preparing to make the third call, to FC Chief of Police Rodney Geller, when they heard more sirens, this time approaching. Two Texas Highway Patrol cars blasted by them, headed for the Marysville Hole.

"If we're lucky," Yune said, "maybe one of those troops is the guy who talked to the Boltons. Stape, I think his name was."

"Sipe," Holly corrected. "Owen Sipe. How's your arm?"

"Still hurts like blue fuck. I'm gonna take those other two Motrin."

"No. Too much all at once can damage your liver. Make the other calls. But first go to Recents and delete the ones you made to Mr. Samuels and Mrs. Anderson."

"You would have made a hell of a crook, *señorita*."

"Just being careful. *Prudente*." She didn't look away from the road. It was empty, but she was that kind of driver. "Do it, then make the rest of your calls."

26

It turned out that Lovie Bolton had some old Percocets for back pain. Yune took two of them instead of the Motrin, and Claude—who had taken a first aid course during his third and last stretch in prison—bandaged his wound while Holly talked. She did so rapidly, and not just because she wanted to get Lieutenant Sablo some real care. She needed the Boltons to understand their part in this before anyone official showed up. That would be soon, because the officers from the Highway Patrol would have questions for Ralph, and he would have to answer them. At least there was no disbelief here; Lovie and Claude had felt the presence of the outsider two nights ago, and Claude had been feeling him even before that: a sense of disquiet, dislocation, and being watched.

"Of course you felt him," Holly said grimly. "He was plundering your mind."

"You saw him," Claude said. "He was hiding in that cave, and you saw him."

"Yes."

"And he looked like me."

"Almost exactly."

Lovie spoke up, sounding timid. "Would I have known the difference?"

Holly smiled. "At a glance. I'm sure of it. Lieutenant Sablo—Yune—are you ready to go?"

"Yes." He stood up. "One great thing about hard drugs—everything still hurts, but you don't give a shit."

Claude burst out laughing and pointed a finger-gun at him. "You got that right, brother." He saw Lovie frowning at him and added, "Sorry, Ma."

"You understand the story you have to tell?" Holly asked.

"Yes, ma'am," Claude said. "Too simple to screw up. The Flint

City DA is thinking of re-opening the Maitland case, and you-all came down here to question me."

"And you said what?" Holly asked.

"That the more I think about it, the more I'm sure it wasn't Coach Terry I saw that night, just someone who looked like him."

"What else?" Yune asked. "Very important."

Lovie answered this time. "The bunch of you stopped by this morning to say goodbye, and to ask if there was anything we might have forgotten. While you were getting ready to leave, there was a phone call."

"On your landline," Holly added, thinking, *Thank God they still have one.*

"That's right, on the landline. The man said he worked with Detective Anderson."

"Who spoke to him," Holly said.

"That's right. The man told Detective Anderson the fellow you-all were looking for, the real killer, was hiding out in the Marysville Hole."

"Stick to that," Holly said. "And thank you both."

"We are the ones who should be thanking you," Lovie said, and held out her arms. "You come here, Miss Holly Gibney, and give old Lovie a hug."

Holly went to the wheelchair and bent down. After the Marysville Hole, Lovie Bolton's arms felt good. Necessary, even. She stayed in their embrace as long as she could.

27

Marcy Maitland had grown exceedingly wary of callers since her husband's public arrest, not to mention his public execution, so when the knock came at her door, she first went to the window, twitched aside the drapes, and peeped out. It was Detective Anderson's wife on the stoop, and it looked like she had been crying. Marcy hurried to the door and opened it. Yes, those were tears, and as soon as Jeannie saw Marcy's concerned face, they started again.

"What is it? What's happened? Are they all right?"

Jeannie stepped in. "Where are your girls?"

"Out back under the big tree, playing cribbage with Terry's board. They played all last night and started again early this morning. What's wrong?"

Jeannie took her by the arm and led her into the living room. "You might want to sit down."

Marcy stood where she was. "Just tell me!"

"There's good news, but there's also terrible news. Ralph and the Gibney woman are all right. Lieutenant Sablo was shot, but they don't believe it's life-threatening. Howie Gold and Mr. Pelley, though . . . they're dead. Shot from ambush by a man my husband works with. A detective. Jack Hoskins is his name."

"Dead? *Dead?* How can they be—" Marcy sat heavily in what had been Terry's easy chair. It was either that or fall down. She stared up at Jeannie uncomprehendingly. "What do you mean, good news? How can there be . . . Jesus, it just keeps getting *worse.*"

She put her hands over her face. Jeannie dropped to her knees beside the chair and pulled them away, gently but firmly. "You need to get yourself together, Marcy."

"I can't. My husband's dead, and now this. I don't think I'll ever be together again. Not even for Grace and Sarah."

"Stop it." Jeannie's voice was low, but Marcy blinked as if she had been slapped. "Nothing can bring Terry back, but two good men died to redeem his name and give your girls a chance in this town. They have families, too, and I'll have to talk to Elaine Gold after I leave here. That's going to be awful. Yune has been hurt, and my husband risked his life. I know you're in pain, but this part is not about you. Ralph needs your help. So do the others. So pull yourself together and listen."

"All right. Yes."

Jeannie lifted one of Marcy's hands and held it. The fingers were cold, and Jeannie supposed her own weren't much warmer.

"Everything Holly Gibney told us was true. There *was* an outsider, and he wasn't a man. He was . . . something else. Call him *El Cuco*, call him Dracula, call him the Son of Sam or of Satan, it doesn't matter. He was there, in a cave. They found him and killed him. Ralph told me he looked like Claude Bolton, although the real Claude Bolton was miles away. I talked to Bill Samuels before I came over here. He thinks that if we all tell the same story, everything will be okay. It's likely we can clear Terry's name. *If we all tell the same story.* Can you do that?"

Jeannie could see hope filling Marcy Maitland's eyes like water filling a well.

"Yes. Yes, I can do that. But what is the story?"

"The meeting we had was *only* about trying to clear Terry's name. Nothing else."

"Just about clearing his name."

"At that meeting, Bill Samuels agreed to re-interview all the witnesses Ralph and the other officers questioned, starting with Willow Rainwater and working backward. Right?"

"Yes, that's right."

"The reason he couldn't start with Claude Bolton is that Mr. Bolton is in Texas, helping out with his mother, who's not well. Howie suggested that he, Alec, Holly, and my husband should go down there and question Claude. Yune said he would join them if possible. Do you remember that?"

"Yes," Marcy said, nodding rapidly. "We all thought that was an excellent idea. But I don't remember why Ms. Gibney was at the meeting."

"She was the investigator Alec Pelley hired to check on Terry's movements in Ohio. She got interested in the case, so she came down to see if she could give further assistance. Remember now?"

"Yes."

Holding Marcy's hand, looking into Marcy's eyes, Jeannie gave her the last and most important part. "We never discussed shape-changers, or *el cucos*, or ghostly projections, or anything that might be called supernatural."

"No, absolutely not, it never crossed our minds, why would it?"

"We thought that someone who looked like Terry killed the Peterson boy and tried to frame him for it. We called this person the outsider."

"Yes," Marcy said, squeezing Jeannie's hand. "That's what we called him. The outsider."

FLINT CITY

(After)

1

The plane chartered by the late Howard Gold landed at the Flint City airport just after eleven o'clock in the morning. Neither Howie nor Alec was aboard. Once the medical examiner finished his work, the bodies had been transported back to FC in a hearse from the Plainville Funeral Home. Ralph, Yune, and Holly shared the expense of that, as well as a second hearse, which transported the body of Jack Hoskins. Yune spoke for all of them when he said there was no way the sonofabitch was going home with the men he had murdered.

Waiting for them on the tarmac was Jeannie Anderson, standing next to Yune's wife and two sons. The boys brushed past Jeannie (one of them, a husky preteen named Hector, almost knocked her off her feet) and bolted for their father, whose arm was in a cast and a sling. He embraced them with his good arm as best he could, disengaged himself, and beckoned his wife. She came on the run. So did Jeannie, her skirt flying out behind her. She threw her arms around Ralph and hugged him fiercely.

The Sablos and the Andersons stood in family embraces near the door to the little private terminal, hugging and laughing, until Ralph looked around and saw Holly standing alone by the wing of the King Air, watching them. She was wearing a new pantsuit, which she had been forced to buy at Plainville Ladies' Apparel, the nearest Walmart being forty miles away, on the outskirts of Austin.

Ralph beckoned her, and she came forward, a little shyly. She stopped a few feet away, but Jeannie was having none of that. She reached for Holly's hand, pulled her close, and hugged her. Ralph put his arms around both of them.

"Thank you," Jeannie whispered in Holly's ear. "Thank you for bringing him back to me."

Holly said, "We hoped to come home right after the inquest, but the doctors made Lieutenant Sablo—Yune—wait another day. There was a blood clot in his arm, and the doctor wanted to dissolve it." She disengaged herself from the embrace, flushed but looking pleased. Ten feet away, Gabriela Sablo was exhorting her boys to leave *papi* alone, or they would break his arm all over again.

"What does Derek know about this?" Ralph asked his wife.

"He knows that his dad was in a shootout down in Texas, and that you're all right. He knows two other men died. He asked to come home early."

"And you said?"

"I said okay. He'll be here next week. Does that work for you?"

"Yes." It would be good to see his son again: tanned, healthy, with a few new muscles from swimming and rowing and archery. And on the right side of the ground. That was the most important thing.

"We're eating at the house tonight," Jeannie said to Holly, "and you'll stay with us again. No arguments, now. The guest room is all made up."

"That would be nice," Holly said, and smiled. Her smile faded as she turned to Ralph. "It would be better if Mr. Gold and Mr. Pelley could sit down to dinner with us. It's very wrong that they should be dead. It just seems . . ."

"I know," Ralph said, and put an arm around her. "I know how it seems."

2

Ralph barbecued steaks on a grill that was, thanks to his administrative leave, spandy-clean. There was also salad, corn on the cob, and apple pie *a la mode* for dessert. "Very American meal, *señor*," Yune observed as his wife cut his steak for him.

"It was delicious," Holly said.

Bill Samuels patted his stomach. "I may be ready to eat again by Labor Day, but I'm not sure."

"Stuff and nonsense," Jeannie said. She took a bottle of beer from the cooler beside the picnic table, pouring half into Samuels's glass and half into her own. "You're too thin. You need a wife to feed you up."

"Maybe when I go into private practice, my ex will come around. There's going to be a demand for a good lawyer here in town now that Howic—" He suddenly realized what he was saying and brushed at his cowlick (which, thanks to a fresh haircut, wasn't there). "A good lawyer can always find work, is what I meant."

They were quiet for a moment, then Ralph raised his beer bottle. "To absent friends."

They drank to that. Holly said, in a voice almost too quiet to be heard, "Sometimes life can be very poopy." No one laughed.

The oppressive July heat had let up, the worst of the bugs were gone, and the Anderson backyard was a pleasant place to be. Once the meal was finished, Yune's two boys and Marcy Maitland's two girls drifted to the basketball hoop on the side of the garage, and began playing Horse.

"So," Marcy said. Even though the kids were a good distance away, and absorbed in their game, she lowered her voice. "The inquest. Did the story hold up?"

"It did," Ralph said. "Hoskins called the Bolton house and lured us to the Marysville Hole. There he went on a shooting spree, killing Howie and Alec and wounding Yune. I stated my belief that it was me he was really after. We've had our differences over the years, and the more he drank, the more that must have eaten into him. The assumption is that he was with some as yet unidentified accomplice, who kept him supplied with booze and drugs—the medical examiner found traces of cocaine in his system—and fed his paranoia. The Texas HP went into the Chamber of Sound, but did not find the accomplice."

"Just some clothes," Holly said.

"And you're sure he's dead," Jeannie said. "The outsider. You're *sure*."

"Yes," Ralph said. "If you'd seen, you'd know."

"Be glad you didn't," Holly said.

"Is it over?" Gabriela Sablo asked. "That's all I care about. Is it really over?"

"No," Marcy said. "Not for me and the girls. Not unless Terry's cleared. And how can he be? He was killed before he got his day in court."

Samuels said, "We're working on that."

(August 1st)

3

As the light of his first full day back in Flint City dawned, Ralph once more stood at his bedroom window, hands clasped behind his back, looking down at Holly Gibney, who was once more sitting in one of the backyard lawn chairs. He checked Jeannie, found her asleep and snoring softly, and went downstairs. He wasn't surprised to see Holly's bag in the kitchen, already packed with her few things for the flight north. As well as knowing her own mind, she was a lady who did not let the grass grow under her feet. And he supposed she would be very glad to get the hell out of Flint City.

On the previous early morning when he had been out here with Holly, the smell of coffee had awakened Jeannie, so this time he brought orange juice. He loved his wife, and valued her company, but he wanted this to be just between him and Holly. They shared a bond and always would, even if they never saw each other again.

"Thank you," she said. "There's nothing better than orange juice in the morning." She looked at the glass with satisfaction, then drank half of it. "Coffee can wait."

"What time is your flight?"

"Quarter past eleven. I'll leave here by eight." She gave a slightly embarrassed smile at his look of surprise. "I know, I'm a compulsive early bird. The Zoloft helps with a lot of things, but it doesn't seem to help with that."

"Did you sleep?"

"A little. Did you?"

"A little."

They were quiet for a time. The first bird sang, tender and sweet. Another responded.

"Bad dreams?" he asked.

"Yes. You?"

"Yes. Those worms."

"I had bad dreams after Brady Hartsfield, too. Both times." She touched his hand very lightly, then drew her fingers back. "There were a lot at first, but fewer as time passed."

"Do you think they ever go away entirely?"

"No. And I'm not sure I'd want them to. Dreams are the way we touch the unseen world, that's what I believe. They are a special gift."

"Even the bad ones?"

"Even the bad ones."

"Will you stay in touch?"

She looked surprised. "Of course. I'll want to know how things turn out. I'm a very curious person. Sometimes that gets me in trouble."

"And sometimes it gets you out."

Holly smiled. "I like to think so." She drank the rest of her juice. "Mr. Samuels will help you with this, I think. He reminds me a little bit of Scrooge, after he saw the three ghosts. Actually, you do, too."

That made him laugh. "Bill's going to do everything he can for Marcy and her daughters. I'll help. We both have a lot to make up for."

She nodded. "Do what you can, absolutely. But then . . . let the fracking thing go. If you can't let go of the past, the mistakes you've made will eat you alive." She turned to him and gave him one of her rare dead-on looks. "I'm a woman who knows."

The kitchen light went on. Jeannie was up. Soon the three of them would have coffee out here at the picnic table, but while it was just the two of them, he had something else to say, and it was important.

"Thank you, Holly. Thank you for coming, and thank you for believing. Thank you for making *me* believe. If not for you, he'd still be out there."

She smiled. It was the radiant one. "You're welcome, but I'll be very happy to go back to finding deadbeats and bail-jumpers and lost pets."

From the doorway, Jeannie called, "Who wants coffee?"

"Both of us!" Ralph called back.

"Coming right up! Save a place for me!"

Holly spoke in a voice so low he had to lean forward to hear her. "He was evil. Pure evil."

"No argument there," Ralph said.

"But there's something I keep thinking about: that scrap of paper you found in the van. The one from Tommy and Tuppence.

THE OUTSIDER

We talked about explanations for why it ended up where it did, do you remember?"

"Sure."

"They all seem unlikely to me. It never should have been there at all, but it was. And if not for that scrap—the link to what happened in Ohio—that thing might still be out there."

"Your point being?"

"It's simple," Holly said. "There's also a force for good in the world. That's something else I believe. Partly so I don't go crazy when I think of all the awful things that happen, I guess, but also . . . well . . . the evidence seems to bear it out, wouldn't you say? Not just here but everywhere. There's some force that tries to restore the balance. When the bad dreams come, Ralph, try to remember that little scrap of paper."

He didn't reply at first, and she asked what he was thinking about. The screen door slammed: Jeannie with coffee. Their time together alone was almost up.

"I was thinking about the universe. There really is no end to it, is there? And no explaining it."

"That's right," she said. "No point in even trying."

(August 10th)

4

Flint County district attorney William Samuels strode to the podium in the courthouse conference room with a slim folder in one hand. He stood behind a cluster of microphones. TV lights came on. He touched the back of his head (no cowlick), and waited for the assembled reporters to quiet. Ralph was sitting in the front row. Samuels gave him a brief nod before commencing.

"Good morning, ladies and gentlemen. I have a brief statement to make in regard to the murder of Frank Peterson, and then I will take your questions.

"As many of you know, a videotape exists showing Terence Maitland attending a conference in Cap City at the same time Frank Peterson was being abducted and subsequently murdered here in Flint City. There can be no doubt of this tape's authenticity. Nor can we doubt the statements given by Mr. Maitland's colleagues, who accompanied him to the conference and attest to his presence there. In the course of our investigation we have also discovered Mr. Maitland's fingerprints at the Cap City hotel where the conference was held, and have obtained ancillary testimony that proves those prints were made too close to the time of the Peterson boy's murder for Mr. Maitland to be considered a suspect."

There was a murmur from the reporters. One of them called, "Then how do you explain Maitland's prints at the scene of the murder?"

Samuels gave the reporter his best prosecutorial frown. "Hold your questions, please; I was just coming to that. After further forensic examination, we now feel that the fingerprints found in the van used to abduct the child and those found in Figgis Park were planted. This is uncommon but far from impossible. Various techniques for planting bogus fingerprints can be found on the Internet, which is a valuable resource for criminals as well as law enforcement.

"It *does* suggest, however, that this murderer is crafty as well as perverted and extremely dangerous. It may or may not suggest that he had a grudge against Terry Maitland. That is a line of investigation we will continue to pursue."

He surveyed his audience soberly, feeling very glad indeed that he would never have to run for re-election in Flint County; after this, any shyster with a mail-order law degree could probably beat him, and handily.

"You would have a perfect right to ask why we proceeded with the case against Mr. Maitland, given the facts I have just reviewed for you. There were two reasons. The most obvious is that we did *not* have all these facts in hand on the day Mr. Maitland was arrested, or on the day he would have been arraigned."

Ah, but by then we had most of them, didn't we, Bill? Ralph thought as he sat dressed in his best suit and watching with his best law enforcement poker face.

"The second reason we proceeded," Samuels continued, "was the presence of DNA at the scene, which seemed to match that of Mr. Maitland. There is a popular assumption that DNA matching is never wrong, but as the Council for Responsible Genetics pointed out in a scholarly article titled 'The Potential for Error in Forensic DNA Testing,' that is a misconception. If samples are mixed, for instance, the matching can't be trusted, and the samples taken at the Figgis Park scene were indeed mixed, containing DNA from both perpetrator and victim."

He waited until the reporters had finished scribbling before going on.

"Added to this, the samples were exposed to ultraviolet light during the course of another, unrelated, testing procedure. Unfortunately, they are degraded to a point where they would have been, in the opinion of my department, inadmissible in a court of law. In plain English, the samples are worthless."

He paused, turning to the next sheet in his folder. This was mere stagecraft, as all of the sheets in it were blank.

"I only want to touch briefly on the events that took place in Marysville, Texas, subsequent to the murder of Terence Maitland. It is our opinion that Detective John Hoskins of the Flint City Police Department was in some sort of twisted and criminal partnership with the person who killed Frank Peterson. We believe Hoskins was helping this individual to hide, and that they may have been planning to perpetrate a similar horrible crime. Thanks to the heroic efforts of Detective Ralph Anderson and those with him, whatever plans they may have made did not come to fruition." He looked up at his audience soberly. "Howard Gold and Alec Pelley died in Marysville, Texas, and we mourn their loss. What we and their families take comfort in is this: somewhere at this very moment, there is a child who will never suffer the fate of Frank Peterson."

A nice touch, Ralph thought. *Just the right amount of pathos without getting all sloppy about it.*

"I'm sure many of you have questions about the events that occurred in Marysville, but I am not at liberty to answer them. The investigation, which is being jointly conducted by the Texas Highway Patrol and the Flint City Police Department, is ongoing. State Police Lieutenant Yunel Sablo is working with both of these fine organizations as chief liaison officer, and I'm sure that he will have information to share with you at the appropriate time."

He's great at this stuff, Ralph thought, and with real admiration. *Hitting every damn note.*

Samuels closed his folder, lowered his head, then raised it again. "I am not running for re-election, ladies and gentlemen, so I have the rare opportunity to be entirely honest with you."

It gets even better, Ralph thought.

"Given more time to evaluate the evidence, this office almost certainly would have dropped the charges against Mr. Maitland. Had we persisted and brought him to trial, I'm sure he would have been found innocent. And, as I hardly need to add, he *was* innocent, according to the laws of jurisprudence, at the time of his death. Yet the cloud of suspicion over him—and consequently over his family—has remained. I am here today to dissipate that cloud. It is the opinion of the district attorney's office—and my personal belief—that Terry Maitland had nothing whatsoever to do with the death of Frank Peterson. Consequently, I am announcing that the investigation has been re-opened. Although it is currently concentrated in Texas, the investigation in Flint City, Flint County, and Canning Township is also ongoing. Now I will be happy to take any questions you may have."

There were many.

5

Later that day, Ralph visited Samuels in his office. The soon-to-be-retired DA had a bottle of Bushmills on his desk. He poured them each a knock, and raised his glass. "Now the hurly-burly's done, now the battle's lost and won. Mostly lost in my case, but what the fuck. Let's drink to the hurly-burly."

They did so.

"You handled the questions well," Ralph said. "Especially considering the amount of bullshit you slung around."

Samuels shrugged. "Bullshit is every good lawyer's stock in trade. Terry's not completely off the hook in this town and never will be, Marcy understands that, but people are coming around. Her friend Jamie Mattingly, for instance—Marcy called to tell me that she came over and apologized. They had a good cry together. It's mostly the videotape of Terry in Cap City that turned the trick, but what I said about the prints and DNA will help a lot. Marcy's going to try to stick it out here. I think she'll succeed."

"About that DNA," Ralph said. "Ed Bogan in the Serology Department at General ran those samples. With his reputation at stake, he should be squawking his head off."

Samuels smiled. "He should, shouldn't he? Except the truth is even less palatable—another case of footprints that just stop, you could say. There was no exposure to UV light, but the samples began developing white spots of no known origin, and now they're completely degraded. Bogan got in touch with State Police Forensics in Ohio, and guess what? Same thing with the Heath Holmes samples. A series of photos shows them basically disintegrating. A defense attorney would have a ball with that, wouldn't he?"

"And the witnesses?"

Bill Samuels laughed and poured himself another drink. He offered the bottle to Ralph, who shook his head—he was driving home.

"They were the easy part. They've all decided they were wrong, with two exceptions—Arlene Stanhope and June Morris. They stand by their stories."

Ralph was not surprised. Stanhope was the old lady who had seen the outsider approach Frank Peterson in the parking lot of Gerald's Fine Groceries and drive away with him. June Morris was the child who had seen him in Figgis Park, with blood on his shirt. The very old and the very young always saw most clearly.

"So now what?"

"Now we finish our drinks and go our separate ways," Samuels said. "I just have one question."

"Shoot."

"Was he the only one? Or are there others?"

Ralph's mind returned to the final confrontation in the cave, and to the greedy expression in the outsider's eyes as he asked his question: *Have you seen another one like me somewhere?*

"I don't think so," he said, "but we'll never be completely sure. There might be anything out there. I know that now."

"Jesus Christ, I hope not!"

Ralph made no reply. In his mind he heard Holly saying *There's no end to the universe.*

(September 21st)

6

Ralph took his coffee with him into the bathroom to shave. He had been slipshod about this daily chore during his mandated time away from the police force, but he had been reinstated to active duty two weeks before. Jeannie was downstairs making breakfast. He could smell bacon and heard the blare of trumpets that signaled the beginning of the *Today* show, which would open with the daily budget of bad news before moving on to the celeb of the week and many ads for prescription drugs.

He set his coffee cup down on the little table and froze, watching as a red worm wriggled its way out from beneath his thumbnail. He looked in the mirror and saw his face changing into Claude Bolton's face. He opened his mouth to scream. A flood of maggots and red worms poured out over his lips and down the front of his shirt.

7

He woke sitting up in bed, heart pounding in his throat and temples as well as in his chest, hands plastered over his mouth, as if to hold in a scream . . . or something even worse. Jeannie slept on beside him, so he hadn't screamed; there was that.

None of them got in me that day. None of them even touched me. You know that.

Yes, he did. He had been there, after all, and he'd had a complete (and overdue) physical checkup before resuming his duties. Other than slightly elevated weight and cholesterol, Dr. Elway had pronounced him fine and fit.

He glanced at the clock and saw it was quarter to four. He lay back, looking up at the ceiling. A long time yet until first light. A long time to think.

8

Ralph and Jeannie were early risers; Derek would sleep until he was rousted at seven, the latest he could be allowed to sleep and still make the school bus. Ralph sat at the kitchen table in his pajamas while Jeannie started the Bunn and put out boxes of cereal for Derek to choose from when he came down. She asked Ralph how he'd slept. He said fine. She asked him how the job search for Jack Hoskins's replacement was going. He said it was over. Based on his and Betsy Riggins's recommendations, Chief Geller had decided to promote Officer Troy Ramage to Flint City's three-man detective squad.

"He's not the brightest bulb in the chandelier, but he's a hard worker and a team player. I think he'll do."

"Good. Glad to hear it." She filled his mug, then ran a hand down his cheek. "You're all scratchy, mister. You need to shave."

He took his coffee, went upstairs, closed the bedroom door, and pulled his phone off the charger. The number he wanted was in his contacts, and although it was still early—*Today*'s opening trumpet flourish was still at least a half hour away—he knew she would be up. On many days, the phone at her end never got through the first ring. This was one of them.

"Hello, Ralph."

"Hello, Holly."

"How did you sleep?"

"Not so well. I had the dream about the worms. How about you?"

"Last night was fine. I watched a movie on my computer and corked right off. *When Harry Met Sally*. That one always makes me laugh."

"Good. That's good. What are you working on?"

"Mostly it's the same old same old." Her voice brightened. "But I found a runaway from Tampa in a youth hostel. Her mom has been looking for her for six months. I talked to her and she's going home. She says she'll give it one more try even though she hates her mother's boyfriend."

"I suppose you gave her bus fare."

"Well . . ."

"You know she's probably smoking it up right now in some bumblefuck's crash pad, don't you?"

"They don't always do that, Ralph. You have to—"

"I know. I have to believe."

"Yes."

Silence for a moment in the connection between his place in the world and hers.

"Ralph . . ."

He waited.

"Those . . . those things that came out of him . . . they never touched either one of us. You know that, don't you?"

"I do," he said. "I think my dreams mostly have to do with a cantaloupe I cut open when I was a kid, and what was inside. I told you about that, right?"

"Yes."

He could hear the smile in her voice and smiled in return, as if she were in the room with him. "Of course I did, probably more than once. Sometimes I think I'm losing it."

"Not at all. Next time we talk, it will be me calling you, after I dream he's in my closet with Brady Hartsfield's face. And you'll be the one to say you slept fine."

He knew it was true, because it had already happened.

"What you're feeling . . . and I'm feeling . . . that's *normal*. Reality is thin ice, but most people skate on it their whole lives and never fall through until the very end. We did fall through, but we helped each other out. We're still helping each other."

You're helping me more, Ralph thought. *You may have your problems, Holly, but you're better at this than I am. Far better.*

"And you're all right?" he asked her. "I mean, really?"

"Yes. Really. And you will be."

"Message received. Call me if you hear the ice cracking under your feet."

"Of course," she said. "And you'll do the same. It's how we go on."

From downstairs, Jeannie called, "Breakfast in ten, honey!"

"I've got to go," Ralph said. "Thanks for being there."

"You're welcome," she said. "Take care of yourself. Be safe. Wait for the dreams to end."

"I will."

"Goodbye, Ralph."

"Goodbye."

He paused and added, "I love you, Holly," but not until he ended the call. It was the way he always did it, knowing if he actually said it to her, she would be embarrassed and tongue-tied. He went into the bathroom to shave. He was in his middle age now, and the first speckles of gray had begun to show in the stubble he covered with Barbasol, but it was his face, the one his wife and son knew and loved. It would be his face forever, and that was good.

That was good.

AUTHOR'S NOTE

Thanks are due to Russ Dorr, my able research assistant, and also to a father and son team, Warren and Daniel Silver, who helped me with the legal aspects of this story. They were uniquely qualified to do so, as Warren spent much of his life as a defense attorney in Maine, and his son, although now in private practice, has had a distinguished career as a prosecutor in New York. Thanks to Chris Lotts, who knew about *el cuco* and *las luchadoras*; thanks to my daughter, Naomi, who hunted down the children's book about "*el cucuy.*" Thanks to Nan Graham, Susan Moldow, and Roz Lippel of Scribner; thanks to Philippa Pride at Hodder & Stoughton. Special thanks to Katherine "Katie" Monaghan, who read the first hundred or so pages of this story on an airplane, while we were on tour, and wanted more. A writer of fiction never hears more encouraging words than those.

Thanks, as always, to my wife. I love you, Tabby.

A final word, this about the setting. Oklahoma is a wonderful state, and I met wonderful people there. Some of those wonderful people will say I got a lot wrong, and probably I did; you have to be in a place for years before you get the flavor just right. I did the best I could. For the rest, you must forgive me. Flint City and Cap City are, of course, fictional.

Stephen King